CHAMELEON

Trisha Hughes

ABOUT THE AUTHOR

Trisha Hughes is the Australian author of her best selling autobiography **'Daughters of Nazareth'** as well as several exciting crime thrillers. Her Historical Trilogy is based on the British Monarchy throughout the ages. This is Trisha's 9th book.

Trisha Hughes is returning to Australia from Hong Kong this year to resume her life with grandchildren and fur-babies.

Contact the author
trisha.hughes.books@gmail.com

For updates and discounts on new releases,
join Trisha's mailing list at
https://www.trishahughesauthor.com/contact

Cover Illustration by Anita Rodgers

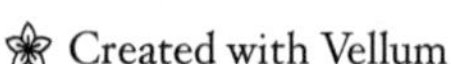 Created with Vellum

ACKNOWLEDGMENTS

Once again my biggest thanks goes to my husband David for his support and encouragement. He has patiently read every draft and consistently talks through ideas with me over a glass or two of wine. Well, okay. Three.

Another big thanks goes to Anita Rodgers, the author of Dead Dog trilogy for simply being a friend in need. She has shown her versatility with designing the cover of this book, and for that, I will always be grateful.

Most importantly, I want to thank my readers who have faithfully read my historical books and have supported me in my crime series. You know who you are. Thank you.

❧ I ❧

Don't make a sound!

My mind was screaming the words over and over in my head.

I was crouched in an industrial bin up to my knees in God knows what muck while a man by the name of Jimmy Preston paced around outside my foul-smelling sanctuary with a long-blade knife, looking for me.

As I moved my hand slightly, I felt something ooze gently between my fingers and a pathetic yelp escaped my lips, just loud enough for Preston outside to hear.

The lid of the industrial bin suddenly opened, allowing me enough light to squint and see his silhouette seconds before his hand grabbed my hair, yanking me out headfirst to land in an untidy heap at his feet.

Being an ex-policeman, I have been well-trained in weapons and hand-to-hand combat, but it's been a while since I've had to perform anything like a direct skirmish and I'm sorry to admit I'm not as toned as I'd like to be. To tell the truth, I wasn't ready for the pure panic, the tingly, unpleasant numbness in the legs, the way adrenaline mixes with fear and drains your strength.

True fighting is nothing like you see on TV. You would never, for example, mess around with a high kick to the face and you would never try anything involving turning your back on an opponent, spinning and leaping like they do in movies. Even as I think about that much activity, I break out into a sweat and imagine the next six months spent in traction.

Think about the physical altercation you may have seen in a bar or at a sporting event. The battle almost always ends up in an untidy grapple on the floor. On TV, people stand and hit each other and no one ever goes down. In real life, one or the other ducks down and grabs the opponent and they fall to the ground and wrestle untidily. It doesn't matter how much training you have, if the fight reaches that stage, I would always lose.

All of these things ran through my head at the same time but instead of immediately kicking behind me, trying to take out a knee or stomping down on an instep, I worked on instinct and used both my hands to pry my hair from his grip. It did not work.

Okay, next move. You aim for the vulnerable spots on the body. The nose was good and it usually makes your opponent's eyes water, which is when you make your move. The eyes, of course, are also good. A gouge to an eye can shut down any will to fight further. The groin is, well, obvious. You always hear that. But the groin is a difficult target because a man is prone to defend it. It's usually better as a decoy move. Fake there, and then go to one of the other more exposed, vulnerable spots. But if an attacker knows what he's doing, every move you make becomes pretty close to useless.

While these thoughts stumbled around in my head, Jimmy had his other hand on the base of my head, holding my skull in a vicelike grip. I could feel the fingers of one hand digging into my gums and pushing against my teeth while the knife in his other hand bit deep into my cheek. His hands were so powerful that I was sure he could crush my skull like an eggshell. I felt a trickle of blood run down my face as he squashed it hard up against the industrial bin.

Jimmy must have read my mind because his legs tensed so that I couldn't go for his groin. His small beady eyes and uneven teeth were pressed close to my face and his breath smelt of malt liquor and a range of other odours I didn't have time to identify. There was dirt under his nails and a rash on his neck, the heads white, as if he'd shaved with a blunt razor. A tiny scar on his forehead, blended into the creases.

I was familiar with the Jimmy Prestons of the world. Jimmy was poor and dangerous with some wild idea that the world owed him something. The threat of violence hung around him like a cloud, obscuring his judgment and influencing others so that when he stepped into a pub or picked up a pool cue, sooner or later trouble would start. Jimmy didn't pick fights. Fights picked Jimmy.

So far, he hadn't killed anybody and nobody had managed to kill him. I'd heard people describe him as an accident waiting to happen, but he was more than that. He was a constantly evolving disaster.

I knew a little about Jimmy's past. He had a rap sheet a mile long that began when he was in school, from disrupting classes to petty larceny to DUI, receiving stolen goods, assault, trespassing and disorderly conduct. The list just went on and on. He was an adopted child and had been through a succession of foster homes in his youth, each one only keeping him for as long as it took the foster parents to realise that Jimmy was more trouble than the money from social services was worth to them. That's the way some foster parents work: they treat the kids like a cash crop, like livestock, until they realise that if *this* chicken acts up, you can't cut its head off and eat it.

The options are limited in the case of a problematic, delinquent child and no one had any idea how to handle Jimmy. There was evidence of abuse by many of his foster parents and suspicion of serious sexual abuse in at least two cases. With issues like that, it takes some pretty special skills to tame these kids and not too many people can claim that ability.

Jimmy was one of the ones who had not been tamed. They say that some men carry their personal war with them all of their lives and some men can put it behind them like an old pair of shoes. And then, I guess, there are others who go on fighting even though they have no idea who they are fighting with or why it's so important not to give up. That was the Jimmy breathing in my face me now.

He wasn't bad looking if you could get past the bad case of acne, which comes from using steroids. He was twenty-nine, built like a bull, his greasy shoulder-length blonde hair parted in the middle with a definite resemblance to a young Viggo Mortensen I'd see in some movie not so long ago. The muscles on his arms were like huge hams, his hands thick and broad and his fingers almost swollen in their muscularity.

One of his hands was clasped hard around my neck and as I stared into his bloodshot eyes, he forced me upwards, my toes barely touching the ground. By now, the knife had pressed deeper into my cheek beneath my left eye and I could feel blood dribbling to my chin, taking my mind off the odours from his snarling mouth. *Rancid onions and garlic,* I thought. *And blue cheese.*

While my mind was registering just how bad an idea it had been to cross Jimmy, he pulled me forward and slapped me hard across the head, open palmed, with his enormous right hand, then pushed me up against the side of the bin again, his huge forearms holding me in place. My head was ringing from the blow and my ear ached. I thought my eardrum had burst but then the pressure on my neck started to increase and I realised I might not have to worry about my eardrum for much longer.

The knife twisted in his hand and I felt a fresh burst of pain. The blood was running freely now, spilling from my chin onto the collar of my white shirt. Jimmy's face was purple with rage and he was breathing heavily through crooked, clenched teeth, spittle erupting as he wheezed out. He was completely focused on squeezing the life out of me.

I managed to move my right hand to the inside of my jacket and miraculously, I felt the cool grip of my gun. I wrenched it free and moved my arm enough to stick the muzzle into the soft flesh beneath Jimmy's jaw before I passed out.

"Don't make history," I squeaked.

Jimmy went crossed-eyed trying to focus on the gun.

"I've never shot anyone before. Not even when I was a cop." I've actually killed a couple of people when I was a cop, but Jimmy didn't need to know that. "You'll be my first."

We eyed each other silently for a good five seconds, the red light in his eyes flaring briefly and then fading.

"We all need to step back and think about this for a bit," I wheezed.

His arms were frozen as he stared at the barrel of my gun then up at me, then back to the gun again. He looked like he had the shit scared out of him. I was feeling a little rattled myself.

"Put the knife down Jimmy."

I sounded tougher than I felt and it must have made an impression on Jimmy because his head nodded slowly and the pressure on my neck eased. Finally, the knife slid out of the wound and I slumped to the ground, still keeping the gun on him even though he'd turned away. My throat ached and I pulled shallow, rattling breaths into my starved lungs. Now that his tide of rage had begun to ebb, he seemed unconcerned about the gun and about me.

He took a pack of cigarettes out of a hip pocket along with a bic lighter and shook a cigarette out then lit up. He leant down and offered the pack to me, a friendly gesture that belied the fact that he'd been trying to choke the life out of me two minutes ago. I shook my head slowly so that it didn't fall off my shoulders and land at my feet. When the pain in my ear started raging again, I decided to stop shaking my head.

"You shouldn'ta got me fired, man," Jimmy muttered as he raised his head and exhaled smoke into the night air.

That's how this had all started. I'd been doing some private detecting work for the Vikings Surf Life Saving Club at Elephant Rock in Currumbin. Bazza, aka Barry Nesmith, had noticed that things weren't adding up in recent weeks. They were making a lot less money and the bottles of Scotch were not making the same number of drinks that they used to. Something didn't add up.

Bazza employed ten part-time bartenders in his establishment, a couple of them he paid in cash and off the books. Jimmy was one of them. It worked for both parties. Jimmy didn't have to declare an income and pay tax and Bazza didn't have to pay money into a superannuation fund for Jimmy. But very quickly, I zeroed in on Jimmy who was taking the odd bottle or two home with him.

When I told Bazza my conclusions, I don't think he believed me at first. His eyes narrowed but otherwise he remained stone-faced. Then his jaw tightened. He nodded sadly. The surprise that had washed over his face a moment ago transformed into something else.

"I trusted him, Jack," Bazza said.

"Don't take it personally. It happens."

The disadvantage for Bazza of paying Jimmy in cash was that it was illegal. It also meant that Bazza couldn't go to the police and charge Jimmy with theft without putting himself in hot water as well. His hands were tied.

He stared down at the top of his desk and shook his head. Outside, Jimmy was tending the bar as we sat in the office deciding his future.

Bazza's eyes returned to staring at the door and I had a pretty good idea what he was thinking. Jimmy was history. I had hoped that Bazza would leave my name out of it. Obviously, he hadn't.

Jimmy took another drag on the cigarette as he watched me slowly uncurling my body and rolling over, trying to get to my knees. I pushed my butt in the air and as I did, something furry brushed my face and I stifled a yelp. I managed to duck walk up to a stand, holding on to the dumpster to support myself.

"Ya gonna get me another one?" he asked.

I didn't want to sound offhand about him losing his job and get him agitated again but I really didn't want to get in to it with him either. The human brain is an amazing organ that no computer can duplicate. It can process zillions of stimuli in a hundredth of a second with a curious mix of chemicals and electrodes. We understand more about the planets and the cosmos than we do about the brain and its workings. And like any tricky compound, we are never sure how it will react to a certain catalyst.

"You'll get another job, Jimmy. Just don't rob the guy that pays your wages, that's all."

"I never robbed him! I never took a cent of his money!"

I remember a psychological term I'd heard when I was beginning my police training. It involves unintended acknowledgement of guilt through the expression of denial. Like when Lee Harvey Oswald was in custody for killing President Kennedy, he answered truthfully most of the questions asked by cops and prosecutors. But he continuously refused to admit ownership of the rifle found on the 6th floor of the Texas bookshop. It was the one piece of evidence that linked him unquestionably and inextricably to the crime but he continually denied it. Jimmy was doing the same. He lifted booze not money but Jimmy didn't see that as stealing from Bazza.

I brushed my hands together to dust away the remaining gravel and mushy bits of banana skin, trying to breath evenly at the same time. It wasn't easy.

He took another drag of the cigarette and watched me silently as the first soft patter of rain made tinging noises on the dumpster.

All I wanted to do was go home and have a hot shower, get something to eat and a cold beer. Not necessarily in that order. My head was aching but I didn't want to get him upset again. I was pretty sure he was in what I call, the 'bozone' layer. It's the layer that surrounds stupid people and it stops any bright ideas from penetrating into their brain.

"You need to be smart about this, Jimmy. Just turn around and start again somewhere else. Maybe go to Sydney."

"I tried Sydney," he mumbled. "Didn't like it."

"Fine," I sighed. "Try Melbourne. Just don't rob your next employer," I repeated.

A couple of minutes later, I left Jimmy to his thoughts and limped to my car with the full intention of heading home.

As I turned the key in the ignition, lightning blistered the sky. Ten seconds later, as I pulled out onto Pacific Parade, making my way to the Gold Coast highway, trees and buildings seemed to shudder as a loud crack reverberated, like the mantle of the earth had split. Seconds later, rain began to fall with tropical intensity as my car splashed along road. In this deluge, it would take me almost an hour to get home.

$$\maltese \quad 2 \quad \maltese$$

Beth

From one block down, the noise level from Alto's was ear splitting. Friday evenings were always the same: nearly manic in its energy, and everyone determined to party, gearing up for the weekend.

"Come on someone. Leave," Beth mumbled impatiently.

She was driving maddeningly slowly, her eyes flicking from one side of the road to the other, looking for a place to park. It was already her third time around the block, and if she didn't find one soon, her only other option would be to drive to a public car park a kilometre away in the touristy section of Broadbeach and walk back in steaming heat.

She glanced quickly down at her watch. It was already 5.55pm and she was going to be late.

Miraculously, a car pulled out from a spot on the opposite side of the restaurant's entrance and she gasped in delight before indicating quickly and manoeuvring her car in. As she leant forward to switch the engine off, she craned her neck around the steering wheel to read the sign on the sidewalk that would tell her how much time she had before she needed to find another spot.

"Please. Please. Please," she muttered as she read, then gave a whoop of delight when she saw it was a 30-minute parking slot up to 6pm, but unlimited from 6pm to 6am.

She glanced in her rear-view mirror, checking for traffic, and saw the traffic lights one block behind her had changed to red and cars were idling impatiently as sunburnt tourists with towels slung over their shoulders shuffled across the pedestrian crossing on their way back from the beach.

According to the Weather Bureau, the weekend would be hot and humid with temperatures soaring into the 30s during the day. That would mean people would be heading down to any of the beaches along the 25-kilometre stretch of the Gold Coast to continue soaking up the nuclear heat. When they were done to a crisp, they'd be off to pharmacies for a jumbo container of Aloe Vera with heat radiating from their bodies, but fully intending to repeat the process the next day.

She shook her head and smiled at the senselessness of it as she stepped out of the car, locked the car with her remote, and jogged across the road just as the traffic lights turned green.

Instantly, the mouth-watering smell of cooking meat hit her nostrils as she walked along the boardwalk and her stomach grumbled loudly, drowning out the sound of the cars whizzing past behind her. Lunch had been a few carrot sticks and some leftover hummus at 1 o'clock and she suddenly realised she was famished. What she needed was a cold glass of white wine and maybe even a barbequed steak to celebrate. At the thought, her stomach grumbled again.

She idly lifted her arms and twisted her long dark hair over her left shoulder as she turned into the entrance of Alto's. The tailored pants and long-sleeved blue shirt she was wearing had been perfect for the air conditioning in the office but in the open-aired bistro, at the end of a long hot summer's day, she was regretting not going home first to change into something a little less constrictive. Instead, she'd opted to stay behind to finish off a report that was due first thing on Monday morning. The short walk from her car had already dampened the hair at the base of her neck and her shirt stuck uncomfortably to her back.

The coolness of the air-conditioning felt almost moist against the skin of her bare neck. She absently pulled her damp shirt from her back as she made her way to the bar, letting her eyes wander instinctively over the occupants of the tables. The habit never left her, even after almost a year.

As she approached the bar, she was relieved to see that her friend Sue hadn't arrived yet just as an Italian-looking bartender, dark-haired and dark-eyed, appeared before her. His badge said Antonio, and although she didn't normally do 'coquettish', in her present happy frame of mind, she gave it her best shot.

She smiled her best smile at him as she pushed her dark-framed glasses high on her nose.

"Chardonnay please, Antonio."

Her smile was wasted on him. Without saying a word, his eyes travelled over her face, hesitating at her cheek, before he nodded and dropped his eyes to a tray in front of him. He picked up an empty wine glass and turned to the fridge behind him for an opened wine bottle leaving her to blink self-consciously at the face reflected in the mirror behind him.

Large gazelle eyes stared back at her and she noticed the jagged scar on her cheek was looking fiery red tonight in the halogen lighting.

I look like the kind of timid animal that always gets eaten by a lion or a leopard in the end, she thought. She noticed blonde roots appearing in her part line and made a mental note to pick up some Clairol on her way home to do a touch up over the weekend.

She quickly turned away from the reflection to dig around in her purse for the correct change, ready to pay cash for her drink. She had no need to be reminded of why people stared at her face.

While she waited for her drink, she turned and let her eyes wander around the room. She and Sue had been to Alto's many times and they always loved it. Being just around the corner from the office, the girls shared lunches there regularly because the restaurant served food that was edible by most people's standards and at reasonable prices. The casual décor had an air of sophistication about it somehow, from the soft lighting to the comfortable seating overlooking palm trees and the shimmering ocean in the distance. In summer, the bi-fold doors were pulled back to allow any breeze to circulate but in winter, they were closed and bar heaters on the ceilings were turned on. No matter what season, the atmosphere was always inviting, almost electric.

Beth placed the correct change on the bar top and received a half-hearted smile from Antonio just as she noticed a couple rise from a booth under a shade cloth that bordered the outside walkway. She grabbed her drink and quickly manoeuvred herself through the crowded tables, around a potted plant, hurrying to the table before anyone else took it.

The spot was perfect. It was secluded enough to make her almost invisible yet close enough for her to still feel like she was part of the vibrant atmosphere. She could feel the air moving from the fan near the bar and the ocean breeze that wafted from across the sand dunes on the other side of the road brought the scent of seaweed and salt with it that she loved so much. Today, mixed in with the ocean smells, came a hint of coconut oil from the holidaymakers who had been making the most of the glorious sunshine. She wriggled a little so she could watch the entrance and the television above the bar at the same time. The 6 o'clock News had just started.

As she sipped her wine, she watched the ticker-tape headlines travel across the bottom of the screen. Three people mugged in Sydney. Another kid off to Syria to join ISIS. A man was rushed to hospital after being stabbed outside a Sydney bar. The Prime Minister's next budget was out and no one was happy. The Gold Coast mayor was making it plain that he was bringing the bikers into line and *everyone* was happy with him.

Just as the ticker-tape was repeating, Beth glanced up to see Sue standing at the entrance, looking like she was on her way to a rock concert. She'd obviously ducked home to change out of her skirt suit she'd worn to the office this morning because she was now wearing a soft, lemony cheesecloth top embroidered with cascades of elaborate delicate flowers on the front and a pair of jeans. She'd taken her hair out of the braid she'd worn to work and now her hair was a mass of tumbling curls cascading over her shoulders.

The outfit meant tonight she'd gone hippy. There was loads of ethnic jewellery on her wrists, a dozen bangles that Beth knew would jingle and tinkle when she flicked her hair over her shoulder. Dangling from her ears were huge silver hoop earrings brushing her neck. An oversized crocheted bag hung from her shoulder and she hoisted it up as she stepped inside. This week her hair was auburn. Last month it was light blonde and the month before it had been a warm caramel. With Sue, you never knew what hair colour would greet you from one week to the next.

Beth began waving and Sue's eyes stopped roaming as she caught sight of her. Her eyes lit up and a huge smile stretched across her face as she threaded her way towards the table.

Sue's smile had always been spectacular, Beth noted. She'd heard a guy once say that Sue's smile was the kind that made you think of poetry and spring rain, a dazzler that can change your day. A bit poetic, if you asked Beth, but no one has ever said that about *her* smile.

"Hey Beth!" Sue beamed as she plonked down in the booth, dropping her bag heavily on the spare seat beside her. "God! 6 o'clock and it's still humid out there. My bet is it's going to bucket down later on."

"You're late again," Beth pouted, not mentioning she'd only arrived herself five minutes before. "I've had to start without you."

She sulkily held up her half empty wine glass to show her how much she was suffering.

"Oh, poor Bethy," Sue grinned back as she grabbed the eye of the bartender. She held up two fingers and pointed to Beth's glass then rewarded him with her stunning smile. He did a double take and smiled back at her, his eyes flicking quickly to Beth, then back to Sue, before turning back to the fridge behind him.

Beth watched him open the frosty door and remove a wine bottle before jerking her head at him.

"What's it with you and Fabio? He barely took the time to look at me." Beth flicked her hair away from the jagged scar travelling from her temple to the underside of her cheekbone. "Am I just too good looking, do you think?"

Sue laughed, showing perfectly even teeth. "Honey, he's just not your type!"

Beth gave her a *how-do-you-know* look as she did an eye roll.

"Don't take it personally but..." Sue stuck her thumb in Antonio's direction, her bangles jingling like gypsy bells, and Beth's eyes flicked towards the bar. While he was pouring their wine, Antonio was already chatting up another girl. This one wore leather and had so many piercings, if she'd gone through a metal detector, she'd have sent bells clanging madly.

The girls were still laughing as their drinks arrived barely one minute later by a different waiter.

Sue gasped and said, "Ooh wait a sec, please," then reached over to her voluminous bag and began digging around in it. She pulled out her mobile phone, held it up to do the visual id, then touched the screen on an icon showing a camera before thrusting it at him.

"Can you take a photo of us, please? We're celebrating."

The megawatt smile she gave him worked a charm. He held up the phone, took the photo, then handed it back to Sue with a wink.

"Gorgeous," he grinned.

"I'll be the judge of that," she grinned back.

She dropped her eyes to the phone and held it over so Beth could see the screen as well.

Both girls stared critically at the phone for a few seconds. The photo showed them smiling widely as they hugged and held up wine glasses. Behind them, a sparkling blue ocean glistened in the sunlight between the palm trees, making it look like they were sitting in a tropical paradise.

"Oh, that's perfect! Thanks so much," Sue beamed at the waiter who had already turned to head back to the bar. He smiled over his shoulder but kept walking.

Beth pointed to the screen and muttered. "You can see my scar."

"It's not a scar," Sue admonished. "It's a survival talisman and you deserve to show it off. Fate threw you a serious challenge and you survived it. You're a warrior and you're beautiful."

As Beth stared at the screen, her heart did a somersault at the tame word, 'challenge'. Sue had no idea that 'challenge' didn't even begin to describe what Beth had been through. Trauma was more like it. Debilitating, devastating trauma.

Beth fixed a brave smile on her face, despite her stomach tumbling and her heart hammering, as she turned back to face Sue.

"Let's not think of the past, Bethy," Sue whispered. "Let's look to the future. Our future."

It was as if Sue could see behind the mask Beth was wearing. Right through to her heart. Sue was everything Beth wished *she* could be. People gravitated to Sue like iron filings to a magnet. And it wasn't just her beauty. She radiated confidence. She was always the first to suggest a new place to eat, a new bar to visit or just the right clothes to wear that complimented Beth's pale skin and newly-coloured black hair. It sounded like Sue was a bit bossy and maybe she was. But in that bossiness, Beth found security and trust where she'd never found it before.

Sue raised her wine glass and smiled happily.

"Congrats, Beth! We've done it! We're on the road to fortune and fame if we play our cards right. You and me. The dynamic duo."

Beth's pulse jittered. Sometimes, she thought she was dreaming. Tricked by an over-active, sleep-deprived imagination.

Both girls worked in what pretentious people call 'advertising' and she had no idea why Sue had gone out on a limb for her. Eleven months ago, Sue had talked her boss into giving Beth a chance and for that Beth loved this girl. It was the worst part of her life and Sue had been there for her from the very beginning.

Beth had no idea why her boss employed me. She had no experience to speak of which indicated Sue's formidable influence and magnetism. Perhaps he just felt sorry for her. After all, she turned up to the interview with a fading black eye and a split lip. And a scar. Maybe he knew that she would be the perfect for the job. Someone who would work hard and never aspire to anything more than a poorly paid office worker, saving him the bother of ever having to look for a replacement when she told him she was getting married or going on a honeymoon or requesting maternity leave.

What Beth found was that advertising was hard work. You were constantly trying to make a rubbish product come out looking fantastic. But Sue was a genius and Beth was happy to follow along in her wake and pick up pointers along the way. The 'creatives' like Sue were the legends and the rest are merely supporting artists. You can tell just by looking at them who was the star and who got paid minimum wage. Back office staff couldn't afford designer clothes or trendy haircuts. But then, what need did Beth have for them?

In the time she'd been at the agency, no one except Sue cared what Beth did. She was barely noticed. Whether it was because she fit in perfectly or because people heard the phrase *office worker,* and automatically fill in the blanks – lady doing photocopying, typing, answering phones.

Beth wasn't complaining. She was actually delighted. She had become the perfect chameleon. She was Elizabeth Delaney. Five feet four, pale skin, green eyes behind large-framed glasses and shoulder-length black hair. Average weight, average height, unexceptional in every way. Except for a disfiguring scar. What she had managed was more than she had ever imagined in her wildest dreams. She had turned herself into someone else and managed to hide herself in plain sight.

Her ultimate goal had been to successfully camouflage herself as a woman without a care in the world. And she had succeeded. To anyone looking, there was no hole in her life and no missing pieces to puzzle over. With Sue's help, she knew which clothes to wear and what shoes to wear with them and she knew what makeup to apply to conceal. She had become an efficient office worker who knew how to blend in with anyone. She could be doing the same job anywhere issuing invoices for vegetables, shoes or Valium.

It did sometimes feel like she didn't really exist and that she was a figment of her own imagination. And there were days when she felt like she was just a shadow connected to earth by a gossamer thread. A strong wind would blow her away and no one, except for Sue, would notice. She would simply blow away like the tiny seeds of a dandelion and disappear.

Then Beth would do a rethink. The job was perfect for her. She didn't have to communicate with people. It was too risky to do that, and there was too much at stake. Her phone didn't ring often – it made her jump when it did – and she was happy. All she had to do was pretend that everything was better than it actually was. And pretending was what she did best. She'd had a lifetime of experience in pretending. Even now, she pretended that she didn't care how people reacted to the contour of the scar. She turned heads all right.

Sue touched Beth's hand softly and she was brought back to earth.

"I can't believe it," Beth almost whispered, the words barely audible above the din of the restaurant. "I think I've been shaking my head in disbelief for days now."

She was actually amazed because the contract was so big. And she meant really BIG! A couple of million dollars big.

It wasn't as if Beth was some prodigy. Sue was the brains of the agency. Beth was just the copy editor and layout manager. This time, however, Sue had come in to Beth's cupboard they called an office and sat down heavily in a chair.

"What's your take on this?" Sue asked as she pushed a copy of an email towards her.

That was how it had all started. Together they sat night after night at Alto's and 'brainstormed' as Sue called it. And it had worked. The client loved what they came up with and the boss actually acknowledged Beth's existence. She had visions of both of them sitting in some rooftop bar sipping Martinis in skimpy, glittery boob tubes in the company of sultry anonymous men with cheekbones you could cut a steak with. A bit wild, but it was a dream that filled her lonely nights in her one-bedroom apartment.

They sat and chatted for a while sipping and planning their next project. It was then her eyes shifted to a couple at the bar, standing beneath the television positioned high on the wall, and her wine glass paused halfway to her mouth.

The girl was maybe seventeen, her figure slim and curvy beneath the black, strappy silk dress. She was beautiful and her lustrous blonde hair had been haphazardly pushed back behind her ears and fashionably ruffled to give a sexy appearance. As if she'd just risen from her lover's bed, satiated and satisfied. As if she had no need to worry about the finer details of whether her hair was brushed into shape or not.

But Beth's eyes weren't staring at the girl. They were riveted on the man standing beside her. He was standing with his back leaning against the bar rail, a glass of red wine in his hand. The look he was giving the woman beside him was all care, love and concern. As if nothing in the world mattered except the woman he was talking softly to, safe and secure by his side.

Beth felt sweat pop out on the back of her neck, dampening her skin as she turned her body towards the boardwalk in shock. Outside, a crescent moon hovered behind a patchy cloud and at any time, she expected to see Elliott and ET gliding across in front of it.

How could everything still look the same when her world had just tilted?

Beth tried to remember the breathing exercises she'd been shown by her therapist to put things back on track during a panic attack. *In, two three four. Out two three four. Have faith in yourself,* she'd said. Beth made a mental note to tell her therapist at the next session that when things start to unravel it's hard to hang on to that faith. Especially when you're back in your nightmare again and you have nowhere to go.

Somewhere in her thoughts, Sue's enthusiastic voice filtered through, like a soft persistent noise in the background.

"What about we share nachos as a starter?"

Beth turned her eyes back to Sue. Dragged them back. Sue's head was down, her teeth worrying her bottom lip in concentration as she read the menu, oblivious to the palpable tension that now filled the air around the table.

"And then, to celebrate, let's have a big juicy steak." Her head lifted and the smile she gave Beth would have brightened a dark room.

Beth glanced back at the couple standing at the bar, her heart pounding. She tried to surreptitiously conceal her stare but her eyes were captivated by the man's familiar face. The perfectly straight nose. The ice-blue eyes. The cheekbones high and sharp. His mouth stretched into a smile that didn't quite hide the fierce look of concentration she remembered so well. Nor did it hide the brooding look that she had always called his 'bad boy' look.

The past year had been kind to the man. He was still lean and broad in the shoulder and his hair was still dark and rumpled in the casual look he preferred. She still remembered how he used to wash his face and then simply run his hands through his hair. As always, the clothes he was wearing, the dark charcoal grey handmade suit, cut to his figure, and crisp white shirt made him look impressive. Radiating a sense of comfortable power had always been uppermost in his itinerary and because of that aura, women seemed to gravitate to him.

Beth's eyes dropped to his hands. He was still having manicures, his nails polished and buffed until they almost shone. Some people would call it feminism but he was anything but feminine.

Eleven months. Three hundred and twenty-eight days to be precise. Plenty of time for wounds to heal you'd think.

Beth wiped a trickle of perspiration off the side of her bloodless face. *RUN!* Her brain screeched out a manic warning and without meaning to, a whimper escaped her lips.

In, two three four. Out, two three four.

"Beth?" Sue's voice cut though her reverie. The smile had disappeared from her face and she was looking around to see what had caused her friend to pale so suddenly.

Almost in shock, Beth's eyes glanced over to the man again talking animatedly to his beautiful companion.

"What's the matter, Beth? You look like you've seen a ghost."

Almost as if he could sense their scrutiny, the man's eyes lifted and his head swivelled slowly in their direction, scanning the room.

Beth's hand gripped her glass as his gaze swept past her, then paused and swept back, settling on her. His blue eyes bored into hers. For a moment, her vision fragmented and she had a horrible feeling she was going to faint. That would not do. Even in her shock she knew *never* to let him see her weakness at the sight of him.

For a second there was no reaction. Then his eyes opened wide and a slow smile, flat and cold, spread across his face. Not a nice smile, it was something verging on evil, and everything inside of her contracted. Her heart pounded and her insides felt like water. She was shaking so much, she could feel her limbs trembling as if from the cold. She couldn't move. She just sat holding her breath as blood pounded through her body and Sue stared at her.

Beth forced herself to breathe as she casually took in his thick black hair and athletic frame, trying to keep the look on her face neutral. As if she didn't care. She allowed her eyes to roam over his chest, his sculptured mouth and his cold eyes as her body shook. Recently, she read that eyes are the window to the soul and if she'd known that a year ago, she would never have walked through hell for six months.

Beth forced herself to appear offhand but she knew that if she glanced in a mirror, her gazelle eyes would be staring back at her and the scar would be glowing a deep red.

Instead of intimidating him, her casual scrutiny only made his mouth quirk wider. She remembered stories from her childhood about the bogey-man. *There was no such thing*, the nuns said, *so he can't get you*. But Beth knew better. Experience had taught her that the bogeyman *did* exist and he can get you at any time. He is not afraid of anything and he doesn't respect boundaries.

Suddenly, she remembered the taste of coppery blood filling her mouth as she gingerly felt the cut on her lip with her tongue. That had been before she felt the burning sensation down the side of her face. She remembered the enormous buzzing going on in her brain and millions of stars crossing her vision. And she remembered an adage from my teens, *'When a fox hears a rabbit screaming, it comes running.... but not to help'*. For years it's stuck in her mind because as it turned out, she was his rabbit and he was the epitome of that fox.

But Nature's least likely fighter is the rabbit. This animal is made for defence with its camouflaging coat, ears that rotate to home in on any threatening sounds and eyes that see for 360 degrees. It's even an herbivore with chiselling teeth and claws that are intended to claw at leafy pants. But when it's cornered, where there's no chance of flight, it will attack its adversary with a shocking ferocity.

Beth watched as he turned to the woman beside him and leant in close, eyes never leaving Beth's, whispering in her ear. She still remembered the sound of his voice. She still heard it in her nightmares.

As he whispered, the girl's eyes moved around the room, finally resting on Beth's. They dropped quickly as she gave a tiny nod and turned her back on Beth and Sue. That was when he smiled at Beth again, almost in slow motion.

Keeping his eyes on her, as if he thought she would disappear again, he placed his glass on the bar behind him. Beth heard an intake of breath as he began walking towards her and she realised it had been her own.

As he reached their table, Sue looked up questioningly, a tiny puff of air escaping through her nostrils. Beth, however, was poised, *en garde,* as she always was with him.

Perhaps it was stupidity, but Beth spoke first.

"Please go away."

Such audacity, Beth thought. She surprised herself.

He snorted softly, a contemptuous sound that sent a fresh chill down her spine, setting the nerve endings in her arms on edge and the hairs standing up.

"Hello Christine. I like the hair. The colour suits you."

Sue's eyes opened wide as they spun towards Beth, her mouth open in surprise.

"And the glasses. Nice touch." He nodded his approval.

That voice. *In, two three four. Out, two three four*

He chuckled at the panicked expression on her face.

"Don't worry. I promise not to bite.

It was a stupid thing for him to say because he'd done everything else to her. She dragged her eyes away from his and glanced around the restaurant. How could no one hear her heart hammering in her chest? There was a whooshing sound in her ears and she wondered again if she was going to faint.

"Where have you been for the past year, Christine?" he grinned. "I've looked everywhere for you."

Beth closed her eyes for a second and almost whimpered. When she opened them, he was watching her, his mouth curled into the semblance of a smile.

"Any new admirers? I'm all ears."

The words were conversational, but the venom was there. His eyes held Beth's and she watched as they glanced down to the scar on her face and linger. An eyebrow twitched and she knew he was remembering that final night.

Sue's eyes moved from Beth to him, startled and uneasy.

"Who the hell are you?" Sue asked.

He turned to Sue, the half-smile still on his face. "Nice to meet you too. And you would be...?

"Leave her out of this!"

Beth tried to sound confident but the quaver in her voice, the voice edged with fear, was unmistakable.

He looked back at Beth, his glance flashing again to the scar.

"Does it still hurt, Christine? Not my best moment, I admit, but I hope you'll find it in your heart to forgive me. You caught me unawares and it was just instinct to lash out."

Sue looked on in silent shock, her eyes swivelling from one to the other.

"If ... if you don't leave, I'm calling the police," Beth stammered.

The words were meaningless. Stupid actually. They meant nothing. He knew she couldn't call the police. The words didn't even make her feel safe and secure. They made her realise that once again she was vulnerable.

He threw his head back and laughed.

"Really? What for?" He looked around and held his arms wide and grinned. "We're just old friends talking. Shooting the breeze. Friday night out on the town."

Not taking her eyes off him, she reached for her handbag on the seat beside her and pulled it onto her lap. His eyes watched closely as she rummaged around, scorn written all over his face. She was desperate to find her mobile. Desperate to show him she had the situation under control.

She let out an involuntary gasp of relief as her hand connected with it and wrenched it out of her bag. Even though she was close to the brink of hysteria, she felt a surge of anger surpassing all of her emotions. She could feel the saliva drying up in her mouth, more solid than liquid, and knew her voice would emerge as a falsetto.

She held the mobile phone up in front of his face like a cross in front of a vampire, taking a deep breath to slow the ones that were coming too fast.

"Leave, or I'm calling them."

She felt so brave saying those simple words. Her voice had risen slightly, and she had to force herself to calm down. She took a shuddering breath to calm herself.

"You think you're so smart." His voice was like syrup. "But you're not."

His whispered words were almost lost in the noise of the tavern. People still laughed and glasses still tinkled.

He chuckled. "Moriarty can rest easy when it comes to you."

His laugh was the light sound of someone enjoying an amusing chat with a friend.

Suddenly, the laughter stopped and his voice changed to something cold and hard. He leaned in close, anger simmering just below the surface, and whispered, "And now I've found you."

Beth's eyes widened involuntarily as the remark hit home. She pushed herself back in the seat involuntarily and she saw Sue's eyes widen in fright.

"Beth?" Sue whispered.

He glanced at Sue and laughed before turning back to Beth.

"Beth? Is that what you call yourself now?" He glanced around to see if anyone was watching before leaning in even closer. "Do you remember how you got the scar, Christine?" he whispered as a vein pulsed in his forehead.

In the silence, Beth heard Sue's intake of breath. She became aware that her hands actually hurt because she'd been clenching them tightly into fists for so long. She could hear her heart beating abnormally fast. So fast it reminded her of a tiny sparrow she'd held not so long ago that had fallen out of its nest. She'd cupped its furry body in her hands and felt its heart beating so rapidly it seemed like a constant vibration rather than a heartbeat.

Then like nothing had happened, like her heart wasn't thrashing around in her chest, his face clouded over.

"I'm sorry, Christine. That was unnecessary," he purred.

His intense eyes watched her every reaction.

Beside her, Sue shook her head as she fidgeted with her wine glass with one hand and clutched her bag with the other, looking like she was ready to run.

Be careful of the wolf, Beth thought. *It's sniffing at the door again. Sniffing and raising a paw. Beginning to scratch. Breathing over my shoulder, panting. Lurking. Today a wolf, tomorrow something worse under the bed or in a closet.*

All Beth wanted to do was let him know he had no control of her anymore. She hadn't seen his mouth compressed into a tight line or the tic in his left eye for almost a year. She'd almost forgotten the anxiety that would start in her stomach when it began. Almost.

She knew what she had to do.

"I've remained silent for almost a year now."

She kept her voice even, working hard not to let a wobble infiltrate it and betray her.

"I've spoken to no one about you and your friends' nasty little secrets and for the moment, they're still safe with me. I've proven I can keep quiet. But don't push me. Not now."

She saw the redness creep up his neck and his pupils dilate until they were dots in a sea of blue. On the other side of the table, Sue's eyes swung between them, silent, scared and puzzled.

Beth shook her head so slightly, urging her to keep quiet, and Sue nodded just as slightly.

Beth turned back to the man. She put her wine glass down shakily on the table and some of the liquid splashed over the side.

"Leave. Me. Alone." She held up the phone again, her eyes boring into his. "I swear. I'll do it. I know things that you and your friends won't want me to tell the police."

Keep it together, Beth. Keep cool. In, two three four. Out, two three four.

The atmosphere around the table crackled with tension as he stared back into Beth's eyes. In the silence, Antonio walked past, glancing first at Beth, then to the man, then back to Beth again. His face remained impassive but she could read the uncertainty. Slowly, he returned to the bar, his eyes glancing over hesitantly.

The man turned to glance at the girl waiting for him at the bar. Her head was still lowered as if she was watching something of immense interest at her feet. When he turned back, his smile had returned.

"It's been nice seeing you again, *Beth*, but I have to go. As you can see, I have someone waiting for me." His smile did not quite reach his eyes. "I'm very pleased to hear you're doing so well. Let's catch up again sometime." His eyes twinkled. "Actually, I insist. I won't take no for an answer."

He turned to Sue. "And it's been a real pleasure meeting you."

He drummed his fingers on the table lightly before leaving.

It was only when he left that Beth found she was crying softly.

Sue leaned forward and whispered, "Who the hell was that?"

Beth's breath was still ragged but she willed herself to calm down. She shook her head as she answered.

"Someone I knew once upon a time. It's nothing, Sue. Forget it. Please."

"But he called you Christine. And he was threatening you."

"It's over Sue. Really. Forget it." She hesitated before continuing. "Please. I'm trying to protect you."

"Protect me?" Sue yelped. "From what? Him?"

"And others. Drop it, Sue. Please. I'm begging you."

They sat in silence for a few seconds, a troubled frown on Sue's face as her eyes travelled over Beth's face.

"Okay," Sue nodded uncertainly. "I guess you'll tell me when you're ready. But I'm here for you Beth. Don't forget that." She hesitated before continuing. "I'm trying to work out what we should do," she said shakily. "It's not easy. Stabbing him seems to be the best solution right now."

Her forehead was puckered into a frown and her mouth was turned down at the sides as she shook her head.

Beth almost laughed as she sniffled. She ran the back of her hand under her nose and calmed herself, sniffling again. She took a sip of her wine to calm herself. As she did, she saw the couple heading towards the exit: the girl scrambling on six-inch high stilettos behind him trying to keep up, him talking earnestly into a mobile phone pressed to his ear. He smirked and nodded one quick nod at her and then he was gone.

The storm that had been threatening for most of the afternoon had arrived in full tropical force and Beth watched in silence as the couple ran towards a black Mercedes on the other side of the road, parked not too far from her own car. The woman ran to her side of the car, wobbling on her too-high heels, while he ran to his side, leaving her waiting, drenched and shivering in the rain. Twin lights flashed on his rear bumper and he quickly opened his door and sat down. The girl quickly opened her door and hurriedly stepped into her side.

As they drove away, rainwater flooded the gutters and poured down unrelentingly. The wind howled and people hovered under umbrellas on the sidewalks, their clothes hugging their bodies tightly while they waited for the downpour to abate.

"Will you be okay?" Sue asked half an hour later, the plate of nachos sitting barely touched on their table.

Beth smiled. "Of course I will. Go home, Sue. I'll see you on Monday. We have a shiny new project to sink our teeth into."

Sue did a little thing with her shoulders, showing pretended excitement.

"That we do," she grinned weakly.

"I'll be fine." Beth reached over and squeezed Sue's hand, smiling as reassuringly as she could. Inside, her heart still thumped in her chest.

"Okay then." Sue paused uncertainly. "If you're sure. I'll see you Monday."

Beth waited until Sue disappeared. While she waited, she kept her eyes riveted on the road. Watching. Waiting.

She didn't have to wait long.

3

We all make mistakes, there's no doubt about it. And to be honest, my track record of late is pretty grim. But sometimes the worst decisions you make start with good intensions.

Her black hair was plastered to her head, her shoulders hunched over to protect her already drenched clothes against the deluge. Over her shoulder was a large black purse she clutched close to her body like it was a lifeline.

She was watching my car with her thumb stuck out, water splashing around her ankles, as I approached the traffic light close to her. She straightened a little in anticipation, moving forward slightly, a tentative smile on her face.

No way, I thought. Picking up a male hitchhiker was stupid enough. But a teenage girl? A guy in his mid-forties picks up a girl by the side of the road on a dark rainy night? Well, you can see it now. I've done a lot of stupid things in my life but that would be an all-time low for me.

Up ahead, the traffic light changed to amber, then red, and I silently muttered *fuck*. My eyes swivelled involuntarily towards the girl, then back again to the road as I placed my foot lightly on the brake. For a second, I considered running the red light but there was too much traffic on the road. Apart from that, it would be just my luck for a red-light camera to pick up my registration plate as I sailed past. In the end, I thought *toughen up* and kept my eyes straight ahead as the car slid to a stop.

That's when I heard the tap on the window.

I kept my eyes focused straight ahead at the traffic light, ignoring her and desperately willing the light to change to green as my stomach lurched.

Sometimes you know something bad is going to happen. You can feel it in the air and in your gut. I put it down to the abundance of bad decisions I've made in my life of late. While my good angel and bad angel squabble over what I should do, I invariably make the wrong choice. Three years ago, when my ex-wife Sally asked me, almost begged me, not to take the promotion to Sergeant because she didn't want to answer the phone one day and hear that I'd been killed on duty. I didn't listen. Sally left me, taking our daughter with her and now I live alone with a cantankerous cat. After a particularly horrific crime involving young boys buried on Mount Tamborine, Inspector Grayson advised me to accept counselling. Again, I didn't listen. Instead I ignored him and resigned from the police force without any prospects on the horizon. Not the smartest thing to do I grant you, but at the time, I wasn't thinking too far ahead. Then to top it off, I had an affair with my best friend's fiancée and it ended badly for everyone. Hiroshima bad. But that's another story entirely. I should have listened to my good angel and stepped away. Once again, I didn't listen.

The tap sounded again, this time more urgently.

My eyes involuntarily swung left and I saw her there, bending down with stringy hair in her eyes, looking at me hopefully. Even in the shadows, the scar running down her cheek stood out, red and cordy. I shook my head but she did a little spin with an index finger, indicating for me to wind down the window.

I powered it down a notch, took a deep sigh and began shaking my head before saying, "Look. I'm sorry. But I can't..."

"Please. I just need a ride home. It's not far. My car's broken down and I don't have roadside assistance." She looked up at the sky quickly then held her phone out to me. "It's pouring out here and my phone's dead."

She shook the phone like that was going to make it start again.

"Please." Her brow furrowed as she continued to plead. "I think some-one's following me."

Her words were coming out in a rush and whether the part about someone following her was a ruse to get into the car I don't know, but from then on, everything changed for me.

I think someone's following me.

Having been a cop, those words meant a lot to me. Some things never leave your life.

If I'd been smart, I'd have taken more notice of the unsettling feeling in my gut, uncurling like a snake. It was telling me that on the snakes and ladder board of life, I was definitely headed towards a snake.

I should have listened to the feeling, but like I said, I never listen. Instead, I trusted my instincts.

I've always believed that no matter what, I can see through any lie or deception and come up with the truth. And without sounding egotistical, my instincts have mostly worked for me. But up until then, I would never have thought I'd be stupid enough to pick up a teenage girl who was hitch-hiking. I'd have to be a total fool, and mostly I believe that's not me. Not totally anyway. It wouldn't be too bright on her part either but right now it's *my* stupidity I'm talking about.

I took a resigned breath, jerked my head and muttered, "Okay. Get in."

Her eyebrows shot up and her eyes were as big as saucers.

"Really?" She sounded like she was surprised that her line had actually worked.

I paused again, allowing myself another second to think about what the hell I was doing. Then I repeated, "Yeah. Okay."

Someone behind me sat on his horn and I glanced up to see the light had turned green. I opened my side window and made a hand gesture to the guy behind me to drive around. As he drove past, he gave me a one-finger salute and a snarl.

She pushed the hair out of her eyes and her weak smile widened.

"Oh wow. Thanks," she gushed.

The door was opened in a heartbeat and she slid in, moving her phone to her left hand so she could reach behind her shoulder to pull the seatbelt down. In one fluid motion, she clicked the belt in place and leaned forward to throw her bag at her feet. Water dripped on the seat and she turned to me, looking a little shamefaced.

"Sorry about your car."

Her eyes drifted to the oozing cut on my cheek and the collar of my shirt splattered with blood and they widened a little. *Out of the fat and into the fire*, my mother would have laughed, but I didn't say that to the girl. She looked like she'd had enough frights for one night.

"An accident at work," I consoled her, knowing the thoughts that must be running through her mind.

If she were smart, she'd be opening the door right about now and making a run for it in the rain. Instead, her chest rose and fell steadily and her eyes stayed glued to my face.

She was a bit older than I had originally thought when I first glanced her by the side of the road. She would maybe be around nineteen, twenty at most, and probably good looking on a better night. But right now, she was so wet, rivulets of water were running down her hair and the tailored pants she was wearing looked like someone had driven past and splashed water on her. She looked like a shaggy dog coming out of the ocean. It made me feel a little sorry for her but then I remembered the sticky spot I was putting myself into.

I waited until she came to a decision. The guy following her must have scared her senseless because she wriggled in her seat, adjusted her seat belt and sat back, silently staring straight ahead.

"All right then. Let's get going," I said, noticing the light was still green. "Where are you headed?" I asked, glancing sideways quickly.

"Oh yeah," she said with a weak smile. "Just keep going straight for a while and head towards Runaway Bay."

I turned my head and glanced over my shoulder to see if any cars where coming before putting my foot on the accelerator. While I pulled out into traffic, she dug around in the bag at her feet and pulled out a band for her hair. She put the phone in her lap and quickly gathered her hair together at the back and haphazardly made a ponytail. As she worked, the smooth skin of the scar running down the side of her face took on a light of its own, making it almost glow in the dimness. She settled back, clutching her phone again, and glanced every now and then at the watch on her left wrist.

Neither of us said anything for a few minutes but her eyes kept turning nervously to the side mirror. I glanced in my rear vision mirror and saw a SUV close behind so I slowed down a little to let him pass. He stayed right there on my tail. The girl seemed to be taking a lot of interest in it as well.

"You okay?" I asked as I watched the car in my mirror. "Boyfriend stuff?"

"What?" She saw my attention focused on the mirror and made a soft noise through her nose as she shook her head. "No. That's not it."

Her eyes swivelled again to the side mirror.

"You seem a bit nervy," I said, watching her shoulders rise and fall in time with her quick breathing.

In the silence, the only sound was the windscreen wipers swishing from side to side.

"Are you sure you're okay?" I asked again.

There was a ponderous pause before she nodded her head a little too hard.

Not a good liar, I thought.

We were on Marine Parade. On my right, The Spit was lost as the horizon became black and immense. The water looked like dark blue ink robbed of any other colour by the driving rain while along the boulevard, the lights were bright and cold against the deep shadows of the ocean. The wind was blowing hard and I could see luminescence from the whitecaps out in the bay. The ocean pounded on the small beach of the normally sheltered Broadwater and the force of the waves created a plume of spray that marched from right to left. The salt water would have been eye stinging further out in the ocean.

As the long slender arm of the Broadwater curved around Marine Parade heading away from Surfers Paradise, the last of the fast food joints and surf outlets whipped by on the left. An old man lost hold of his umbrella and it went dancing away in the wind, pirouetting and whirling into the distance as he scampered after it. Adding to his distress, a red hatchback whizzed past, right through a puddle that sent a wall of water crashing over him. He just stood, arms still reaching out for the umbrella, dripping, staring after the disappearing car. Oblivious to the man, businessmen were scurrying from shop to shop on their way home, trying to protect their well-defined hairdos from the rain, talking into their mobile phones with one hand and clutching their laptops protectively in the other. In my youth, laptops were a whole other pleasure.

We drove on for a few minutes in silence, my wipers squeaking against the windscreen and thumping at the end of each smeared arc.

I cleared my throat. It was still aching from where Jimmy had pressed the knife.

"Are you going to tell me where home is or do I have to guess?"

"Oh yeah." she smiled weakly as she shifted her legs in the footwell. "Can we just keep going on this road for about two kilometres? I'll let you know where to drop me off."

Her eyes kept glancing in the rear mirror and as she clenched and unclenched the handle of her bag nervously at her feet, the leather made a creaking noise.

I took my eyes off the road and glanced at her but I said nothing for a while. When I spoke, I kept my voice low.

"Sometimes it helps to talk to someone."

The wipers thumped loudly in the silence.

"Someone told me once," I continued just as quietly, "that when you're afraid of something, what you want more than anything else is for your life to go back the way it was before you found out there was something to be afraid of. You want to build a high wall around yourself and keep your life behind it, safe and sound."

She turned her head and watched me intently, not saying anything. She was barely breathing.

"But nothing ever stays the same," I continued, "and it's not a safe life at all. It's your new life with a wall around it."

Even to my own ears, I sounded wise.

"I'm not saying talk to me," I continued. "But you have friends. Talk to one of them."

She snorted through her nose and shook her head as she turned her attention back to the window.

"You sound like my therapist," she mumbled. "You know nothing."

My eyebrows raised at the mumbled words *therapist*.

"So tell me," I said softly.

This tactic always worked when I was a cop. The softness of my tone invited confidence and before I knew it, they were opening up like we were old friends. Except this time, it sparked a bitterness that surprised me.

She turned back to me, her face twisted in a sneer.

"I don't want my..." she put two fingers up as quotation marks, "...*old life*...back." She harrumphed scornfully then grew quiet. "What I want is to be allowed to live my *new life* in peace."

The last words had been whispered and I let them settle in the silence.

"What's your name?" I asked.

She hesitated. "It doesn't matter."

She glanced nervously in the mirror again and I did the same. Something was bothering her about the SUV sitting close behind me. The headlights suddenly switched to full beam and I instinctively put my hand up to cover my eyes from the brightness in my mirror.

"What the...?" I said, as I adjusted the mirror to block the full force of the headlights.

"Can you pull over and let me out here, please?" Her voice sounded panicked.

"What?" I turned quickly to face her, registering alarm.

"Right here."

I could hear the urgency in her voice and even in the dimness of the car; I could see the dark hollows of her eyes in the pale face.

"This will do. Just there." She pointed through the windscreen. "At the corner."

I knew *where* she was pointing. I just didn't understand *why* she wanted me to pull over all of a sudden. I'd committed myself to driving her home, but I put the indicator on anyway and began to pull over. Before I'd even come to a stop, she was looping her purse over her shoulder like she was planning a quick getaway.

"Hey, if someone's following you, maybe you shouldn't be getting out here. I'll take you all the way home. Okay?"

"Look. Don't worry about it. This has nothing to do with you."

"Are you in some kind of trouble?" I asked, glancing in the rear mirror.

"Just stop the car!"

She was beginning to sound terrified. She had her seat belt unbuckled and was grabbing the doorhandle even though the car was still moving. I didn't think she'd actually open it but she did. Just a little way to make me even more nervous.

My foot slid off the accelerator.

"SHIT!" I shouted. "Shut the damn door until I stop! Are you out of your mind?"

"I WANT TO GET OUT," she turned and screamed at me, opening the door a little wider. The shouted words were loud enough to make a couple of heads turn and look our way. Her fear was pretty palpable.

She didn't say anything for a second, then she spoke in a little girl voice. "Please."

I gripped the steering wheel tightly and my insides twisted as I swerved into a park and hit the brakes hard.

With the engine still running, I turned to face her. "Look. Like I said. I can take you all the way home. I'll even promise not to talk. You don't have to get out. It's still raining." I turned and looked over my left shoulder through the back window then turned back to face her. "And that SUV is still there. Come on. Be sensible. Let me take you home."

She threw open the door and swung her legs out, ignoring the rain that was drenching the legs of her jeans. As she snatched her bag off the seat I realised she wasn't listening to me at all.

I leant over and yelled. "Okay. Okay. But are you sure you'll be alright?"

"I'm sure." She glanced up as the SUV, recognisable now as a Subaru, passed us but slowed down to a stop fifty metres ahead.

She raised her purse above her head to block the soft rain and said, "Look, thanks. I saw someone I know inside Montezumas and they can take me the rest of the way home."

She gave me a half-hearted smile then turned ran back in the direction we'd just come from, glancing once over her shoulder. She gave me a little wave and just like that, she was gone, her feet splashing through the puddles.

I glanced over to the Subaru and squinted, trying to see the driver. The window was tinted so heavily I couldn't even make out if it was a male or a female inside.

If I was still a cop, I could have radioed the incident in. I would have been able to look up the licence plate number of the owner and see if there were any priors. I could have seen if the car was stolen or if the owner had any outstanding offences against them. But I couldn't do any of that. I couldn't even see the license plate number.

I glanced back at the restaurant but I couldn't make her out anymore.

Here I was, late at night, worrying about a girl I didn't know, who I'd given a lift to only five minutes ago. I knew I should have known better than to get myself into this position but after she mentioned that someone was following her, what could I do? What I should have done was give her my mobile to call someone and ask them to pick her up. But even then, I knew I was only kidding myself. I'd agreed to give her a ride and see that she arrived home safely and by doing that, I'd made her my responsibility.

I glanced back to the Subaru again. It was even hard to see the colour because of the rain. I turned and scanned the inside of the restaurant again. A couple sitting there with two children. A boy and a girl in their late teens by the window and a guy at the counter putting in his order. No girl.

My heart was pounding. I'd lost her. I hadn't wanted her in my car in the first place but now I felt a little panicked that I couldn't see her.

When I looked back towards the Subaru, it was gone.

My mind raced as I tried to form a plan. Should I call the police or just forget the whole thing? What the hell would I tell them anyway? Even as I was thinking, I knew it was stupid. The Subaru was gone and so was the girl. And I hadn't even been able to get the licence plate number.

Just this morning, I was sitting in traffic listening to the radio competing with honking horns and squealing tyres. I was blissfully unaware that in just a few short hours, there would be this.

I took one last look at the restaurant before pulling out of the parking space and headed home.

$$\maltese \quad 4 \quad \maltese$$

One Week later

Looking out of my office window, there wasn't even a gust of wind to rearrange the fronds of the palms bordering the esplanade and I knew the air would be still and steamy even by the usual Surfers Paradise standards. The calendar had officially ticked over to autumn but summer still lingered on, here in the subtropical coast of Queensland. Only the angle of the sun and its rising and setting times suggested that summer was ebbing. According to the Channel 9 weathergirl, the heat would ease in the next day or so but of late, I've lost a little faith in her. She never seemed to get it right.

During the day, the temperature gauge has hovered around 32 degrees Celsius during the day, hot enough for me to wear t-shirts, light chinos and overpriced sunglasses to work like some wannabe actor out of a B grade movie. It only drops to 24 degrees at around 6 o'clock at night. Inside my office, however, the temperature sat at a pleasant 23 degrees all day, which is why I was spending as much time as I could in my office with the air-con on full blast working out how to pay my bills.

Being a Friday night, smarter people than me had already left work behind and taken off for the weekend. Tomorrow, some would be heading to the beach while others would head to public swimming pools, which in my opinion were about one-half chlorine and the other half screaming kids. Others would be standing shoulder to shoulder in air-conditioned pubs drinking their way through the oppressive heat wave because sometimes the humidity is so high, the moist air makes you feel like you're breathing water.

I was ensconced in a halo of warm, sleep-inducing light and the subdued sound of the television suspended on a bracket in the top corner of the ceiling was the only sound in the room apart from the coffee machine gurgling in my tiny kitchenette. The coffee was to counteract the narcolepsy that afflicts me at the approach to anything connected to money matters.

I pushed my Code Word puzzle book to the side and lay my head down in the warm glow of my desk lamp, the crown of my head pressed up against my laptop, as I listened forlornly to the gurgling of filtering coffee. As I listened, I realised that the smell of Irish Cream was not quite sufficient to stimulate my senses. Five more minutes and I would be out like a light, drooling on my desk.

That's when I heard the soft tap on the door.

My head jerked up and Karen popped her head around the door without waiting for me to reply, one hand on the door handle the other spanning the lettering on the door. The words *'Jack Curtis. Surfers Paradise Detective Agency'* glinted through her fanned fingers.

"Hey, handsome. I was just leaving and saw the light on. What are you still doing here? It's a Friday night for goodness sake."

I sublet my office from Karen's law firm, Barclay and Davidson, on the 13th floor of the Regus Building in Cavill Avenue. It's a good-sized room with a view over the street and a private door leading directly out to the corridor, which is particularly helpful since my working hours vary depending on my clients.

Five months ago, I'd helped Karen with a case concerning an ex-friend of mine, Joseph Banner. I call him an ex-friend because I was instrumental in putting him away for life for murdering his fiancée, so he doesn't call me a friend anymore. The fact that I had begun an affair with her weeks before the murder didn't help matters either. At the end of the case Karen arranged an employment contract for me at her firm, along with some office space, because she believed as an ex-policeman with a twelve-year background on the force, I'd be invaluable to the firm.

Being a private investigator isn't rocket science. Most people associate my line of work with a car chase in zero visibility followed by a standoff and a shootout. But there is nothing further from the truth. It's more sitting around and trying to stay awake at all hours of the night. Husbands and wives cheat on each other and go missing just as often as cars do and it's been my experience that *things* are often missed more than *people*. If someone stole your car, there was no question that you wanted it back. But if your cheating, scotch-drinking, lying husband failed to come home one night, you had to ask yourself if it was good fortune that was smiling down on you.

Somehow, this lifestyle suits me. I am self-supporting, although only just, and I am cursed with a doggedness that makes private investigation a viable proposition for someone with a senior pass at school, a certificate from the police academy and an inability to work with, or for, anyone. However, I am reliable, conscientious and obey most laws but I will lie at the drop of a hat if I have to. This inconsistency has never troubled me because I'm not what you'd call a 'people person'. During my twelve years on the force, I was content with being what the general public called *'you people'*, as if I belonged in an exclusive club and I was only allowed out to view the horrors of their world from time to time.

"I'm just tidying up a few things here and then I'll be gone too."

I clicked SAVE on the document on my laptop and closed the lid as I removed the readers from my nose. The Channel 9 news updates had begun and I reached over to mute the television with the remote.

Karen stepped in and glanced towards the kitchen, her black pencil skirt and white blouse as pristine as the moment she paced into her office at the start of the day. Without even seeing the French braid on the back of her head, I knew it would be as tight as it had been at seven o'clock this morning, her usual starting time. Twelve-hour days mean nothing to Karen.

Her nose twitched. "Is that coffee I smell? Irish Cream if I'm not mistaken."

She sniffed again as her eyes swivelled back to me, a grin on her face.

"You seem like a nice enough man but what have you done with the real Jack Curtis?"

Her grin widened at the look of confusion on my face.

"Coffee? At 6.30 on a Friday night? That's not the Jack Curtis *I* know."

"Oh hardihaha. Aren't you the funny one?" I grinned back. "One more coffee to finish off these bills and then I'll be revelling with the rest of the world."

I was hoping I sounded convincing. The short and sweet of it was I had nowhere I needed to be and no one was waiting for me.

She stood still for a few moments, looking down at my desk and the solitary photo frame holding my daughter's picture: a poorly taken photo of Jasmine from my iPhone at the beach, smiling up at me with the sun shining behind her like a halo.

Karen glanced down at it then up at me, her right eyebrow high on her forehead with the usual quizzical expression on her face. She said nothing because she knew I was lying. It's been a long time since I've felt like revelling. Six months to be exact. Since Shannon's murder.

After the court case, for almost a month, I watched summer die around me in technicolour, fortifying myself for an unknown future. I sat for hours in Anzac Park with nothing but time on my hands. Every day, I watched the bright yellows, reds and burnished orange leaves float from the branches and collect on the grass. Unable to sleep, I watched the sun break free of the clouds turning the sky a deep blue and the windscreens of the traffic on Marine Parade into hard squares of orange light to the tune of honking horns and squealing tyres. I stared at grey clouds of seagulls hovering over the car parks of McDonalds and KFC scrounging for scraps of food as the compelling scents of salt, seaweed, motorboat fuel along with the aroma of French fries wafted towards me. It blended into a heady mixture you couldn't find anywhere else in the world if you grid-searched every inch of it. Palm trees swayed, children laughed, and all seemed right with the world until a claustrophobic sense of futility and paranoia suddenly enveloped me. That and the fact that bills were piling up around me and I had no income to speak of.

You could say Karen saved me. She offered me a job investigating for her firm and now I'm a private detective, sitting in an office, lurching from month to month, wondering if I'll still be operational in thirty days' time, while I wait for my next client to walk through the door.

When I look into the future, I try to see myself sitting by a pool in the hot sun with a nice cold beer in one hand and a bottle of sunscreen in the other hand, smelling like a freshly baked macaroon. I try to imagine a bright and prosperous future ahead of me. A nice home with all the modern conveniences: a beautiful view, a marina where I could park my tinny when and if I bought one, and there would be a pub close by. Doesn't sound out of the question, does it? Well, I'm still working on it. For all that, you need a nice fat pay check and for that, you need to have clients and work. A viscous circle and the tiny pilot light of hope abruptly goes out.

"How about I take you out into the big bad world and buy you a drink?" Her hand waved at the desk. "Surely, this can wait."

I wonder how many men's hearts have stuttered when watching that teasing smile sweep across Karen's face, her head tilted invitingly to one side. Even in my state of drowsiness, I did a double take. Then I had a mental picture of myself as if I was looking down from the ceiling. A dishevelled forty-something-year-old man with hair beginning to recede a little and down-curving lines at the corners of my mouth that seem a little judgemental at times. When I catch sight of myself in a mirror, I've even noticed that when my face is in repose, I look tired, even a little pissed off.

I had a vision of sitting opposite Karen in Gilhooleys trying to be charming. Being out of practice, I knew pretty soon I'd be turning into Barry Manilow, wailing about my misfortunes.

I straightened up a little before replying.

"I still have a few things left here to do. And the sooner you leave the sooner I can finish up. I swear, you're worse than a wife."

I picked up my glasses and placed them back on the top of my nose before lifting the lid of my laptop. I took a short tentative breath, splayed my fingers over the keyboard and let them hover momentarily before touching the keyboard to take the computer out of sleep mode.

Karen grinned wider when she saw my involuntary grimace as a sharp *doink* told me I'd hit several keys at the same time.

Typewriters were so simple. If you hit several keys and it seized up, you just had to reach in and pull apart the arms that had bunched together.

The worst that could happen was you'd get ink on your fingers. And there was never a 'printer failure.' All you had to do was wind the spool a few times with your finger and keep typing. Instead now, when I've almost finished typing a report, a window opens up and says *'A fatal operating error has occurred. The operation will shut down ...'* and then the seconds start ticking down to zero. Then I know I'm cactus. Needless to say, in my office there are two cursors. Typewriters will always be monuments to a less stressful time before firewalls, spyware, google, twitter, Instagram and bloggers.

I looked up at her over my glasses with a look on my face that said, *Are you still here?*

"Go." I waved my hand dismissively at her. "Have fun."

She stood there for a second, unsure of what to do. Finally, she said, "Okay. Okay. I get the point. But remember, all work and no play makes Jack a dull boy." The smile widened. "Hey. I just thought of that! That was funny."

"Yeah. You're hilarious." I lifted my hand and wiggled my fingers at her. "Now go."

"Okay. Have a good weekend and I'll see you Monday, Jack."

With a small smile, she was gone, leaving me alone to battle with the computer.

I stared gloomily at the desk littered with invoices. The room was silent now that the coffee had stopped gurgling and, in the silence, I picked up the remote again and unmuted it. The weather girl was just finishing up.

"We can expect a little rain tonight but tomorrow will be another gloriously hot day in Paradise so make sure to slip slop slap before heading down to the beach."

She turned to her left, a megawatt smile on her face, teeth glowing a brilliant white in the studio lighting. *"And now it's back to you Carl."*

I shut the lid of the laptop again and was in the process of switching the television off when the newsreader's face appeared on the screen.

"The search continues for missing teenager Elizabeth Delaney and the police are still unable to locate her whereabouts. Elizabeth disappeared one week ago from a Surfers Paradise restaurant and has not been seen since last Friday night. A friend of Elizabeth contacted the police when she failed to turn up for work the following Monday."

The first thing that hit me was Elizabeth Delaney's photo. Her head was cocked a little to the side; black hair falling over her forehead and around her shoulders and tucked behind her ears. A thick scar running down the side of the face was clearly visible.

I froze, my mouth opened in shock.

Sometimes there's a moment when you know things will never be the same. I had a feeling like I'd stumbled into a Twilight Zone episode. Suddenly, I felt a little light-headed and there was sweat on my face that wasn't there an instant ago. I felt it in my hair, on my forearms and behind my knees. The skin on my forearms tingled.

It was the same girl I'd picked up that rainy night one week ago. The same one who watched the SUV in my rear vision mirror nervously. The same one who jumped out of the car and disappeared into the night.

She was dressed pretty much identically as the night she sat in my car. Tailored pants and a lightweight blouse buttoned up the front. But in this photo she was sitting in a restaurant amid tropical plants with a huge smile on her face. Beside her was an auburn-haired girl who looked as if she had come straight up from Byron Bay: wild auburn hair, a cheese cloth top, jeans, large hoop earrings and gypsy bangles. Even though the pair looked incredibly mismatched, they were hugging each other and holding up wine glasses as they laughed into the camera lens.

I leaned forward and concentrated on the photo filling the television screen. One week ago, her long dark hair had been wet and hanging limply around her face, but it was definitely the same girl. The skin tone was about the same, almost porcelain, even though I'd never gotten a really good look at her in the darkness of the car. But she looked about the same height and build. Skinny, about five feet three, maybe four. And there was the scar. It was definitely her.

"If anyone has any information or if you have seen Elizabeth, please contact the police immediately on this number.

A phone number appeared at the bottom of the screen and I stared at it. I knew that number well. My ex-partner, Detective Samantha Neil.

I'm not a part of Sam's world anymore. A disturbing case involving five missing boys, buried alive in the lush greenery of Tamborine Mountain, put an end to that career. I hover here now, on the fringe of reality, like a ghost. Nine months can feel like an eternity when the future stretches before you like a prison sentence.

Carl's voice brought me back to my small office.

"That's the news for tonight folks. We return you to your regular viewing program. Good night."

The small intuitive part of my Irish brain, that part that always suspects the worst, had taken possession of my body. Half an hour ago I was waiting for my coffee to finish brewing, wondering what I was going to do with my weekend. Well, now I knew.

There are moments in your life when you know you have to make a decision that will affect your life. Everyone is scared of taking that first step, especially when you can't see the whole staircase. The decision might come after long deliberation or after no more than a second of thought, but it carries the potential to change the direction your life takes and whether conscious of the fact at the time, looking back, you are aware of the changes that decision brought. I was having just that kind of moment.

I stood up and walked into the kitchenette with my half empty coffee cup. For a long moment, I just stood at the sink, my hands splayed on the counter, staring at myself in the mirror. The face that stared back at me was somehow unsettling. Not the expression, but something in the eyes. There was something there – a kind of hunger. Almost desperation. For months I've been focussed on nothing except my job and building up my reputation and business. But now, I wanted to be a part of this investigation. I *needed* it.

When everything in your life is right on track it's easy to believe things happen for a reason. It's easy to have faith. But when things start to go wrong it's hard to hang onto that faith. It's hard not to wonder why things happen. All of a sudden, you find yourself in the middle of your life, and you're nowhere near where you were going. How do you find a way from the person you've become to the one you know you could have been?

Some people, and that would include me, spend their lives hoping for something to happen that will change everything. They look for power or love or the answers to their biggest questions. I think what they're looking for is another chance. Some way to lead another life where all the mistakes they've made will be erased. Nothing bad has happened yet and all the possibilities are still in front of them.

Slowly I smoothed back my hair then picked up the phone and called Sam.

❦   5   ❦

On the horizon in front of The Grand Hotel at Labrador, dark thunderclouds were rolling in fast, bringing a damp smell of seaweed. In the bay, at a distance, I could see fishing boats lurching as they tried to bring in their catch. Waves crashed on the shore and a dog walked out of the surf, shaking himself, sending a cascade of droplets into the air where they glittered momentarily before falling to the sand. It was starting to drizzle and tiny beads of water shimmered brilliantly in the darkening sky. Just as I reached the entrance to the hotel, a salty breeze hit me and with it came the salty smell of the surf and coconut oil.

The doors opened suddenly and a knot of revellers spilled out of the front door. Some guy toppled sideways, taking two women with him and the three of them lay at the entrance laughing and giggling their way to their feet. A woman's voice hiccupped, "You're rat-arsed," and the three of them erupted into a fresh round of giggles as I stepped around them into the welcomed coolness of the air conditioning.

Music pounded against the walls and cigarette smoke drifted on the night air in wisps and curls. On a small platform towards the right-hand side of the bar, a dark-haired singer/drummer and blonde guitarist were singing and flirting with several girls and encouraging them to sing along with them. A group of teenagers playing pool were laughing and swaying in time with the music.

Through the bi-fold glass doors leading to the front veranda, I could see most of the tables and stools overlooking the ocean were gone. In the distance to the west, lightning rippled across the mountains and within an hour, I knew everyone would be scurrying inside out of the deluge the weather girl had predicted. The water frothed white around the rocks as a gull circled close enough that a wing brushed against a palm frond, leaving a soft grey feather floating in the air currents.

Closest to the door sat a trio that caught my attention. Sitting with her back ramrod straight was a sixtyish looking woman, looking tanned and wrinkly, like she'd been scrunched up and then spread smooth. From the expression on her face, she could have provoked Mother Teresa into using the F word. Even from my vantage point near the door, something about the her made me think of a bird of prey. Maybe it was the eyes too close together or the way she cocked her head sharply when she spoke. Whatever it was, my inner voice said '*Whoa*'. Beside her was a much younger woman who could have been her daughter.

With them was a still-trim elderly man who had the figure of an ex-tennis player, a little scrawny but fit. He had the unfashionable good looks of a silent film star, Valentino maybe, whose features I always thought were a little too prominent and his eyes too moody. This guy's hair was so black, it made me question if Clairol had some say in the colour. On closer look, his eyebrows matched.

Who am I to judge? I thought. Valentino was the heartthrob of thousands of women in his day.

I steeled myself and pushed through the crowd on my way to the bar, scanning the assembled patrons for Sam, and hoping I was doing the right thing by seeking her out. She hadn't arrived so I ordered a beer from the bartender who poured it without taking his eyes off the television set hanging from the ceiling. I glanced up to see the program was Friday night football and the score at the bottom of the screen told me the Broncos were losing again.

I stood with my back to the bar while I waited for Sam to arrive. When a couple nearby left their table, I stepped over quickly and sat down.

While I drank and waited for Sam, her lop-sided grin and chocolate brown eyes swam around in my mind. I suddenly realised I missed her. I missed her looks of reproach, her sarcastic comments spoken with a grin and I even missed the crinkles at the corners of her eyes when she smiled.

I know it sounds like I have a soft spot for Sam and I probably do. But not in the way you may think. She represents what I miss most. Being a cop. I have this new life now but it isn't how I'd seen my career three years ago when I left Hobart. Sam was a big part of my old life and it was a life I missed terribly.

It's not the lack of friends, the too many hours alone or my poor social-isation skills that makes my life lonely these days. It's more than that. I began with the police force twelve years ago and there has never been anything else for me. We teach our children that they are special, but I actually lived it. I had a job where I was respected and looked up to. Reporters chased me. Other policemen and women asked my opinions and watched everything I did. And then one day, poof – all gone.

I've absorbed enough from Dr Phil to know that bereavement affects everyone differently. I have been through the bewildered stage, the denial stage, the angry stage and I am now in the resigned stage. Dr Phil also said people are lonely in this world for different reasons. Some of them have something in their disposition. Maybe they were born cruel or maybe they were born too tender. But most people are brought to where they are by circumstance, by calamity or a broken heart. But they certainly haven't planned on it. He was right on the mark. Being a survivor is bloody hard work. Harder than I thought it would be.

A burst of laughter came from across the room. A couple were dancing as friends looked on. The guy was doing a combination of Mick Jagger and Peter Garret moves that looked more like epilepsy than dancing. Watching him made me question whether he had a day release pass from the local mental care hospital.

Very faintly through the laughter, I could hear the ocean roaring outside and I knew the tide was coming in and smashing on the shore. When I looked outside, all I actually saw were the same old palm trees, the same old seagulls and the same relentless green everywhere.

I had just finished my first beer when I saw Sam's car pull into the car park across the road in front of Charis Seafoods and my heart did a little stutter.

I couldn't help but think of all those old movies where trains separate lovers, steam billowing from beneath, the conductor calling a last warning, the whistle blowing, the chug-chug as the wheels begin to move, one lover hanging on and waving, the other running along the platform. I don't know why I thought of this because the Sports Bar at The Grand Hotel is about as romantic as a pile of elephant muck with dung beetles inside it.

I sat and watched as Sam crossed the road and walked slowly towards the front door. Within seconds, she was standing in the doorway, eyes moving around the crowd looking for me.

Tonight, she was dressed in designer blue jeans, all scraped and torn a little in parts. *Distressed* they called it. In my day, distressed meant *upset* but then, that's just me showing my age. Her billowy shirt was a soft, pale caramel colour that went well with her dark eyes. A suede bag dangled from her shoulder and she hoisted it up to her shoulder as she stepped inside.

I'd always thought Sam had Italian somewhere in her background. She had a "European' complexion and with those fiery eyes, I'd always imagined a Sophia Loren personality to go with the colouring. As it turned out, I was wrong. The colouring and eyes were pure Black Irish, descended from Spain when the Spaniards crossed the Bay of Biscay into the Celtic Sea and settled in Cork centuries ago.

I'd been wrong about the heritage but I hadn't been wrong about the depth of passion in those Black Irish eyes. As I watched her, they stopped moving as she caught sight of me and for a moment, we just stared at each other.

I suddenly remembered one of my psychology classes where an instructor flashed different faces from a projector onto a screen and students were supposed to identify the emotions portrayed. It was astonishing. Almost everyone could accurately differentiate between disgust, fear, surprise and joy.

For me, I've always thought voices reveal just as much expression and that our brains are capable of deciphering and categorising almost imperceptible nuances in tone. By the look on Sam's face, I'd missed the nuance in her voice when I'd spoken to her earlier on the phone. I had thought she sounded pleased to hear from me. In actual fact, it looked like she would rather be anywhere else in the world but here tonight.

She stepped forward a little tentatively and I waited for her to smile. Tonight, the smile was tight somehow. And it looked pained.

I've had my fair share of bad breaks in life. A divorce. No living family, apart from a daughter with a bad attitude. To give Jazz a bit of leeway, she *is* fourteen and hormonal. But it surprised me that this woman watching me with guarded eyes had once been my friend in the darkest of times and no matter how much of a mess I'd made of things, she had always been there for me. It pained me to see that hesitant look on her face and I wondered if she was holding the smile back from me deliberately.

Then I remembered what had dimmed the wattage.

I'd heard that she had recently been messily divorced, the marriage over for about four months now. The disintegration of her marriage would have pained her in a particular way, I knew. She came from a broken family herself and she had always wanted to do better than her parents had done.

I stood up as she approached the table and glanced over my shoulder towards the bartender. I caught his eye, held up two fingers and mouthed 'white wine' and he nodded.

She stopped a metre from me, neither of us sure if the proper protocol called for a hug or a handshake. We did neither.

I walked around and pulled a chair out for her and after she sat down, I returned to my chair and sat down as well. Neither of us spoke for a few more seconds. We just looked at each other.

"Hi," I finally said.

"Good to see you still have all the smooth lines," she smirked awkwardly.

My heart gave a little tug at that lop-sided grin of hers.

I feigned a rakish grin. "Hey, baby, what's your sign?"

She did a little tilt of her head from side to side. "Better."

"Come here often?"

"Good. Now say, 'haven't we met before?'"

"Nah," I wiggled my eyebrows. "No way I'd forget a foxy lady like you."

We both laughed, both of us trying too hard and we both knew it.

I toyed with the napkin dispenser as I watched Sam's face begin the subtle sequence of expressions I've seen a thousand times. Embarrassment, sympathy, and just the slightest recognition that a seemingly perfect life is not so perfect after all.

"You look nice," I said, trying to break the silence.

She had changed, but not much. She was thinner. Her dark hair was pulled back and tied into a ponytail. Most men like a woman's hair down but I've always liked a woman's hair tied back; the openness and exposure of it, I guess, especially with Sam's cheekbones and neck.

"So do you," she lied.

I smiled my Mel Gibson at her. "Well, handsome was never the hard part for me."

She grinned back and said, "Let me tell you something important for future reference. Sisters look nice. Colleagues look nice. Even mothers look nice." She hesitated. "I look great."

She blushed a little and gave me a self-conscious smile.

"I stand corrected," I laughed.

A waiter appeared and put the drinks down on the table in front of us, slopping wine onto Sam's coaster. She waved him away good-naturedly as he began to clean up the spillage and quickly took a sip of the wine. The phrase 'Dutch courage' crossed my mind.

There was a brief silence as we both looked through the bifold doors. Outside, the tables had filled up but beyond them you could see the ocean sparkling like diamonds had been scattered on the waves in the last bits of reflected sunlight and lightning.

A group of small sailboats were heading off to the Southport Yacht club determined to catch the last of the happy hour. From here, the boats were almost too small to be seen with the naked eye, each one seeming to rise from the water like ghosts on the horizon. The wind had picked up with the promise of that thunderstorm the Channel 9 girl had predicted and their sails fluttered in a swirling dance as they maneuvered between what I thought were two red buoys.

We both sat watching for a few seconds and I pretended to be envious of someone who was sitting on a heaving platform, braving the inclement weather while things with sharp teeth and stinging tentacles swam right below them in the ocean.

"Nice wine," I mumbled.

She nodded, sipping her wine. Her eyes swivelled from me to the view outside, like she was watching the world's most confusing game of ping pong.

"Nice view," I gestured with my glass.

She nodded again. We looked awkwardly at the menus, even though neither of us had any intention of ordering food. I shut mine with a snap.

"Okay," I said. "I'm out of comfortable clichés and forced banter."

"Phew," she grinned.

A few strands of hair had escaped from her ponytail and fell across her face. It took all my willpower to stop from pushing them away.

She took another sip of the wine before speaking.

"So," she sighed, putting the glass on the table, spinning the stem a little between her fingers. "How have you been", she hesitated, "um...since the last time I saw you?"

It felt like the air went suddenly still.

There it was. The elephant in the room. *Shannon.*

I closed my eyes and it was all there again.

The past never dies.

I remembered a cliché my mother used to say to me: *'Don't stare at the sun or you'll go blind.'* Everyone knows not to stare into the sun. But sometimes you want something so badly that you'll risk going blind for just a glimpse of what it might all be about. Imagine darkness and then imagine that bright light. That's how it was for me with Shannon.

My eyes welled up suddenly. That never used to happen to me before Shannon's death. Now, I'll be having dinner with a friend or mowing the lawn or I'll hear a song on the radio, normal things, and then wham, I get blindsided. Don't get me wrong. I don't spend all my days crying. I still live. I am bereaved, sure, but not all the time.

When I first met Shannon, I had thought she was my great, unrealised love and I had clung to that idea as if that golden future was being unfairly denied me. You meet someone who looks a certain way or has something in their smile and eyes and maybe that's all that falling in love is.

I know now that Shannon and I were never meant to be together and if she hadn't died, there wouldn't have been a happy ending anyway. I've come to terms with that. I've cried my tears and what's left now is anger. But for the short time that we had been together, there had been a light at the end of the lonely tunnel for me. And I missed that light.

I have tried in recent months to discover a means of erasing the memory of her death mainly by accepting offers of work that sound like they could involve any serious form of risk. Just to divert my mind. The trouble is there are not many jobs available in my line of work that necessitates risk of some kind. Instead, I'm left with the memories.

What gets me, what gives me that surprise *wham*, is the way grief seems to relish in catching you unawares. It enjoys leaping out of nowhere, startling and mocking you, stripping away your pretence of normalcy. Grief lulls you, thus making that blindside all the more jarring.

I suddenly realised I had been silent for several minutes. Sam's glass had paused halfway to her mouth as she watched me intently, and the glass was nearly empty. I caught the eye of the bartender again and held up two fingers to indicate two more drinks as I downed the last of mine.

Sam's eyes were scanning my face for emotions. She knew me well.

"I'm sorry, Jack."

She said the words as she put the empty glass down on the table. She sat looking at me, her features unreadable and for an instant, she seemed like a stranger.

I was still nodding when the second round of drinks arrived and we both waited until the waiter had left before continuing. I watched her twisting her glass, making circles on the table, and I realised the sadness I saw was actually a depth of experience. An air of having experienced suffering and having overcome it. There was loss, grief, maybe even depression in her eyes, and my heart gave a little tug of sorrow to know she was probably still becoming accustomed to the changes in her life. It wasn't going to be easy for her and it was going to take time. Ask me. I'm an expert on the subject.

Watching her had given me a little time to put things in order in my mind. I'd already mentioned to her over the phone that I had information regarding Elizabeth Delaney, knowing she wouldn't be able to refuse me. Now it was time to tell her my story.

As if reading my mind, she put her elbows on the table and clasped her hands together, fingers entwined.

"Okay. Tell me why you wanted to see me about Elizabeth Delaney," she said.

This was the Sam I remembered. Once she knew something was up, she became still and alert. Her eyes took on a sharpness and most people would think it was cynicism. I knew it was concentration.

I took a deep breath.

"Okay. Down to business," I said.

A burst of laughter came from across the room and we both waited for it to die down before I continued.

"I may be able to give you a little help with your investigation," I began.

She cocked her head to one side. "Enlighten me."

I took another deep breath. "Let me tell you a story. I was on my way home a week ago and a girl was standing by the side of the road, hitchhiking. I gave her a ride."

Her eyebrows shot up and there was a microscopic twitch. She sat back and picked up her wine glass.

"You picked up a hitchhiker?"

She sounded surprised. Shocked even. She was staring over the top of her glass incredulous.

I held my hand up, palm facing her, to stop the backlash I thought was coming.

"Not my best moment and probably not the smartest thing in the world to do. But yes. I picked her up. She tapped on the window when I stopped at a red light and said her car had run out of petrol, or broken down, I can't remember which one. Her phone was also dead and she thought someone was following her. What could I do?" I shrugged.

I knew I had a reprimand coming by the way she folded her lips together.

"You could think first before you expose yourself to so much risk. That's what you could do."

She was shaking her head in disbelief and the softness of her voice belied the tone of recrimination.

"What were you thinking, Jack? A man your age, picking up a young girl by the side of the road, late at night? Seriously?"

The words were out before she had time to think about them and a thrill of mutiny surged through me at her flippant remarks.

I tried to smile even though they had hit their mark.

"May I continue please?"

Her mouth opened slightly to say something, but then she had second thoughts about what she was about to say. Instead, she cocked her head to the side again and sighed.

"Okay," she nodded. "So you gave her a lift."

"I did."

I breathed for a second, summoning up the courage to tell her the rest of the story.

She reached over to lift the wine glass to her lips but her eyes stayed glued to mine over the rim.

"Are you going somewhere with this, Jack?"

I looked her straight in the eyes. "That girl was Elizabeth Delaney."

The words echoed in the silence at the table as her eyes widened a little. She blinked a couple of times, her antennae quivering.

She put the wine glass down slowly to the table. I could read the thoughts hurtling around in her brain, building up steam for an eruption on the same scale as Vesuvius.

"You're not telling me it was the night of her disappearance, are you? I assume you know the exact date?"

When I didn't answer, she sat back in her chair. "You are!"

"I know the exact date and yes, it was the night of her disappearance."

I tried to make my voice sound nonchalant, but she wasn't fooled.

Her eyes were like chips of stone, cold and hard.

"And what time was this?"

"Around 8pm."

She shook her head as if she couldn't believe what she was hearing. Her glinting eyes never left my face. There would be a hundred questions going through her mind right now and she would be trying to work out which one to ask first.

She took a deep breath and I knew she was trying to calm herself. Her good angel was fighting inside with her bad angel and I was hoping the good one was going to win this time. I've seen Sam explode before and there is always fallout.

When she spoke, her voice was controlled, but tense.

"It's been a week, Jack. Why haven't you let the police know before now?"

"I only just found out tonight, Sam. That's why I called and asked you to meet me."

"You don't watch the news?"

Her voice was a little loud and brusque, even over the music, and she looked around self-consciously.

"Her disappearance has been all over it," she leant forward and almost whispered. She gave a little smirk and snorted. "You've missed some really great shots of me and Cavanaugh."

Cavanaugh was Sam's new partner. They'd been assigned as partners after I'd left the force and it still stung. During Shannon's murder enquiry, he had been part of the investigative team and at the murder trial, he stood silently beside Sam and watched closely.

"So where did you drop her off?"

She was looking at me intently. I had a bad feeling because the story stretched the limits of credibility even to me.

"She told me to pull into the carpark of The Lucky Lobster. I did as she asked and she took off."

"Whoa ... whoa." She put both hands up, palms facing me, as if she was trying to stop me from talking any further. "She just got out?" She made a little harrumph, then continued. "What...that didn't concern you? Really? Even after she'd told you she thought someone was following her?"

I was beginning to think I'd made another bad decision in coming here tonight.

"She demanded to get out of the car, Sam." I shrugged. "I let her out."

My voice came out louder than I'd have liked but I was seriously regretting getting involved at all in the whole business.

"Don't give me attitude, Jack. I have one of my own."

She was trying to calm down but she was still talking angrily through her teeth.

"When she got in your car, did she say where she wanted to go?"

"Home is all she said. She told me to drive straight ahead. She didn't give me an address."

"So, she just stepped out of your car into the rain and didn't look back?"

I nodded.

She was looking at the table and shaking her head.

"This is madness. Crazy!" She looked up. "You know she never made it home, don't you? Apparently that was the last time anyone saw her. It puts you in the firing line, wouldn't you say?"

"I know." The thought had already crossed my mind. "At the time, I thought she may have had a fight with her boyfriend."

She cocked her head to the side. "Because…"

"She kept looking at the rear mirror. And there was a dark coloured SVU behind us that perhaps, and I repeat Sam, *perhaps*, hadn't been there before I picked her up. Nothing conspicuous but enough to make her nervy."

Sam opened her mouth to say something and I had a good idea what that was. I jumped in.

"I'm not sure what make of car it was. My guess is a Subaru. It was raining hard but it was *maybe* a Subaru, dark paintwork, dark tinted windows. I couldn't tell if it was a male or female driving."

"Jesus, Jack. A week I've been working this. A whole week! I gave you more credit than this."

It had seemed like the right thing to do at the time but I couldn't help wishing it was possible to turn back the clock and erase those few hours from my life.

"You know, hindsight's a wonderful thing, Sam. Don't you go pointing the finger of blame at me. I was just at the wrong place at the wrong time."

She locked eyes with me. "Is that the best you can come up with? That's like *'the dog ate my homework.'*"

I stared at her for a second, annoyed. How was I supposed to hang on to righteous anger when she was absolutely right?

Trying to soften my voice, I said, "I thought you should know."

There was a five-second pause as she sat, staring at me.

"Can I ask a question now?" I asked.

"Go ahead," she said. Her voice was brittle with anger.

"Why are you investigating this? You're homicide, or you were the last time I saw you. Elizabeth Delaney is a missing person."

One eye flickered. I knew she was weighing up what to tell me.

"I'm mainly Vice these days," she said hesitantly.

"Vice?"

I couldn't keep the surprise from my voice. She spent years working hard to get into Homicide. Vice was a step backwards.

Sam simply nodded.

"Vice as in drugs, pornography and prostitution?" I asked.

She stiffened almost imperceptibly but I caught it. *What the hell was that about?*

Again she nodded. But I knew her well. She was holding something back.

"What aren't you telling me, Sam? The kid was involved in ... what? Prostitution?"

She said nothing, just twirled the wine glass.

"Drugs?" I pushed.

Still nothing. Still twirling.

"Both?" I pressured.

She stopped twirling the glass and glared at me.

"For God's sake Jack. I can't talk about this. It's an ongoing case and you're not a cop anymore. You've done your civic duty, okay? You informed me about picking her up. And it's appreciated. That's the best I can offer you."

"Bullshit!"

The word came out louder than I wanted it to but I was angry. Seriously angry. It may be an ongoing case but she knew me. We'd worked together for more than a year. Day in and day out. She knew everything about me, professionally and personally. And she knew she could trust me.

She blinked and the colour rose in her cheeks as she watched me glower at her.

She exhaled in a little puff and waggled her head from side to side. "What do you want of me, Jack?" Her voice was quiet, defeated almost.

There was another little awkward silence as we stared at each other. Then I took a deep breath before answering.

"I need ... I'd *like* ... to see the file."

Her eyes widened for a second.

"I know. I know," I muttered before she could talk. "It's an ongoing investigation." I shook my head. "Sam, I *know*."

I raised my glass and finished my drink in one gulp.

What I wanted more than I cared to say was I wanted in on the investigation. I wanted that part of my life back. The part I'd thrown away. I wanted to feel the adrenaline rushing through my veins again and I wanted to prove to myself that I wasn't a lousy detective. I wanted all of that but I couldn't say any of that to Sam. My pride wouldn't let me.

Instead, I looked Sam in the eyes and said, "You know me. I want answers, just like you. And like it or not, I'm involved. It's not like you have any leads so far."

I could see I'd wounded her. She inhaled sharply and her eyes widened.

"That's not fair, Jack." She leant forward and reached for her wine glass as a flush crept up her neck, her mouth tightening mutinously. "I'm doing everything in my power," she snapped defensively.

"I know that, Sam," I said as placatingly as I could. "But what about a little help? Could you use a little assistance on the side? That's what I'm offering here. Assistance. A *quid pro quo*. You help me and I'll help you. That's all I'm asking."

"That's a serious ask, Jack." She was shaking her head as she spoke. "Give you the file? That's my job right there if someone finds out. At the best, it will take years off any promotion I can expect. It'll create a storm at the station and I'll be at the centre."

She was frowning, exposing fine wrinkles I hadn't seen before, and the lights of the bar highlighted a few silver strands near her ears.

It's odd how things stand out. I'd noticed it in my own face. Months would go by and then suddenly one morning in the mirror, I'd catch a sideways glance and see new lines etched in my face. When I get out of bed these days, my back protests and I've started making 'old man noises' when I get up from a chair.

Unlike me, these subtle changes in Sam didn't detract from her good looks. They enhanced them and I found myself liking the look of them.

"I don't even know how I could get it out without being seen," she mumbled.

"Life isn't about waiting for the right moment, Sam. It's about taking chances and learning to dance in the rain." I smiled knowingly.

Her eyes widened and she blinked a couple of times. "You did *not* just make that up! You read it somewhere and you've been waiting for the right time to quote it."

"My words." I put my hand over my heart to show her I was telling the truth. I was actually lying because I *had* read it somewhere, but I wasn't going to admit it to her, especially when I could see a look of admiration in her eyes.

"Seriously, Sam. No one will find out. Just make a copy of the file and say you're going through it at home. That's all. A copy. Anything I find out comes right back to you."

I waited for her to say something. She swirled her wine but said nothing for a good minute. Then she seemed to come to a decision.

"Okay," she sighed, blowing breath out of her pursed lips. "I'll drop by your office tomorrow with copies of everything in the file, okay? You'll be there?"

Tomorrow was Saturday and I normally wouldn't be in the office over the weekend unless I had an active case. Which I didn't. But I would jump through hoops of fire so I could be there when Sam came in tomorrow with the file and I was still proud enough not to want her to know it.

"All morning," I lied with a smile.

She finished her drink and reached down for her bag, digging around for her purse.

I put my hand up to let her know the bill was mine. She hesitated for a second and muttered, "Thanks."

"If I'm not there, just leave it at reception and Karen will make sure I get it."

Sam's eyes darkened momentarily at the mention of Karen's name. I had no need to remind her who Karen was. For a month, Sam had seen me sitting next to Karen, working closely with her in the courtroom as my best friend sat on trial for Shannon's murder.

Then the thought came to my mind that the file shouldn't be left on the receptionist desk of Karen's firm for the world to see.

"On second thoughts, let's meet at Charlie's in Cavill Avenue tomorrow morning. Is 10am okay for you?"

For a moment, she looked like she was going to say something. She opened her mouth and took a breath but changed her mind. She simply nodded.

"See you tomorrow morning, Jack."

One minute later, she was gone, leaving a faint perfumed smell of jasmine behind.

I paid the bill and crossed the road, walking past my car in the car park and onwards to Harley Park. I needed to clear my head. The heady smell of pinecones filled the air and in the distance, storm clouds were rolling in, bringing with it the damp smell of seaweed.

The ocean has always drawn me in during turbulent periods of my life. The relentless waves crashing on the shore, then receding, casts a spell on me, telling me life will still continue no matter how desolate I feel. I heard someone say once that solitude is dangerous because it's so addictive. It becomes a habit after you realise how peaceful and calming it is. I hate to admit it but they had a point.

I sat on a bench overlooking the Broadwater watching the fishing boats bring in their catch, while thoughts rampaged through my head. A man in a hooded raincoat, better prepared for the weather than I was, jumped from his boat to the boat ramp and shooed away a couple of seagulls that were standing nearby, looking at the ocean like yard ornaments. I heard somewhere you weren't supposed to feed the seagulls. They just kept coming back for more. They only have two sections of brain: one larger part in constant search of food and one smaller part that stores information on where food has been scrounged from.

A dog barked in the distance and I could see his coat standing straight out from his body like an echidna. While I sat, a warm breeze ruffled my hair and all sound seemed louder. Laughter from the people at The Grand, dogs barking, cars shushing past. The sounds echoed around me, making me feel even lonelier.

Out of the blue my father's face popped into my thoughts.

My father's life was pure Irish: full of great loves (my mother) and great tragedies (my brother's death) without backing down or giving up. If I had a dollar for every time I heard him say, *'If life punches you in the face, stick your chin out and take it'* I'd be a rich man. But that was before my younger brother Adam was killed in Afghanistan.

The last time I saw Adam, his head was shaved and his ears stuck out. His face was tanned and his nails were clipped and above his shirt pocket were new ribbons he had already earned himself. He looked invincible as he turned and waved to us the morning he left to go back overseas. All smiles and eagerness.

That was seven years ago. Two years later he was dead and the wind just went out of my father's sail.

People say life goes on. But when you suffer grief, it's all consuming. It blocks out everything in its intensity. And when that grief ebbs away, what's left? You have to go on. But that's the hard part. Trying to pretend.

My father died five years ago. Despite his gruff exterior, he was an emotional man. They say he died of a stroke but I believe it was from a broken heart. I can still hear his full-body sobs and see his chest heaving and his shoulders trembling. I thought he would break in half as his endless anguish continued for weeks after we heard the news of Adam's death. Not long after my father died, my mother followed him after being diagnosed with breast cancer. When the results came back from her tests, she simply gave up. Within months, she was dead too. Now Shannon was gone, along with her sad smile, her lips the colour of blood and her hair the colour of coal.

"She's dead!" I shouted to the dark ocean. "Dead!"

The words skimmed across the water like a flat stone.

"It's over," I whispered.

My mother always had a saying for every occasion. No matter what it was, there were always some words of wisdom she would dredge up to impart to me. I remember months after my ex-wife left me and moved up here to Surfers Paradise, I was devastated and barely able to function. My mother stepped in with a saying: *When sorrow sours your milk, it's time to make cheese.*

It was a very Irish way of saying *'stop hanging on to the past and do something about it'*. All my life she'd said things like that and I missed her more than I can say.

I ran a hand through my hair that was turning grey over my ears at an alarming rate then rolled my shoulders, trying to ease the tension I could feel rippling through my neck muscles.

For some people, a simple hot shower at the end of a long day can ease tired muscles and calm the brain but the big stuff, the end of what could have been the *love-of-my-life* stuff, needed something more turbulent, more dramatic and cinematic even if the *love-of-my-life* was purely in my own imagination.

But the memories of Shannon weren't my imagination. You can wade into the ocean and find tiny fish that you can pull out from time to time, like memories. You can hold those memories in your hand if you want or you can let them swim away. But the deeper you go into the ocean, the darker the water becomes and you lose your grip on the sand and your lifeline. You can't see the fish either, or your feet, but you can feel them brushing against you in the darkness. But some of the fish are sharks and they belong out there, left alone. Watching the waves crash on the rocks felt much the same way my life had unfolded.

Above the thrashing palms I heard a baleful cry of a crow. It stopped then rose again: a chilling sound carried high on the wind.

❧   6   ❧

Coomera Waters is the kind of suburb they call 'family friendly'. Not well-to-do or upscale, but acceptable. People have barbeques and garage sales and they love Sunday markets.

I am a rare creature here. I'm straight, I'm single and there are no visible children. I'm not social. I hate mowing. I don't like gardening and I don't like barbeques. And I don't care if the exterior of my house looks exactly like my neighbour's house. I never have any visitors and of late, my job has me leaving for work at night and catching five hours sleep in the quiet hours before dawn until the sound of mowers and school buses wakes me. I'm about as common as the Pope at a Bat Mitzvah and I have to work hard to come across as normal. To bypass any suspicion, whenever I see someone I manage a smile. Sometimes I even wave and call out a cheery hello because most people are easily fooled by mundane gestures. There was a time when guys like me were considered confirmed bachelors, even eccentric. Nowadays, people wonder if we're paedophiles. So I work hard to alleviate that fear.

I parked the car in the garage then walked back outside towards the front door. The comforting smell of a late BBQ cooking somewhere in the neighbourhood wafted over as I unlocked the front door and turned on the light.

The house was quiet. All my ghosts were sleeping.

Sherlock was sprawled out on the kitchen floor and he eyed me with a contemptuous look on his face. He lifted one baleful eyelid as I entered – *you again* – and let it drop.

If he was a dog, he'd have been all over me but that's not what cats do. They're disdainful and aloof and none are more indifferent than Sherlock.

I dropped my keys on the side table near the front door and ambled into the kitchen, flicking on the switch for the air conditioner on my way.

The soothing predictable sounds of my house echoed around me. A ticking clock. The drone of the refrigerator. The mozzie zapper on the back veranda.

Sherlock did a dramatic show of aloofness, stretching and yawning before grudgingly walking over to greet me.

"Hey! You're happy to see me too," I said as I leant down to scratch him behind his ear. "How was your day?"

Sherlock is a refugee from my local RSPCA. I rescued him after my marriage breakup thinking that having an animal around would somehow break the silence. A dog needed attention, something that I wasn't able to provide in my past occupation but a cat...now that was different.

At the compound, he seemed relaxed, even laid back. *The cat version of me,* I thought. It was only after bringing him home that I found out it was a ploy. It turned out that Sherlock likes nothing more than dipping his paw into glasses of beer and knocking then over, his meow sounds like he's being put through a mincer and he prefers drinking from dripping taps in the bathroom, even the toilet bowl, rather than his dish. Having said all that, I've grown accustomed to having him around.

A soft *prrrrr* followed me to the fridge as I opened the door.

"It's about time you started to pull your weight around here," I commented as we both stared at the sorry contents. "What do you do around here all day anyway?"

Another *prrrr* sounded, apologetic this time I'd like to think, as I stared at the only edible looking things in the fridge. Last night's leftover spare ribs. And half a can of sardines sitting next to it.

I took the ribs out for me and emptied what was left of the sardines onto his plate and put it down hopefully in front of him.

He took one stiff at it then turned and scratched the floor, like he'd just used the litter. Then he walked to the cat door and let him outside into the garden without a backwards glance at me. I couldn't blame him.

I popped the lid off a beer and drank it straight down while the ribs warmed up in the microwave. Instead of feeding the mosquitoes on the back veranda, I grabbed myself another beer and took it, and the warmed-up ribs, into the lounge room. I set them both down on the coffee table as I pulled my boots off, one at a time, then dropped myself into my swivel chair like a bag of wet sand, tipping back and forth slightly, listening to it creak.

As I stared out through the front window, the scattered lights of a few houses and a streetlight shone like a halo through the moisture sheen. A thin crescent moon hovered behind a dark cloud, making shadows dance in my darkened front yard.

I reached for the TV controls and switched it on, flicking through the channels until finally settling on the remains of the late news while I ate and drank.

Scott Morrison stood on a podium telling Australians about his upcoming budget. Protesters were picketing a dog show demanding an end to selective breeding and to *'no more exploitation of animal beauty in an exhibitionistic performance no less repugnant than the degrading of young women in topless bars.'* Then came plans to get big, painted, fibreglass dolphins installed across Surfers. As if the cows weren't enough. The Premier of Queensland was also making it plain that she was supporting the New South Wales Premier who was mounting a political campaign based on gang violence and corruption especially in the outer suburbs of Sydney. Our Premier's mission was to bring the bikie gangs into line and the people of Surfers Paradise were more than happy with her. The Bandidos and Hells Angels, on the other hand, were revolting, excuse the pun. The rules were being touted as the toughest organised crime laws and they included increased sentences for child exploitation rings, financial fraud and drug trafficking. The gangs, however, believed they were being targeted unfairly because a growing percentage of crime in Surfers Paradise was not necessarily committed by actual bikers. Much of the crime was committed by a splinter group of non-riding members or associates of these gangs, they said, bringing into question whether these individuals were being sheltered by the name 'bikers'.

For a long time, Vietnamese and Middle Eastern gangs conducted extortion against nightclubs. More recently, drive-by shootings have become more common with tit for tat drive-by events occurring in return. A Crime squad was set up in 2006 following revenge attacks, including stabbings and assaults and since then, the gangs have increased their repertoire to drug trafficking, child pornography and child exploitation. Fourteen years later, the people of Surfers Paradise have had enough and were happy to 'outlaw' motorcycle gangs and put an end to the violence.

Surfers Paradise is the sixth biggest city in Australia and is about twenty minutes from my house. But it could have been another planet away. It's a city of more than half a million people that balloons to three or four times that number during the warmer months when tourists come here to improve their tans and attend the weekend events like the jazz festival at Broadbeach. They shop in quaint gift shops on Tamborine Mountain, cool off in the hinterland of Natural Arch or they shop on downtown Cavill Avenue where shop owners were struggling to hold onto customers who preferred the air-conditioned comfort of Pacific Fair Shopping Centre.

But even in Paradise, we lock our doors. We're not stupid. And there are parts of town you would just not go after dark. Shopkeepers had even begun to draw metal doors down at night to protect their storefronts at close of business. Sometimes there were helicopters with searchlights hovering at three in the morning.

I downed the last of my beer and looked at my watch. 11.30 p.m. I had a feeling that sleep for me tonight would be sporadic again but over the years, I've learnt to function on very little because of my job. You have to learn to cope with whatever you can.

Tonight, my thoughts would ruin my sleep and wake me in the morning like a vulture on the bedpost. Exhaustion always makes me maudlin.

I turned the television set off and walked to the bathroom. I stripped down, brushed my teeth then turned off the light before slipping into bed.

As predicted, my mind refused to disengage and for a long time, I just stared at the ceiling asking myself questions. Why was Elizabeth Delaney being followed by the guy in the SUV? Was she involved in drugs? Prostitution? Was she just missing or was she dead? Why would someone want to kill her? If she was alive, where was she hiding? And why? What was Sam holding back from me?

For me, dreams always come in the last few moments of sleep. The cognitive areas of the brain attempt to interpret signals and I always wake up, seconds later, gasping. Of course, Shannon is always in my subconscious and in the months after her death, when I not only lost the woman I thought I loved, but also my best friend, sleep became even more sporadic. Sometimes it takes a while but in the end, I always end up blaming myself. You don't have control over the things your subconscious decides to push to the forefront of your mind. You just have to deal with them one they're there.

It's the small hours of the morning that all my doubts and fears come to haunt me. They're like demons, standing silently at the bottom of my bed, watching and waiting for the grey dawn to arrive so they can recede back into the dark recesses of my mind.

Around four o'clock, the wind suddenly died as the sky became as pale as bleached bone, as if the colour had been drained out of it. Rain clouds disappeared over the eastern horizon and I knew in an hour or so, the rising sun would ascend like an egg yolk. Suffused light gradually filled the sky making the water look like liquid fire.

And then I fell asleep.

7

My sleep had been so deep, there was no slow swim to the surface. One moment I was drowning in black and the next, my eyes flipped open and I saw Sherlock asleep on my chest, his breath smelling like week-old dirty socks. On the floor was a dead mouse. I pushed him off, cursing as I picked up the mouse and walked through the kitchen to toss it over the back veranda into the garden.

My neighbourhood wakes up early. Finches chirp, butcherbirds sing, sprinklers come on, car doors slam and then cars back out of the garage. As my coffee brewed, I watched the sun filtering between the trees with a soft golden light. The sky a soft pink shot with gold and I listened to the birds singing happily as they swooped low in long loops. The air had a hint of flowers.

The fires of summer hadn't started yet but when they did, it would be big news. Every news channel would be filled with pictures of news choppers diving close enough to ignite because next to terrorist activity and Nicole Kidman, fires are our biggest interest.

My pantry produced very old Frosted Flakes and I knew that I would find ground coffee in the freezer. The combo would help but I'd only had three hours sleep and there's only so much that caffeine and sugar can accomplish.

I made a mental note to pay a visit to the supermarket this afternoon and made a disgruntled noise as I poured my coffee. I hate grocery shopping. Irrational, but there it is. I'll make any excuse to avoid the supermarket. And then I pay the price when I arrive home late to any empty fridge and pantry.

I had a quick shower, downed another cup of coffee before locking the door behind me on my way to the garage. As I waited for the garage door to rise, two dogs rushed passed me along the quiet street, followed by a woman giving chase and yelling. She was dressed in a blue maxi halter dress that swept the ground and would have been perfect to wear if she was nominated for an Oscar performance. Her hair was piled high, lolling from side to side as she galloped towards me. When she saw me, she slowed down a little. I recognised her as my neighbour's big-boned niece who he boasted had 'inner beauty'. Her name was Bronwyn and he had been trying to set me up with her for a while now but so far I'd managed to come up with an excuse every time to evade a date.

I held my hand up in a tentative greeting. She flashed a rueful smile at me and I waved back cheerily like an idiot. I didn't want to start a conversation, but again, I had to keep up appearances.

She hesitated and shrugged before hitching her dress high above her knees with both hands and taking off again at breakneck speed, giving me a full view of the glittering thongs on her feet.

My mind wandered on the drive to the office and the lack of descent scenery on the road helped. The stretch of M1 between my house and the office is one of the ugliest pieces of land on the coast, treeless and flat with a brown stubble interrupted only by power lines. While I drove, I rotated my shoulders stiffly and tapped impatiently on the steering wheel. By 8.30am, I was in my office washing up the coffee cup from last night. A skin of solid milk had formed on the surface of the half-finished coffee but was now sitting in the sink.

If I ever decide to head into the office on a Saturday, most of my morning is spent listening to any messages on my machine and following up on them. It never takes too long. I glanced at Monday's calendar and noticed it was looking unsurprisingly empty. For once, it didn't annoy me because it meant I wasn't compromising any current investigations and my time was free to start on the file Sam was about to give me.

I was itching to head off to my meeting with Sam but before I could do that, I had to finish off a couple of reports and have them ready to give to Karen on Monday morning. This was bread and butter stuff that paid the bills so I couldn't neglect them.

I managed to finish the reports, fighting the urge to leave the office early until I couldn't stand it anymore. I put the reports in my top drawer, locked it afterwards, then shut my door and began the walk to Paradise Centre and Charlie's Café at 9.30am. I didn't want to be too early and look too needy if Sam arrived early. I planned on looking cool and calm when she walked through the door.

As I stepped into the sun and began walking, I knew it was going to be a scorcher. It was already 28 degrees and the sun was shimmering in a cloudless sky.

Of late, the city has been doing a clean up, and in a sense, it made my life a little more difficult because there's not as much work around. The runaways and homeless are in the open now and more obvious, except they're not always pretty. They vomit and they soil themselves because they often can't find toilets. Enough said. You can sit on one of the prettiest streets in the country and if you've been sitting long enough, you begin to see the ugliness.

Sadly, St Vincent de Paul still loses a lot of kids. More than they save. And you can forget the 'syphoning out the weeds' analogy. It's stupid because it implies that we're getting rid of something bad and preserving something good. In fact, it's just the opposite. Try this one instead: the street is more like a cancer. Early screening and preventive treatment is the key to long-term survival. Not much better, but you have the idea. I know Vinnies turns lives around but I also know that what happens here on the streets, in what can be regarded as a cesspool, never leaves these people. The damage has already been done. The people from Vinnies try to work around it and they may even help kids to move on. But a lot of times, the damage is permanent.

One block from Charlie's, a guy stepped out from a darkened doorway. He looked worse for wear, but then again, my bet was he hadn't started out too sparkly in the first place. His hair was Aerosmith-long, parted in the middle and on the greasy side, his eyes spiderwebbed with tiny red veins. The patches of skin visible under the beard were pockmarked. His jeans looked like they'd been trampled on by a pack of dingoes and the waist was too big, giving him that ever-desirable butt-crack look. Hair crawled down from his armpits towards his rib cage and a pack of Marlboros was rolled up in his sleeve like he'd stepped out of the movie 'Grease'.

On one side of the door, the blacked-out window sign read ADULTS ONLY. On the other side, a poster of a girl in nothing but thigh-high black boots and miniscule bikini bottoms was stuck to the window. She had a finger in her mouth and a look on her face that could not be confused with anything else in the world. The sign said Candy Wrapping and 'More inside'.

I'm a guy and I have urges like any other man but I've never been able to understand how anyone could confuse filth with eroticism. It made me want to have a shower and a shot of penicillin.

Having said that, there are negatives to hiding the sleaze. When sleaze is obvious, you can scoff and feel superior. People need that. It's an outlet for some. Another advantage to in-the-open sleaze is the question: what would you prefer - an obvious frontal assault or a snakelike danger hiding in the long grass? Finally, and maybe I'm looking at this too closely, you can't have a front without a back. You can't have an up without a down. You can't have light without dark, good without evil or purity without sleaze.

Aerosmith scratched his crotch and looked me up and down slowly as if he disapproved of my looks.

"Shows about to start," he said through nicotine-stained teeth, jerking his head towards a sign that said, SHAVING RYAN'S PRIVATES.

"Sorry I'll miss it," I replied and continued walking towards the coffee shop. I glanced at my watch and saw I still had twenty minutes until Sam arrived so I walked on a little further towards the beach.

The sky was clear after last night's rain and across the road, through the Surfers Paradise arch, the beach was already filling up with glistening limbs as sunbathers lazed on towels. Most had phones in their hands, some scrolling their fingers continually up the screen, checking their social media while others took enviable selfies to send to friends and relatives. A scattering of surfers floated about, hoping for the gentle swell to grow into a rideable wave and on a high steel-form seat sat a lifesaver in red budgie-smugglers, his baseball cap on backwards but his hand over his eyes to block the sun, watching people swim between the yellow flags.

To my right, the Surfers Paradise Surf Life Saving Club occupied the same prime location overlooking the beach that it has for decades. The gleaming two-story building overlooks the white sand and I knew that on the lower floor, behind the outside tables in the shade of the deck, surf boats, ropes and jet skis sit ready for action. On the top level, the bar and restaurant waits patiently for customers, its foyer lined with darkening wood honour-boards and trophy cabinets as silverware darkens slowly in the salty sea air.

From memory, to the right of the entrance, black and white photos of smiling young men, standing shoulder to shoulder holding surfboards, line the walls and to the left there's a counter with the usual pad for casual visitors to sign themselves in before ordering a drink and a meal. High-backed stools line the bar and behind them, round tables and chairs wait for diners to order from the bistro menu. On a screen above the bar, the cricket would be on the TV and through a partitioned off area stood the pokies, hidden away from sight.

The foyer is one large open space and at this time of day, the glass doors would be concertinaed open to allow unfettered access to the deck overlooking the beach. The sea breeze would be wafting through and the atmosphere would be happy and lively.

I was beginning to regret not telling Sam to meet me there when I glanced at my watch again and realised I had ten minutes to hightail it back to Charlies before she arrived.

I'd just found a table overlooking the mall and ordered the coffees when she walked up to me at 10am on the dot. To my relief, she was carrying a file tucked under her arm. She looked fresh in black pants and a soft pink shirt and without looking in a mirror, I knew she wouldn't be saying the same thing about me.

"Skinny cappuccino still your preference?" I asked, pushing a mug in front of her as she sat down. After the night I'd had, a long black was the only beverage that would dust away the cobwebs.

The waitress had delivered the coffees only moments before, along with the toasted bacon and egg sandwich I'd ordered for myself. Steam was still rising from the rim of the mugs and the smell of the sandwich wafted towards my nostrils, grabbing my stomach. I reached for one half, carefully grabbing it with both hands, and took a bite just as Sam sat down.

"Thanks for the coffee," she mumbled. She almost smiled as she spoke but it stopped quite short of the blazer I remembered from the past.

"I see you brought the file with you," I mumbled as I chewed, catching a dollop of tomato sauce with a fingertip just before it fell on my tie.

"Yep." She blew on the coffee and took a tentative sip. "I bought the file with me." It was face down in front of her on the table, and I could see she was not willing to pass it over just yet.

I put my sandwich down and wiped my hands and face with a napkin before reaching out for it just as she slapped her hand down on top of the file. It looked like I had a lecture coming.

She put her cup down on the saucer before continuing, her eyes glinting.

"As I said last night, this is still an ongoing investigation, Jack. You know I'm going out on a limb here showing this to you. I don't need to tell you the amount of trouble I could get into if someone finds out that I've shown this to you. This has to be kept between you and me."

She'd developed a little tic at the corner of one eye, I noticed. It showed vulnerability and it's something I'd never seen in her before. I was hoping I wasn't the cause.

"I know, Sam," I nodded. "And I appreciate it." Even to my own ears, I sounded like Michael Bolton – all whiney and needy. I made a mental note to work harder on the tone. It was becoming a nasty habit of late.

I raised my eyebrows and dipped my head towards the file. I knew she would interpret it as a request and she pushed the file towards me with one hand while reaching out for the coffee with the other.

She looked deep into her cup like a psychic reading tea leaves before lifting her head.

"Go ahead". She nodded her head at the file, her eyes a little bright and intense.

She watched me over the rim of her coffee cup as she blew softly to cool it down. I moved my mug out of the way to make way for the inch-thick folder.

Emblazoned on the front in bold font were the words: REPORT OF

SOUTHPORT POLICE DEPARTMENT - ONGOING INVESTIGA-
TION – NOT FOR CIRCULATION.

It was a pretty small folder considering Sam's statement that the investigation had been ongoing for a week.

In any investigation, the first few days are always the most important.
If you don't find anything much in that time, the scent grows colder by the
day and you're left with hearsay and nothing tangible. People forget things
they see a week ago in the daily effort of living and working.

I opened the file and right on top was the photo of Elizabeth Delaney
and the auburn-haired gypsy I'd seen on the news, both laughing into the
camera lens. I stared at it for a few seconds feeling a twinge of regret that I
hadn't had a hand in changing Elizabeth's fate that night. I put the photo
aside and began shuffling through the scant few photocopies of reports in
the folder.

I raised my head slowly to look Sam in the eye.

"I don't need to tell you that there's not much to go on here, Sam."

She picked up a spoon and stirred her coffee with a diligence that was
impressive.

"Like I said before," stir, stir, "you can't be seen to be investigating this,
Jack."

"What about cash withdrawals? Or credit card transactions?" I tapped
the file with my index finger. "There's nothing in here about those."

She hesitated, stirred some more, and took a few breaths before she
answered. She was holding back something and I had no idea what that
'something' was.

"She doesn't have a credit card," she finally said. "And there's been no
activity on her bank account for the past week." She hesitated again.
"There was however, a maximum limit withdrawal from an ATM in Surfers
Paradise on the night you gave her the lift. At around 10pm. But nothing
after that."

The look she gave me was penetrating. I gave her a look of my own.

"Last night you said I was the last person to see her alive. That transaction exonerates me. She got out of my car at 8pm and the CCTV camera
will have taken a photo of her making the withdrawal at 10pm. She was
alive and well two hours after I saw her." I gave her a grin. "I'm in the
clear."

I was innocent of everything except stupidity but it felt good to know there was now proof of that innocence.

She shook her head. "We only have your word on that time frame, Jack."

I sat back hard in my seat, stunned. "You're doubting me, Sam?"

"You know *I* don't, but facts are facts. And I don't need to tell you there are others involved in this investigation."

"Meaning Cavanaugh."

She nodded. "Meaning Cavanaugh. And he does everything by the book."

I nodded to the file. "So why wasn't that ATM transaction included in this file you gave me?"

She shook her head in exasperation. "Look, you're unorthodox. I understand that and it's fine. Really it is. But I repeat. You can't be seen investigating this. Okay? If certain people find out, it could be my job. And I can't have that."

When she talked about 'certain people finding out', I knew she meant other than Cavanaugh. She was referring to Inspector Grayson. Broad chested, thick necked, totally bald with eyebrows like furry black caterpillars. The last time I saw him, his face was the colour of a ripe tomato and I knew his blood pressure was still over the top. I hadn't wanted to make it any worse and resort to performing mouth to mouth on him.

What I do concede is he's a good cop. He has good instincts and he's tireless. Before he became chief and spent a large chunk of his day behind a desk, I'd heard he would knock on doors all day and night if needed to get a good result. He'd go on searches for days, getting less than four hours sleep a night, until he found what he needed. But like Cavanaugh, he was a cop who worked strictly by the book and anyone who worked with him knew to be careful. Everyone covered each other's asses when it came to working with Grayson.

I looked down at the almost empty file. This wasn't Sam. She was diligent and a strict believer in paperwork. If nothing else, I'd taught her that. But here was the file of an ongoing investigation and it was almost empty.

Then I knew why. I looked up at her.

"You've taken most of the notes out of here, haven't you?" I asked incredulously.

She didn't reply but I knew the answer anyway.

"You don't trust me, Sam? Seriously? After all the cases we've worked together? You still don't trust me?"

My voice came out sounding wounded, and to be honest, I *was* hurt. Shocked and hurt. I'd seen Sam as a friend, a past colleague who knew me better than anyone else, so this side of her left me dazed.

I know I looked hurt and her voice softened as she spoke.

"You can't go around interrogating people like you used to, Jack. You always get too involved."

I felt like some kid being told off by his mother when he was blameless.

"In case you've forgotten Sam, I'm a private investigator now with a licence and a gun. I'm allowed to," I did the quote thing with the fingers of both hands, "go around interrogating people."

I was intent on my conversation with Sam when the door opened behind me and a gust of air blew a napkin off a nearby table. I saw the look on Sam's face when she glanced towards the door. Her eyebrows went up and her mouth opened in a little 'o'.

I turned to look and in the doorway stood a man of about forty with a Tom Cruise innocence about him. He was dressed in jeans that looked like they had been washed a thousand times and a Gucci t-shirt that had probably cost more than I earned last week.

My first meeting with Detective John Cavanaugh had been six months ago when he and Sam had been called to investigate Shannon's death. At the time, I'd taken him for about thirty-five years old despite the grey streaks in his blondish hair and the crow's feet around his blue eyes. He had a 'cop look' about him due to the way he carried himself and the build that comes from working out three or four times a week. Not big. Just muscular.

I'd also mistaken him for a clotheshorse, assuming he was someone who would glance at himself every time he passed a mirror. It turned out I was wrong. He may look in mirrors but only to see what was going on behind him.

He did an all-in-one scan of the room then his eyes rested on mine for a second before he paced over to the table.

Sam paled a little as he sat down at our table, calm and still. I hate walking on someone else's eggshells.

I took a breath, about to speak, but he shot an arm out with his palm towards me, like he was telling a dog to stay. Then he looked at Sam and said, "If this gets out," he tapped the file on the table between us, "you'll be dancing a jig at the Centrelink Unemployment Office."

"Is this a testosterone thing, Cavanaugh?" I asked him, sounding genial. "Did you overdose on your Testogel this morning?"

There is something truly delicious about being the bad guy and I can see how some people get off on it.

He didn't react immediately, which was an indication that he believed he was in charge of the situation. He simply looked at me without blinking and I was reminded that he was someone I had to wary of.

"I know I only just arrived at this little party but I wasn't born yesterday. I know you and Sam have a history." He put his hand up to silence me again as I opened my mouth to interrupt. "Let me finish."

I made a gesture to him that said *go ahead.*

He nodded and continued. "I'm fine with that. But this," he glanced down at the file and tapped it again with his index finger, "this goes beyond friendship. This is breaking all the rules in the book. And it's putting her career in jeopardy."

There was a time when I was under the illusion that I was an honourable man. I believed I had ideals and my behaviour was governed by a set of high-minded principles. But as I get older, I start to realise every day is made up of compromises. Bending the rules doesn't seem worth losing sleep over anymore.

I'd crossed the line six months ago during Shannon's murder investigation. Actually, I pole-vaulted over it. I ran at it flat out and jumped as high as I could. One-part mourning. One-part rage. Mix them together and watch out for Jack Curtis. What I told myself at the time was I'd landed on my feet like a cat does. Looking back, I'm not proud of some of the things I did to prove Joe's part in her murder. But the end justifies the means, right?

But just because I'd crossed the line back then didn't mean I couldn't step back over the line and become the pillar of respectability again. I actually have. I work hard at building my reputation and maintaining a reputable business. It may not be profitable at the moment, but it's still early days.

As we held each other's stare, I knew he was right. What I was doing now was stepping over the line again, and worse still, I was dragging Sam with me.

No one spoke for a moment. When I did, I tried to sound reasonable.

"I don't remember inviting you to sit down Cavanaugh. This is a meeting between old friends. And you weren't invited."

Butter wouldn't melt in my mouth.

"That's interesting, Jack." His voice did not reflect his statement and I suspected it was his way of being polite. "I wouldn't have thought sitting around holding hands and singing Kumbaya was your style."

Most people have an off switch but his didn't look like his was going to turn off just yet.

"I would also have thought that you weren't the type to put friends into situations that could cost them their jobs. This," he tapped the file, "puts Sam in a very dangerous spot."

Sometimes it's better to say nothing. Don't commit to anything and you won't put yourself in any deeper than you already are. But that's not my way and this wasn't one of those times. Old habits die hard.

I smiled and shrugged. "As Jiminy Cricket once said, *Let your conscience be your guide.*"

The comment came out a little glib, which hadn't been my intention. I *knew* Sam was putting her career on the line, even though she'd taken out most of the information, and I knew the implications. I just didn't need him reminding me of it.

"Are you here out of concern for my welfare, Cavanaugh?" I asked. "Why am I not feeling all warm and fuzzy?"

Finally, I hit a nerve.

He leaned forward in his seat with his face inches from mine, just to make his point.

"Do you want to waste the next few minutes discussing your feelings? You don't seem too concerned by the situation here and the consequences of what I'm saying."

The words were spoken carefully and slowly, like I was a child with a learning disability.

He turned to Sam. "And I thought we were way past all of this Sam. I'm your partner. Remember? We look out for each other and we can rely on the other one to help when necessary. Even when one partner steps over the line," his head nodded towards the folder on the table, "the other one is always there to pick up the pieces. That's what we said. Remember?"

I supressed a tiny spark of appreciation. If I were honest, I'd admit that I liked him in a strange sort of way. He reminded me a little of myself, the way I used to be.

I sat back and watched them. Sam looked uncomfortable as they held each other's gaze for a few seconds. Then Cavanaugh said, "What's really going on here, Sam?"

Sam looked at me then lifted her coffee up and finished the contents in one gulp before dropping it back on the saucer with a thunk. She took a deep breath like she had just made a decision. Then she reached over and shoved the file towards Cavanaugh without saying a word.

He looked down at the name on the cover, then looked back at Sam.

"This is an open case."

She glanced at me quickly before speaking. "There's nothing of value in there, Cavanaugh. See for yourself. I removed most of it."

I raised my eyebrows at Sam, mimicking *seriously?* She acted like she hadn't seen it.

Cavanaugh opened the file and flicked through the meagre contents and I felt another moment of annoyance surge.

They did the exchange-a-glance thing and Cavanaugh quietened down a bit after a tight nod to each other. No words, just a look and a nod, and instantly they were on the same page. I felt like the only fire hydrant at the dog park.

Cavanaugh slammed the file shut. "What's it got to do with Curtis?"

It was as if I wasn't at the table. I felt like I was in a production and I was the only one who didn't know the lines.

Sam turned to me. "Tell him Jack."

They were both holding out on me and I probably would have done the same thing had the roles been reversed. But I needed more information and the only was to do it was to tell the story and be nice. Sometimes you have to give a little to get a little.

I forced up a charming smile and told the story again while Cavanaugh placed his left elbow on the table and his fingertips on his forehead, like this was going to give him a headache.

Five minutes later, I had finished the story without any comment from him. But I knew that was just a temporary thing.

"We need to be very clear on something here Curtis," Cavanaugh sighed. "You've got your way of doing things, and I respect that, but you come to us with everything you find." His eyes bored into mine. "And I mean *everything*."

I was a little shocked. What he'd just said meant I was in.

He saw the look of surprise on my face and said, "Don't go thinking the band's getting back together again here. Don't be so stupid as to think that." He let that sink in. "What I'm saying is you play things straight with us or things won't work out so good for you. You don't want to get in the middle of something here," he tapped the file, "more than I want you there. And you come to us with EVERYTHING! Got it?"

I was feigning dubious but inside I was squirming to get into action. Keeping my tone calm and professional took a great deal of effort, especially since my heart was racing.

"Absolutely," I said, practising my lying skills.

He sat back abruptly and nodded. His eyes flicked to the waitress who had been watching us silently from the counter as if she was expecting one of us to leap over the table at the other and start a fistfight, like at the OK Corral.

Cavanaugh's eyes flicked back to me and he smiled.

"Of course, that goes both ways." he conceded. "If we have anything useful, all you have to do is ask and we will be happy to share."

I didn't believe him for a minute. Don't bullshit a bullshitter. But then again, I didn't know him well enough to know. I was also wondering if he'd always been like this and I was the one who'd been blind.

"Any guidance on how I'm going to do that?" I asked sceptically. "Because from where I'm sitting, it doesn't look hopeful."

He shrugged and I interpreted it as '*I don't care*'.

"This isn't a free ride, Curtis. But you could try saying 'please' a lot. People like good manners."

He looked up at the ceiling as if he was remembering something. "My mother used to say, '*Good things come to those who wait.*' Maybe you could try that, Curtis. Nothing else seems to be working for you."

Maybe it was just my present state of mind but I was over the bottomless repository of fridge-magnet philosophy like *'Good things come to those who wait'*. Because they don't. And take *'Tomorrow is another day.'* Well, thank you Einstein for cracking the Georgian calendar. Then there is *'It wasn't meant to be'*. Who are you? Buddha? God? Worse still is saying *'Time heals all wounds'* because it doesn't. It heals the anger and it dries up some of the tears. But it doesn't heal the pain. And what about *'Don't sweat the little shit.'* Are you kidding me?

I could feel the redness creeping up my neck and as it reached my face it burned with anger and irritation. Why did I care what he thought?

I willed myself to be quiet. To let the anger settle before talking again. He would see the anger as a weakness and I didn't want to give him that satisfaction.

Instead of an angry response, I didn't say anything. He was just pounding his chest, so I let the silence linger on for a bit to let him have that round.

He watched me control myself, letting his eyes roam over my face before seeming to come to a decision.

He turned back to Sam. "If we do this, you don't just need to control him." Cavanaugh's eyes were boring into Sam's. "You need to put him on a leash."

Again, I sat and let the words sting for a second before replying. "Sticks and stones, Cavanaugh," was the best I could come up with.

He looked at me as if I was something he'd scraped off his shoe. "I'm sure that sounded different in your head."

He suddenly stood up. "The fact is you have always painted outside the squares, Curtis. But this time, kindly remember you're not the centre of the universe."

He nodded to Sam and then did the same to me before leaving.

"Well, that was enjoyable," I mumbled as the door shut behind him.

"He's not that bad, Jack, once you get to know him." She shrugged. "He's kind of anal but he's a good cop."

As she spoke, she was picking up her handbag that had been resting on the ground at her feet.

I leant forward and said, "Mmm. Anal. Isn't that another word for an asshole?"

Her mouth twitched but she said nothing.

She hitched her bag over her shoulder and muttered apologetically, "I have to go Jack."

Surprise must have been evident on my face. My heart skipped a beat at the thought of losing the only opportunity I had.

"But I still have some questions, Sam. Come on. This file is practically empty! You said so yourself!"

"Sorry Jack. But I have to go," she repeated. She nodded at the file. "There's a list of Elizabeth Delaney's known contacts in there so you may want to start with those. It's not a long list but it's something. The name of the girl who reported her missing is Susan Bishop. Her details are in there too."

She hesitated for a second; like she wanted to say more but wasn't sure if she should.

"Hayley Johnson is another known contact but..."

She hesitated again, opened her mouth as if she was about to tell me something, then closed it again.

Strange.

"What aren't you telling me, Sam?"

I watched as her chest rose and fell but she remained silent.

"Have a good day, Jack," she said. And then she was gone.

❧ 8 ❧

Less than half an hour later I was sitting at my desk. I leaned my six-foot frame into my chair and kicked my shoes off at almost the same time. Thoughts were rampaging around in my head, urging me to make notes in my computer before they disappeared. I wiggled the mouse and the screen popped up with the prompt for me to put in my password. I sighed and did as I was told and after a few seconds, it blinked awake and the desktop came alive. This time the message said, *Download an upgrade.* What the hell did that even mean? I pressed the *later* option and it came back and asked *when.* It was like being married all over again.

I managed to click out and opened up a new file on the desktop, renaming it *Elizabeth Delaney,* but in the time it took to do that, the whole train of thought had gone and I was left sitting in front of my Mac wondering what it was I'd been thinking to type in the first place. I pulled the file back in front of me and glanced through it again.

The list of friends was the second page after the photo. A couple of names from her apartment building, all of whom, it stated, had been contacted and had no information to offer the police. A work friend by the name of Susan Bishop who had reported Elizabeth missing. And the name

Hayley Johnson with no information next to it at all. That was it. Elizabeth Delaney was worse than me.

I put the sheet aside for later and started on the rest of the file. The first page of the report stated her car had been found and listed among the contents was a small quantity of cocaine found in the glove box along with a gun.

At the words, cocaine and gun, my eyebrows shot up. *Where the hell did she get a gun? Had the gun been in that oversized bag she hugged when she was in my car?*

Crime has always existed throughout history. It exists in all cultures, committed by all races, in all time periods. But Australia is this isolated little country at the bottom of the world and even though it seems like Surfers Paradise never sleeps, it's certainly not Miami even though we try to make it seem like we are part of the same set.

Like Miami, Surfers Paradise is beautiful. Ask anyone. On any given day, the sky over the Gold Coast is a deep, sharp blue, washed clean of dirt and chemical elements that sometimes colour the skies. We get melanoma candidates like Miami who strip off and soak up the sun on some of the most beautiful beaches in the world. Like Miami, shirtless young men and girls with ponytails walk along the sidewalks overlooking the ocean while palm trees sway in the breeze and male and female joggers, bodybuilders with great tans and tourists move through the endless streams of people. Like Miami, everyone is smiling and the ocean stretches and sparkles for as far as the eye can see.

But that's where the similarity ends.

The big difference is this is Australia and you can't just walk into a shop and buy a gun. There are strict procedures and protocols to go through and with the threat of terrorism these days; it puts you on the radar as far as the police are concerned. If you want to get a license to carry a gun, you have to have a valid reason. And believe me, I know. I'm a cop turned private investigator and I still had to jump through hoops of fire to get mine.

So here was a twenty-year old girl with a gun and I knew the only way she could have purchased one was to buy it illegally. But why did she feel she needed a gun to protect herself? And where did she get it?

I pushed the questions to the back of my mind and read on.

Fingerprint analysis revealed three sets of prints on the gun with no identification for any of the prints despite an intensive data base check. If they weren't in the system, it meant the fingerprints belonged to people who didn't have a police record. Or they hadn't been caught yet. The only print on the bag of cocaine matched one set from the gun, and the assumption was that *that* one was Elizabeth's.

The next sheet showed questions concerning her state of mind at the time. Was she anxious? Nervous? Depressed? Had she planned on killing someone with the gun or had she planned on simply going somewhere to take her own life?

I could attest to the first three. She was definitely scared of something. And then there was the SUV following her. But suicide? It's a difficult thing to do, taking one's own life. Especially putting a gun to your head and pulling the trigger. Most people would require a little Dutch courage to help them on their way and there were drugs in the glove box that could have helped her with that.

But there were some problems here. From the short time she'd sat in my car, there had been none of the tell-tale signs of disturbed personality of the type likely to attempt suicide. And anyway, she'd gone missing and left the gun in the car. If she'd planned on killing herself, or anyone else, she'd have taken it with her.

It's also an established fact that women rarely commit suicide with guns. Although there are rare exceptions, women don't seem to have the same fascination with firearms as men and they tend to pick less obvious violent ways to end their lives. I knew Sam would be thinking the same as I was.

I picked up the contact list again. The first name was Susan Bishop. It provided a contact number but no address. I pulled a notepad over and prepared to take notes. I wrote Elizabeth Delaney at the top of the pad, then the date and time underneath. Under that, I wrote *#1: Rang Susan Bishop to organise a time to meet.* Then I picked up the phone.

A female voice answered after the first ring. "Hello?"

"Hello," I replied. "Is this Susan Bishop?"

There was silence on the phone. I could hear noises in the background, a voice over a loudspeaker announcing specials and a general hum of shoppers.

Eventually she asked, "Who is this?"

"My name is Jack Curtis, Susan. I'm a Private Detective helping the police with their investigation into Elizabeth Delaney's disappearance. I'd like to ask you some questions, if I may. Can we meet somewhere?"

"How do I know you're who you say you are?"

It was a strange thing to say and it made me hesitate. Her voice sounded cautious, nervous even, and the hairs on the back of my neck rose.

"You can call Detective Samantha Neil at Surfers Paradise Police Station to verify my name, if you like. I believe she interviewed you when you made the missing persons report? You can also Google my name. I'm an ex-policeman, now a private investigator, working in Surfers Paradise. There may even be a photo of me."

"I'll call you back." And then she hung up.

I sat back and blinked.

There is a theory that 10,000 hours of practice makes you an expert on any given field. After twelve years on the force, it was my humble opinion that I was damn good at what I did. And that was detecting. But over the past six months, I had not been given an opportunity to use that expertise in my role as a private investigator. Now, if my instinct was right, Susan Bishop was about the change all that. She was nervous of something, or someone, and the whole case had taken on a new twist.

I had to admit, I was zinging. In the space of one day, I'd gone from writing a boring report on a cheating husband for Karen to investigating the disappearance of a girl I'd given a lift to one rainy night a week ago. I felt like I was back in the driver's seat and my prayers had been answered.

I made a note under the first item. *#2 Susan Bishop confirming my identity. Call back to make appointment to meet.*

I pulled the list back over again. The second name on the list was Hayley Johnson. This time there was an address but no contact number.

I stared at the name for a few seconds, remembering Sam's odd behaviour when she mentioned Hayley's name at Charlie's. Every instinct I owned told me Sam was hiding something. I was sure she'd been tossing up whether to tell me something or not but in the end, she'd opted for silence.

Instead of accepting her silence, it had fired me up to find out what that *something* was.

I jiggled the mouse of my computer again and opened Safari to Google

Maps, typing in the address from the file. I found it easily enough and saw it wasn't too far away.

I made another note. *#3 Go to address given for Hayley Johnson at* I looked at my watch and added an hour to the current time at the end of my note.

Before heading over to talk to see Hayley, I wanted to go over the file one more time. I'd only managed a quick glance at it so far and I wanted to make sure I'd read all of the paperwork, leaving nothing out.

Fifteen minutes later, my stomach grumbled and I was working on making coffee in the kitchenette when I heard a knock on the door.

I lifted my head tilting it in that direction, like a dog on alert. I wasn't expecting any clients so I walked slowly towards the door just as the knock was repeated.

"Yes?" I asked tentatively, craning forward to listen.

A woman's muffled voice said, "I'm looking for a man by the name of Jack Curtis? From Surfers Paradise Detective Agency?"

"We're closed," I called through the door.

"I'm sorry. I can't hear you," came a muffled reply.

I sighed heavily and opened the door a crack, enough to see who was on the other side. The woman was smaller than me by perhaps eighteen inches, and probably two decades younger.

"We're closed," I repeated.

"You *are* Detective Curtis, aren't you?" she asked.

I sighed. "I'm not a police detective anymore."

"May I come in?" she asked, her blue eyes glowing softly.

"We're closed."

She remained standing at the door, staring silently at me.

"My name is Susan Bishop," she finally said.

She watched my eyes widen in silence.

It was the gypsy girl from the photo. Except now she was dressed conservatively in a pair of jeans and a Foo Fighters t-shirt. And her auburn hair was pulled back in a pony tail instead of cascading over her shoulders. I barely recognised her.

I opened the door for her and with one glance over her shoulder, she walked past me into the office.

Conscious that the coffee machine was gurgling and spitting in the back room, I offered her the chair on the other side of my desk. She put her oversized bag on the floor next to her feet and wiped her hands nervously on the pants of her jeans before placing them in her lap. I caught sight of the puzzle book still sitting on my desk as she arranged herself so I moved the book hurriedly out of sight into my in-tray.

"Can I offer you a coffee?"

The machine was making the strangling noises it does when the process is complete.

She shook her head. "No thank you."

The smell of Irish Cream wafted through the office but I opted not to make myself a cup until I'd talked to her.

"So. Susan," I smiled. "You checked up on me."

She shifted a little from side to side in her chair. "I needed to be sure."

"Of what?"

"You," she replied.

"O...kay," I nodded. "I assume you've done your check and you're happy to talk to me about Elizabeth?"

I leant back in my chair and tented my hands over my stomach as she nodded.

"Tell me about her then. Before the night she disappeared. Just to give me a bit of background."

She hung her head, swallowing hard. I kept quiet and let her begin in her own time.

Taking a deep breath, she began.

"It's a bit complicated and it's a long story. I met Elizabeth," she did a jiggle of her head, "Beth, about eleven months ago and we just clicked. She's quiet and I'm rowdy but we got along just great. I feel like her big sister."

She breathed deeply.

"I work at an advertising firm and she came in for an interview for the job of copy editor." She hesitated. "I could tell she'd been in a really bad relationship because she'd covered up the last of a black eye with some makeup and when she smiled, I could see her bottom lip had been cut and was healing. It was still a little swollen." She sighed. "But she was determined to get the job and I wanted to give her a chance because, well," she shrugged, "we were pretty desperate. The previous girl left us without notice so I convinced the boss to take Beth on and we've never looked back since."

She stared out of the window for a long time lost in thought and I almost started to ask a question when she looked back at me and continued.

"I used to wonder why she wore these big sunglasses that practically hid her face. She said she didn't want to scare people. But she was really pretty, even with the scar."

I kept quiet. In the silence, the coffee gurgled one last time before I heard a click. The machine had switched itself off automatically.

"And she was so secretive," she continued. "She barely went out except when I wouldn't take no for an answer."

When she turned back to me, her eyes were shining.

"But I never asked why and now I wish I had. Somehow I knew something bad had happened to her and if she wanted to talk to me, then I'd be there, ready to listen." She breathed deeply. "But she never did. Instead, she buckled down and we became best friends."

Her smile was sad as she took another deep breath and stared at her hands resting in her lap for a second. Then she lifted her eyes to hold mine.

"Then, one week ago, we met at Alto's Restaurant in Broadbeach. We'd just clinched a big deal on an account and we were celebrating."

She smiled to herself, lost in the memory. "We'd worked so hard on this together and it finally paid off."

I nodded again, encouraging her to finish. She looked up at me with her worried eyes.

"That night, at the same restaurant, there was this guy I'd never seen before. He was with another girl and it shook her. Badly." She was talking nervously in short, sharp sentences.

I raised my eyebrows, ready to say something wise about jealousy. She saw the sceptical look on my face because she cut in before me.

She shook her head. "No! It wasn't like that." She leaned forward, intelligence sparkling, grief set aside for the moment. "Hear me out. He saw us and came over to our table. And he was," disgust was evident in every line of her face, "slimy. That's the only word I can find that fits him. Slimy."

She wiped the underside of nose with her hand and sniffled.

"She was shaken but I could tell it wasn't because she was jealous," she said. "She was shaken because there was something else happening that I didn't know about."

"I'm sorry for interrupting," I said, leaning forward. "This is the night Elizabeth disappeared?" I turned and pulled my notepad towards me, ready to take down notes.

She nodded.

"And you've told this story to the police?"

She nodded again. "When I reported her missing the following Monday. She didn't turn up for work and she wasn't answering her phone. I knew something was wrong. She always answers the phone to me."

I'd just read through the file and none of this was in it.

"You're sure you told all this to Detective Samantha Neil?" I repeated.

"Yes, I did. Is something wrong?"

I felt a flush of anger rise at Sam for removing this vital part of the file.

"No, nothing. I have a copy of the file here," I pointed to the manila folder to my right, "but I haven't read that report yet." I smiled. "I'm just getting the time line correct."

I swallowed my annoyance. "Okay," I managed. "Please. Continue."

She nodded. "When he came over to our table, he started out like this macho type guy, all tough and smarmy, looking down smugly at her, almost threatening her without actually saying anything threatening. He looked at her scar and said something like, *'Does it still hurt, Christine? Not my best moment, I admit, but I hope you'll find it in your heart to forgive me. You caught me unawares and it was just instinct to lash out.'*

She leant forward. "He actually called her Christine. And it shook her, I could tell. But then something happened. Something changed. *She* changed. Her face grew ... hard ... that's all I can say. And Beth is not a hard person. Then, it was like *she* threatened *him* and it took him a second or two to recover. Not in so many words but there was this veiled threat in *her* voice. She said something like, *'I've remained silent for almost a year now. I've spoken to no one about your nasty little secret. It's still safe with me. I've proven I can keep quiet. Until now. Don't push me.'* I saw the look on his face and I saw the redness creep up his neck. What she said sent him running."

She reached down to her feet for the bag the size of a small suitcase and rummaged around. Finally, she pulled out a small packet of tissues and took one out.

"She was upset but she stood up to him. And he didn't like it. He left us eventually, but she was definitely shaken by the whole thing."

She watched me as I rolled my pen in my hands, trying to find the right words to say.

"Did the two of you discuss what happened afterwards?"

She shook her head. "She refused to talk about it. She said she wanted to protect me. And then like the good friend I was, I left her to go home."

The last words came out with a little sob. I saw the pleading in her eyes and heard the quaver in her voice.

"That was the last time I saw her. She didn't turn up for work on the Monday and she wasn't answering her phone. The boss let me go over to her flat but she didn't answer the door. I have a key but when I let myself in, it didn't look like she'd been there for a while. I filed a missing person's report that morning." She bit her lip. "And she's still missing."

I took a few moments to absorb what she'd told me before answering. If I was honest with her, I'd tell her that if the police hadn't been able to find her in a week, chances were, I wouldn't either. Everyone who watches Law and Order knows the first 48 hours are the crucial ones. But I wasn't about to be honest with her. I wasn't going to tell her I'd picked Elizabeth up that night, wet and scared by the side of the road. I wasn't going to tell her that her friend knew someone was following her and she was terrified. I wasn't going to tell her I watched her run into the darkness and I just let her go. What I was going to say was I was invested in this and like the bulldog I am, I wasn't going to let go until I found Elizabeth and the truth.

She watched me play with my pen.

"Would she hide from you Susan?" I eventually asked. "If she was trying to protect you, I mean?"

She was shaking her head vigorously.

"She wouldn't hide from *me*." She swallowed noisily, trying to hold back emotion. "I'm all she's got."

I hesitated before I said the next sentence. I didn't want to scare her.

"If she wouldn't hide from you, and I'm sorry to say this, it could only mean she is in danger. Or worse."

I watched as she folded her lips inwards and her eyes glistened before she leant down for the black handbag at her feet again.

"I've got money, Mr Curtis." She placed the bag on her lap and hugged it close to her body.

I envisioned a tidal wave of twenty-dollar bills spilling out of the bag, like money at a crack bust, and the way she clutched the bag only emphasised it. I smiled despite myself but I couldn't let this go any further.

"Put your money away, Susan," I began. "With all the resources the police have, if she's alive and they can't find her, it probably means she really doesn't want to be found."

Even to my own ears, it sounded callous.

She was still shaking her head as I talked, and she seemed to have wilted right in front of me. Her shoulders sagged and everything about her screamed pain.

She reached into the oversized bag and pulled out a manila folder. "I've written down the names and addresses of a couple of places she goes, but she didn't go out much. There are the names of some of the people in her apartment block as well as a girl she said she used to know. Hayley Johnson. She once told me she hadn't seen Hayley for almost a year though."

Elizabeth's words spoken by Susan a moment ago echoed in my head. *I've remained silent for almost a year now.* And now Susan was saying Elizabeth once told her she hadn't seen Hayley for *almost a year*. Was this my first decent clue? Was this the connection I was looking for? Was the stranger at the restaurant and Hayley somehow connected?

Susan pushed the folder over the desk towards me. Her hand was shaking gently and pieces of paper fell out onto the table. She scooped them together and pushed them across the table to me along with the folder.

"That's an old couple one floor above her. And there's this guy one below she talked about sometimes. There are a couple of other names from work she was friendly with but I spoke to them and they said they never went out together. They was just work acquaintances. It's the best I can do but it may help you." She shrugged. "It obviously hasn't helped the police so far."

As I glanced down the list, I was pleased to see Sam's list matched this one and she hadn't left any names off.

"They told me what you just said," Susan continued. "That she doesn't want to be found. But that's can't be the case. She would never do that to *me*. Never." She shook her head vigorously. "Something's happened to her." She moved a quivering hand from her lap and placed it over her heart. "Believe me, I would know."

She straightened her back and took a deep breath.

"I Googled you and read things about you. You were a good policeman once and you're a determined man. And a fair one. I want you to look into this to make sure the police are covering everything."

She pressed her fingers to her lips and swallowed audibly. "Just tell me honestly what you think," she mumbled. "If you think as the police do, then so be it. But I want to know the truth."

I'd been listening to her with my cultivated non-expression, absorbing her words.

"You're a good friend, Susan," I said softly.

She stood up abruptly and slipped her bag over her shoulder.

"My phone number is on the inside flap of the folder. Please call me if you find out anything. That's all I ask."

She was halfway to the door before I stood up. I moved quickly from around my desk to open the door for her.

"I know Detective Neil," I said, opening it wide as she turned around to face me. "She's good at what she does and she won't leave any stone unturned."

She swayed a little and smiled her wan smile at me again before turning her back on me and walking out.

I tucked the file Sam had given me under my arm and shut the office door at around 2.30pm. Hayley Johnson was the first person on my list.

≫ *9* ≪

The house at the address in the file was a small low set, set back off the street with a wide front lawn that needed a mow. Sitting in the middle of the yard was an oversized ornate fountain, like a Jag ornament sitting on a Getz. The house looked like the average house in a very nice street, which according to the real estate agent who rented me the house at Coomera, is better than the best house in an okay street. A white Hyundai was parked in the driveway so I knew someone had to be home. I pulled in behind it, parked, then walked up to the front door and rang the bell.

I could hear muffled sounds from inside and a man's voice calling out, "Are you going to get that?"

I waited, figuring someone would come to the door sooner or later.

A man in his mid-fifties opened the door. He looked like he'd just arrived home from work: his tie was loosened and askew, the top button on his shirt was opened and the cuffs of his pants rested on black socks instead of shoes. The big toe of his right foot peeked out through a hole. In his hand was the largest wine glass I'd ever seen, filled halfway to the top with white wine.

"Yeah?" he asked.

"Mr Johnson?"

He looked down at the folder under my arm and did a little 'tsk' with his tongue and said, "Whatever you're selling, I'm not buying...."

"I'm not selling," I interrupted. "I'm here to...."

A female voice from inside yelled out, "Who is it, Mike?"

He swivelled his head and yelled back, sounding slightly annoyed, "I don't know yet," then back to me. "Like I said, I'm not buying."

"And I'm not selling," I repeated. "My name is Jack Curtis. I'm a private detective."

I stuck my hand out with a business card in it.

He changed the glass to his left hand and took the card gingerly, like it would bite him.

"A detective?"

I took my wallet out and held my license up for him to see but I didn't bother to hold it out for long.

A woman appeared at the door with a matching glass of wine in her hand except it was just about ready for a refill. Her hair was pulled back into a ponytail and all that remained of her lipstick was a smudge. The rest was on the rim of the glass. Her cheeks were glowing and her eyes were bright so I had an idea this wasn't the first glass she'd had this afternoon.

"Can we help you?" the woman asked with just a hint of slurring. She wasn't drunk yet but that was probably her intention.

"He's a detective, Jane."

"The police?" The rosiness suddenly left her cheeks and her spare hand fluttered to her chest.

I repeated my name and said, "I'm not with the police. I'm private."

She hesitated a split second, her eyes swivelling to Mike and back to me again, then asked, "What's wrong? What's this about?" She was still checking to see if her heart was beating.

Mike gave Jane a look that said *be quiet* and then turned to me, shaking his head.

"Jane always assumes the worst."

"If the police come to the door, it's not to ask you to a party," she snapped.

It looked like Mike was going to say something snappy back and my guess was it would start a heated conversation between the two of them.

"May I come in, please?" I asked quickly.

"What's the problem?" Jane asked, still baring the door. "Is this about Hayley again?"

It seemed a long leap for her to assume that I was here about Hayley but who knows, maybe Hayley had a predisposition for trouble.

"Well … yes," I admitted. "But as far as I know there's no problem." I quickly added. "Is Hayley here? I'd like to talk to her if I may."

"No," Mike Johnson said a little too quickly. "She's not here."

The speediness of the reply made me wonder whether she actually was.

"The police have already asked us questions last week about Hayley and where she is. We told them the same thing we're telling you. We don't know where our daughter is."

That piece of information hadn't been in the file either and I silently vowed to bring it up with Sam the next time I saw her. I was covering ground they'd already done and it was wasting my time. Then again, if I found out something they'd missed, I'd quote *'All good things come to those who wait'* back at Cavanaugh. The thought was a pleasant one.

I repeated my request to come in and they reluctantly led me through to a small lounge area just off the dining room. As I walked in, I caught a glimpse of a kitchen through an archway with dishes piled by the sink and an almost empty bottle of wine sitting next to a packet of Cornflakes. Unless they were planning on having Cornflakes for dinner with the wine, that box had been there all day.

By contrast, the lounge room was pure Laura Ashley. Two two-seaters, with perfectly positioned thrown cushions in matching beige tones on each of them, sat facing each other. The soft, thick carpet left indentations of my shoes as I walked to one of the two seaters and sat down. A sideboard sat elegantly under the front window and held nothing except a bouquet of yellow roses in what I suspected was a crystal vase. No photos. No smiling faces of happy couples or laughing children. The place was immaculate: like a cover shot from House and Garden.

Mike tossed one of the cushions onto the ground and it hit the beige broadloom carpet with a soft *poof*. Jane scowled at him slightly and I guessed if I hadn't been there, Mike would have had a talking to about his contempt for her decorating touches. She sat down next to him and they both watched me, expectantly.

"Can you tell me where Hayley is right now?" I asked.

They exchanged looks.

"No," Mike said. "We have no idea. She's always been one to come and go whenever she wants and she's never felt the need to tell us where she's going."

While Mike was talking, Jane was nodding. She was either agreeing with him or she was happy with the story he was telling.

Her eyes had been riveted on something in her glass but she glanced up suddenly and said, "We really need to know why you're asking these questions."

"I'm working with the police in the disappearance of Elizabeth Delaney. Did you know she is missing?"

They exchanged another look. "We heard about that. Dreadful. Really dreadful. But Hayley doesn't know anything about that."

Which meant they'd seen Hayley recently, definitely in the past week, to know that she didn't know anything.

"I need to talk to Hayley," I repeated.

"We told you, we have no idea where she is," Jane said a little too quickly. "She never comes home anymore. She leaves her things here, for safe keeping, but she rarely visits us."

"She lives here though." I was making a statement more than asking. "Right?"

"Well, *technically* she does," Jane said. "But she's a big girl now and she spends a lot of her time with her friends instead of us. She could be anywhere."

She put the wine glass to her lips and drained the last of wine. A frown creased her forehead for a second like she couldn't believe it was all gone. Mike had been watching his own wine swirl around the glass as his wife spoke.

In the silence, I could hear a dog barking outside and the drone of the air conditioning. Neither of them seemed particularly inclined to say anything else to me.

"I'm not here to judge Hayley."

I used my mild-mannered cop voice and tried to sound reassuring but the statement got their attention. Both heads jerked up and both sets of eyes widened.

"I just need to ask her some questions about Elizabeth Delaney. Does she have a phone number I can contact her on?"

Jane rolled her eyes. Now that the wine was finished and she realised it was more about Elizabeth than Hayley, she had become a little less tense.

"Are you kidding? It's like it's surgically attached to her hand."

Mike put a restraining hand on his wife's leg and said, "If we see her, we'll let her know you were looking for her, okay?" I had the feeling I would be shown the front door again in a very short time. "What will I tell her?"

"It would be easier if I had Hayley's number, sir. It's long and it's complicated and it would be best if I could talk to her myself."

Mike hesitated but stood up and left the room, heading towards the kitchen.

Jane fiddled absently with the rings on her fingers.

"We did the best we could with her, you know." Her eyes lifted and caught mine as she almost whispered the words. "She was always wild. Always in and out of trouble. But she's been better of late." She hesitated for a second and took a breath as if she realised she'd said something she shouldn't have. Then she exhaled and fiddled with the rings again, saying nothing.

Mike walked back in with a number scribbled on a post-it note. Beside the number was an address.

"She never answers it. You'll have to leave a message and hope she gets back to you. You might have better luck with her ex-boyfriend. I wrote his name down as well. It's Jason Brady."

He pointed to the post-it note.

"That's the address Hayley gave us for him. From what she said, she doesn't see him anymore. He was in with some unsavoury types. He came by a week ago looking for Hayley and I told him she wasn't here. He didn't take it too well and I told him not to come back again. I threatened to call the police if he did. She used to shack up with him on weekends but that was a while ago."

Jane snorted through her nose. "Shack up. Goodness Mike." She shook her head mockingly. "She was only seeing him because he had a car."

"What kind of car?" I asked.

"Pardon?" she asked.

"What kind of car does Jason drive?"

She looked at her husband. "It's black, Mike, isn't it? Something big. What do kids today call them?"

"An SUV, Jane." He rolled his eyes at me. A little male bonding thing going on with the word *women* understood.

I took the post-it note from Mike's hand and said, "If you see Hayley before I reach her, can you ask her to give me a call please?"

He looked down at my business card without really looking at it and showed me to the front door. I heard it shut firmly behind me before I'd stepped down off the top step.

Ten minutes later, I was driving slowly up the street Mike had written on the note, looking for the number on a letterbox in front of Jason Brady's house. I always wonder why people make it so difficult to find the letterbox. If you didn't want to make it easy for the fire department, then have a little pity for the pizza delivery guy and the postman.

The houses on my right side were even numbered so it had to be on my left. I was doing a count when I saw a car pull out of a driveway up ahead and reverse across my path. He did a quick turn like he hadn't even noticed me before accelerating off so fast he fishtailed.

They were right. It was a SUV. A black Subaru SUV and when I looked at the number of the house he'd come from, I knew it had to be Jason. As he sped past me, I saw a young man wearing a baseball cap backwards, the way most kids wear them these days, thinking they look like some kind of rap star.

As he roared down the street, I did a fast three-point turn and tried to catch up. He'd disappeared around a corner so it seemed likely he hadn't seen me do the turn.

Five minutes later, I was in the car park of a tavern, watching him walk up to the entrance.

He wasn't running but he was in a hurry and he moved like he'd done athletics when he was in high school.

Once he disappeared inside, I parked my car and entered the bar as well.

It was like a hundred other bars. The first thing that hit me was the smell of nicotine, like a curtain you had to pass through. It meant I'd be making a trip to the cleaners for the suit I was wearing.

After the smoke came the combo stench of stale beer, sour dish clothes and perspiration, mixed with a little vomit on the side. It filled my nostrils and I knew that if I needed to go to the toilet, which I didn't, the urinal wouldn't flush.

Of the fifty or so people standing around, some were at the bar, some were at tables and over a dozen were hanging out by the pool tables, the clack of pool balls blending with the music. Mounted on the walls were two television sets, both showing a soccer game between Chelsea and Liverpool with the sound turned off, which didn't really matter. No one was watching.

I wasn't the oldest guy in the room but I was close to it. From an ancient juke box near the men toilets, Jimmy Barnes was screaming out lyrics telling anyone who would listen the dubious benefits of cheap wine and a three-day growth. Glancing around, it was kind of appropriate. From what I could see, there couldn't have been a person here who was alive when that song first came out.

I scanned the room for Jason and found him standing at the bar, two-deep with drinkers, talking to a couple of tough looking guys. Besides the baseball cap, Jason had on a black t-shirt and an old pair of jeans with rips around the knees I knew had cost him a pretty penny. The other two were not as discerning. One was clean-shaven with bony shoulders and a sunken chest, accentuated by a V-neck t-shirt and a pair of jeans sitting so low, I could see what is delicately called a 'plumbers crack'. The other was his physical opposite. His chest was big and his heavy arms were crossed over a beer belly hanging over a pair of scruffy chinos. From where I was standing, it looked like the three men were speaking heatedly.

A few eyes turned towards me then returned to their drinks disinterestedly as I walked up to the bar and ordered a beer, watching the three of them out of the corner of my eye. The bartender watched them as well, eyes bouncing from the beer he was pouring for me to the door, to them, to the waitress, to the tables, and back again to the beer, taking it all in and on alert.

There was a pillar about two feet away from him so I took my beer and leant against it. There was too much noise for me to hear what was being said so I pushed myself off the pillar and walked towards the pool tables. From there, I could watch Jason as I sipped my beer.

Whatever he'd come in for was over and done with quickly and he was walking fast towards the exit.

I set my almost full beer glass on the bar and hurried out after him. He hadn't gone far from the front door when I called out.

"Jason Brady?"

He swivelled around and squinted at me.

Jason was a big guy. I stand at six feet tall and he was a good two inches taller than me. And 20 kilos heavier. All faux gangster with greasy blonde hair falling out of the cap and tribal tattoos on his bloated biceps.

"Who's asking?" he asked.

His voice was light and a little high-pitched. Michael Jackson light. Except this guy must have been gobbling steroids for years. His skin was bad and his arms were bigger than my legs. He reminded me of Popeye.

I sighed. "To my question, you answered, *'Who's asking.'* Like you're being cagey. But by saying that, you've already told me you *are* Jason Brady."

He hesitated and frowned. "Huh? Do I know you?"

He stared at me waiting for me to answer. That's the problem with steroids. Some of them scramble your head and this guy didn't look like he'd started too far up on the food chain to begin with. He looked mean, sullen and stupid. Not a good combination but this was no personality contest.

"My name's Jack Curtis."

"So?" He shrugged. "Like I said, do I know you?"

"Can I have a few words with you? I'm a private investigator helping out the police with the investigation of Elizabeth Delaney."

The reaction I received wasn't quite what I expected. He flushed crimson and clenched his mouth shut so tight that his lips were two white lines. I could see two pulses on both jaw lines, which meant he was clenching and unclenching his teeth. He raised a hand with his palm facing me, taking a step back and shaking his head violently at the same time.

"I don't know anything about that, man."

I've had reactions before but this took the cake.

"You don't even know what I want to ask you, Jason."

"Whatever it is, I've got nothing to say to you. Leave me alone."

I'd seen his type before. Full of bravado. Too young to be smart and too stupid to know better.

He took a few steps away from me so I stepped forward to fill the void.

"The police haven't been able to find out where Elizabeth is. Maybe you could help me out. It will only take a couple of minutes. Just a couple of questions. That's all."

I could hear the whine in my voice again and I made another mental note to improve my approach in the future. It was getting to be a bad habit.

As I talked, the door opened behind me and the ear-splitting music spilled out.

"Can we go somewhere quieter?" I yelled. I didn't feel like getting into a conversation right in the open doorway with people going in and out all around us.

It was like I'd poked a dog with a stick.

"GET LOST OLD MAN!" He shoved me hard enough to move me back a step.

Maybe it was my frame of mind but he had a very 'punch me' face and I was itching to help him out with that.

It's not in my nature to back away from things just because they're difficult. Another thing my father told me was, *Plant your feet and stay firm. The only thing is knowing where to plant your feet*.

I stepped forward and planted them a foot away from him and made my voice sound firmer.

"Jason. It's with me now or later with the police." I gave him my Dirty Harry look and kept my eyes locked on his. "Your choice. Then it won't be this nice guy standing in front of you."

I smiled at him. Lots of teeth. When he didn't respond, I turned on my nice-guy sparkle. I even changed to my Tom Hanks smile. It probably came out more like a snarl but that's the way it goes sometimes.

He gave me a nasty look in return then it was as if a light bulb had switched on over his head. Like in a Roadrunner cartoon when Wile E Coyote has a bright idea.

"Oh," he said. "I get it." The grin turned into a short laugh. "Good. Very good. You almost had me."

My eyebrows rose. "I almost had you? You think I'm joking?"

"No man. Just tricking."

"Really? Do I look like I'm tricking?"

He stepped forward but I didn't move quickly enough to stop the fist from connecting. The blow caught me on the side of the head and I went down. As I hit the ground, stars burst in my vision as two feet ran off towards the car park.

"Shit," I muttered. I'd landed on my butt. I rolled over and brought myself up to my knees, making sure I didn't topple over. People were walking past me shaking their heads. Someone even muttered, "Bloody drunk." From the car park, I heard the squeal of tyres as the Subaru scattered loose stones behind it.

If I wasn't angry before, I was now. I don't like being punched and I don't like being reminded of my advancing years. I know there are people who believe in the 'forgive and forget' motto but I only go along with that sentiment if I can get even first.

I could feel the lump on the side of my head not far from the cut Jimmy had given me but I had no want to see what they had done to my good looks. Mentally, I was sharpening the metal toes of my shoes before heading back to Jason's house to pay Jason a little visit at his home.

❧   II   ❧

Jason's car wasn't in the driveway when I drove past but a newish looking Hyundai was. I didn't really expect him to be home but you never know sometimes. Not many criminals are rocket scientists, which is why they're criminals. If they weren't criminals, they'd be doing something else to screw up people's lives, like running for an election.

I parked on the curb and walked up the driveway, listening to soft music filtering through the quiet afternoon from inside the house. The music meant someone was at home.

A woman answered the door and I found myself just looking at her for a few startled seconds. That's what people say when they can't afford to buy something. *'Just looking, thanks.'*

Something about being in the presence of a beautiful woman puts a man at an immediate disadvantage. It doesn't matter how tough you are or how confident you feel, when a woman who looks like this is in your presence, she has the upper hand every time.

Almost of their own volition, my hands brushed the creases of my suit ineffectually and I pushed my tie up closer to the collar of my shirt. As I did, I realized I had grit on my hands from falling in the car park and the bruise on my face must have been glowing.

"Good afternoon. My name is Jack Curtis."

"Charmed," she said, although she sounded anything but charmed. I'd seen warmer eyes in shark aquariums and the smile was so fleeting it made the average flight attendant seem gushy.

"Can I help you?" she asked looking me up and down.

"I'm looking for Jason Brady." I turned to the driveway and said, "I see his car isn't here."

It was a stupid thing to say but it was out before I could stop it. I was still annoyed and reeling from my encounter with Jason and in hindsight, I'd have been better off having a shower and coming back another day.

She stared at me in silence for a second before saying, "Jason is my son. My name is Pauline Brady." She looked me up and down again. "And you are from where?"

Pauline Brady had once been a beautiful woman. I guessed her age at about forty-five if Jason was about twenty-five, but I could be wrong. She could have been younger. Even at forty-five, the ruffled blonde hair, blue eyes and full lips would turn heads. She had a soft golden tan and curves in all the right places. When she spoke, she had an occasional lisp that would send flutters down anyone's spine. But you could see the heart and soul had been ripped out of her.

"As I said, my name is Jack Curtis. I'm a private investigator."

I gave her a super friendly smile - *See how harmless I am* - and the bruise on my cheek complained.

I took a card out from the inside pocket of my suit and handed it to her.

"I was a police detective working at Surfers Paradise Police Station. I have my own agency now and I'm investigating the disappearance of Elizabeth Delaney."

For some reason, I had the urge to tell her that I had once been someone of importance. Ego is like fame and it's more addictive than heroine. Adults who lose fame, one-hit-wonders for example, usually tailspin into depression, though they try to act like they're above it. They don't want to admit the truth. Their whole life is a lie, a desperate scramble for another dose of that most potent of all drugs. Fame. That's what screws you up. Your ego.

She put her head to the side. "Curtis? Are your relatives the Curtis family who own a large sheep property out west?" The tiniest of lisps made the question sound coquettish.

"No relation, I'm afraid," I smiled. "My family is in beverage distribution."

My father worked six night shifts a week in an Irish bar in Hobart when I was growing up. If he'd heard my description of the family as 'distribution', he'd have laughed himself into a case of hiccups.

She looked at the card then used it as a fan as she spoke.

"Why would you be looking for Jason?"

Suddenly, I saw the futility of my situation. Jason wasn't here and I wasn't going to get anything out of his mother. I was hungry and I needed a drink, a shower and a cold pack for my face and again, not all of that necessarily in that order.

We stared at each other for a few moments while my good angel and bad angel jostled yet again. My bad angel said Jason needed to be taught a lesson while my good angel reminded me that my usual vile behaviour had brought me nothing but grief and that you catch more flies with honey than you do with vinegar. That was all well and good but hey, Jason started it.

But something in her evasiveness surfaced above my anger. It was pretty clear she wasn't going to tell me anything.

From inside the house, a thump sounded and my eyes flicked to the darkness behind her.

Without looking, she said, "Cats," then flashed me a wry smile. For a second, I was reminded of Snow White's stepmother, Maleficent.

"The charity is finished, Mr Curtis," she said abruptly. "Jason isn't here but if he were, he wouldn't be able to help you. It would be best if you left him well alone."

There it was again. The little lisp at the end. I could imagine in another life and once upon a time, I might have fallen a little in love with that lisp, if I weren't in such a foul mood.

Without another word, she shut the door on my face and left me standing in the growing darkness on her front porch.

I glanced down at my watch. It was almost 5.30pm. I hadn't eaten anything since the coffee and sandwich with Sam this morning and I could feel the first beginnings of the shakes. It meant my blood sugar was dangerously low and I knew I was finished for the day. Tomorrow, I would go through the file in more detail and make plans.

12

Problems started early for me on Monday morning. The bruise on my cheek had turned aubergine purple, my left eye was turning black and I'd resorted to wearing sunglasses like some self-important movie star from Movie World. But I had recuperated enough to be looking forward to getting back to my office to start the week off on a positive note, even though after two days I was still no better off than when I started on Friday night.

On the way to my office, I passed the usual Monday morning faces in the front office – sagging, gaunt and resigned – hovering around the coffee machine. I attempted a cheery greeting that wasn't returned and walked down the corridor to my office. At the door, I stopped dead in my tracks, slowly taking my sunglasses off.

The door was slightly ajar.

I glanced at the lock to see if it had been broken but all seemed in order. Someone had opened it and I could only assume they either had a key or had talked Karen's receptionist into letting them in and waiting for me. I knew I didn't have any appointments this morning so I was instantly on my guard.

I pushed the door softly, trying not to make a noise as I glanced in, taking the time to peak around the door. I've seen enough movies to know that bad guys hover there with something big in their hands that will no doubt hurt or break body parts.

The last person I expected to see was Frank Fitzroy sitting in my client's chair, chewing on the end of a pencil with my Code Word puzzle book open in front of him. Unless I'd forgotten to lock the door, which I knew I hadn't, he'd broken in and had made himself at home.

Frank's sleazy reputation is widely known. It's been five months since I've last seen him and it wasn't under the best of circumstances. Frank had helped me put Joe behind bars for the rest of his life and as Frank drove away after the sentencing, I'd believed it was the last I'd ever see of him. At least I was hoping it was.

A cup of coffee with the steam still coming off it sat in front of him and the heady aroma of Irish Cream filled the small office again.

Frank glanced up at me as I walked in. He leant back in the chair and as he did, it let out a large squeak and the fake leather made an embarrassing farting noise. He ignored it and smiled a wide shark grin at me, exposing his crooked teeth.

"How've you been, mate?" His voice was still throaty as if his larynx had been damaged years before.

"How the hell did you get in?"

I found myself staring at Frank. I'd almost forgotten how ugly he was. His face was round and his ears stuck out like handles. His nose was a blob and there were scars from stitches on his jawline. As he sipped the coffee, he waved me in with his free hand and pointed to my chair. I remained standing stiffly at the door.

"I can't reveal all me tricks," he said, ignoring my body language and pointing at the chair again. "You know that, Jack. But friends in high places always comes in handy. I did a favour of sorts for the guy on security years ago and now he thinks he owes me." He put his free hand out to the side. "Who am I to argue?"

He picked up the puzzle book and waved it at me.

"I see you're still doing puzzles, Jack. Just not crosswords anymore, I see. Good decision, I'd say, because you really sucked at them." He gave a chuckle that came out sounding like a bark. "Now these. These are good." He leant over and placed the tip of the pencil on a vacant word. "See this word? All these 12's?"

"Pardon me?"

"The puzzle you're stuck on. 12 has to be E." He glanced up at me to emphasis his point. "It has to be. So that makes the word Perseverance. Again, has to be."

"Do you mind?"

"Not at all. No need to thank me. That word alone will give you all the clues you need to finish the puzzle." He glanced down again at the book and his eyes roamed around the page before he pushed it across to me. "Looks like you could use the help."

He gave a snort that I imagined was supposed to be a laugh.

"You know me. I love puzzles. It's a talent. Me forte, if you like." He drawled the word *forte* out, making it sound more like *four tay*. "I make sense out of things that don't make sense."

Everything about him was relaxed but from experience, I knew his brain was firing.

"What do you want Frank?"

He tsked a couple of times and grinned. "You haven't even asked how I'm doing, mate."

I said nothing for a moment. Then, "Okay. If it will move things along. How are you doing Frank?"

"Great. Thanks for asking."

I waited again while he settled himself.

"Funny the way things work out, ain't it?" he said. "Perseverance? That could be me middle name Jack." He gave me a lazy smile as he stared at me with his piggy eyes for a long moment.

"Who do you work for these days Frank?"

"These days?" He wiggled his shaggy eyebrows at me. "You know me Jack. I spread m'self around. I'm the helpful kind who likes to solve puzzles bigger than these ones." His head jerked in the direction of the puzzle book.

"Is it still Matthew Simmons?" I persisted.

He snorted. "Simmons?" He snorted again. "Nah. You did a right trick on him, Jack my boy. Simmons is long gone. Along with his reputation." He shook his head. "Nah. I've got m'self a better pay check these days."

He pointed at my chair again. "Sit down. Sit down. Make yourself comfortable. I've got a story you might like to hear. In fact, I *know* you will. 'It happened about a year ago."

Despite my better judgment, I walked to the other side of my desk and sat down. He has a reputation for violence, but up until now, he had never actually been charged with a serious crime, more through good fortune than any great intelligence on his part. He was the kind of guy to whom other lowlifes referred to as having 'smarts', but I had never subscribed to the theory of comparative intelligence where petty criminals were concerned, so the fact that Fitzroy's peers considered him a sharp operator didn't impress me much.

I made a show of looking at my wrist watch. "Okay, Frank. Make it quick."

He leant back in the chair, ignoring the farting noise again, and laced his fingers behind his head, crossing his right ankle over his left leg. It gave me a good view of his red socks that were the colour of blood.

"For the sake of me story," he began, "let's just call the hero Sugar Daddy. Respected. Married. Two kids. High up on the totem pole. You know? Model of society. Except this guy's got a fetish. And it ain't shoes, trust me. Would have been better for him if it was."

He snorted, enjoying his joke.

"Anyway. One day, 'e gets this itch that needs to be scratched see, so he heads off to his favourite place. Safe. Secure. Classy. They know him there and no one's talking, if they know what's good for them. So he gets a room and he's halfway through scratching this itch when downstairs in reception, a lovely young thing walks in. It's the usual piece of fluff Sugar Daddy has been seeing for a year or so but this time she just assumes she's the one he's come to see. She's seen him walk in the hotel and she gives him a little time to get comfortable and freshen up before she walks in and asks reception for the key."

He squirmed a little, making himself more comfortable. Watching him, I knew it was going to be a long story.

"See, they know her in reception," he continued, "so they just fink there's been a change in plans and she's meeting up with him for a happy threesome and a little kinky party. That's what they fink. Everyone's happy. Everyone's larfin'." He gave another snort. "So she gets up to the room and opens the door and there 'e is, busy shagging someone else on the bed."

He unlaced his fingers and uncrossed his feet, sitting up in the chair. He was watching me with his piggy eyes and I knew this was why he'd come to my office today.

"But this isn't a usual shag," he smiled in a semi-feral way. "This time it's a *boy* he's shagging. A *young* boy, if you get my drift." He held his hands up theatrically in horror. "*Real* young."

I felt sweat pop out on my top lip and my stomach clenched, threatening to release the undigested remains of my breakfast. Unwanted visions from my last case as a police detective jumped into my head and my stomach turned a bit more, followed closely by an unpleasant taste in my mouth. Myriads of images bubbled up from my sub-conscious. Images shot through with violence and I steeled myself against them. I could almost smell the sweet, cloying odour of eucalyptus on Mount Tamborine along with musky animal smells as body after body of young boys were discovered under the dappled light filtering through the trees as the cacophony of birds sung in the background.

I had been the lead on the case and as such, I took the full responsibility for the failure to apprehend the murderer of five fourteen-year-old boys, all runaways and all homeless. Not that anyone blamed me for the outcome. In fact, it was the opposite. But it hit me hard and I lost all faith in my ability as a policeman. It was why I left the police force a year ago. Everyone said I needed time to heal but in fact, I was scared. Scared that the same thing could happen again, and my mind would not be able to cope the next time. If it happened again, I would be sitting with Nurse Ratchet instead of with Frank.

It wasn't a new story. The Gold Coast spends millions each year on prostitution control, but 'control' was an operative term. Prostitution wasn't going to disappear, no matter how much money the council threw at the problem, and so it was a matter of prioritising.

It was a different story for the squad tackling the Sexual Exploitation of Children Squad. They had their work cut out for them. 20,000 kids are subjected to sexual exploitation every year, including child porn, of whom over half are runaways or kids who had been thrown out of their homes by their parents or guardians. Surfers Paradise acts like a magnet for them. There are over 3,000 children working as prostitutes in this country at any time and no shortage of men willing to pay for them. The squad uses young-looking female cops to lure paedophile 'johns' into their nest. If caught, most would avoid goal if they had no history but at least they would be in the register as sex offenders and then could be monitored for the rest of their lives.

The pimps are harder to catch because a lot of them have gang affiliations, which makes them more dangerous, to both the girls and the cops. Their connections make them smarter than the average criminal.

"Where are we going with this, Frank?"

My voice came out as a croak as I fought to keep the emotion out of my voice.

He smiled, ignoring my discomfort. "Just coming to the best part, mate." He reached across for his coffee cup and saw it was empty. "What about a refill?"

"Finish the story Frank, then I'll get you another coffee."

"No need to get snooty." He sat back, squirming a little to get comfortable and making the chair fart again. "Okay. Where was I? Oh yeah. So this girl walks in on it all and she's shocked, as you can imagine. And Sugar Daddy doesn't like it. Not one single bit. Works her over, good and proper. She wouldn't be working for a while after that, you know? Not with two black eyes and a split lip. Maybe a couple of loose teeth into the bargain."

I felt my scalp recede because I realised where this was going.

Frank gave me a little Groucho Marx eyebrow wiggle.

"I see you know where I'm going now."

He nodded sagely before continuing.

"Anyway, she manages to get out. She runs to a friend who lives close by and the two of them are smart enough ta know they have to hit the road. But see, Sugar Daddy knows these two shaggers are friends. He knows all about them because he's shagged them both. And he can't have this sort of thing getting out. Not in his position, he can't. He contacts some friends he knows and now his friends are on the lookout for the shaggers. So now we got two shaggers on the run. And believe me, they're in a panic. They're in a car and they take off."

My mind was busy working while he told the story and by now, I'd put two and two together. Frank hadn't just come in to tell me a story. With Frank, there's always a reason. My guess was he knew I was looking into Elizabeth Delaney's disappearance. His story of the two girls could only mean that the one who walked in on the guy and the kid was Elizabeth. The friend was Hayley and together the two of them had tried to get away. When Elizabeth spoke to Susan Bishop, she'd mentioned a friend. That friend had to be Hayley.

"Are you wiff me, Jack? Am I boring you?"

I mentally shook myself. "Just putting the pieces together Frank. Go on."

"Keep up wiff me then, mate. We're just getting to the good part. So, this friend is driving but they're only streets away when she hits this Mercedes. Herr first thought is *'SHIT'*. *How am I gunna pay for this?* You know? The car'd skewed sideways a little on impact but basically it was just a door. But you know panel beaters are like blooming thieves these days."

He chuckled and leant forward as he picked up his empty coffee cup. He glanced at me but I sat still, waiting for him to continue.

"You're hard mate. Anyone ever tell you that, eh?" He settled back again. "Okay. There were two guys in the other car: a guy driving, solid guy full of steroids like Arnie Schwarzenegger, and anuvva guy in the passenger seat we'll get ta later. Straight away she could see Arnie has this cut on his forehead." He pointed to the crease lines on his own forehead. "It's bleeding and he keeps touching his head and staring at the blood on his fingers. Arnie seems a little panicked but the other guy, he's just sitting there, staring at the girls. Takin' it all in. You see. He's the one with the brains, not Arnie."

Frank looked at his empty cup again. A hissing sound bounced off the walls as Frank sucked air in through his crooked teeth.

To move the story along, I picked up the cup with a sigh and walked to the kitchenette to refill it with the last of the Irish Cream. I'd have liked one myself but there was only enough for one cup and making another pot would have taken time to brew. The last thing I wanted was to leave Frank in the office on his own for too long.

While I was pouring the coffee, I noted the time. Every Monday morning, Karen's office begins with meetings and she would be looking for the reports as soon as the meetings were over. At present, they were locked away in my drawer. I didn't want to stop Frank talking while he was on a roll plus I didn't want him to see where my reports were kept. The only option I had was to hope the meetings went long, giving me a little extra time.

I walked back to the desk and handed him the cup then sat down again.

"You'll make someone a great wife some day, Jack me old darlin'." He blew on the contents before taking a sip. "Don't know why you haven't been snapped up yet." He snorted. "I'm tempted meself except my active lifestyle might not suit you."

"Get on with it, Frank."

He raised his eyebrows as if he was offended before continuing. "In a hurry, Jack?"

He put the cup back down on the desk, crossed his legs again and threaded his hands over his stomach, watching me.

"Okay. So Shagger's friend gets outta the car and sees straight away the guy in the front seat needs an ambulance. That's when she realises her phone is still in the car. She yells out to Shagger to call ooo but when she looks closer, she sees Shagger just sitting there, staring, so she runs back to get it herself. As she's dialling, she turns around and sees what Shagger sees. It's the guy in the passenger seat. He's out of the car and he's walking towards them." Frank began to nod. "She sees him clearly. Can't miss him. Big guy, dark suit, shaved head, European looking, mid-forties with this big watch on his wrist. A Rolex. And he's angry. Real angry."

As he talked, his eyes flicked around the room.

"Anyway, the strangest thing happens. As Rolex is walking towards them, another car pulls up and a guy leans out, all nice and friendly like, and yells *'Ay mate, are ya okay? I've called ooo for you.'* In his hand is a mobile phone. Straight away Arnie knows an ambulance, and probably the cops, will be there any minute. He fires up the Merc and drives off with the front fender dragging beside him on the street. Get this though, the dickhead leaves Rolex behind."

He chuckled and wiggled his eyebrows. "Loved to have been there and seen the look on Rolex's face. Obviously the steroids have left Arnie with his brain a little scrambled. Or maybe he wasn't too bright to start with. Wouldn't have wanted to be in his shoes."

He chuckled again. "Anyway, Shagger's friend was trying to memorise the number plates but Rolex has reached her now and he hits her hard on the side of her head. Her head feels like it's about to fall off. The next thing she knows she wakes up in the hospital. She has no idea what's happened to her friend. Or Rolex. And the police are asking lots of questions."

The gears were starting to grind in my head. I remembered a couple of cops talking about this when I was still a detective at the station. It had been big news back then but it hadn't been my case. Or Sam's either because she'd been my partner. But while we were busy investigating that series of unsolved murders of young boys on Mount Tamborine, I remember a couple of guys talking about this case as a career boost. In the back recesses of my mind, I remember them saying that the girl had managed to escape without anyone knowing where she'd gone. Now I knew that girl was Elizabeth Delaney and she'd stayed hidden for a year.

But something had gone wrong. Somewhere in the past week, she'd come across someone who scared her and wanted her out of the way. Susan Bishop told me that. She said at the beginning Elizabeth had been too scared to go out of the house. Then she started going out bit by bit. She'd found a job and managed to rebuild her life. Until one day, a week ago, someone had seen her and then everything fell apart again. Somewhere in that time she'd gotten hold of a gun. Maybe she had it all along. But now I was up to the night I picked her up.

I tapped my fingers on my desk as I thought. Hayley was still a mystery. And so was Jason. Where did he fit into all of this?

Frank sipped the coffee, watching me as thoughts rummaged around in my head. I glanced down at my watch. 10.30. Karen would be leaving the meeting soon.

"You've got 'til midday mate," Frank stated.

"What?"

"Midday." He jerked his head towards Karen's office. "I sweet-talked the secretary, the blonde one in the tight white skirt, and told her you had an important meeting. It couldn't wait, I told her. She said you have 'til midday." He grinned, showing off his crooked teeth. "Charmed her, I did. Wasn't easy." He grinned wider. "But she's only human, right?"

He snorted with what I assume was laughter.

"Her smile was icy to start wiff and her aura was positively glacial. But she's as thin as a rake so I put it down to being hungry. Not like you, mate." He glanced down at my waistline. "Looks like you have a propensity to roundness, which you need to watch like a hawk. Lucky you're good at you job."

With Frank, it was best to let him say what he has to and hope he finishes the story sooner rather than later.

He did a bum wriggle in his chair. "But I knew she'd weaken," he continued. "Girls always do with me. It's a talent, ain't it?" He shrugged and grinned. "Maybe I'm just better looking than you." The grin widened.

I couldn't keep quiet any longer. "Where are we going with the story, Frank?"

"Okay. Okay. So, this friend has lots to say to the cops. She tells them about Sugar Daddy and this new little playmate and how her friend was beaten up and how they both ran for their lives. She tells 'em about the accident and she tells 'em that Rolex hit her hard enough to make her teeth rattle."

Frank looked at me closely and leaned forward as he spoke the next words. "She also asks 'em where Shagger is. And they ask her who's Shagger? And then she tells them the whole story."

He leant back again and tapped his head. "See, I know things Jack." He tapped his head and smiled as if he was Yoda and he'd just imparted the secret of becoming a Jedi. I said nothing because I knew there was more to come.

I was right.

"When the cops hear all this, they get *real* excited, know what I mean?" he continued. "Before she knows it, a sketch artist is sitting there and can you believe it, she's able to identify Arnie and Rolex. Rolex was involved in a Ponzi scam from years back in Sydney and a suspect in a drug case and Arnie is a local no-account thug who does odd jobs for the big guys. All tats and leather with a record a mile long. They've been looking for Rolex for a long time and they've never been closer to putting him away for corruption, both down souff and up here in Queensland than they have on that day."

Frank took a sip from his coffee and eyed me over the top. "You heard of Ponzi?"

This was typical Frank. Jumping from one subject to the other with no logical link. I knew better.

I sighed. "Okay. Ponzi. Let's hear it."

"Carlo Ponzi," he began "was a small-time con man who spent loadsa time in prison before he came up with this scam. Not an original one, mind you. He basically stole the idea, but for a time it was big. He ended up steeling fifteen million dollars and back in his day, that meant serious money."

"When was this?"

"After the First World War."

He took a swallow of his coffee and settled back before he continued.

"The con itself was really pretty simple. People gave him money to invest. He promised them, oh I don't know, let's say forty percent or somefing equally outrageous for a period of ninety days."

"How was he going to make that kind of money?"

"Exactly. He weren't. He was robbing Peter to pay Paul. But he had a good story and he played it well. The first guy in had ninety days to brag about it to his friends. And of course, they had to get in on it as well. Sounded too good to be true." He chuckled. "When the ninety days was up, the first guy got paid off. Full return of the principal plus the forty per cent profit. By then, the profit was coming from the money his neighbours were putting in."

"Sounds like you needed to be the first in on this deal."

"You're smart, mate." He touched his forefinger to his temple. "That's exactly what you needed to do. His partners all agreed to keep milking it. They were each taking a million a year and they were having fun to boot, just getting rich. They'd invented the golden goose. But of course, someone always kills the golden goose. It stopped working the day everybody wanted their money back at the same time. A guy wrote an article for the Post during the Depression declaring that Ponzi was insolvent. He stated that even though Ponzi was claiming to have \$7 million in funds, he actually was \$2 million in debt. And of course, everyone panicked. And they all panicked at the same time. That's when he was screwed."

"Okay. Good story, Frank. What's it got to do with this case?"

"Rolex had the same scam going in Sydney. Made big bucks from it before it turned belly-up and with the funds, he disappeared and got into the drug trade. The cops have been looking for him for years. And here he is," he winked, "right here in Paradise. Making good friends in high places."

He fell silent for a minute, watching me think.

"Okay, Frank. Again. What's it got to do with Elizabeth Delaney?"

"When you spoke to your friend the cop on Saturday, did she mention that the cops assumed Sugar Daddy'd put a hit on the girl a year ago and he called in Rolex to do it?"

When you spoke to your friend the cop. The statement meant that Frank had been watching me with Sam and Cavanaugh at Starbucks on Saturday. I didn't see him, but then I'd only have seen him if he wanted me to. I felt a prickle go up and down my spine and the skin on my forearms began to tingle. Aside from being totally unaware of his surveillance, another part of me was annoyed at how much Sam was hiding from me. I'd never suspected she'd deliberately hold back so much vital information.

I looked Frank hard in the eye and he snorted.

"Didn't fink so. Can't be a coincidence that Rolex and Arnie just happened to be driving a Merc at the exact same spot where the two girls were, can there? Anyway, the cops had the names of the two in the Merc and they sent a coupla detectives to get a search warrant from a local judge so they could search Arnie's pad because they didn't have an address for Rolex. The plan was, once they had Arnie, they'd make him talk and then he'd spill the beans on where to find Rolex. They put the girl in safe custody and set the ball rolling."

Frank was watching me closely, his eyes not leaving my face, and I knew the next part of the story was important.

"The judge is all professional like, and he's asking questions like, *'Where did all this come from?' Is she sure about the two in the car?'* They tell him the story I just told you and the judge then asks, *'Where's the girl now? Is she safe?'* all concern and sympathy, like. And of course, the cops tell him everything. They tell him Shagger is missing but they have the friend in safe custody ready to finger Rolex and Arnie when they have them in a cell. Once they have the two safely tucked away, they'll know who Sugar Daddy is and they'll have the proverbial 'at trick."

He grinned. "But see, the judge hesitates. 'He's not sure they have enough evidence for a search warrant. He says, *'How can the girl be sure it was Arnie in the car?'* he asks. *'Didn't she say there was blood all over his face? How could she possibly identify him?'"*

His eyes were boring into mine. "This is when it all starts to fall apart. The judge says he can't grant the warrant. There's not enough evidence, he says. The next day, Shagger's friend sees a newspaper. She reads the story about Arnie and Rolex, aka Preston and Cruz by the way, and nuffing's been left out."

My head jerked at the name Preston. *Preston? Jimmy Preston?*

My eyes wandered over the room as my mind spun. Fragments of Frank's story drifted back into my brain. *'There were two guys in the other car: a guy driving, solid guy full of steroids like Arnold Schwarzenegger'.* And then, *'Straight away she could see Arnie has a cut on his forehead.'* I'd seen a scar like that close up while standing in the industrial bin a week ago. *'Obviously the steroids have left Arnie with his brain a little scrambled. Or maybe he wasn't too bright to start with.'*

Jimmy?

I pulled my notepad over and wrote, *Find out who the judge was. And if Cruz's driver was Jimmy.*

Frank's eyes watched me scribble the note but he didn't comment.

"The news reporters were pretty thorough for a change." Frank's voice brought me back from my reverie. "There was a mug shot of them both on the front page wiv pictures of everyone involved including the cops who interviewed her in the hospital."

He reached forward and picked up the coffee cup.

"And then she reads the whole story about how the judge won't issue a warrant."

Frank sipped his coffee before continuing, his eyes watching me.

"Suddenly, she panics. She says she has to go to the bathroom but instead, she hightails it and does a runner. So now, no one can find her and the cops are back where they were in the first place. Except now they have two missing girls."

"How do you know all this Frank?"

He smiled his ugly smile, giving me the full spectrum of his crooked teeth.

"Finger in a lot of pies, Jack me old sod," he said as he leant forward and put the coffee mug on the table.

I had no idea of which pies Frank was referring to. The last time I had dealings with Frank, he worked as an investigator for Matthew Simmons from Simmons, Ryan and Holzman. But he'd said Simmons was gone now and he had a better 'pay check'. My guess would be Frank had come up with the information because someone had hired him to look into the disappearance of Elizabeth Delaney as well. But why would this be of interest to them? It was still an active case with the police, not a law firm. And how did Frank get all his information? Could he have spoken to Hayley? Somehow I didn't think so. If Frank had that sort of information, he'd have sold it to the highest bidder long before coming to me. No, he didn't know, but he found out the information some way. I decided to keep this insight to myself for a while and dig a little deeper.

"You can do better than that Frank," I countered.

"Come on, Jack." He was looking down at his hands like there was something fascinating about his fingernails. "You think I'm gunna hand over my technique to you? I'd be out of business before the end of the day. I'd be like you." He looked around the office. "I'd be stuck in a one room cupboard you call an office, doing Code Word puzzles and peeking through hotel windows, taking photos of wayward husbands in their jockey shorts. And at night, I'd go home and watch *Bachelorette* or summat like that on the tele. As appealing as all that sounds, I'd rather stick ta what I do best and keep me mouth shut."

He scratched his head and I watched the white flakes drift down to his shoulders. "In any case, I'm not here to exchange pleasantries. I'm here to put that tiara back on your head."

There it was. The dangling carrot. I knew it was coming. Frank never does anything for nothing.

"What is it, Frank? Are you trying to make a deal with me?"

I let that sit in the silence for a few seconds to let him know I was on to him.

"I know how you work Frank," I said. "Wheels within wheels, remember. You probably have two paying jobs linked to Elizabeth Delaney already and you're on the lookout for more."

"You're smarter than you look, Jack." He grinned. "But not smart enough. Her name? It's not Elizabeth Delaney. It's Christine Buchanan."

I remembered the story Susan Bishop told me. The man who walked up to them at Alto's had called her Christine so I knew Frank was telling the truth.

"How do you know all this, Frank," I asked again.

He ignored the question. "It's a sweet deal I'm offering. Everyone wins."

I sighed, letting him know it wasn't going to be easy.

"Go on."

He grinned. "Has your big brain started to ask why she did a runner? She was safe. Cops everywhere. Even one outside her room 24 hours a day. Your good friends, the cops, offering round the clock protection. She identifies two of the guys and then what…she runs? Doesn't make sense, does it?"

He leant forward again. "And anuvva fing. Who was the pervert in the hotel with the kid?"

He spoke the words slowly and I was silent for a bit, waiting for him to continue. He stared at me, waiting for me to catch up and say something. I had nothing

"Do *you* know who he was?" I asked hopefully.

He harrumphed. "What? I've got to do your job for you too? Ask your friend the cop. It's her case now that Elizabeth Delaney's done a scamper."

He was right. I was tempted to ring Sam as soon as Frank left and drop this little revelation at her feet like golden retriever would do with a dead bird. But I stopped myself in time. Why not wait for the flock of dead birds

Frank stood up, pulling his jacket off the back of the chair.

"What's the deal Frank? Why'd you come to me with all this?"

"You're a pal, Jack. Pals help pals." He showed me his teeth again. "Maybe we should team up. Maybe even work togevva."

I leant back in my chair and laughed.

He stopped shrugging into his jacket, one arm in while the other arm stopped searching for the sleeve. "Is that funny, Jack?

"Yes." I was still smiling. "It's funny. It's so funny, it's ridiculous.

"Why is that Jack?

I lifted an eyebrow and gave him my most incredulous expression

"Seriously? You think we'd get along?"

He continued shrugging on his coat. "We don't need to get along. We'd be partners. Part time if you like. You scratch my back and I'll scratch yours. It's always worked throughout history."

I sat and smiled at him some more. "I hope you're not developing Stockholm's Syndrome for me, Frank."

He nodded and grinned but said nothing.

"There's something you're not telling me Frank," I said watching him hitch his pants up slowly. "How did you get all this information?"

"If I told you that, who would trust me, eh?"

"It's the guy who was shagging the young boy, isn't it?"

He wiggled his eyebrows.

"He hired you to find Elizabeth and now you're here hoping I'll hire you to find her too." I grinned back at him. "One job, two pay cheques. Wheels within wheels, Frank. I know you better than you think I do."

"Just fink about what I said, Jack old mate." He smiled his toothy smile. "I'll be in touch."

He was almost to the door when he turned back.

"By the way, how old is that laptop of yours? Ten years?" He shook his head and snorted. "If you even hope to make it in the private sector, mate, you'll have to improve your skills on it. Download a few apps and programs. Go into the dark web."

I looked at him blankly. *The dark web?*

"I have skills that would make your mind boggle, mate. I can dig so far down and get into systems you could only dream of infiltrating." He chuckled and winked. "Togevva, Jack. We'd be unbeatable."

He tipped an imaginary hat from the door. "Don't forget that report in your drawer there for that pretty young lawyer."

Then he left.

I was missing something important. I knew it in every fibre. It was right there but just out of reach and Frank's story had pulled it to the forefront again. Something was running around in my head and I just wasn't sure what it was. I was remembering the Johnson's evasiveness. The glances they exchanged before answering my questions. Hayley's father putting his hand on his wife's knee to stop her from talking too much. What was I missing?

Then it hit me.

＃ 13 ＃

ayley's mother was wearing a tailored grey suit and a pristine white blouse tucked in to the waistband. I'm no fashion guru but the outfit looked expensive.

There was a tiny frown on her forehead when she saw me standing on the porch. The frown turned into two tiny seagulls across her forehead. She leaned out a little and swivelled her head from side to side and I knew she was checking to see if anyone else was with me. She leaned back inside when she saw I was alone and stood in the doorway, cradling another wine glass, like a sentry. Her eyes flickered to the bruise on my cheek and the frown deepened.

"Detective? My husband isn't here."

She pulled the hem of her skirt down to cover her knees with her left hand, as if she was afraid I was going to have my wicked way with her right there on the doorstep. The shirt had loosened a bit at the band sometime in the past hour, somewhere between the second and third drink, was my guess. Either Happy hour had started very early or she was having a liquid lunch.

"I came to see *you*, Mrs Johnson." I gave her a smile Mel Gibson would be proud of. "May I come in?"

She inhaled sharply and asked, "Why?" in a small voice.

"I'd like to talk to Hayley." As an afterthought, remembering Cavanaugh's advice on good manners, I added, "Please."

I looked over my shoulder, just to make her a little more nervous, like I suspected someone was hovering behind a bush listening to our conversation. "And I'd rather do that inside."

She took a few breaths, her chest rising and falling, her eyes searching mine.

"We told you. Hayley's not here."

I looked down at my feet for a second, then lifted my eyes back to her face.

"We both know that's not true."

Her teeth nibbled her bottom lip as she thought. I was silently grateful Mike wasn't at home. I may have ended up with the door slammed in my face.

Maybe my Mel Gibson look was improving because she came to a decision. Her eyes raked the street behind me and she stood back, waving me inside.

I walked past her into the house. The same Laura Ashley throw cushions in matching beige tones were sitting precisely on each two-seater. The only difference in the room was a couple of yellow rose petals had fallen from the crystal vase and sat dejectedly on the wooden sideboard.

I sat down in the same two-seater I had last time and she sat on the other one facing me with both knees pressed tightly together. Both hands were wrapped around the wine glass like she thought I was going to snatch it away from her.

"Mrs Johnson," I began, "I need to talk to Hayley."

She shook her head. "I told you before, detective. We don't know where she is."

I drew in a deep breath and looked down at my hands resting in my lap before I looked back up at her. She had raised the wine glass to her lips and was watching me over the rim of the glass.

"You're her mother. I respect that. But this isn't just about Hayley anymore. It's about finding Elizabeth too. Whether you realise it or not, both girls are in danger now."

I watched her face pale as she gingerly placed the wineglass on the table with a shaking hand.

"I know she's here." I kept my voice soft, and nothing moved except her eyes, which widened.

I watched her in silence as she thought. It's one of many tricks in my bag that tends to unsettle people. Silence affects people in different ways. My silence made her feel awkward, as I knew it would. She was thinking, *Should I lie and deny it or should I just come out with the truth and get it over with? Maybe I should just throw him out?*

I've seen that look a thousand times before. It's always the same. First the eyes widen then the pupils dilate. Without realising it, the eyes do a little dance, first left then right. Left first because that's the side of the brain that forms the lies.

Her mind was working so furiously, I could almost hear the gears crunching. Thoughts ran across her face as she went through the motions. Her hands were visibly shaking which is probably why she put the wine glass on the coffee table. She clenched her hands together in her lap and I waited until she'd decided which way to go. But it didn't matter. I wouldn't give her the chance to speak.

She opened her mouth and I held up my hand, palm towards her, silencing her.

"I know, Mrs Johnson."

"You do not," she scoffed.

"What I know is almost a year ago Hayley came back home to you, scared for her life. She told you everything that had happened from when Elizabeth called her for help." I paused for a second. "Or perhaps I should say Christine called her for help." Her eyes snapped open and I knew I was right. She knew the whole story.

I continued as I nodded knowingly. "From Christine calling Hayley for help, to hitting the Mercedes, to Christine disappearing, to Hayley ending up in the hospital. Hayley would have told you how she ran from there because she was scared again and you've been protecting and hiding her ever since." I let sympathy soften my voice. "You've done an amazing job and it can't have been easy with the cops knocking on your door, as well as goons in five-thousand-dollar suits." I let that sink in before continuing. "You hid her and she's been here all along."

She waited for me to continue as she worried the skin around a fingernail.

"She has to be getting restless by now." I spoke softly. "She will be getting hard to handle because she will be thinking surely she's safe by now. She'll want to get out into the world again. But that was before Elizabeth went missing and now you're back where you started from. Hiding Hayley from the cops and the goons."

She closed her eyes and a small sob escaped her lips, followed by a sharp intake of breath.

In all my years of training, I've always taken a sharp intake of breath as a sign of surprise at my intuition. And as a rule, it was always followed by a show of anger as a means of diverting attention away from the question. Jane Johnson was no exception.

"You know nothing!" she spat at me.

Every time, I thought.

"But she's not going to stay hidden for much longer," I continued softly.

Something changed in the room. You could feel it like crackling electricity.

She sat back in shock. "How?" she asked in a distraught voice. "How did you know she was here?"

Patience always works. Not my best quality and it takes a lot of effort on my part. But I always make an attempt.

"The cornflakes packet on the kitchen bench at three in the afternoon," I said.

Her hand shot to her mouth, the knuckles pressing hard on her lips.

That's when Hayley stepped into the room.

"Settle down, mum. It's okay."

A kind of hushed calm came into the room.

The cut-off t-shirt Hayley wore came to well above her navel, exposing four inches of bare midriff above jeans that hung low on her slender hips. Her blonde hair was scraped back into a ponytail that came to the middle of her back and without makeup she could pass for sixteen years old.

Petulance shone from her intense blue eyes.

"Leave us, Mum. Let me talk to him alone."

Her mother was shaking her head vehemently. There was no way she was leaving the room with just the two of us there.

"No way, Hayley! I'm staying. Like it or not! I'm your mother and I have a right to know."

I had a million questions to ask Hayley but through my experience as a policeman, the best method is to wait it out. They were both staring each other down.

Eventually Hayley sighed heavily and her shoulders and head dropped wearily.

"Okay mum. Okay."

Her mother patted the seat next to her and Hayley grudgingly sat down beside her. Her mother nodded gently and steeled herself as she looked at me. It was my turn.

"Where's Christine, Hayley," I asked.

Hayley's head shot up. "I don't know."

I raised my eyebrow, giving her my most incredulous expression.

"I don't! That's why I'm hiding here. I haven't seen her for a year."

Something made me believe her. "Well, if you want to help find her, you have to tell me everything you know. Leave nothing out."

There was silence while she processed my statement. When she nodded, I knew I'd won.

She took a deep breath.

"We were kind of wild, you know? Christine and me." As she spoke, she idly massaged her right thumb into the palm of her left hand. "We did a lot of things together we shouldn't have."

She stopped and glanced at her mother who was nodding her head silently. There was more to come so I didn't interrupt. I let her tell the story in her own way.

"We've known each other since school. Seven years. She was the most important thing in my life, deciding where we'd go and what we'd wear so often that I had no idea who I was without her. She decided what films we watched. What music I liked. Every CD I own was recommended to me by my other half. Christine." She smiled sadly. "She was so strong. 'Try this Hayley, you'll adore it.' 'This will smell wonderful on you.' 'Blue is absolutely your colour.'" She swallowed as tears surfaced. "What do I do without her now?"

The description given by Susan Bishop was an entirely different one from Hayley's. Susan's version painted Elizabeth as a timid mouse who was scared of her own shadow. A follower not an instigator. Hayley's version was of a strong person who could influence anybody to her way of thinking, be it right or wrong. Maybe a couple of black eyes and loose teeth had changed Christine from a troublemaker to the anxious Elizabeth Susan knew.

I tucked the thought to the back of my mind as Hayley continued.

"On the night Christine called me, we were living in a flat together. We looked out for each other. We never brought anyone home but we watched out to make sure no one followed us home. When I answered the phone that night, she was sobbing and begging for help. She told me she'd walked in on her john and he was," she hesitated and glanced up at me, "he was with this kid of about twelve or thirteen."

So far it was the same story Frank had told me a short time ago and once again I wondered how he'd managed to uncover the story. Sam wouldn't even tell me. Who had told him?

Hayley took a shaky breath before continuing.

"I didn't know the details but she sounded scared and desperate. She was begging me to come and get her." She shrugged. "I knew where she was because, like I said, we watched out for each other. We told each other where we were going and what time we were meeting our johns. I'd been to the same hotel with a john of my own."

She stopped and took a deep breath, glancing sideways quickly at her mother then back to me. Jane Johnson was concentrating on her hands clenched in her lap.

"She was like a broken doll," Hayley said. "Her face was bruised and bleeding. Her lips were cut and swollen and her dress was torn."

Her mother winced and folded her lips together, trying to hold back her emotion. Hayley noticed and turned to her. She reached out and picked up one of her mother's hands.

"Mum. I want you to leave us." Her voice was soft but firm.

There was a hesitation on her mother's part and Hayley jumped on it.

"Please mum. It's best you do."

Tears came to her mother's eyes but she did as her daughter asked. As she stood and moved towards the kitchen, her eyes caught mine and I thought I saw a silent plea. Then she dropped them before disappearing.

"It's painful for mum hearing this," she said unnecessarily as she watched her mother disappear.

"Of course it is," I said.

I let her gather her thoughts again for a second.

She folded her lips inwards and chewed the bottom one with her teeth as she tried to gather herself. "Christine wouldn't like me telling you all this."

I kept my eyes on hers, never wavering. Who was I to judge other people's behaviour? We all have secrets. Some things we want to keep hidden. It could be something as simple as a boyfriend who beat her or it could be as complicated as having an affair with your best friend's fiancée. But nothing stays hidden forever.

Her eyes danced over my face, from on eye to the other, watching and waiting.

"Do you know who this john is?" I asked, keeping my voice soft.

"No." She was shaking her head before I finished my sentence. "He kept that a secret. He didn't want anyone to know. None of them do. They deliberately never tell you much."

She gave a watery smile and I nodded, waiting for her to continue.

"But he was someone important. I know that. You could tell just by looking at him."

"Okay, Hayley. Describe him for me," I nudged.

She took a deep breath and looked at the ceiling as if the answer was up there.

"He was fortyish, I guess. Average height, dark hair, blue eyes. Not movie star handsome but good looking. He had pale skin and his nails were so nice," she smiled. "Perfectly even and buffed. Not long but not short either. Like he had regular manicures. Like he'd never done a day's work in his life."

The description was good. The hard part was where was I going to start looking?

"Okay. Let's get back to the night Christine called you. You picked her up," I urged. I didn't want to tell her I'd heard the next part from Frank. I wanted to hear it from her.

She swallowed before telling me her version of the story, from the time she picked Christine up to the time she ran out of the hospital. To give

Frank credit, he was pretty accurate with the details. I made a mental note again to ask him where he'd found the information.

A small sob escaped. "What if I'd stayed in the car with her?"

Her voice came out ragged and pained. Each syllable was a new pain.

"What if I'd stayed in the car with her instead of getting out?" She choked off the sob again.

I could feel the guilt coming off her in waves. Any psychiatrist would tell her that she was blameless. But then there's 'survivor's guilt'. It's an emotion when people who have been intimately involved in a traumatic event live to talk about it. People embrace guilt instead of confronting the agonising truth that it is beyond their control. They are helpless. The moments leading up to the event play on their minds like an endless movie. She will forever think about it at night before she goes to sleep and in those endless hours before dawn, analyse actions as a choreographer might review the sequence of steps in a dance.

I waited as she lowered her head to her hands. Seconds later, she took a deep breath and lifted her head, tears shining in her eyes.

I gave it another moment before saying, "Then you'd both have been missing. Or worse. You'd both be dead."

I watched as reality began to trickle in.

"But Christine escaped, Hayley. She became Elizabeth Delaney and began a new life. She changed her appearance, found a job and was putting it all behind her. Until a week ago. Someone recognised her, someone who didn't want her around, and now she's gone again. Either she's disappeared on her own or she's dead. My job is to find out which it is."

The words were brutal but there was no way around it.

She stared silently at her hands clasped in her lap and her eyes swivelled from side to side. As she squeezed her eyebrows together, I knew unpleasant images were running through her brain.

"Okay. You don't know who he is," I continued. "Tell what you *do* know."

She did a little so-so thing with her head. "He liked a certain look, you know. Blondes with long hair were his favourites." She was thinking, her eyes travelling around the room as she concentrated.

"He liked blondes?" I asked, a frown on my forehead. Even in the rain,

Elizabeth's hair had been dark, almost black. And the photo Sam had shown me was of a girl with black hair.

She nodded. "I know. You've seen the recent photo of her in the papers. She wasn't always a brunette. She's a natural blonde."

She's a natural blonde. Present tense, meaning she believed Christine was still alive.

She stopped for a few seconds and thought some more.

"At first he was like everyone's best friend. That's what I thought at the time anyway. And then things began to change. He didn't like what I wore. My arse was flabby. Things like that." She swallowed noisily. "And then he started to get rough."

I repeated the same question I originally asked her.

"Do you know where Christine is, Hayley?"

"How would I know that!" she snorted angrily. "I've been stuck here for a year!"

It was best to say nothing while waiting the anger out.

She gathered herself and looked a little shamefaced.

"Okay," I conceded. "You don't know where Christine is."

Although doubt still lingered in her eyes, she visibly calmed herself.

"But we still need to find her," I added.

I said *we* so that she would feel included in the search.

"Is there anyone else who may know where she is? Another girl he saw besides you and Christine?"

She chewed her lip and a little frown appeared on her forehead.

"There *was* this one girl. Simone. I think she saw him a couple of times before Christine arrived on the scene. Once he saw her, he dropped everyone else."

"That's great. Where can I find this Simone? Maybe she can give us an idea of who this guy was."

In a little girl voice, she said, "You could try a club called *Dolly's*. She used to work there on weekends. She always waits around near the clubs after ten o'clock. She may be able to tell you. She's a lot older than Christine and me. She's about twenty-three and she's been around a lot longer than either of us."

I hid my smile at the age reference. "What does she look like, Hayley."

"I told you. She looks like Christine and me. Long blonde hair and thin."

I took my notebook from the inside pocket of my jacket and wrote down the name, *Dolly's* and *after 10 o'clock*.

She was chewing on a ragged thumbnail as she talked. As she chewed, a half-formed idea was forming in my head.

"I don't think it's safe for you here, Hayley," I began slowly so as not to scare her too much. "If *I* found you, it's only a matter of time before the bad guys do. Jason's been around here and he knows the guys who want you and Christine dead. Now that Christine has resurfaced, they'll be more insistent. You could be putting your parents at risk."

She paled visibly but nodded her head. "I've had time to think about this and yeah, I worked that out."

"And so did Christine. She changed her appearance and her name to Elizabeth Delaney so she could escape them. But it wasn't enough. They found her." I let that settle in. "And eventually, they'll find you too."

The thought that niggled before resurfaced and I let it grow.

"How would you like all this to go away?"

She raised an eyebrow and mumbled, "Of course I would."

"What if there was a way to find Christine and get your life back? Would you be interested?"

The look was sceptical but behind the eyes I could see a spark of hope.

"What are you saying?"

"I'm saying what if we could get rid of these guys? For good." Again, not *you. We.* "What if we could find out who this guy was and expose him?"

What I was planning would make me a hypocrite. Again. I was once a policeman, sworn to uphold the law, and over the past year I'd tampered with evidence in order to take revenge on my best friend for the death of Shannon and now I was planning on hiding a witness from the police in order to draw out a seriously dangerous cartel of drug traffickers and paedophiles. I wasn't happy with the alternatives or the ultimatums involved but there was a young girl out there who may or may not need my help. Not a great justification but one just the same.

"What if you came with me?" I added. It wouldn't look good when Sam and Cavanaugh found out but what the hell.

Her eyes widened.

"I could hide you," I insisted.

In my mind, I was hearing Frank say, '*We could work together. You scratch my back and I'll scratch yours.*'

"I have a partner," I lied. It was a small lie that could in fact be a truth in the near future. "And together there'd be someone with you all the time while the other is working on a plan to draw them out. Your own personal bodyguard."

She gave me a look that said *are you shitting me?*

"Why would I let you do that?"

"I'm not going to sugar-coat it." I nodded and shrugged, letting her know it was up to her. "We're talking about dangerous people here with a lot to lose. And they want you and Christine dead."

I hesitated before continuing, just enough for her to process the information.

"This guy tried once when he sent Cruz to get you. It was just plain bad luck that someone saw the accident and had already called ooo. If that hadn't happened, you would both be dead now. It shows they mean business. Have no doubt in your mind, they *will* find you and they *will* kill you both." I let that sink in before continuing. "It's just a matter of time."

I looked towards the kitchen and added another incentive. "The longer you stay here, the more you put your parents at risk."

She was shaking her head. "How do you expect to beat this guy? He's a powerful man."

I grinned. "My father told me once that if you buckle down, really buckled down, and you get the planning and the execution right, a hundred per cent right, you are bound to succeed."

She smirked. "That sounds like something Bruce Willis said in one of his *Die Hard* movies." She was shaking her head again. "You don't know this guy and I'm sorry, you're not Bruce Willis."

"Maybe not. But I've known men like him. They all have one thing in common. They all have an ego to feed."

"So how do we do it?"

We.

"We exploit the sensible part of his nature. His smart, organised, bureaucratic, cautious and painfully rational."

"O.K." She looked sceptical as she waited for me to continue.

"We do something a rational person in his position would never even consider. Something unhinged. We draw him out into the open."

The room had a hush to it now. The only sound was the hum of the refrigerator and the distant cacophony of the parakeets in the backyard. She was barely breathing as she watched me.

Her eyes were intent as they bored into mine.

"And how are you going to do that?" she finally asked.

"Something ingenious," I grinned, trying to reassure her.

"Use me as bait, you mean." Her voice had risen, part panic part shock.

I did a so-so thing with my head. "I prefer the word 'lure'," I said.

She gaped at me. "Same thing from where I'm sitting. I end up dead either way."

"There is no way I'll let that happen."

I watched her chew her lips.

Keeping my voice low, I said, "There's no one else you can trust."

I watched her swallow and glance towards the kitchen as her mother appeared from around the corner and stood in the walkway.

"How do I know we can trust *you*, Mr Curtis?" she asked.

"Who else do *you* have, Mrs Johnson?"

14

I called Sam and asked her to meet me for coffee at 3pm. I'd missed lunch again and my blood sugar was starting to get dangerously low. Soon I'd be swooning like a druggie begging for a fix.

The excuse I gave Sam was I had some updates for her on the case knowing it would be too juicy a carrot for her to pass up. It would also guarantee she'd drop everything and meet me sooner rather than later.

In actual fact, I wanted to see if she was going to part with some information. She'd obviously kept me out of the loop regarding the accident a year ago as well as omitting the part about Hayley being in the hospital. My pride was hurt and maybe if I sulked a little she'd feel sorry for me and fill me in on some of the details.

I'd ordered a coffee and a toasted panini and I was taking the first bite, brushing the sesame seeds from my tie while I watched a news report on a television mounted high in the corner.

The news was still on, showing a report on a fire at Sovereign Island early that morning. A large crowd of people had gathered, no doubt attracted by the flames and excitement, and they were now being kept back by police officers. Several police cars and official vehicles were parked along the verges of the street, which was still muddy in places. Two fire trucks and an ambulance were parked outside the property, lights flashing red, blue, red, blue. All hoses had been deployed, and the medical examiner, plus four paramedics were walking across the scorched front lawn.

The gardens had once been beautifully tended with clipped hedges, palm trees and what I imagined had once been azaleas. Now, leaves hung in blackened shreds and there was a general air of neglect after the fire debris had worsened the view. Small puffs of smoke still smouldered around the ruined walls and roof. A large crowd of people had gathered, no doubt attracted by the flames and excitement, and they were now being kept back by police officers. A reporter held a microphone out to one of the officers but he quickly reached out and put his hand over the microphone. The reporter muttered something to him and by the expression on her face, she wasn't wishing him a good day.

A picture of a balding sixtyish man flashed on the screen from what could only have been his entertainment area. He was wearing an emerald green smoking jacket I'd only ever seen Elmer Fudd wearing and he was smiling as he held up a frosty glass of white wine to the camera. In the background, a topaz blue pool sparkled and further on in the distance, sunlight glistened off the ocean like it was jam-packed full of diamonds.

An on-air television reporter walked amongst the police, a woman I'd seen a hundred times on the local news, talking with her camera operator close by her side. The cops were pushing gawkers along the footpaths yelling *'Clear the area'* but no one was taking any notice. Above, a television helicopter spiralled down for a closer look and I knew that the news of this fire would beat whatever Nicole Kidman were doing tonight.

One word could sum it all up. Chaos.

As I chewed and watched, Sam walked in and sat down opposite me.

"How did that happen?"

She was referring to the bruise on my cheek.

"Long story," I replied.

A waiter appeared at the table and while Sam waited for her coffee, I told her a condensed version of the Jason incident, leaving out the part where I was sprawled on my butt watching him drive away.

I took another bite of the Panini and went straight for the jugular.

"Okay Sam," I said chewing slowly. "When were you going to tell me about the accident a year ago involving Elizabeth Delaney and Hayley Johnson?"

Her eyes darkened. "And how did you find about that, Jack? That's classified. It wasn't even in the file I gave you. But here you are, asking me that question. How is that, Jack?"

Her coffee arrived at the table and while I waited for her to stir a sugar sachet into it, I thought about how I was going to play this out.

Instead of answering her question, I deflected it.

"You lied to me, Sam. The information in the folder. You lied about it."

She blew softly on the frothy surface then pressed her lips together.

When she didn't answer, I said, "I'm not stupid, Sam. I saw the look you and Cavanaugh gave each other the other day. Now I have information that proves it."

She put her coffee cup down and reached for a paper napkin in a dispenser on the table.

"I didn't lie, Jack. I just didn't tell you everything."

Can you trust anyone in this world? Shannon lied. Joe lied. Even Sally lied when she said she'd always love me.

"Not a good start to a working relationship, is it, Sam?"

She dabbed her mouth slowly with the napkin. She was stalling for time and I knew it.

"How did you find out, Jack?" she persisted, unfazed.

"I've been doing some private detective work of my own."

Two could play her game. I reached over and pulled a napkin of my own out of the dispenser and wiped my fingers slowly, taking my time while I thought about what to say.

My problem was how much did I tell her. I wanted her to think I knew more than I actually did and, in the process, she'd part with some piece of information I didn't know. It was going to be tricky because Sam could always read me.

"Okay." I wiped my mouth and scrunched the napkin up before tossing it on my empty plate. It was time to give a little information to Sam so she'd be obliged to give a bit back. Quid pro quo.

"I found out with the help of Frank."

I said the words nonchalantly but I knew they would make an impression. I wasn't disappointed.

Her eyes widened in shock over the rim of her coffee cup and she almost dropped it back on the saucer.

"Frank!" she squeaked. "Do you mean Frank Fitzroy?"

When I didn't say anything, she sat back as she tried to process this new piece of news.

The statement wasn't strictly true. He'd come to *me* with the information but I wasn't about to tell her that. Fair's fair, right?

"You have *Frank* helping you now?" she repeated, shaking her head. "Oh for God's sake! Are you mad? You know what that man is capable of. He has no morals at all and he'll turn on you in a heartbeat like the weasel he is."

"You want answers and so do I." I shrugged, like it was a done deal. "You've given me precious little to go on and Frank has contacts. And I seem to remember you and your buddy Cavanaugh saying that as long as I share information with you, you'll do the same. So far, it's all talk on your part. I've given you information but you haven't held up your end of the deal as far as I can see."

She held my gaze for a second while I stared back unblinking. Then she sighed, probably thinking she was in deep already so why not go all the way?

"Okay." She hesitated, glancing down at the coffee for a few seconds collecting her thoughts. Then she raised her eyes and continued. "Hayley identified the driver. But he's just small fry. It's the gorilla she identified that interests us."

Us, she'd said. Her and Cavanaugh. I knew they were partners but it still riled me.

"His name is Manuel De la Cruz. He has connections to a drug ring working out of Sydney and the Federal police have been watching him for years. He's making money as an Import/Exporter," she harrumphed sarcastically, "with a whole lot going out but not much coming in. There's no balance and the Federal police know it. He's got an accountant by the name of David Farmer who cooks the books for him. Red flags have gone up on him too but there's nothing they can pin on him. So far, they've been sitting on their hands because they want to get the whole team. But they're watching closely, you can bet on that. Then Hayley went missing and they lost the best lead they've had in years."

We sat staring at each other for a second like we were on a date and there wasn't going to be another one. She looked uncomfortable with me and I assumed it was because she wasn't here with Cavanaugh. After the last dressing down he'd given her, she'd be reluctant to cross the line again.

When Sam began talking again, I could hear the frustration in her voice.

"All right, Jack. Elizabeth Delaney's real name is Christine Buchanan."

I kept my face as neutral as I could. I didn't want her knowing I already knew Elizabeth's real name. It was a test of sorts, to see how much Sam would tell me. She continued unaware that she'd passed a test.

"Hayley was going to stand up in court and tell the whole story of what happened that night with Christine. We were never able to find her so Hayley's testimony was vital. Then Hayley disappeared as well. The police thought that if she could stand up in court, the judge could make Cruz open up his books. David Farmer is Cruz's moneyman with no criminal background or history of violence but if Farmer is indicted then all of Farmer's assets will be frozen along with his projects. Cruz won't want that to happen because it's *his* assets that will be frozen. Now, one year later Elizabeth suddenly appears out of the blue and then disappears again, presumed dead. To top it off, we still haven't been able to find Hayley."

I kept quiet about Hayley.

As we were talking, I saw a Porsche pull up at the southern end of the Starbucks car park. Behind it, a black Subaru SUV pulled in and parked behind it. Sam saw me jerk forward and her head spun around towards the car park.

A guy the size of a Beluga whale unfolded himself from the front seat of the Porsche and walked a few steps to open the back door for the passenger. When the guy in the back seat alighted and straightened up, it was like one of those action toys that starts out as a dump truck but ends up something huge and menacing. This guy was massive. From what I could see, he was touching six and a half feet tall and 110 kilos with broader than normal shoulders and a head like the size of a basketball. His ears stuck out and light glistened off his shaved head. His brow was heavy, his eyes tiny, his cheekbones high and his chin was square. Every about him screamed Cro-Magnon.

He brushed his suit with the back of his hands, one of those gaudy silk ones that Italians think are fashionable. Then I noticed a chunky watch, probably a Rolex, and an even chunkier gold pinkie ring. He looked like a bald Tony Soprano gone heavy. He was not the sort who blended into a crowd and I knew it was Cruz. Looking at the two of them, I felt practically dainty.

Most people who live and work in Surfers Paradise every day take life for granted. When they first arrive, they see the bright lights and tourist traps and even if they close their eyes, the images are still there, imbedded in their mind. But like sunspots, the images eventually begin to fade. They begin to see the flaws. They see the homeless kids and they see the drunks lying in the parks with empty bottles of cheap booze lying by their side. They see the ten-year olds on pushbikes, one hand on the handlebars to steer and a can of beer in the other hand. And then one day, like me, they see the monsters lurking around corners waiting, and waiting.

"Jesus Christ," Sam breathed.

"No. I don't think so," I muttered. "No sandals. No beard."

Sam gave me a *'you've got to be kidding* look' as Jason Brady scrambled out of the SUV, feet first and slow. He steadied himself and stood up to face the giant who was staring at him silently. As I watched the scene play out, Sam was scrambling for her mobile phone in her bag, her eyes locked on the car park. She found it and dropped her eyes to it for a second, pushing a button and holding the phone to her ear as she watched the scene play out.

Cruz moved forwards a few steps slowly because of his bulk, which gave me time to see the butt of a gun shoved into a holster under his left armpit.

They still wear those things? I thought.

Then his lips moved but only the bottom half of his face worked when he spoke, like the jaw of a skull. He asked a question but I couldn't make out what it was he asked.

"Cavanaugh." Sam's voice was all business as she spoke into the phone. "I'm sitting in Starbucks on Cavill Avenue and Cruz is in the car park. I don't know how long he'll be here but get a car here asap to follow it. It's a red Porsche. You can't miss it. Licence number TLG 691." She read the number out then pushed the hang up button, focussing back on the car park.

Whatever it was Cruz said to Jason, he looked panicked. He just shook his head violently and breathed, his hands by his side. He gave a shrug and the giant repeated the question. This time, Jason answered, his lips barely moving but his head kept shaking from side to side. Whatever he was saying, he was trying to let the giant know it wasn't his fault.

While the giant processed the information, Beluga's head swivelled slowly, eyes not resting, scanning for onlookers. While he scanned, the giant's head was nodding up and down a degree, as if processing the information Jason had imparted. He was quiet for a moment before a smirk came to his lips. His body language was exaggeratingly friendly but Jason was cringing. From my angle, Jason was looking more and more uncomfortable. And anxious. Even a little terrified.

And then Cruz moved. With astonishing speed for someone so huge, a fist came out and landed on Jason's face and it must have loosened a few back molars, assuming he had any. His brain must have been bouncing around in his skull. His head moved backwards and smashed against his car door, then he bounced down to the concrete.

"*Shit*," squeaked Sam.

I was watching Jason shaking his head groggily. "This guy must have missed the 'Leadership Skills' module when he was doing his training," I muttered.

Cruz was standing still, looking down at Jason and Jason was still shaking his head. But now he was talking too. But in a rush. Like he was trying to stop the next punch by saying something Cruz might like to hear. When he finished talking, he was staring up urgently like he was waiting for Cruz to say something. Suddenly, he had Cruz's attention.

"We've got to do something Jack," Sam urged. She was almost out of her seat when I reached out to stop her.

"Stop!" The words came out louder than I expected and an elderly couple at a nearby table, tucked away so they couldn't see what was happening in the carpark, looked up at us alarmed. A couple of young mothers, babies asleep in strollers, stopped talking mid sentence to snap their heads our way. Four tables away, a girl wearing jeans and a green hoodie nursing a mug of something, raised her eyes, glanced out to the carpark, then dropped them quickly again.

I quietened my voice. "You *do* know you weren't born with the ability to throw fireballs, right? Remember what I always told you? Never interrupt a criminal when he's making a mistake. It's almost over anyway." I jerked my head in their direction. "Look. The kid said something important. Cruz is not going to do anything more. Not in full view of half of Surfers anyway. Just wait a minute."

Cruz's expression remained rigid. Then he smiled stiffly, more like a grimace. This time, I read his lips. '*Of course.*' And then he nodded.

The look of intense relief on Jason's face was unmistakable. I saw his chest rise and fall as Cruz patted him on the head like he was a dog. Whatever Jason had said, it had appeased him for the time being.

I was wondering what Jason said that had put a halt to the conversation when Cruz looked up and I could have sworn he was looking straight at me.

I watched a wildlife show not so long ago and it explained how some animals have the power of super scent. The wolverine, a thickly furred snow mammal, is bearlike in strength and somewhat in appearance. But it is the biggest species in the weasel family and it has the strongest sense of scent in the animal kingdom. It can smell food up to a kilometre away even buried in the snow. If we were to spread out all our human olfactory sensors, ours cover the size of a bottle top whereas the wolverines cover the size of a dinner plate. It was as if Cruz had scented me and knew exactly where I was. And he was watching me.

The look only lasted for a few seconds, but I could have sworn it was longer. The intense scrutiny was there and then it was gone but for that length of time I felt my scalp recede.

As Cruz turned and stepped back towards the Porsche, Beluga opened the door to the back seat and Cruz folded himself back in. Jason did a bum walk backwards towards his own car, and even from my position in the restaurant, I could see sweat glistening on his forehead.

Within seconds, Beluga was revving Cruz's car before they moved off into traffic. It was all over within a couple of minutes as if nothing had happened. Jason was up and back in his car before Cruz turned the corner.

"What the hell was that all about?" Sam whispered, looking over at the couple whose eyes had dropped to their coffee.

"From Hayley's description, that was Cruz. Big, burly and mean."

Her head spun towards me like the kid out of the Exorcist, eyes wild and open. She mumbled the 'f' word and asked, "What do you mean 'from

Hayley's description'? How the HELL do you know what Hayley has to say, Jack?"

I waved off the question and gave her a look that said *Come on.* I didn't want to tell her I'd heard it from Hayley but I had to tell her something.

"Frank told me."

She almost spluttered. "And how the hell does Frank know?"

I didn't want to go into it because when Frank was on your side, he could be as leaky as Julian Assange and I needed all the help I could get from him right now. If I said too much, Sam would have him in for questioning and that would be the end of any help I'd get from him in the future.

I deflected the questions again by saying, "I'd say Cruz wants Hayley badly. Elizabeth too, if she's still alive. But definitely Hayley. She's the one who identified him and she's the one who will stand up in court. If the judge lets her, that is."

I knew the judge was pulling the shots but I didn't want to ask Sam if she knew, just in case she didn't. I wanted to keep a trick or two up my sleeve, just in case. I could use it as leverage for later.

She was silent as she sat back in her chair. Her eyes travelled over my face and I could almost see the cogs working in her brain. I'd seen this look before on Sam. She knew something and she was contemplating whether to fill me in.

I cocked my head to the side. "What, Sam?" I asked.

She sighed heavily. "Have you seen the latest news?"

I shrugged not knowing where she was going. "Some," I said. "Why?"

"The judge you're referring to," she hesitated, "is dead."

I leant forward, placing both hands on the table, and blinked.

"Dead? When?"

"This morning. There was a fire at his house on Sovereign Island. Apparently he was drunk and smoking in bed. The Fire Chief thinks he fell asleep with a cigarette in his hand and it dropped onto the carpet and ignited while he was sleeping."

My head automatically swivelled to the television mounted in the corner, my mouth gaping open. I'd only just seen the news report.

The information banged around in my skull for a few seconds while I processed it.

I turned back to Sam, surprised at her lack of shock. The implications were astonishing. I was still trying to get my head around it while she sipped her coffee in silence.

"You don't think that's a little," I shook my head and paused, looking for the right word, "well, coincidental?"

She hesitated. "No, I don't, Jack. It's terribly unfortunate and sad, yes. But that's all. He had nothing to do with our investigation except for the fact he couldn't find enough probable cause to issue a warrant to the police to search ..." She stopped and blushed, knowing she was about to let a piece of information slip out. "He was just doing his job," she managed.

I was shaking my head, ignoring the slip because I already knew about the search warrant.

"Unfortunate?" I asked. "That's what you think this is? Unfortunate?"

She stared at me, puzzled and sceptical.

"I don't believe in coincidences, Sam. You know that."

Her sceptical look didn't change. I dropped my eyes to the table as if the answer was right there, between my coffee cup and empty plate. It may be nothing but it didn't feel like nothing. Something wasn't right but I couldn't put my finger on it.

"What about what you just saw out there?" I jerked my head towards the car park. "Maybe that's what was going on in the car park. Cruz got lucky because of that judge. And by the looks of it, Cruz is just as surprised as I am that the judge is dead."

She blinked, slowly understanding that I already knew about the warrant. "You knew about the judge refusing to issue the warrant?"

I waved the question aside.

"For years now," I continued, "Cruz has been able to sit within the judicial system with impunity. I'm not saying there are judges on the take, or that they're warped, but well, some are. And Cruz is different. From what I've read, you don't mess with him unless you want to wake up with your pet parakeet's head in your bed."

The disgusted noise she made sounded like something my mother use to make when I'd tried to talk her around to my way of thinking. She was never a pushover and neither was Sam.

"Is it too big a stretch of the imagination to think that the judge was taking a little bit of cash on the side from Cruz for looking the other way?" I asked.

"Isn't that taking it a bit too far, Jack? A conspiracy? Seriously?" she harrumphed. "People smoke in bed all the time. Houses burn down all the time. Let's not try to make something more out of this than it is."

"I repeat. I don't believe in coincidences."

Suddenly, I realised what Frank had been inferring when he sat in my office. He'd told me how the judge had ruled because there had not been enough evidence for a search warrant. But I could sense there was something he was leaving out. The thought had been so strong but it was right there in front of my face. The young boy that Elizabeth had walked in on, where had he gone? Was the judge Sugar Daddy? Immediately, I disregarded the thought. The judge who died had looked like Elmer Fudd and he was not the same person that Hayley had described. No, there was another man involved in this. Another powerful, influential man. And if this guy Frank called Sugar Daddy knew where to procure one young boy, did he know where to find more?

Suddenly, I gripped the table with both hands. The case of the murdered boys Sam and I had been investigating had occurred at exactly the same time that Christine Buchanan had disappeared a year ago. Exactly. Sam and I had talked to the detectives involved in the case at the same time that we were investigating the murders. Was this case connected to the murder of young boys on Tamborine Mountain a year ago?

There were so many thoughts rushing through my brain, I was struggling to put them into some sort of sequence.

"What happened to the boy, Sam?" I almost whispered.

She just stared at me. "How do you know about…?"

"I know. All right! Just tell me!" I stopped and took a breath, trying to keep my temper in check. "Where has the boy gone?" I repeated a little calmer. "The one Christine walked in on." I was swapping the names Christine and Elizabeth and it was beginning to confuse me.

When Sam didn't answer, I placed my elbows on the table and put my fingertips to my forehead, resting my head there for a few seconds, my eyes closed.

"Is this case connected to Tamborine Mountain, Sam?" I asked softly.

I glanced up to see her liquid brown eyes watching me.

She answered quietly. "Maybe."

I inhaled sharply. "And you didn't think to tell me?" My eyes held hers. "That case ended my career and almost my life. It took everything away from me. My job. My life. Almost my sanity." I shook my head sadly and gaped at her. "And you couldn't find it in your heart to let me know I wasn't the incompetent loser I thought I was?"

She stood up quickly and grabbed her handbag that was hanging from the back of the chair.

"I can't talk about this, Jack. I have to go. I have to see if they've managed to follow Cruz." She hesitated. "I'm sorry. Truly I am. I was just following orders."

When I didn't answer, she sighed heavily. "Please make sure to ring me with updates."

"Sure thing," I lied.

The look she gave me would have curdled milk.

"I'm serious, Jack. Everything. Cavanagh's not someone you can mess around with. He'll be back," she warned.

"Super," I smiled.

❦ 15 ❦

After meeting Sam, I headed home. I had a few things to organise. Firstly, I had to call Frank and make plans for him to come to my house and babysit Hayley. I had a few things scheduled for the night and I'd promised Hayley I'd pick her up around 10pm when it was dark and the likelihood of nosy neighbours seeing her leaving the house would be minimal. I remembered Frank's words about us being partners and I decided tonight was as good as any to test him. What I had planned, I couldn't do alone. And I estimated I'd need his help for the next three days.

Surprisingly, Frank agreed to the plan without asking too many questions. He'd be here to keep Hayley safe while I continued the search. What I had in mind for this evening, I couldn't do in broad daylight. I needed the cover of darkness if it had any chance of success.

While I waited, I went over my notes, adding a few new ones to the list.

After the sun dipped below the horizon, I pulled out a dark hoodie and a pair of sweatpants from the back of my wardrobe and put them on over my clothes. Then I chose a black baseball cap and pulled it low over my forehead. I didn't want an over-zealous rookie cop pulling CCTV footage and see my face light up the screen. Even at night, there would still be enough moonlight to highlight my features.

Checking myself in the mirror, the first word that came to mind was lumpy. But the look would work, especially with a baseball bat hidden behind my leg. It cost nothing to be careful. I knew I would be in plain view so I had to ask my questions and get away quickly. Chances were people would see what was happening and they'd call ooo for assistance.

With everything in place, I locked up and went back to Jason's house. His SUV was parked in the driveway behind the Hyundai I knew had to be his mother's. The house was lit up like a Christmas tree with lights were on in every room of the house making me wonder who was paying the electricity bill. Apparently crime does pay.

I drove down the street and parked so I could see when he left. There was barely enough light for me to write up my plans for the next couple of days so I switched on the torch on my mobile phone and shone it onto the notepad. With one hand on the phone and the other holding the pen, the pad kept slipping on my knees so eventually I just gave up and watched.

Stakeout is not the heart-racing excitement it's cracked up to be. It's boring and tedious and it involves a lot of waiting. While I waited, I dug around in the glove compartment looking for something, anything, to eat. A furry piece of gum and a peanut of dubious origins was all I could find and my stomach growled loudly, sounding like a rusty hinge groaning open in a horror movie. I picked the lint off the gum and popped it in my mouth.

About half an hour later, Jason came out of the house in a hurry, carrying what looked like an oversized canvas duffel bag, and sped off. Like I said, detecting isn't rocket science. It's being at the right place at the right time and taking full advantage of it.

I started my car and followed behind at a safe distance until he pulled into a service station. I turned in and parked around the side of the building within view of his car, watching him fill up with petrol and walk inside to pay. It was all going to plan.

I stepped out of the car and crouched beside a dumpster hoping that from where I crouched, I would be invisible in the darkness. He'd have to come out sooner or later and when he did, I'd be waiting for him. This time, I wasn't going to let him get in the first punch.

I threw the gum away and waited.

My heart was racing and I was sweating in the thick sweatpants. I couldn't believe I was about to do this. *Re-think this,* my good angel whispered. *Nah. Be honest,* said the bad one. *You're loving this too much.*

A few minutes later, he came out with a bag of crisps and a canned drink. My stomach growled again as he leant into the car and threw them both on the front passenger seat. This was my chance. I had a very small window of opportunity between someone inside calling the cops and me hearing the sirens approaching. Maybe two to three minutes. Four if I was lucky. More importantly, I had to keep my face averted from the CCTV pointed down in my direction.

Before he stepped into the car, I did what I never thought I'd ever do. I pulled the hood over my head and jogged over to him, going for him first, skipping like a boxer.

When Jason saw me, all his previous bravado disappeared and his arms went up in a defensive pose. His elbows raised and he looked like he was ready to land an enormous punch on my face.

Not this time pal, I thought.

Keeping my back to the CCTV, I got the flat of my left palm on the underside of his elbow and pushed up hard, bringing his upper arm past vertical. I reached behind him and grabbed the waistband of his pants and pulled them down. His ass fell instantly to the ground and I heard the breath *oomph* out of him. The look on his face was the same look he'd given Cruz in the parking lot.

"Where's Elizabeth Delaney?" I asked.

He lay on his back, leaning on his bent elbows, making a pretence of thinking about it, as if he was trying to remember. But his eyes flickered. Then he shrugged.

I smiled down at him. It wasn't a nice smile, because I wanted him to know I meant business.

"Were you the one following her the night she disappeared?"

His eyes flickered again as he frowned, wondering how on earth I knew that little piece of information.

"And did you turn on Hayley and give her up to Cruz?" I persisted.

Time was ticking along with him just watching me. Time I didn't have. I stepped forward, keeping the bat out of sight, and said, "Her parents told me you and she were an item once." I saw the glint in his eyes and continued. "They also told me they didn't like you."

He snorted but I could feel fear coming off him in waves. Not surprising because I'm a respectable-sized man and not a five-foot four woman.

He stayed put on the ground looking up at me. "No offense to Mr Johnson, man, but he's being a bit dramatic. Sure, I saw Hayley a few times. We used to go out for a while. That's all. I heard her friend went missing a week ago and I went to Hayley's house, just to make sure *she* was alright. I haven't seen Hayley for a year, man. I didn't even know if she was still with her parents."

Like I told you, criminals are not smart. He'd just told me that he knew Elizabeth Delaney had gone missing a week ago. To know that, someone must have told him they'd seen her recently. Like a week ago in Alto's.

"How did you know Elizabeth went missing a week ago, Jason? Shouldn't you have said a year ago?" I asked threateningly.

"It's all over the news, man!"

He kept looking to the left and I couldn't remember if that meant a lie was coming or if it was just memory. It didn't matter. I didn't believe a word that came out of his mouth anyway.

"So why all of a sudden do you turn up at the Johnsons asking to see Hayley?"

"I was concerned! I couldn't understand why they wouldn't let me talk to her a year ago. We were dating, man, and they wouldn't even let me see her! I could see they were holding out on me. Like she really *was* there but they weren't going to let me near her."

The indignance in his voice sounded almost real. "I wanted to make sure she was alright. That's all. The two of them were once good friends."

He was watching me closely as thoughts ran around in my head. Human nature is so predictable. A liar embellishes, trying to 'up' the story so you share the outrage. I use the word embellish but it's downright lying.

"Who's the giant who hit you in Starbucks car park, Jason?" I asked.

The perplexed look was priceless. He was wondering how I knew to ask that question and I let it sit in the silence for a few seconds until he realised I'd been watching him.

"My God," he said with almost awe. "You have no idea, do you?"

I didn't like the way he said that with such confidence.

"Can I phone a friend?" I asked.

This time, there was no evasion in his eyes.

"He'll kill you, man. And not even think twice about it. Or worse, he'll kill someone you love. Maybe he'll make you watch while he kills them. And then kill you. Me, too."

I'd seen Cruz at work but this sounded a little dramatic.

"You sound a little paranoid here, Jason. This isn't Hollywood and it isn't an episode of Criminal Minds."

He was shaking his head while I spoke. "He will. He will." He pointed to the bruise on the side of his face. "This was because I didn't get what he wanted. He was *annoyed.* You don't want to see him when he's angry. Leave it alone, man."

I was getting tired of being told to step away. I pulled the bat from behind my back and stook a step closer.

One of the biggest questions in life should be *'am I willing to go one step further?'*

I could see the panic on his face. "Oh, come on, man. What's that for? What else do you want?"

"What didn't you get for Cruz, Jason? Or should I say who?"

His eyes flickered when I said Cruz's name but he stayed silent. I couldn't wait any longer. I lifted the bat high overhead, the way I'd seen baseball players do it on television. Bat back, elbow up. Putting all my weight and leverage into it, I bought it down on the fleshing part of his thigh.

You're probably wondering how I, an ex-cop who was sworn to uphold the law, could justify what I just did. I can't. I'm a hypocrite. *This is what you've sunk to*, the voice in my head said. *Beating up kids who are lying on the ground, defenceless.*

He screamed and held his hands up to stop me. "Please, man. Stop!"

In the background, I could hear a siren heading our way.

I turned my head towards the sound, listening and trying to judge how far away it was. In that split second when my attention was diverted, he began fumbling in his back pocket and brought out a gun. He was slow and adrenaline had cut in for me so it was easy work to snatch the gun out of his hand.

"Don't be a moron!" I ejected the clip and put it in the back pocket of my jeans. I didn't know if there was a bullet in the chamber so I pointed the gun to the ground and fired. There was enough noise with the siren getting louder so the shot that echoed around the car park was almost lost. Almost, but not quite.

I needed to get away and I needed to do it quickly. I tossed the gun back at him and he was on his feet in an instant. I'd hit him hard but he jumped up as if nothing had happened. If it weren't for the lump rising on his cheek and the limp as he turned to run, I'd have doubted I'd hit him at all. He inched toward the open car door getting ready to make a run for it.

He turned and said, "Leave it alone, old man. He's out of your league."

I watched as he jumped into the front seat and fumbled the key into the lock before roaring away. With the sirens getting louder and louder, I dropped my chin to my chest, avoiding the camera, and walked briskly away to my own car, annoyed I had nothing to show for my efforts.

Two streets away, I pulled over and threw the hoodie and cap into a 7-Eleven dumpster. The cops probably wouldn't bother with the CCTV cameras since there was no one complaining and they wouldn't bother dumpster-diving into the remains of strawberry slushies. I was hoping they'd put it down to a drug deal gone wrong and wipe their hands of it. Just two gang members disagreeing.

My job was done. I'd scared the hell out of him. I decided to head home and prepare for the second part of my night.

16

It was almost 8pm by the time I got home and my stomach grumbled louder this time in protest. I had a full night planned and if I was going to have my wits about me, I needed to eat something.

I dug around in the freezer to find something edible and lifted out a Tupperware container with something brown in it. I sniffed the container dubiously and remembered the curry I'd saved from a meal a couple of weeks ago. Satisfied, I popped it in the microwave to warm while I took a beer out of the fridge and popped the top. Two minutes later, I walked over to the dining table with the meal and the beer and pulled out a chair.

While I ate, Jason's words surfaced about the possibility of Cruz killing someone I loved. There weren't too many to choose from. My daughter Jasmine was the first who came to mind but it was a long shot for Cruz to find her. My ex-wife Sally had changed addresses twice in the past twelve months.

It's easy to act tough and say I can't be intimidated but I had to be realistic. What were the odds I'd find Elizabeth alive? Very long. What were the odds I'd find Cruz and bring him in to face justice? Even longer. And then, what were the odds that someone close to me would suffer because of my determination to solve the case? I didn't even want to think about that. If I was smart, I'd just step back and hope the police had it covered as I stepped away from it all.

Except I couldn't. Adrenaline was zinging through my body for the first time in over a year. And I hate to admit, I loved the feeling.

As I spooned the last of the curry into my mouth, I pulled my laptop over and typed in the password, planning to Google the newspaper article for Cruz's photo. It took me longer than most people because of my ineptitude with computers but eventually the piece began to appear on the screen. While I waited for the page to come up, I thought about Frank's comment on improving my computer skills.

It had been big news. Front page stuff. And I'd missed it. As Frank had said, Cruz and Preston's mug shots were there.

The curry did a little turn in my stomach as Jimmy Preston's face gazed back at me from the article. I gulped some beer as I stared at the screen. The picture had been taken a few years ago but I'd never forget that face. I'd seen it up close a little over a week ago staring down at me as I hid in the industrial bin. The acne wasn't as prominent back then but neither were the muscles. And the scar was missing.

Obviously, in the past couple of years, he'd worked hard on building up his body, supplementing his job at the bar with work that required muscle. There was very little information about Jimmy but I didn't need to know much. What I needed was how to find him now.

I pulled a pad over and jotted down a note. *Get Jimmy Preston's address from Bazza.* Then I turned back to the article.

The bulk of the article concerned Cruz. As I sipped my beer, I read. The Ponzi scam was mentioned as well as the fact that many prominent men and women got burnt trying to make some quick and easy money. No names were mentioned. In my experience, anything quick and easy has to be shady and is always best avoided. Someone should have told these 'prominent men and women' my theory before they forked out the cash in the first place.

Then I googled Cruz' name and another article popped up. The picture of Cruz had probably been taken in his early twenties and the article was from quite a few years ago. Maybe ten. His face stared back at me over his shoulder as his lawyer pushed him forwards, away from the reporters. The face of the lawyer was that of a younger Elmer Fudd, minus the green smoking jacket.

The lawyer had the kind of face juries loved. The nice uncle who belonged on a Rotary Club steering committee. The kind who always bought the first round of drinks, invited friends over for a barbeque on weekends and never forgot the receptionist's birthday. My guess was Cruz had to pay a huge wad of cash for this guy. And then he'd become a judge and Cruz hit pay dirt. I kept reading.

Like Jimmy, Cruz wasn't as big back then and the word 'steroids' popped into my mind again. Without a doubt, Cruz, Jimmy, Beluga and Jason were all taking them and it wasn't too far a reach to believe they were getting the product from the same source.

From what Sam said, Cruz had dropped out of sight after this and reappeared in Surfers, buffer and meaner, probably due to too much testosterone. One thing was for sure; he still needed a lawyer on his speed dial.

Under *Get Jimmy Preston's address from Bazza* I wrote *Find out who Cruz's new lawyer is.* I had no idea how to do that.

Frank's parting words on the 'dark web' popped back into my head. I Googled the words and a page popped up. As I read, I drank the last of the beer.

The dark web is a part of the internet that isn't indexed by search engines. You've no doubt heard talk of the "dark web" as a hotbed of criminal activity — and it is. Researchers Daniel Moore and Thomas Rid of King's College in London classified the contents of 2,723 live dark web sites over a five-week period in 2015 and found that 57% host illicit material.

A 2019 study, 'Into the Web of Profit' conducted by D. Michael McGuire at the University of Surrey, shows that things have become worse. The number of dark web listings that could harm an enterprise has risen by 20% since 2016. Of all listings (excluding those selling drugs), 60% could potentially harm enterprises.

You can buy credit card numbers, all manner of drugs, guns, counterfeit money, stolen subscription credentials, information, hacked Netflix accounts and software that helps you break into other people's computers. Buy login credentials to a $50,000 Bank of America account for $500. Get $3,000 in counterfeit $20 bills for $600. Buy seven prepaid debit cards, each with a $2,500 balance, for $500 (express shipping included). A "lifetime" Netflix premium account goes for $6. You can hire hackers to attack computers for you. You can buy usernames and passwords.

. . .

THIS WAS HOW FRANK WAS GETTING INFORMATION. ACCESSING information by breaking into other people's computers. The only way he could have accessed the information Hayley told me was by hacking into the Police Department's computer and bringing up the reports. I made a mental note to ask him about it.

I glanced at the clock on the wall. It was 9.30pm and time to head off to pick up Hayley.

I shut the laptop and put the dirty bowl in the dishwasher before grabbing my keys and heading out the door.

❄ 17 ❄

Hayley's house was in darkness as I drove down the street, as were the other houses. I drove up to the junction and did a U turn, scanning both sides of the road as I slowly drove back to the house. As I approached, two silhouettes appeared at the front door, hovering on the front porch in the darkness. I came to a stop and a third one slipped out and ran down the driveway to my car. I could be mistaken but I could swear I saw Mike glare at me as his daughter ran to my car.

Once inside the car with Hayley buckled up, I did another U-turn and headed towards the freeway and home.

"You okay?" I asked in the silence.

Hayley nodded but said nothing.

Trying to ease the tension, I said, "My partner Frank and I will both be watching you around the clock so you'll be fine, Hayley." I was trying to sound reassuring. "And your bedroom will be right next to mine."

She turned her head slowly to face me. "Don't you go expecting any favours from me." She scowled at me. "You know what I mean. I'll turn on you so fast your head will spin. I know how to protect myself."

Her statement hung in the air as the road noise filled the car.

"I promise to behave," was all I could manage without laughing.

The drive back to my house was awkward with Hayley hugging the door. Not that it bothered me. I was happy for the silence. I had a head full of thoughts that needed sorting out and I was beginning to regret my impulsive idea to hide Hayley at my house. The logistics alone was going to be a nightmare. One of us had to be with her at all times and if I was busy trying to find Elizabeth, that only left Frank.

In the back of my mind, I knew Frank would assume I'd folded and was including him in on the case. He'd suggested we be partners but I'd laughed at him and yet here I was, asking him to help. What he didn't know was there would be no cash in it for him. I wasn't getting paid for my work which meant neither was Frank. I made a mental note to tell him that vital piece of information. But only after we managed to keep Hayley safe and after I came up with a plan.

Half an hour later, I was back at the house and Frank was sitting in my lounge room watching television. I'd phoned him on the way to Hayley's house and told him where I'd put the key but in the back of my mind I had a feeling he already knew. Months ago, during Joe's trial, someone had ransacked my house looking for a vital piece of evidence and even though Frank denied it, I knew it had to be him.

Hayley was sullen as she walked beside me into the house.

"Frank, this is Hayley Johnson," I said as we both walked in. I'd decided the less Hayley knew about Frank the better.

Frank could sense I didn't want to talk in front of Hayley so he gave her a smile. I think that's what it was.

"I'm starving," she said petulantly. "This guy only wants sex."

Frank didn't miss a beat. "He's like that with me, too, but we've learned to adjust."

Hayley blinked then burst out laughing.

"Thank God *you* have a personality," she laughed. "This guy is like a corpse."

"He's Mister Personality when you get to know 'im," Franked grinned, showing her the full range of his crooked teeth. "Then you can't shut 'im up."

I sighed as the two of them chuckled, already at ease with each other.

"Three rules, Hayley," I said. "No drugs. No men. No booze. While in this house, you're Doris Day."

"Who's Doris Day?" she asked.

"Mother Theresa's sister. You get the point?"

She glanced at Frank, a smirk on her face and he wiggled his eyebrows at her and mouthed, *Hormones*.

She giggled.

"Give her something to eat Frank," I sighed. "I'll fill you in tomorrow. I have to make a phone call and go out again."

I jerked my head in the direction of the three bedrooms. "Choose whatever bedrooms you want. Just remember, mine is the one with the ensuite at the end of the hallway."

"La di da," Frank mumbled and Hayley chuckled beside him.

＊ 18 ＊

As well as a restaurant and a bistro, *Dolly's* has several different bars, one for shows, another for poker machines and a public bar where most of the locals seem to congregate. From the outside, the yellow glow of mercury-vapour lights streamed across the gleaming tops of parked cars. Near the entrance, girls were lounging against the walls, their eyes following as a succession of vehicles cruised by. The double doors were closed keeping in the cool air and the cigarette smoke out.

After leaving Hayley and Frank to search through my near empty freezer, I called Sam. I didn't tell her I'd found Hayley and I didn't tell her I had her stashed at my place. And I definitely didn't tell her about Frank because the plan I had in mind involved him and it didn't involve her and Cavanaugh. Not yet anyway.

What I wanted was to look like I was sharing information with her. It was a little give on my part that could pay off big time for me in the future. What I told her was I'd talked to Susan Bishop and she'd remembered something. Sam wasn't happy that Susan hadn't given her the information first but I said she'd only just remembered. The part I was definite about was if Sam wanted me to give her this information, I was to be the main investigator.

It took a bit of persuasive talk on my part to convince her but in the end, she reluctantly agreed. I told her about Simone and where we may be able find her and my plan to talk to her at the club. What I needed from Sam was a picture of Simone. All I knew was she was blonde and thin. Not much to go on when half the young women in Surfers Paradise fitted that description. But if she'd been in the business for a while, Sam would be able to lay her hands on a photo. It was the only reason I was including Sam in on this. The quid pro quo she was talking about. I bring her along if she brings the photo.

It was eleven o'clock and Sam and I had both driven our own cars. We circled the parking lot twice, looking for parks. We each found one, locked our cars and headed towards the front entrance. As we walked, Sam shoved the photo of Simone into my hand, scowling at the same time. I had a good look at it then placed it in the inside pocket of my jacket along with the photo of Elizabeth Delaney.

We walked into the bar and heads turned. I didn't think anyone recognised Sam as a police officer: they were all probably wondering if we had any form of business to offer, namely drugs. I could smell the dope as reefers were passed from hand to hand and I saw Sam's nostrils twitch as she looked around.

Music blasted from the dance floor. The very air smelled briny from the beer on tap. A light show twinkled on the ceiling simulating twilight on the ocean and the walls were painted in various shades of blue graduating downward from a calm blue to the midnight hues of the deep.

Tables were tucked into alcoves made to look like coral reefs. The lighting was muted, much of it emanating from massive aquariums where fish undulated endlessly. Reproduction antique navigational charts were embedded in polyurethane on every tabletop, and the world they portrayed was one of vast unpopulated oceans with treacherous creatures lurking at the outer limits. Not so different from the patrons themselves. All the waitresses were dressed in skin-tight body suits and I had to guess they were hired on the basis of their build: slim hips and no breasts to speak of.

Sam stayed close to me and leaned in once to say something but the noise in the place obliterated her voice. We found a vacant wall with an unobstructed view and leaned there, people watching. The volume of the music would necessitate a hearing test later. I'd once fired a gun in a small tunnel and had been plagued by an intermittent hissing deep inside my head for weeks later. These people were going to need hearing aids by the age of thirty.

"There's no sign of her." Sam yelled over the music. "Are you sure this information is legit?"

"She'll be here somewhere. For these girls, this is like the unemployment office."

I spotted Simone across the room and touched Sam's arm and pointed. My mouth formed the word *Simone* and she followed my gaze. Simone was standing near the door, apparently alone, though I had to guess she wouldn't be for long.

"Lucky break," I shouted above the music. "The lady's not having a profitable evening so far."

Hayley was right. She had the look, apart from the age.

On American television, prostitutes have a certain look. Their make-up is usually a Gaugin palette of colour with rosy cheeks, red lips and sparkly eye shadow. Add tasteless clothing to the ensemble and you get the picture. This was not the case with Simone.

Her perfectly cut blonde hair flowed down her back and even from this distance, I could see her flawless make-up, slim hips, a flat belly and the almost non-existent breasts that could have been taken for early adolescence. A body like that is much admired by postmenopausal men. She was wearing loose, black satin pants and a sparkly halter-neck top that left very little to the imagination. Over her shoulder was a black sequined handbag with enough tassels to embarrass Liberace.

We made our way across the room and at some point she spotted our approach. I jerked my head towards the front door and her eyes shifted from me to Sam, sizing us up. Sam and I had both worn suits, making it look official, and she noticed, adding two and two together and arriving at the conclusion we'd hoped. *Cops.* She pivoted, walking ahead of me, making a production of it, and every male eye was crawling up and down her bare back.

Outside, the temperature rose dramatically, the air smelling fresh and moist.

Up close, I could see the skilful use of cosmetics in the battle she must have fought for adolescent looks. Her insolent blue eyes raked me up and down and I knew she was one of those people you instinctively know nurses a reservoir of anger they can draw upon when needed.

"Is this supposed to be a bust?" she asked warily. "Because if it is, you're wasting your time. I haven't done anything wrong."

"It's not a bust and I'm not a cop." I let that sink in. "Is your name Simone?"

"What if it is?"

"I'll take that to mean yes," I sighed. "My name's Jack Curtis and I'm a private investigator. We just want to talk to you about a client you had a few years ago."

She threw her head back and laughed. "A few *years* ago. You've got to be kidding."

When she finished chuckling, her eyes fixed on mine but her head jerked once towards Sam. "Who's she?"

"Detective Neil," Sam said.

"A cop." She almost spat the word, shaking her head in disgust. She looked steadily at me for a few seconds. "I'm telling you Curtis, you better not be setting me up." Her complexion was as perfect as a child's but her eyes flashed at me, mean as a snake.

"It's not a setup, Simone." I pointed to Sam. "*She'll* even pay you for your time."

Sam's eyes looked startled and she gave me an astonished look.

Simone's eyes scoured the parking lot and then strayed back in Sam's direction.

"I don't do women," she said sullenly.

"Hey," Sam said a little too loudly, "neither do I. In case anybody gives a shit."

I ignored Sam's outburst and addressed Simone.

"It's just a few questions, Simone. Then we'll be on our way. It's about a guy who hurt someone you know."

She thought about it, looking off into the distance.

"Come on. Help us out here," I coaxed.

"Okay," she said grudgingly. "But I'm doing it here at the casino. I'm not going down to the station."

She looked hard at me and I nodded.

"Let's get it over with then," she said. "And you better not be conning me."

"Trust me," I said.

"Trust him," she snorted. "What a joke!"

She said the words to no one in particular as she headed off around the corner away from the incoming patrons.

"Have a smoke if you want," I offered. I'd have liked one myself.

"I don't smoke," she snapped again, screwing her face up in distaste. "I hate smoking. It's bad for you and it stinks." She toed the ground petulantly before continuing. "Enough of this shit. I've got work to do. What do you want to know?"

From my inside pocket, I brought out the picture of Elizabeth Delaney and handed it to her.

Her eyes roamed the picture then handed it back to me. "Her hair was a different colour when I knew her. But yeah. I knew Christine." She looked down at her feet. "What's she done?"

"She's missing, Simone. Presumed dead. Except she calls herself Elizabeth Delaney now."

Her head snapped up and she blinked a couple of times. "Shit. She's the one all over the news. The one who's missing." She shook her head. "I didn't recognise her."

"Then she did a good job of hiding herself. We're trying to find the man who made her do that. And we think you may know his name. Apparently you knew him before he met her."

Her eyes widened before she spoke. Her little girl eyes contradicted the outfit she was wearing.

"I hope you don't think I had anything to do with it. If it's the guy I think it is, I met up with him a few times but that was years ago. He started getting rough and I kept that in mind. The next time he hit me, it was worse and I decided then and there not to see him again. He paid me and I left and I made sure never to see him again. That was it. The end. Christine took over from me." She sneered. "I was getting too old for him, anyway. He likes them young."

"So you *do* know who he is?"

She'd made a mistake and she knew it. If she were smart, she would have just denied knowing him at all. Instead, she'd embellished.

She started nibbling on a hangnail. Her nails were bitten to the quick. "I don't know his name."

I watched her pull on a cuticle before asking, "What are you afraid of Simone?"

"What am I afraid of?" she sneered. "I'm afraid of losing my teeth and I like my nose just the way it is, thank you very much."

"So maybe you should go down to the station with Detective Neil here and talk to her about it," I said.

"Oh right. Maybe I should go ahead and check myself into the morgue as well. Save myself the messy middle step," she snapped. "She should have taken my own personal advice. Earn money and learn not to depend on anyone else. You can do anything you want if you're independent. Some guy mistreats you, you get the hell out. You walk. Know what I'm saying?'

"That's my philosophy," Sam almost whispered beside me.

I glanced at Sam. For an instant, I glimpsed the ghost of an expression that could only be called despair. Then it was gone, leaving me feeling like I'd seen something I shouldn't have. She turned and stared at me, as if she'd read my mind. She said nothing before turning her attention back to Simone.

"Yeah, mine too." Simone was warming up to the topic. "I got a little money saved up and I try to stash it away. It's not much but it's enough and I'm not going to touch it. I'm going to leave it in the bank and let it collect interest. I'm not about using a stockbroker because it's a perfect excuse for some asshole to come along and rip you off. How about you?" she said to Sam. "You got savings?"

"Yes, I do," she nodded.

"Where've you got it?"

It felt strange standing there listening to financial strategy from a girl who worked the streets.

"In the bank," Sam replied.

"That's good. Keep it there. That and long-term stuff. If you have money, you have power, and no guy can come along and punch your lights out."

She turned her attention to me.

"How much do you earn?" she asked me.

I stared. "That's pretty personal."

"Yeah, I know. But this is between us. You tell me and I'll tell you. How much did you earn last year? What you paid taxes on?"

I didn't want anyone knowing how little my agency was making.

"I've only just opened my agency," I answered. "It doesn't count."

"Eighty," Sam piped in. "Before overtime."

Now it was Simone's turn to stare at Sam. "That's *all*? I bet I earn more than you do in six months without getting out of bed. I earn fifty on top of your eighty. No kidding."

"By the looks of it, you got your nose broken too," Sam said a little defensively, defending herself.

"Yeah, but I bet you get worse. No offence. You're not bad looking but for eighty thousand? You get punched in the chops same as me, am I right?"

"I try not to look at it like that."

"Don't bullshit yourself. Your job is dangerous the same as mine only with half the pay. You ought to switch. Not that I'm promoting my line of work, mind you. I've seen plenty of girls should be worrying more about algebra and zits. Instead they're here in this life." She shrugged. "Some make it. Some don't."

I knew exactly what she meant. Every day teens wanting to be models try to escape abuse or boredom or poverty at home and arrive in Surfers Paradise. Every day pimps cruise the bus stations watching for backpacks and hopeful faces. Then like the predators they are, they offer a photo shoot and a party. Most of the kids end up junkies and prostitutes. The unluckiest arrive toes-up at the morgue. As a cop, I had been powerless to stop it but I always felt grief. I always will.

Sam smiled at Simone's statement, oblivious of my silence.

"Thanks. If I decide to change careers, I'll come to you for job counselling." As an afterthought, she asked, "What do you charge?"

I stared at Sam and my eyes said *what?*

"Two hundred bucks," Simone replied.

"*An hour?*" Sam yelped.

"What's the matter with you? Two hundred bucks *a trick*. Nothing about sex takes an *hour*," she laughed contemptuously.

I put my hands up to stop the conversation.

"Can we just get back to the reason we're here please? The man Elizabeth Delaney was servicing?"

She nibbled nervously at her bottom lip. "He's an asshole and he's got a temper..."

The words trailed off as emotions flitted across her face. Her eyes raked back to mine.

"Do you think it could be him?" She swapped her lip for her fingernail again and began working it.

"It's early days. We don't know yet but we would like to talk to him. Do you know where we can find him?"

She said nothing but continued to work on the fingernail.

"Simone?"

"I'll tell you something I've learned over the years. Keep your mouth shut. I slipped up a couple of times and swore I'd never do it again. You know what I mean?"

"We won't let him hurt you." I kept my voice soft.

"How are you going to stop him?" she snorted. "You going to send someone around to protect me?" A smirk appeared on her face. "Huh? You going to do that?" Her eyes scanned mine in the silence. "I'M A PROSTI-TUTE," she yelled at me. "Remember? We don't rate that kind of protec-tion against people like him."

People like him.

"Just tell me where we can find him and no one will know where we got the information. I promise."

"Sure you do," she said as she put her tassled bag on her shoulder. "What the hell? Like I said. I don't know his name. And I don't want to know. What I *do* know is this guy is *someone*. You know what I mean? Someone *important*. And he's got connections."

"Connections?"

"Yeah. Connections. Are you thick, or something? Someone like him, he knows people in high places. When he was leaving this one time, he was talking on his phone as he walked out. I heard him call someone '*Your honour.*' So yeah. Like I said. Connections."

Sam and I both knew *your honour* meant a judge. Which meant the guy was more than likely a lawyer. *And* he had connections to a judge. It wasn't much but it was something and it all added up.

Suddenly I remembered the article I'd googled this evening. The picture of Cruz with Elmer Fudd pushing him forwards and my thought that Cruz had to have a new lawyer on speed dial here in Surfers. Now it looked like he had a judge *and* a lawyer on it.

"And he had soft hands." She put the finger back in her mouth and chewed. "His nails looked like they'd been manicured. All even and shiny. Not with polish but kind of ... buffed. Not long but not short either. But nice."

She hesitated.

"What, Simone?"

"His voice," she mumbled. "I used to think it was kind of sexy. You know. Soft and whispery. Gentle." She snorted. "That was before he hit me and I realised there was nothing gentle about him."

She hitched her bag higher over her shoulder. "But that's it! The next time you need information, bring money," she added. "You got the money, I got the mouth." She laughed dryly. "So to speak."

She wiggled her fingers at us as she walked away.

Sam and I said our goodbyes at our cars, her saying she'd let me know if there were any updates and me promising the same with my fingers crossed behind my back.

Half an hour later, I was pulling into my driveway. The house was in darkness as I turned the key in the door and stepped inside. The clock ticked loudly as I glanced at it. 12.40. In the background I could hear snoring.

I walked quietly towards the bedrooms. The first door was shut and I eased it open, hoping it wouldn't creak. Hayley lay curled up asleep in a foetal position under the covers.

The next bedroom door was open and Frank lay sprawled out on top of the bed fully clothed, mouth open and snoring loudly.

I made my way to my own room hoping the sound of his snoring wouldn't filter through the walls. I needed a good night sleep.

❧ 19 ❧

Over coffee in the morning, while Sherlock sat on the kitchen bench balefully eyeing Frank, I explained the financial situation to him.

He grinned crookedly at me and said, "Later mate. We'll sort it out later. We're pals, right?" He stopped slurping the coffee and added, "But you pay for the food. There's bugger all in your fridge and we have ta eat something besides cat food. I'll order some things online at Woollies and get them delivered so leave me your credit card."

Maybe it was a stupid thing for me to leave him with Hayley but I had no other choice. I had some things I needed to do. I needed to find out if the man Elizabeth had seen at Alto's, on the night she disappeared, was the same man Simone remembered.

It was almost 10.30am when I left Frank at the house, him waving me goodbye with my credit card in his hand as Hayley continued to sleep through the morning.

Lunch at Alto's was half an hour away. Tables were still being set and from behind a door, pots and pans collided with hot plates. The restaurant was definitely a step or two up from most pubs on the coast. There was no stench of stale beer and no sticky floor and no smell of vomit wafting up from said floor.

It didn't take long to find the bartender who'd served them that evening. All it took was Elizabeth's photo.

Antonio had a pensive look on his face before nodding.

"Yeah. That's her. She was nice looking," he said. "You can see that. Except for the scar. If she did something about that, she'd have been smoking hot."

"Do you remember the guy who walked over to their table?"

He thought for a second, a frown creasing his forehead. "Yeah. Mean eyes. Dark, mean eyes. Like *don't-mess-with-me-or-you'll-be-sorry'* eyes." He snorted. "Not to the girl at the bar with him though. To her, he was all smiles." He winked. "She comes in here lots. Waits at the bar and they all gravitate to her like bees to a honey pot. Now *she* was hot."

"What else do you remember about him?"

"He was wearing a suit. A dark grey one that must have cost him a fortune. I remember because it was 30 degrees outside and here's this guy thinks he's God's gift to women wearing a suit. Had a Lacoste shirt underneath it and kept putting his hand on his hip and pushing the coat aside so the logo could be seen. Even had the collar turned up like a dickhead." He snorted again and smiled as he remembered.

"What did he look like?"

"Mid forties, I guess. Dark hair, big nose, mean eyes." He shrugged. "Nothing special but he must have had something going for him 'cause you could see the girls eyeing him up and down. Who knows? Maybe girls like dickheads." His eyes opened wide as he remembered something. "Oh, and his nails were manicured."

Bingo.

"Like a ponce," he continued. "Kept looking down at them and admiring them."

"Who came in first? The girls or him?"

"The girls." He nodded his head to the photo. "Her first, then the other one maybe ten minutes later. They were drinking over there," he nodded to a booth near a large potted plant. "He walks in and starts talking to the hottie at the bar. When he saw the two over there," he jerked his head again at a table, "his eyes lit up like a Christmas tree."

I could feel my phone vibrate in my pocket. I ignored it.

"You get a lot of pros in here?"

"Sometimes, yeah. If it's quiet over at *Dolly's*, they head over here. There's also a strip club within a kilometre and sometimes the girls do a little business on the side over there."

He suddenly paled when he realised what he'd said.

"I'm not from Vice and I'm not judging."

My phone vibrated again and as I reached in my pocket to grab it, I saw the television screen over the bar was switched to a news station.

On the screen, a helicopter camera zoomed in on a winding dirt road, then closer in to a clump of trees. It could have been one of the roads branching off Mount Tamborine Road but I couldn't be sure. Uniformed cops were standing around and I could see crime scene tape and a suggestion of a half-concealed body lying on the ground. The ticker-tape at the bottom of the screen said, '*Body found in woods on Tamborine Mountain.*'

I had a bad feeling.

"Oh no," I mumbled as I watched an ambulance pull up, lights flashing, followed by the medical examiner's van. Paramedics got out of the ambulance and joined the cops. Another car pulled up, joining the group, and parked behind the van. Both front doors opened and two people stepped out.

Even the view from the helicopter couldn't conceal who they were. One was Sam and the other was Cavanaugh. This time the ticker tape running across the bottom of the screen said, '*Southport Police are not releasing any details as yet*'. I could see more helicopters in the air and guessed the other television channels had joined Channel 9, late to the party.

"Listen man," Antonio was saying as I stared at the screen. "These girls come in and buy drinks. They don't do any harm."

I watched as Sam and Cavanaugh weaved their way through the cops. Then Sam squatted down on the grass beside the medical examiner and her face went ashen.

The medical examiner was Mary O'Brien and I knew her well. Petite, blonde and sweet, with a bright smile for everyone. Too sweet for such a gruesome job. As Mary examined the body, they quietly talked. Instead of the friendly smile I remembered from my days on the force, there were deep furrows on Mary's forehead.

Her reaction didn't surprise me. She could never manage being a cold observer. People were not just tissue and chemicals to her. I've seen her almost cry over John and Jane Does with incredible respect as she performed autopsies on them. There's never any coldness with Mary. There's only quiet compassion.

Antonio shrugged. "Sometimes they leave with guys. Sometimes they don't. None of my business what they do once they're out of here."

Watching Sam and Mary sent me back in time when I knew the drill too. I'd squatted down by bodies many times myself. There would be no emergency and no hustle. No shouting voices to the ambulance to get the stretcher over quickly. No IV lines or breathing tubes and no chest compressions. Dead bodies don't warrant emergency procedures.

"But man, she was HOT!"

I absently fingered the scar on my stomach where the bullet had entered my body over a year ago. A lot had happened since then. My chest tightened as the reality of what had happened suddenly hit me once again. I mentally shook myself and focused on the television screen.

Antonio turned to look up at the TV screen, curious to see what had grabbed my attention.

"Hey! Is that a dead body?"

Cavanaugh stood beside Sam, his face wooden as he looked down at the body covered in dead leaves. A policeman came over and said something quietly and Cavanaugh turned and snapped something at him. It was a bit showy, like something you would have seen on an episode of CSI. The cop took a step back, a surprised look on his face, then he backed away as Cavanaugh looked down at the body again, his face set. All business.

I saw Sam stand up and walk away, her face to the cameras. As she walked across the park, she reached into the back of her jeans and pulled out her mobile phone. I saw her head lower as she touched a number and at the same time, my phone began to vibrate again. I looked down at the screen and saw Sam's number and I looked at the television, watching Sam standing with the phone to her ear and waiting.

I pressed the answer button but before I could say anything she jumped in, "I'm at a crime scene so I can't talk right now Jack but we need to talk."

"Is it Elizabeth?" I asked, my voice a croak.

She glanced over her shoulder at Cavanaugh still looking down at the body.

"No. But we need to talk. And soon." she said, then hung up.

I watched her do it.

Click.

I looked down at my phone, unsettled by the abruptness of the call. I glanced back at the TV and watched her put the phone back in her pocket and walk back over to Cavanaugh. He raised his eyebrows as Sam said a few words to him. His forehead wrinkled up, but he said nothing. He didn't need to. Anger was written all over his face.

❧ 2 0 ☙

I pulled into the house and parked in the driveway after heading back to the office first to check my answering-machine for messages. I knew Sam would be busy at the crime scene for another hour or more so I planned on heading down to the station later on in the afternoon.

It was close to 3pm and the next-door neighbour was out rearranging his sprinkler. He gave me a wave as I stepped out of the car.

"Hey, Jack," he called out over his shoulder.

"Hey Gary," I said. See? Non-threatening. The nice neighbour.

"You got visitors Jack?"

"Yeah, Gary. A distant cousin and his daughter. Just for a few days."

He stood up and dusted his knees. Grassy wet patches circled his knees.

"How's Bronwyn?" I asked good-neighbourly. I didn't really care but I was keeping up appearances.

"She's great. Thanks for asking." He gave me a look that said he was pleasantly surprised at my willingness to chat. "Said she saw you yesterday when she was out chasing the dogs." He laughed and shook his head. "Damn dogs are better at escaping then Houdini was."

I laughed along with him. Mr Nice Guy.

"Hey Jack. Bronwyn has a music recital on the weekend. You want to come?"

I hesitated, not because I had any intention of going, but trying to word my refusal in a way that good Karma will still be on my side. Karma is like this organisation where every event is recorded and at some stage, at Karma's choosing (because Karma is cagey that way) it will step in and make it all right. If you've done good deeds, it may repay you, hopefully with interest. For example, if you help an old lady cross the road Karma will pay you back generously for your erstwhile good deed. Having said that, of late I think Karma is doing the virtual lounging on the couch in his underpants watching Sky Sports oblivious of everything.

I smiled at Gary and said, "I'd love to," while thinking *I'd rather have a kidney removed.* "But work," I shook my head sadly. "You know what it's like. I'm up to my ears in it at the moment." I laughed. "And these visitors. They want to be shown the sights on the weekend. Shouldn't complain, though. Next time?"

I was still waving like an idiot as I headed into the house. I stepped inside and Hayley and Frank looked up from the dining table that was covered in chip packets and coke cans, a card game called Phase 10 in progress.

"Hi," Frank called out cheerily. Hayley just jerked her head as a greeting.

Both dropped their heads back to the game.

I nodded and headed off to the bedroom and started to shed my trousers just as the doorbell rang.

From the lounge room, there was the sound of chairs being scraped across the floor and I quickly threw on a pair of sweat pants before walking out the bedroom door. Frank and Hayley rushed past me on the way to her bedroom, her hands full of cards, his full of chips and soft drink cans.

"You expecting visitors?" Frank asked.

I shook my head. "No. Keep quiet but listen hard." I turned to Hayley. "And you too. Stay quiet."

"Hey! Why are you picking on me?" she whispered angrily.

The doorbell rang again and I looked out the lounge window.

Two cops. They were dressed in plain clothes but there was no mistaking them. I don't know if it's the way they both stood on the front porch or the clothes they were wearing. But there was no mistaking them. They were cops. One male one female.

I walked towards the front door and reached for the doorknob just as the doorbell rang for the third time.

I didn't recognise either of them. The woman's hair was pulled back in a casual ponytail and she was probably mid to late thirties. She was dressed in a pair of jeans and a buttoned-up pale blue shirt but she wasn't fooling me. She was a cop.

The guy was a bit older and his dead-leaf brown pants and purple shirt told me there wasn't a little woman waiting at home for him.

Next door, Gary was still fiddling with the sprinkler, his eyes glancing nervously over to the two visitors, trying not to make it seem too obvious that he was watching and listening.

I raised my eyebrows and the woman gave me a tight smile.

"Jack Curtis?"

"What can I do for you two detectives?"

She hesitated, then smiled. "I'm Detective Philippa Sawyer." She pointed to the guy next to her. "This is Detective Jackson."

I didn't like the vibe I was getting. If I didn't know better, I'd say they were here to deliver some bad news, like someone close to me had died. I've done the condolence bit a few times in my past life as a cop and it's not my forte. Looking at them, it wasn't theirs either. But as pitiful as it may sound, I couldn't imagine anyone coming to deliver bad news to me in a squad car in an official capacity. Apart from Sally, who would probably run over me in her car rather than go around me, my daughter Jasmine was the only other person in my life who I cared about.

I skipped the *nice to meet you* bit and ask, "Is my daughter alright?"

"We're not here about your daughter. Or anyone else in your family."

The only other option was they knew about Hayley.

"What can I do for you?" I asked with a practiced smile on my face.

"Can we come in?" Sawyer asked.

I could hear rustling coming from inside. The last thing I needed was for one of them to ask to use the bathroom and discover a minor, who looked like the love child of Brad Pitt and Barbie, huddled in a back bedroom with a person that looked like Frank. It wouldn't look good.

"Not today," I said. "Cleaning lady hasn't been. Tell me what you want."

The little smile she had slid off her face.

"Can I use your bathroom?" Jackson said.

I groaned.

"Tell me what you want first," I repeated.

"No need to be testy," Sawyer said.

"No need to be coy either," I said staring her down. "Let's not draw this out. I don't want Jackson here wetting his pants on my front porch."

Jackson glared at me and Sawyer put her hand on his arm.

"You're right. We do have bad news."

I waited.

"There's been a murder."

Okay. Not Hayley.

"Are you referring to the one that was on the news earlier today?" I asked.

"That's the one."

I sighed. "Again. What can I do to help you?"

"We'd like you to come down to the station to answer some questions."

That got my attention. Why the hell did they want me to go down to the station with them? And to answer what questions?

"I don't understand," I shook my head.

"The murder victim's name was Jason Brady."

My eyes popped open and I inhaled sharply.

"So you knew him," Sawyer smiled.

When I didn't answer, she asked, "When was the last time you saw him?"

"A couple of days ago. I questioned him in relation to Elizabeth Delaney's disappearance." I frowned. "Detective Neil knows all about this. What's going on?"

"You're sure that was the last time you saw him?"

I kept quiet about the night I'd hit him at the petrol station. If they'd seen the CCTV footage and seen me, they wouldn't be asking me when I'd last seen him. I'd be in cuffs already.

"Yes, I'm sure," I lied. "Why?"

She looked at Jackson and he nodded. Then she turned back to me.

"The murder weapon was found near the body and we have it down at the station. We've already done a fingerprint analysis on it."

She watched me in silence.

"Okay." I finally said. "What sort of weapon?"

"A gun."

I waited while they both continued looking at me in silence.

I shrugged. "Okay again. I'll bite. Whose prints did you find?"

"That's the problem," Sawyer said. "See, the fingerprints on the gun didn't get any hits from the regular criminal database, which means the person has no criminal record."

The hairs on the back of my neck stood up now but I let her finish.

"But they were still in the system." The small smile reappeared. "And we got a hit."

I knew where she was going with this and I tried not to show my shock. I flashed back to snatching the gun out of Jason's hand, emptying the cartridge, and throwing it back to him. I'd been just as stupid as every criminal who watches CSI and thinks they know everything. I'd left my fingerprints on the gun.

I snapped out of it.

"Whose prints do they belong to?" I asked innocently. Just in case.

"They were your prints, Mr Curtis. And we'd like you to come down to the station with us to help us with our enquiries."

The cell smelt fresh and sterile. There was no graffiti and it didn't smell of disinfectant, urine and misery. Yet. It featured a new solid metal door with a small hatch at eye level and in one corner, the red light of a video camera flickered.

I remember the old cells reeking of vomit: the marinated aftermath of revellers trolling the Surfers Paradise bars. There were no cameras in the cells a year ago. Just steel bars behind a corridor beyond. The mayor's budget must have stretched a little for the upgrade. I'd locked a few teenagers up after a night of drunkenness and tomfoolery but never had the misfortune to spend time in one myself. I was wishing that was the case now. On the bright side, it gave me time to think.

I'd made a song and dance about changing out of my sweats and Sawyer had grudgingly agreed. What I needed to do was talk to Frank before leaving so I left them standing on the porch as I headed to my bedroom. On the way, I quickly poked my head into the back bedroom.

Frank and Hayley were both standing behind the door, their backs pressed against the wall.

"Nice work," Frank whispered.

"Thank you," I whispered back. I was feeling mildly euphoric about pulling the changing bit off but nervous at the consequences of my stupidity with the gun.

I looked over my shoulder at Sawyer and Jackson. They were still shuffling their feet impatiently at the door.

"Now it's your turn. Find out what you can, Frank. Where Cruz is. Also ask around about the guy Elizabeth walked in on a year ago." I looked at Hayley. "If you want us to help you, you have to help us. Tell Frank everything you know."

Her eyes were as big as saucers. "We have three people trying to kill me right now! You said you'd protect me! What are we supposed to do while you're away with them?" Hayley jerked her head at the front door.

"Actually, it's only two people trying to kill you. We can exclude Jason now," I said.

"Oh. Sorry if I wasn't more specific!" Her arms were crossed mutinously across her chest. "So what's your strategy?" she asked.

"My what?"

"Oh shit." She leant her head back against the wall. "I'm going to die," she muttered.

Almost an hour went by before I heard the sound of movement outside my cell and I looked up to see Philippa Sawyer standing back and waving me through.

"After you, Curtis," she grinned. "The inspector is ready for you now."

With Sawyer walking behind me, I strode down the same short hallway I'd walked down a year ago, up the familiar flight of stairs and into the same squad room I'd once occupied. A cop passed us by leading a young teenager through the swinging doors on the way to the holding cells. He did a double take when he saw me and nodded a greeting.

The squad room buzzed with low conversations as I approached. Empty doughnut boxes still littered desks surrounded by empty Styrofoam coffee cups as well as KFC boxes, empty chip packets and chocolate wrappers. A policeman's diet.

I took stock of the crowd and saw Sam talking on a phone behind a desk near the window while several other detectives sat at their desks staring at computers. Sam glanced up when I walked in and glared at me. Standing in front of the whiteboard like a teacher about to start a lesson was Cavanaugh and behind him, with half of his ample posterior perched on the corner of a desk, sat Inspector Grayson.

As if sensing my entry into the room, a hush came over the room and Grayson and Cavanaugh turned towards me. No one said a word. In the background, telephones rang and policemen in the corridors stood shouting back and forth to each other. But in the squad room there was total silence and the foot Grayson had been dangling in mid air suddenly stopped swinging.

Grayson hadn't changed much. A little over six-foot-tall, a little over fifty years old and solid looking. He still looked mismatched, as if God hadn't been paying a lot of attention when He'd put him together. Big ears stuck out at right angles from a square head devoid of any hair and a face scarred from childhood acne. His eyebrows hovered over his eyes like great grey caterpillars as he scowled at me. His hairy arms made him look like a monkey in a machine-washable suit. Despite the bags under his eyes, there was a sharpness about him.

I felt an ornery kind of kinship with Grayson. He's tough, emotionless, harsh and mean, all with an overriding competence. He knows his business, he never misses anything and he takes no guff. Once upon a time, I would have said he grudgingly liked me. Looking at the veins popping out on his forehead now, I'd say his opinion had changed.

One of the disadvantages about answering to a man like Grayson, who first couldn't say good morning without putting an exclamation point at the end of the sentence and providing an analysis for it, is.... Don't get me started. With Grayson, I could work my way through to ten with plenty to spare. He was like a dog patrolling his boundaries, barking at anyone who came too close.

I stopped and looked around the squad room as Pete Bridgman spoke from the back of the room.

"Nice to see you again Jack."

He paced determinately over to me, his face stretched into a smile that accentuated the freckles splattered across his nose and cheeks.

On any normal day, Pete was every mother's dream for her little girl. He's six-foot-tall, athletic, his eyes a topaz blue and his curly blonde hair makes him look like Little Orphan Annie after a sex change. He always seems to have an endless supply of pristine suits that look like they have only just come from the cleaners. However, today was not a normal day. Today, his tie was unknotted and his sleeves were rolled up to reveal tanned forearms. As he walked towards me, he swiped his fair hair back from his forehead before holding out his hand.

I cleared my throat and shook it.

"Thanks Pete. I wish it were under better circumstances."

He nodded and walked back to his desk, glancing defiantly at Cavanaugh standing at the whiteboard before he sat down at his desk.

My eyes skimmed the whiteboard. It's where the basic breakdown of any murder is pinned: victim's name, medical examiner's name, laboratory reference number and the crime report number. All around the inside of the board are the details of the place where the body is found and pictures, if any.

From where I stood, I could see before and after pictures of Jason pinned to it. The first one, a buffed up, younger version of Jason than the one I'd seen a couple of nights ago and the second one, his body lying on the grass with blood saturating the ground under what was left of his head.

"Curtis!" Grayson bellowed, standing up. "Get into my office!"

I followed Grayson as he stomped into his office. Sat down heavily in his chair and tented his fingers across his round belly. His office was crowded with box files piled up on the carpet in both corners behind his desk and the edge of one peeked out from under his desk. I could hear the air-conditioner droning away in the background, but it wasn't enough to take away the thick odour of cigarette smoke.

"I see Dr Jekyll has returned. I can't wait to hear what you have to say about this?" His voice was deep and husky, weeks away from throat cancer.

"I didn't do it," I answered as coolly as I could.

He stood up abruptly and began pacing the room, running both hands over his bald head.

"Hell! I know that! That's not what I want to know! What I want to know is why your prints are all over the damn weapon!"

I'd heard that Grayson had high blood pressure and he lived in constant fear of a stroke that had killed his father. Mouth to mouth was something I had no wish to perform on him. I pointed to his chair and asked, "Have you spoken to Sam?"

Thankfully, he sighed heavily and sat back down. He sucked on the inside of his cheek for a few seconds, his two caterpillars working up and down in unison.

"About you being a private investigator now?" His voice had calmed and his face had lost the ruddy glow of only a few seconds ago. "Yeah. She spoke to me about it."

He took a deep breath and emptied another cigarette out of a bent packet and lit it up, breathing deeply. The colour subsided as he harrumphed angrily and took another drag of the cigarette.

"What I want to know is why your prints are all over the gun?" He leant back in his chair. "You've got five minutes to astound me."

I had to word this carefully. Grayson was smart enough to know if I was lying or not, so I wasn't about to lie to him. What I was going to do was omit a couple of things. Like stalking Jason from behind a dumpster in the middle of the night with a baseball bat in my hand.

"In the course of my investigation," I began slowly. Grayson's eyebrows rose questioningly, but he let me continue. "I came across certain information that I thought Jason Brady could help clarify for me. I met with him and he pointed a gun at me. I snatched it out of his hand, emptied the clip and tossed it back at him. End of story."

He punched the stub of his cigarette out in a paper cup already resembling a volcano.

"Don't tell me that because it's just going to piss me off even more!"

His voice was starting to rise again.

I had this paranoid feeling that he thought I wasn't up to the investigation after such a long time away from the job. Paranoia can help to give you an edge and sometimes an edge makes all the difference.

"I watched him drive away and that was the last time I saw him." I insisted. "He's in league with Cruz and I was trying to help Sam and Cavanaugh get to the truth."

"Save the analysis for the gang out there," he jerked his thumb in the direction of the squad room. In the silence, a clock ticked loudly and the air-conditioner droned. He stared down at the top of his desk, shook his head, then stared at the closed door like it was made of glass and he could see right through it. I had a feeling he wasn't telling me something vital. He was tossing it around in his head wondering if he should or if he shouldn't.

"What are you not telling me?" I asked.

His eyes moved back to mine. He nodded as he stared deep into my eyes.

"Whoever killed him tried to make it look like it was a suicide."

He swivelled in his chair, his face the only part not moving. His eyes glowed with anger.

"Your prints being all over the gun that killed the kid doesn't mean much if it was a suicide."

I said nothing.

"Sure, it made us wonder why they were there," he continued, "but if it was a suicide," his hands rose and waved theatrically in the air, "it means nothing. It was just strange. Something we needed to ask you about."

He took a deep breath and the anger settled a little. "But the medical examiner and Walt in the morgue have doubts about it being a suicide. Which is why we brought you in. You see, if it wasn't suicide, then you were our prime suspect. Your prints being on the murder weapon and all."

Were. I sat still, barely breathing, waiting. He waited. Cops are patient. They wait.

He stopped swivelling and leaned forward, his arms folded on the desk as he stared at me.

"I've been working crime scenes way before you were wearing your big boy shorts, and in all that time you're the luckiest man I can remember."

He swivelled some more.

"You see they discovered an anomaly. They discovered something else. Your prints and Jason's weren't the only ones on the gun. If they were, there's nothing your or I, or anyone else, could have done to help you." He let that sink in before continuing. "But they weren't. There were yours, the kid's and a partial that we haven't identified yet." He took a deep breath. "We've checked the system but there's not enough to make a positive analysis."

He sat back and tented his fingers over his ample stomach. "But those partials are your *get out of jail free* prints. They are the only things that saved you." He nodded and smiled. "As I said, you're a lucky man."

He started swivelling again. "What I want to know is what am I going to tell the people upstairs on the third floor when they find out about this?" He nodded his head at me knowingly. "And they'll find out. Trust me on that."

I blinked at him a few times, letting my breath out slowly.

"You could tell them the truth. You could tell them in the course of my investigation, I came across Jason Brady and he assaulted me but I overpowered him and sent him on his way. You could say that Jason Brady was involved with some dangerous characters and any one of them could have killed him." I waited for him to say something. When he didn't, I said, "And you could say you trust me."

I felt like a man who wakes up alone on a deserted island to find that all the boats had been stolen during the night.

Grayson let out a deep sigh as he sat up straight, pulling some files across the table and shuffling them around.

"What I'll do is tell upstairs you're doing some consulting work with us." His head shot up. "Free of charge!"

He nodded a few times, happy with his plan. His caterpillars met in the middle of his forehead, just to make sure I wasn't going to argue.

"Don't make me regret this, Curtis, or I'll do things to you that would make Genghis Khan blush." He let that sink in before continuing. "Just make sure you fill Neil and Cavanaugh in on everything. And I mean everything! And take it easy on Cavanaugh. This will be like kicking a puppy."

He waved his hand at me dismissively. "Now get out of here before I change my mind."

When I walked back to the squad room, Sam was standing in front of the whiteboard and Cavanaugh was butt-leaning on the desk, making the posture look arrogant somehow. They both turned and looked up expectantly.

Sam asked, "What's going on, Jack?"

"I'm sure I don't need to tell you that I didn't do it Sam."

Cavanaugh said nothing. His eyes flicked over to Grayson's office and back again.

"Grayson's letting you go?" he asked in a hushed voice.

"Better than that," I gloated. "I'm now a consultant with the Southport Police Department." I spread my hands wide and grinned. "I guess the band *is* getting back together again."

I was smiling so wide my face felt tight and if I smiled any more, my cheeks would crack. It surprised me how much I loved being the bad guy.

I did my best Bogart. "I'm all yours, shweetheart."

I turned towards the whiteboard with the details of the crime scene spread over it and crossed my arms over my chest. "And now, *you* get to share everything with *me*."

I let my eyes roam over the board while in my peripheral vision Cavanaugh's complexion went from white to crimson.

"What I need first is a copy of the medical examiner's report," I continued unfazed, ignoring Cavanaugh as if he wasn't there. "And the autopsy report if Walt has finished with the body."

I could hear Cavanaugh's teeth grinding and without saying a word, he stood and turned, heading towards Grayson's office and knocking on the door.

"You're enjoying this," Sam said watching him.

"Immensely," I replied with a smile.

"We haven't received the paperwork from Walt yet," Sam said watching Cavanaugh open the door and step inside. She glanced at the watch. "This late in the day, it won't be available until tomorrow morning."

"Tell you what, Sam," I glanced down at my own watch. It was close to 5.00pm. "Why don't you go home? I'll head over to the morgue and see if Walt is still there and if he has anything yet. If he does, I'll bring the report back and leave it on your desk and make a copy for myself before I head home too."

She was still staring at Grayson's door as raised voices echoed through the squad room.

Grayson was right. There was no use antagonising Cavanaugh.

"I won't step on anyone's toes, Sam," I promised. "I'm just consulting." I spoke the words softly. "And it's probably only a once off."

When she didn't reply, I smiled wryly. "He'll be slumping around with a face like a cat's bum for a while, all martyred and woe-is-me, but he'll soon see I'm not about to move in on his territory."

She let out a long, slow breath. "He'll be impossible to work with."

"And I'm sorry for that. But I'm only here to help."

She continued staring at Grayson's door, chewing her bottom lip, but saying nothing.

"While I'm here, I need something else," I asked tentatively.

She dragged her eyes back to me and frowned. When she didn't say anything, I said, "The report from the Fire Department on the house fire at Sovereign Island."

Her eyebrows shot up high on her forehead. "The house fire? You mean the fire at the judge's house?" Breath puffed out of her pursed mouth. "Come on Jack. Why?"

I smiled. "A hunch."

She threw her hands up in the air. The resigned gesture that reminded me I wasn't really an outcast, just not welcome.

"Sure Jack. Why not? If you haven't got enough to fill in your time, sure, go ahead. Chase your tail on this one too." She waved me away. "Go to the morgue. I'll have the file on my desk by the time you get back."

I nodded at the door. "I suppose I'd better..."

Sam was gone before I finished the sentence.

❦ 22 ❧

I'd always believed the word 'morgue' came from the French word 'mort' meaning death, but it actually comes from another French word 'morgeur' meaning 'to peer' from the days when bodies were plucked from the Seine and displayed to the relatives of the missing through the grilles of a Paris prison.

Personally, I hate them. Sure, this one was all white, cool and clean but it's the mixed odours of blood, alcohol, disinfectant and death permeating the cold air that I hate. Maybe it's the formaldehyde. Maybe it's the blood. But whatever smell it is, it infiltrates everything. It's a mixture of decay and chemicals unique to this world. But then again, maybe the thing I hate most about morgues was just the silence that has little to do with the absence of noise. It's a silence that comes from a failed heartbeat, a voice silenced forever and all the senses that have shut down.

I stood at the door and looked around at the overhead microphones, the bars of fluorescent lights spread across the ceiling, the wall of steel lockers and the steel tables complete with a ridge running all the way around them. Drain basins were connected to the foot of the tables into which water, blood or any other matter is channelled. Hanging from the ceiling over each table was a large set of scales.

Most people would recognise all this from TV shows. What they don't experience is a glimpse of what lays *inside* the lockers or the chill and the smell of offal. Dead people on TV are intact, clean and bloodless. Not so in reality.

As I walked into the autopsy room, Walt Mason was sitting at his desk dressed in green scrubs with a Bacon and Egg McMuffin in one hand and a hoodie that had once been a deep green but was now covered in dirt in the other hand.

Walt is forty, balding and totally used to all confrontations with death. He looks like a member of a boy band gone to seed. His underwater fish-belly complexion, from too much time spent in the morgue, glows under the lights, giving him a greenish tinge as if he too is decaying.

In the silence of the room, the second hand of a clock hopped noisily and the overhead lights hummed.

"Has anyone ever told you you're a ghoul?" I asked.

He glanced up with the burger halfway to his mouth.

"Well, hello Serpico."

He tossed the hoodie on to his desk and the half-eaten burger on to a greasy wrapper and began licking his fingers.

"Can't keep a good man down, eh, or is just that no one else wants you?"

Walt is a rough diamond that not too many people take to. He's blunt, again probably from spending too much time alone in the morgue, and he's tactless. But he was one of the few people I liked when I was on the job.

I grinned. "Nice to see you again, too, Walt."

I glanced over to the autopsy table and saw the stainless-steel table had been washed and was laying empty ready for the next body to arrive. On a nearby table, grubby jeans and a pair of sneakers sat waiting for the hoodie to join them.

"I see you've finished with Jason Brady?" I asked.

Walt picked up a serviette that looked like it had already been used several times already and began wiping his fingers with it.

"What are you doing here, Jack?" he said with a small frown creasing his forehead. "Are you back?"

I shook my head. "Just consulting, Walt. If Sam and Cavanaugh let me."

"Hmm," he said nodding. "Well, good luck with that."

He tossed the napkin in the bin.

"Yes," he said. "I've finished with the body and I was just bagging his clothes." He jerked his head towards the hoodie.

"Anything out of the ordinary?" I asked.

He shook his head. "Just what you'd expect after spending a night in the bush. Dirty but intact. Way too early for any material to deteriorate."

He jerked his head towards the out-tray on his desk. "The report's in there ready to be collected."

"Can you give me an estimate of his time of death?" I asked.

Jason's time of death was important. I needed to know how soon after our confrontation he'd been murdered. I had an uneasy feeling that someone may have been watching us then followed him when he left. I didn't see anybody and that made me uneasy as well. Maybe I was slipping.

"It's hard to tell," Walt replied. "When a body's been in the open and in this heat," he shook his head, "nature changes things."

He walked over to his desk and picked up the report. The lights hummed and the clock ticked.

"The first day after death," he began, "flies lay their eggs in the moist, dark places such as the nose, mouth, eyelids and rectum. They tell us a lot. A few days later, I'd expect to see maggots and flies all over the body. An entomologist can take pupae from the body and fix the time of death according to the different stages of putrefaction. The length of putrefaction determines when infestation first took place and gives us the approximate time of death. Eggs have been laid in this boy's body but none have hatched yet. So that would suggest around twenty hours."

He scratched his head. "Adipocere has occurred but only just. After a while, body fats convert to fatty acids and areas of the body are covered with what looks like a waxy surface."

He looked up at me. "I once scraped away the adipocere from a corpse to reveal a tattoo. It was the only way we were able to identify him. But we know who this boy is. His wallet was in his back pocket."

He ran his tongue over his teeth loosening any food particles still lodged between his teeth. While he worked I waited.

"Now lividity," he continued. "Lividity is what happens to a person's blood after death. The heart stops, blood pressure collapses and blood drains and settles into the lowest part of the body due to simple gravity. It stays there and over a period of time it stains the skin purple. Somewhere between three to six hours later, the colour starts to fix and then it fixes permanently, like a developed photograph. Someone who falls down dead on their back will have a pale chest and a purple back. Vice versa for someone who falls down dead on their chest. This boy was found face down and if he'd died there, blood would have pooled on the front of his body because dead bodies don't roll over onto their stomachs after death."

He reached over and picked up a takeaway cup of coke, slurping noisily through the straw. Again, I waited.

He swallowed. "I found traces of lividity on the front of his body which says he died at the crime scene."

I nodded as he turned the page of the report.

"Now, here's the cruncher. The thing that told me it wasn't a suicide. We did a test on his stomach contents and found it contained half digested meats, vegetables and cheese consistent with having eaten pizza a couple of hours before death. Not just that, it contained huge amounts of trichloroethylene, otherwise known as methyl trichloride."

"Translated that means?"

"Chloroform. Pure and simple."

I gaped at him. The hopping hand of the clock ticked off the seconds.

"I thought chloroform was an anaesthetic that you breathed in prior to an operation," I commented.

"It is," he nodded, "although medicine has advanced in the past few years. Chloroform can cause vomiting and after an operation, that's the last thing you need. They use ether these days with better post-operative effects. But getting back to chloroform. You can also ingest it with food. The boy probably didn't even know what he was eating. It's a colourless liquid with a pleasant non-irritating odour and a slightly sweet taste." He picked up the container of coke. "He could have had a coke and he wouldn't have noticed the difference. It was unlucky for the killer that the boy was discovered so soon after death because tests on chloroform are only useful for a short time after you've been exposed to it. Another day or so and we wouldn't have known about it. Unlucky for the killer but lucky for us."

"Are you telling me that you can walk into a chemist and buy chloroform over the counter?" I felt a little twist in my gut.

"No, not a chemist. A hardware store. Chloroform is also a grease solvent used by a lot of dry cleaners. You can also find it in some paint strippers."

"Jesus. So the killer overdosed him on chloroform? What would the symptoms be?"

"Chloroform affects the central nervous system, the cardiovascular system, stomach, liver and kidneys. I read somewhere that in the late 1950's, factory workers in the United States who worked to manufacture lozenges were treated for chloroform vapours exposure. Workers reported symptoms of fatigue, a dull-wittedness along with depression and gastrointestinal distress. And that was an extremely mild dose. Chloroform causes relaxation of the bronchial muscle resulting in airway constriction. It can also cause the tongue to fall posteriorly, which will again aid in obstruction of the airway to the lungs. Put that with the paradoxical fear he must have felt and you'd have a dead body in a very short time.

"What do you mean paradoxical fear?"

"In the case of paradoxical fear, there is massive activation of the parasympathetic division. This fear occurs when someone is backed into a corner where there is no escape route or no way to win. The body responds with a decreased heart rate, constriction of the pupils and decreased diameter of the airways or bronchoconstriction. Add that to the effect of chloroform and you have one heartless bastard to contend with."

He sighed heavily. "And there's something else."

I raised my eyebrows. "You've been busy."

"Welcome to my world."

He sighed again and his voice became quieter.

"We have ante-mort abrasions," he said.

He tossed the report on his desk and looked at me.

"And that would mean..."

"Most wounds have four stages of healing." He held up four fingers and bent them one at a time. First finger. "Scabbing." Second finger. "The formation of epithelial, which is the tissue that forms on the superficial part of the skin and lines the blood vessels." Third finger. Regeneration hyperplasia where there is an increase in the number of normal cells." Fourth finger. "And lastly, the formation of granulation tissue. This new tissue forms across the wound to provide a framework that supports the epithelial cells that migrate into the open area and fill it. The newly formed granulation tissue also secretes a fluid that kills bacteria."

"Wow," was all I could say. "You even sound like you know what you're talking about."

"Okay, okay. What I'm trying to say is that these scrapes were at the second stage which means his body went through about an hour of healing before he died. Realistically he probably walked to the site for half an hour or more before he was killed. From reading the report Sam gave me, he was found in the bush on Mount Tamborine. Am I right?"

I nodded.

"The walk through the bush in his drugged state would have caused the damage because he would have been unsteady on his feet. The healing process would have begun from then. So depending on how soon afterwards he was shot, you have your time of death."

There was a deep silence while I digested this new piece of horrific information.

I was doing the math in my head.

"Are you sure about all this?"

"Are you questioning my skills, Jack?"

"Are we being a little sensitive, Walt?"

He sighed. "If your job meant being surrounded by dead bodies as far as the eye can see on a daily basis, I'd like to see how sensitive you'd become."

I couldn't argue with that.

"So what you're saying is he was drugged, taken to Mount Tamborine, was either led or was forced to walk through the bush, then shot?"

"In my professional opinion, yes."

"Did the shot kill him instantly or did the killer leave him to die?"

Walt was shaking his head. "No Jack. He could never have survived that trauma. He died instantly. The abrasions came from the walk through the bush to where he was killed. Like I said, half an hour, maybe a bit more."

My brain was firing. Hikers finding the body so soon must be pissing the killer off. The burning question was who had Jason gone to see after he drove away from me.

And then another thought popped in. If Jason had been drugged during the meal, there was no way he would have been able to drive his car to Mount Tamborine. That meant the killer had driven the car, probably while Jason was out to it in the back seat. He must have then woken Jason up to do the walk through the bush where he killed him. That means he'd driven the car away afterwards. So where was Jason's car now? I made a mental note to ask Sam later.

"Can you give me the time of death, Walt?" I asked.

"I'd say he's been dead about 20 hours. Rigor mortis has peaked, that happens at about 12 hours, but it hasn't dissipated yet. That happens after 48 hours. My best guess is his body was discovered about 12 hours, maybe 14 hours, after death. That would make time of death at around 10pm last night."

I started doing the math in my head, working backwards. First there was the walk through the bush. So, maybe half an hour? That took us to 9.30pm. And they would have driven to Mount Tamborine from Surfers Paradise. Another half hour. That took us to roughly 9pm. He had food in his stomach, pizza Walt said, so now we're at about 8pm.

The calculations astounded me. He would have met with his killer within an hour after our confrontation and gone straight out for a pizza dinner. He knew his killer well enough to sit down to a meal with him.

Mason handed me the report.

"You can take this with you. Mary's report is in there too. We'll do more tests tomorrow and then we'll know more."

I thanked him and headed back to the squad room to make a copy of the report before heading home to read it through.

❦ 2 3 ❦

True to her word, Sam had left the report of the house fire on her desk for me with a terse note saying to make my own copies.

It took fifteen minutes or so to make copies of everything and put them into separate folders before I tucked all three reports under my arm and headed home. My gut was acid and my head was a bongo.

The house was in darkness when I arrived home and it shouldn't have been. Frank should have been there with Hayley and my gut did a little somersault as I opened the door, switched on the light and pulled out my mobile phone. I'd added Frank to my contact list so seconds later, I heard the phone ringing at his end.

The throaty baritone of Frank came to me over the phone. "Are you ringing to say you miss me?"

I ignored the humour and said, "Where the hell are you Frank? You're not supposed to be out of the house with Hayley. We've discussed this."

"Settle down, mate. I took her back to her place for some more clothes and toiletries. Have more confidence in me. I know what I'm doing. She's inside with her parents and I'm outside keeping an eye open for the bad guys. Nothing's gunna happen to her. Trust me. I'm good at what I do. I told her I'd give her an hour and we've only just arrived so try not to get your knickers in a knot while we're away."

I heard the flick of a lighter and knew he'd lit a cigarette.

"Put the cigarette out, Frank. If anyone's looking, they'll see the glow and wonder why someone's outside skulking in the bushes with a cigarette in their hand."

A strangled chuckle came down the line. "Skulking." He laughed again. "Okay, okay. If it'll make you happy." I heard him stamp and knew he'd dropped the cigarette and stood on it.

"For goodness sake, have a drink, Jack. Ya sound like ya need one. As well as groceries, I bought a six-pack of beer. You can thank me later." He chuckled. "We'll be home soon."

And then he hung up.

He's was right. He was good at his job and that was why I'd asked him to help.

I did as he suggested. I took a can of beer out of the fridge and searched for something to eat. The leftovers of a pizza sat dejectedly under some glad wrap. Beside it sat a cooked chicken, still in the alfoil from Woolworths, several packets of cold meat, cheese, fruit and a loaf of bread.

I took the pizza out and tossed the glad wrap in the bin before seating myself at the dining table, spreading all three files out on the top. I was so hungry I ate the pizza cold.

I opened the first file and saw Jason's death certificate sitting on top. It stated he had died from a gunshot wound to the head but didn't add much else. One other section interested me however.

According to the file in front of me, a 38-calibre bullet was fired at a range of not more than two inches causing Jason's fatal injury. The bullet had entered through the left temple, burning and splitting the skin and singeing his hair above the wound, and shattering the sphenoid bone. The bullet hole was slightly smaller than the diameter of the bullet, since the epidermis had stretched to allow its passage and then contracted afterward. There was abrasion around the hole caused by friction and heating as well as surrounding bruising.

The bullet had exited above and slightly behind the right temple, fracturing the orbital roof and causing bruising around the right eye. The wound was large and its irregularity was due to the damage caused to the bullet by contact with the skull, which had distorted its shape.

The bloodstain pattern analysis was consistent with the injury received and a ballistics examination of the recovered bullet matched up with the gun. Chemical and microscopic analysis of skin swabs taken from Jason's left hand revealed propellant residues, indicating that the gun had been supposedly fired by Jason. The gun was also found hanging from his left hand.

It all looked like a cut and dried suicide. But still, the attending Medical Examiner, Mary O'Brien, had seen reason for doubting that.

A medical examiner can ascribe the manner of death to one of six causes. In order these are: 'natural', 'accident', 'suicide', 'homicide', 'pending investigation' and 'could not be determined'. Mary had opted for 'pending investigation'. In other words, just like Walt, she had enough doubts about the circumstances of Jason's death to require the police to continue their enquiries into the death.

I took another bite of the pizza and opened the second folder. It held the autopsy report from Walt and it stated Jason's body measurements, his physique and state of nutrition at the time of death. All matched my memory. There were no signs of self-neglect indicative of mental disorder or needle marks indicating drug dependency of any kind. The analysis of his ocular fluid found no traces of drugs, apart from the chloroform, or alcohol taken in the hours before his death, and urine and bile analysis also came up negative, indicating he had not ingested drugs in the three days preceding his death. That surprised me because steroid use had been on top of my list for Jason. Blood analysis stated that Jason's alcohol intake had been negligible before his death.

Next came the report on his clothing. Jeans, black t-shirt, green hoodie, sneakers size 13, a wallet with $36 and change in it. No jewellery except for a watch on his left wrist.

One thing I knew was that suicide victims usually shoot themselves in certain sites. The most common are the mouth, under the chin, the forehead or the temple and discharges into the temple usually occur on the side of the dominant hand. That was the reason why Mary had opted for the 'pending investigation'. The watch on the left wrist indicated that Jason was right-handed and a vision popped into my head of Jason lying on the ground, reaching into his back pocket with his right hand, looking for the gun.

So why would he shoot himself in the left temple, using his left hand if he was right-handed? The answer to that was because he didn't shoot himself.

I put the second folder on the table beside the first and picked up the third one. The judge's name stared back at me from the incident sheet as I read the report.

What it all came down to was drinking and smoking in bed. Just as Sam said.

I could almost see it. The bottle tipped over and most of the contents spilt onto the floor. He either didn't care about the spillage or had fallen asleep. The sleeping hand dropped the cigarette onto the carpet. The alcohol-soaked carpet went from smouldering then ignited into a hot flame, which caught the sheets and the blankets as the room filled with smoke then flames.

Normally it would take about ten minutes for the cigarette to ignite the sheets. Ten minutes when he may have smelled smoke, felt the heat, woken up and stamped his foot on the cigarette and that would have been that. But the alcohol would have helped to ignite the fire and because he'd passed out, he couldn't smell the smoke. He didn't have a chance.

It was probably the smoke that killed him, not the flames. They would have come later. Most people who die in a fire, die from smoke inhalation first. It's like the gas chamber because it's really the gas, carbon monoxide that kills you.

He would have been lying in bed drunk, his respiratory system working hard even though his mind had shut down, and those lungs would have just sucked in the smoke and filled until it was too late. He would have suffocated on smoke while he was asleep. A small blessing. He never knew what happened.

It's one of those cruel but kind ironies about house fires. Cruel that it takes your life and all the physical things – your furniture, the paint on the walls, your clothes, books, papers, photographs and all the accumulation of your life and forces them down your throat and into your lungs.

But something still niggled at the back of my mind. *Too coincidental* the voice whispered. *And you don't believe in coincidences* it taunted.

I needed to think this through. I stood up, took another beer out of the fridge and walked out onto the veranda. Snippets of conversation from people on their evening walk drifted over to me as I pulled out my phone to message Frank.

Pick up some more beer on the way home.

Seconds later, a ping sounded and Frank had replied. *Who am I? Your wife now?*

I smiled as I typed, *And pick up something nice for yourself.*

I saw dancing dots appear at the end of my message so I knew Frank was typing a reply. Seconds later the dots disappeared and an emoji appeared. A yellow face blowing me a kiss.

It was another hot humid evening. The air was heavy with the promise of a storm and as I looked up at the sky lightning flashed over the mountains. I knew there was a full moon tonight but there wasn't a hint of it, or any stars, in the dark, empty sky.

Stars have always put things into perspective for me. They're tiny lights dusting through billions of light years in space. It makes you realise you're just one tiny insignificant speck in the middle of nowhere.

I heard a noise beside me and turned to see Sherlock walking towards me. In his mouth, was something that wriggled.

"Oh, come on!" I yelled, throwing a leg in his direction. "Get away with that!"

Sherlock did a quick U-turn and scampered away with the something back into the yard again.

I looked at the near empty can in my hand and remembered someone once saying that every drink kills a thousand brain cells and the first to go were memory cells. I stood up and took another can out of the fridge, ready to murder a few more memories.

Sherlock came back and stared at me with luminous green eyes while I sat and savoured the beer. I poured some of the beer onto the decking and he blinked a few times before walking forward gingerly. He lapped at the beer for a few seconds before jumping onto my lap. I scratched the spot just above the base of his tail, which made his back end rise up to my face. He smelled like cat litter so I pushed it back down again and he began pushing his claws into my pants leg.

As I looked out at what was a black hole in my back yard, I extracted the claws from my knee. It was so quiet, I could almost hear my wristwatch ticking and my heart beating - one of those rare wells of urban silence that gives the city dweller a sense of peace. I basked in it until a squeal of brakes and furious honking broke the spell.

In the darkness, the cicadas were screaming like loud tinnitus in my ears and the wind had picked up. Pieces of litter were floating airborne. House lights were still on, but they wouldn't be on for long. In the distance, Surfers Paradise still glowed a sulphurous orange and I knew the late shift would have their hands full with drunk kids leaving nightclubs and brawling in the streets.

Even as these thoughts crossed my mind, I saw the lights next door switch off and seconds later a few more houses followed.

I took another sip of my beer. It was warm now. Popular with Europeans, I know, but so was blood sausage and Steven Segal, neither of which has ever appealed to me.

Just then the land line rang and I nearly dropped the beer. No one called me on that.

I pushed Sherlock off my lap and walked inside to pick up the phone.

"Hello?" I said tentatively, ready to hang up on a telemarketer.

"How's the tan coming along, Jack?"

Karen's voice was warm and smooth, like a nun with a past.

I felt the smile start deep in my chest and expand like a bubble. Suddenly, the empty house was full of her warmth.

"I assume that's what you're doing because you sure haven't been working in your office for the past two days."

"You may not even recognise me when you see me next. My tan is glowing and I now have a six-pack that any twenty-year-old would be proud of. Women are falling all over themselves to get at me."

"I'm sure I don't want to know."

"Do I detect coolness?"

"You detect indifference. That's not the same thing."

"Ha. We'll see if you feel the same way the next time you see me."

"Let me guess. You've changed your name to Jean Claude Van Curtis?" she taunted.

"Must we play this game?" I laughed.

Hearing the gentle laughter at the other end of the line felt soothing and comforting. Like a diver coming up for air.

A thought niggled at the back of my mind. Did I hear something else in her voice? Did I hear warmth?

Suddenly I had a vision of Karen lying on a tropical beach beside me, Margarita in one hand and bottle of sun cream in the other, her head turned towards me with a suggestive smile on her face. Her trim body was swathed in something soft and flowing and beside her I looked like Clint Eastwood, craggy and sexy, smelling like a coconut macaroon. The vision was so vivid; warmth flooded my body.

I wouldn't mind making her player number two in my post marital lovers but I also think a platonic working relationship is the wisest course. No hassles, no demands, no disappointments, and both partners get to keep all their neuroses under wraps. Whatever shows on the surface, most people come equipped with emotional baggage. With intimacy, the baggage starts to show and I wasn't in any shape right now to pretend I didn't have any, so why complicate life? Get close to someone and the next thing you know, you've given them the power to wound, betray and abandon you. Believe me. I know. I'm an expert on the subject.

My policy is to avoid a lot of unruly emotion and keep my distance. In me, the need for love and the fear of being rejected have been at war since Sally left me two years ago and since Shannon's death nine months ago. My caution is like a wall I've built up to keep myself safe. In psychiatric circles, there was probably a name for people like me.

And yet...

"Ah," I teased, trying to match her smoky tones, "my plan worked. You've missed me."

"You wish." There it was again. The sultry laugh.

The background noise of my backyard was suddenly a million miles away. Here I was at fortyish, feeling like a teenager making a date. I was living like a musician waiting for a gig. I needed to either pawn my instrument or find a place to play it.

Like a movie playing in my head, I saw us melting into each other's arms, lips coming together like a crash of waves. I was kissing and being kissed, my fingers in her hair, skin against skin and I had to shake myself because it had all the trimmings of some trashy novel.

Karen's background noise hummed across the line as I breathed heavily. A soft clink - wine bottle against glass? And I could just make out the beautiful voice of Trisha Yearwood singing softly. Suddenly I didn't want the call to finish.

I sat down on the floor, my back against the wall. "I have a confession," I conceded as I made myself comfortable.

"Uh oh."

"No tan. But I have been busy. And I may need to discuss some things with you. As my lawyer."

There was a moment's silence, and then she said, "Is this true or is this just more Jack Curtis humour? No joking now."

"No joking."

For the next fifteen minutes, I told her the story from the beginning. I told her about the hitchhiker I'd picked up and who was now missing. I told her about Frank coming to see me with a story from a year ago when Elizabeth was Christine and how she and Hayley had escaped only to be caught up in something far worse than anything they could have imagined. She grunted but said nothing, letting me finish.

While I talked, Sherlock ambled in and hopped onto my lap again. He sniffed my chin and stared into my face, looking concerned. Maybe he didn't know I was smiling. Then he began to buzz and he curled himself on my lap.

I told her about Jason, even the part about the baseball bat, and I told her that he was now dead and my fingerprints were found on the weapon. I told her about Cavanaugh and how he was itching to pin something on me but Grayson had come through and included me in on the case.

She grunted. "Some people are assholes."

I grinned. "Let me get out a pen and write that down."

"How is Cavanaugh now?"

"We get through with a minimum of gunshots."

"I hear he's a snake in the grass. And deadly. Watch out for him, Jack."

While I stroked Sherlock, I told her about the fire and the judge's death and how I had a hunch he had something to do with it all but couldn't be sure. I finished by telling her about Cruz and Beluga in the Starbucks car park and the fear in Jason's face.

In the background, Trisha Yearwood began singing about footprints in the sand. I listened to the words that hung in the air before continuing.

"Something keeps niggling in the back of my mind, Karen. Something Frank said."

Karen snorted. "Watch out for him too. Don't let that weasel convince you of anything, Jack. Seriously. He's bad news."

I kept the part about Frank and Hayley both here in my house for another time. Maybe I was just seeing a different side of Frank. Sure, I didn't trust him as far as I could kick him. But he was handing me something on a silver platter and I couldn't quite see what it was.

"I know. I know. But he told me a few things. He also left a few things out. Like he wanted me to join the dots together for myself. Except I can't quite see the finished picture yet."

Sherlock did one final stretch and let out a sigh. I scratched his head and listened to him purr before continuing.

"And I think it was something to do with the judge. This judge who died in the fire was the same judge who ruled that there wasn't enough evidence to make up a search warrant. Because of him, Cruz and his accountant, Fleming, were let off the hook, free as birds. And now that same judge is dead. It can't be coincidental."

"It does sound implausible," she conceded.

It sounded confusing. There were too many bad guys and I was having a hard time keeping track of them all.

"But if the fire wasn't accidental, then it's murder," Karen reasoned. "Those are the only two choices. And if it's murder, then who would want to kill him?"

She let that question hang in the air for a second before continuing. "Certainly not Cruz or Fleming. He's their 'get out of jail free card.' They'd want him safe and sound. So who killed him?"

"I know, Karen. I know. Something doesn't add up." I sighed. "I just don't believe in coincidences."

"Okay. What now?"

"I have a copy of the report from the fire here and it looks like they're going to rule it as an accidental fire. But I want to see for myself. I'm going to have Sam make an appointment for me with the Fire Chief so he can walk me around the scene. It's just a hunch but you never know."

I took a deep breath before continuing. I had to come clean about Hayley but I didn't want to do it over the phone at this time of night. I decided it could wait until tomorrow. I also wanted to tell her about the conversation with Simone and how she thought the guy who beat up Elizabeth was a lawyer. Karen may have some input and ideas on that one. I didn't have much of a description, but I had something.

"There's more. But not over the phone." I hesitated before continuing. "I may have to hire you as my lawyer."

I heard her breathing and I knew she would be biting her lip. It was a quirk of hers when she was thinking.

"I want to see you tomorrow morning when you go in to your office, Jack. Just let Connie know when you're ready and she'll make a slot available. I have a reasonably quiet day scheduled for tomorrow to catch up on some things so you pick a time that suits you best."

I agreed to see her first thing in the morning and hung up the phone before scrolling through my contact list for Sam's name. I wanted to talk to the Fire Chief in person and I wanted to do that at the burned house as soon as possible. It had been over thirty hours since the fire and I knew Forensics would have finished with it by now. It was the best time to go through the house one last time. I wanted to tick that last box, just in case.

I texted Sam asking her to set up a time for me to talk to the Fire Chief tomorrow afternoon at the house. The morning would be spent at the office filling Karen in on what had happened over the past couple of days.

From the veranda, the sky in the east was dark. I breathed the warm night air and listened to the crickets and the cicadas again and thought how fine it was that so much of my being could have so suddenly become focused on one person's phone call.

As I watched the sky, a silent fork of lightning flashed through the distant clouds like a silver spear followed a good ten seconds later by the first rumble of thunder. Another great fork rent the clouds and stabbed towards the earth. The thunder came again like cannon fire across the sky.

My phone pinged with a message. Frank's name appeared on the screen. *On our way home honey.*

❦ 24 ❦

The echo of Karen's heels changed from the soft click on the parquet floor to a soft hush on carpet as I followed her through the air-conditioned coolness of the reception area to the conference room. I'd been there once before when I signed the lease agreement so I knew a smoked glass table and black swivel leather chairs waited patiently for me. From behind, Karen's pencil skirt was as sharp as a knife and her soft perfume blended with the scent of jasmine and orchids wafting from the arrangement on the receptionist's desk.

Before heading over to Karen's office, I'd called Sam to see if she'd made the appointment with the Fire Chief. I had an appointment with Terry Bryson at 3pm this afternoon, so I was free for most of the day. A meeting with Karen was first on my list.

As always, the conference room was spotless and the table gleamed under the myriad of tiny led lights scattered over the ceiling like stars. In the centre sat a black ceramic vase with white lilies. On the only wall that wasn't glass hung a TV screen and on a sideboard beneath it, rested a silver water jug and crystal glasses. The only smell was Karen's perfume, the lilies, leather and money.

"Stop gaping, Jack. Sit down." She settled herself into her seat at the top of the conference table and motioned for me to take the one closest to her. When I was settled, she leaned her arms on the table and laced her fingers under her chin.

"Okay, fill me in on the rest."

Ten minutes later, I'd filled her in on the Hayley situation. She listened in silence as I told her the facts, holding nothing back.

"Are you crazy?" She gaped at me when I finished, astonishment written all over her face.

"I admit this isn't the usual way I go about things but I have a plan," I finished lamely.

"Oh it's usual for you Jack. You jump in first and think later. But this time, you've excelled yourself."

She was shaking her head and biting her lips again as she thought.

"As of now, you are my client," she stated. "Do not talk to any one about this and definitely, you do not talk to Detectives Neil and Cavanaugh. Do you understand?"

Chastised, I nodded.

"I'm serious, Jack. Especially not Detective Neil." She watched me sternly before continuing. "She may have been your partner in the past but that's what it is: the past. She has a job to do and she won't hesitate to pull the rug out from under your feet."

I remembered hearing the same passion in her voice six months ago. It's one of the many things I liked about her.

I crossed my heart and smiled. "Promise."

The heat slowly left her face as she stared at me. "Is there anything else you need to talk to me about?"

I nodded. "One thing that's been bothering me is that no one seems to be looking for the guy who beat up Elizabeth Delaney in the first place a year ago. That's where this all began. He sent Cruz to cut her off after she ran from him but she escaped and has been hiding for almost a year. They're only looking for Elizabeth because she's missing now and they're connecting Cruz to this. But what about this other guy? Who is he? If they're looking for this guy, Sam is certainly keeping that a big secret from me."

"Like I said, she's just doing her job."

"Well, I'm going to follow up on it. Simone and Hayley gave me some ideas so I have somewhere to start."

"Oh? Tell me," she said.

"Both Hayley and Simone said he was fortyish, average height, dark hair, blue eyes. Not movie star handsome but good looking. Probably a lawyer who has connections to a judge or two. And he has regular manicures. Like he's never done a day's work in his life. And he has a whispery voice apparently. It's a start."

While I was talking, Karen paled visibly. I stopped talking and stared at her.

"You know who he is, don't you?"

She shook her head a couple of times, before answering. "But it can't be. The description fits, but it could fit half the lawyers I know." She frowned and looked down at her hands. "The manicures though, *that* stands out. And the whispery voice."

She worried her lip some more then reached over and picked up the phone.

"Connie. Can you phone Cummings and Fraser and see if I can see Simon Parker this morning, please? Call me right back when you know. Ta."

She put the phone down and picked up her pen. "Simon Parker is a partner in a law firm called Cummings and Fraser located in Broadbeach. He's well respected, married with a couple of kids, so I don't see how this can be him." She shook her head. The only sound was the clicking of the pen. "But that description."

Married with two kids, Frank had said. *Respected.*

The phone rang on the desk and Karen picked up. "Yes Connie."

She listened for a few seconds then glanced down at her watch. I glanced down at my own. 9.45am.

"That's cutting it fine," she muttered. "Thanks for that Connie. I'll be out of the office for the next couple of hours but I'll be back for the meeting at midday."

She hung up and looked at me. "If we're there by 11am, he can spare us half an hour."

"You're good," I commented.

"Don't be intimidated by my prowess. Inside, I'm as nervous as hell. Simon Parker has some serious connections."

I stood up and said, "Then let's do it before you change your mind."

The law office of Cummings and Fraser was located in a nondescript glass high-rise building among a series of other nondescript high-rises in Broadbeach. One thing that struck me was it was in walking distance from Alto's.

The parking garage was gated and the gate wouldn't open until a polite security guard in a blue blazer strolled over and asked our names and who we'd come to see. He spoke into his walkie-talkie for a moment and waited for a reply while he kept a close eye on us. A few words more and he let us in.

We left Karen's car in the garage and followed the guard's directions to the lifts that led to the foyer. As we clip clopped behind him, I noticed a sapphire blue BMW parked in a designated parking area with a sign on the wall above it saying SIMON PARKER. Another guard in a blazer smiled at us in the foyer as we changed to another lift that led to the floors above and a third guard just happened to be in the lift with us. I glanced at his name badge. Carl. Like the guards in the garage and the foyer, Carl had the corded neck of a man who spends a lot of his time honing confrontational skills. Corded necks are a dead giveaway.

The painful strains of sitar music blending with cascading waterfalls filled the elevator. This mingling of sounds I find as soothing as fingernails on a blackboard. It was a long way up to the fourth floor.

The outer office was a busy place. Phones were ringing and no doubt a computerised billing device was attached to the phones clicking away every ten minutes and charging for each sixth of an hour. Karen didn't bat an eye.

In the corridor, men in grey Armani suits hurried in both directions, some carrying files, others legal pads, most with coffee in their hands, their bodies storing enough caffeine and adrenaline to keep them going through the day. No rolled-up shirt sleeves or loosened ties here.

Our arrival prompted a range of reactions. Some were openly curious at who warranted a bevy of security guards at this time of the morning. Others dropped their eyes not wanting to show any interest in case they were summoned, thus increasing their already heavy workload. It was only 10.45 in the morning and everyone looked tense. I guess tension is a way of life when it comes to giving animals the best possible defence they're entitled to. Especially at $1000 an hour.

A fashionably thin woman on reception, sporting fashionable glasses and a headset with a microphone, lifted a finger to indicate we should give her a second before talking. While she talked, her eyes travelled up and down Karen.

Seconds later, she asked, "May I help you?"

"We're here to see Simon Parker," Karen said in a cool, no nonsense voice. "He's expecting us. Can you let him know I have ex-police detective Jack Curtis with me as well, please? He is investigating the disappearance of Elizabeth Delaney."

The receptionist hit a button and whispered, then asked us to take a seat, which we did.

There were no House and Garden magazines to flick through while we waited. Just a glossy brochure on the law firm and its partners. Karen sat ramrod straight, head held high with just her eyes flicking from lawyer to lawyer as they scuttled past.

On page three I found the bio and photo on Simon Parker. Fortyish, average height, dark hair cut a little long but perfectly stylish and eyes the colour of sapphires. He *was* movie star handsome but mostly it was those intense eyes that had a slight upward slant that would have attracted the women. The overall appearance was immaculate and his bearing was commanding. From my little experience with the fairer sex, the combination of his good looks, charisma and those eyes would be almost irresistible. I had an idea that when he spoke, he would have the cultured voice of an academic who thought us lesser mortals should just get out of his way.

While I waited, I read, while Karen glanced over my shoulder from time to time.

Parker was a local boy through and through. He attended a local high school and left to travel to Sydney to get his BA at the University before getting his law degree. He was a *'nationally and highly regarded family law practitioner'* and before my eyes blurred with boredom, I read that he chaired this, authored that, and served on this board while receiving awards for excellence in his chosen field.

Before I threw up on the carpet, a tall woman in a tight skirt sauntered over to us.

"This way please."

A Persian carpet made from enough wool to gnarl the fingers of dozens of kids in an Indian sweatshop and long enough to go end to end at Coolangatta airport paved the corridor. Egyptian looking vases filled dimly-lit alcoves while wishy-washy Monet and Renoir prints dotted the walls with halogen-spot lighting specifically chosen for their calming effect. They'd certainly be needed once Parker's clients saw their bills. I've never had much time for art. Pictures like these have always seemed far too expensive for my humble means. Besides that, I prefer the prints of dogs and cats playing pool, but there you go.

God would live here if he could afford it. The carpet was thick and luxurious as we waded through it to the conference table where twenty chairs waited patiently for someone to sit down. Two of the four walls were made of glass overlooking rolling waves and swaying palm trees and not too far away, I could see the roofline of Alto's. Another wall had leather bound books from floor to ceiling. On the last wall sat an original oil painting, vibrant and hideous in overly bright and nauseous colours. It was of the 'trip and spill' school. It looked like someone had tripped while carrying cans of oil paint and fallen over and over again, each time splashing the contents all over the canvas.

The surface of the table was a dark and exotic looking slab of timber that had spent centuries surviving on the floor of some primeval forest only to be harvested to be made into this table. In the middle of the table was one of those speakerphones with countless buttons.

We sat in silence for fifteen minutes while Karen kept glancing at her watch before the tall woman returned.

"Ms Sawyer. You have a phone call."

Karen looked up, a frown on her face. She looked at me and held a finger to her lips, telling me to be quiet, as she reached over and pushed a flashing button on the speakerphone.

"Sawyer," she said.

A male voice said, "Karen?"

Another frown. "Yes?"

"What are you doing at Cummings and Fraser's office, Karen?"

"I'm here to talk to Simon Parker regarding a case a client of mine is working."

"And what case would that be?"

"The disappearance of Elizabeth Delaney."

"Which our office is not handling. Am I right?"

"I'm just following up on a lead."

"No, Karen, you are not following up on a lead. You are bothering a prominent lawyer who is friends with at least two local judges that I know of. One of those judges just called to inform me that one of my partners is harassing a practicing attorney."

Karen gave me a *'see what I have to deal with'* look but she said nothing.

"Do you understand what I'm saying, Karen?"

"Yes sir. We're leaving now."

"Please come into my office after the midday meeting is completed to discuss this."

My bad angel was yelling *'Up yours'* but I managed to keep quiet.

"Yes, sir," Karen said apologetically.

As Karen disconnected the call, the tall woman opened the conference room door, ready to escort us out. We followed her back down the Persian carpet silently where she deposited us at the elevator before turning to leave.

"I'm sorry about that Karen," I said contritely.

She nodded stiffly but said nothing.

The elevator doors opened and Carl stood back allowing us to enter.

In the garage, as we walked to Karen's car, I noticed the sapphire blue BMW was no longer in its space.

❧ 26 ☙

It was the second time in two days I'd driven into the car park of Alto's.

Karen had dropped me back at the office and I promised to keep her informed on everything. I'd opted for an early lunch and headed straight back to Alto's. If I was right, Simon Parker was having an early lunch too after scampering away from us at his office.

I pulled into the parking area and saw his BMW parked in the middle of an almost empty lot. He'd chosen to park well away from the other lesser beings in case one of us put a scratch on his $200,000 car.

I checked the entrance. No sign of him. I parked my car next to his, hugging his right side so there were mere inches separating my passenger side from his driver's side. There was no way he could squeeze through and reach his door, forget opening it. If he chose to get in through his passenger side, he'd have to climb over the console, arse in the air, to reach the driver's seat. Something told me he wasn't the type.

Then I waited. I'm good at waiting. It doesn't bother me. It wasn't true surveillance because he wasn't going anywhere in a hurry. I eased my seat back all the way and pulled out my notepad, running through my notes and updating them.

It didn't take long.

At 1.00pm, Parker walked out of the restaurant, talking on his phone. As he drew closer, he fished his remote out of his pocket and grabbed the key fob, still talking. I heard the little beep-beep noise of the door unlocking and I waited some more.

When he stopped short, I knew he's realised the parking situation.

I heard a muffled, "What the fuck?"

I lifted my own phone to my ear and pretended to talk to someone. With my other hand, I took a firm hold of the door handle.

"Hey!" he yelled. "Hey, you!" No whispery voice here. But then again, I wasn't thin, blonde and adolescent.

I ignored him and kept the phone to my ear, which really got him angry. He came around to my side of the car and using what I assume was his wedding ring, he tapped on the window.

"Hey! You couldn't find another parking space?"

I turned towards him and gestured with the phone to indicate *I'm kinda busy right now*. His face reddened some more and he knocked louder. I gripped the door handle tighter.

He leaned in closer. "Listen, assho..."

I opened my door fast, smacking him in the face. He fell backwards, landing hard on his butt and his phone flew out of his hand then crashed to the asphalt. I couldn't tell if it was broken but the fall couldn't have done it any good.

Before he had time to recover, I said, "I've been waiting for you, Simon."

He put his hand to his face as if checking for blood.

"No blood," I said. "Yet."

My bad angel yelled *Woo hoo bad boy*.

"Are you threatening me?" he asked incredulously.

The whispery voice had returned.

"Could be." I put my hand out and said, "Here, let me help you up."

He stared at my hand as if I was holding a turd in it. I gave him one of my Mel Gibson *crazy eye* looks and he scuttled back a bit.

Still grinning, I said, "I'm here to save your career, Simon."

"Who the fuck are you?"

"Jack Curtis."

A look of understanding flicked across his face. This was a man who was used to being in control, to make the rules, to making his problems go away with phone calls to well-placed sources. He is not accustomed to out-of-control conflicts, and if I played it right, I could take advantage of that.

"I'm calling the police," he muttered.

"No need," I said, spreading my arms. "I work with the police. What can I do for you?"

"You're a police officer?"

"Yep," I lied.

His face turned red again. "I'll have your badge!"

"For bad parking?"

"For assault!"

"The car door?" I smiled and shook my head. "Simon. That was an accident. I'm sorry. But, sure, let's call the cops. You can see about having my badge for opening a car door when you were standing way too close. And I," I point to myself, "can see if we can firstly have you disbarred and secondly, have you arrested."

He was still on the ground as I hovered over him, not really giving him room to rise without my help. It's a common power play and I was enjoying the feeling. I reached out my hand again and this time, he took my hand and pulled himself up.

He walked over to the phone and picked it up and I could see the cracked screen from where I was standing.

He glared at me. "You'll pay for this damage."

I smiled back at him again. "Nah."

He glanced at his car but mine was still blocking the driver's door and I can tell he was calculating the pros and cons of crawling across the passenger seat and driving away.

"You tell me what I need to know," I said, "and we keep this between us."

"And if I don't?"

I shrug. "Then I destroy you."

He snickered. "You think you can do that?"

"Not sure, but hey, I won't rest until I give it a good shot. I have nothing to lose, Simon. I don't care if you," I make quote marks with my fingers, "'have my badge'. I'm single and I have no social standing. Which means, I have nothing to lose."

I took a step closer.

"You, on the other hand, have a family, a reputation and what the papers like to call," again with the quote marks, "'*standing in the community*.'"

"You can't threaten me!"

I smiled wider. "I just did."

He huffed and puffed for a few seconds until I asked, "Where's Elizabeth Delaney? Is she dead?"

His eyes roamed my face. "I don't know any Elizabeth Delaney."

"Sure you do," I smiled. "She used to be Christine Buchanan. Pretty, blonde. Except now she's a brunette. Oh, and she has this scar running down the side of her cheek." I drew a finger down the side of my face where I knew the scar began and ended. "But you know all about the scar, right Simon?"

His expression moved through surprise, confusion and settled on alarm.

He hesitated before answering, "I don't like what that statement implies."

I ignored his statement. "After seeing her at Alto's..."

His eyes opened wide and his mouth opened, ready to talk. I put my hand up and said, "I know, okay. I know. Let's just leave it at that." I started again. "After seeing her at Alto's, she disappears. My question is, did she disappear of her own accord or did someone, i.e. you," I actually said that, *i.e. you*, "take her." I hesitated before adding, "and did you have her killed?"

His eyes roamed my face and I could see his mind working hard.

"And while we're having this little chat, let me ask you another question, where is the boy?"

He inhaled sharply but before he could say anything, I jumped in.

I grinned. "See? I know a lot more than you think I know."

His face twisted into a snarl but he said nothing.

"You'd want to protect your life and keep *that* nasty secret from your wife. No matter how good a lawyer you think you are, your wife is going to win custody of your kids and keep the house and a good chunk of the money."

"I haven't seen or touched Christine since that night!" he snarled.

Deep inside, I could believe that. Generals don't go into battle. They send their pawns in to do their dirty work. And pawns are expendable.

"Jason Brady," I said. "Was he one of your pawns?"

Parker's laugh reminded me of Frank's. It was somewhere between a growl and a bark.

"Are you that naïve?" he snarled. "Pawns who sleep with snakes get bitten. Same old story."

His statement took me by surprise. What was he taking about? Was he saying Elizabeth was sleeping with Jason? The last I heard, he had been seeing Hayley.

A man in a white shirt and maroon waistcoat I assumed was the manager of Alto's stepped out of the restaurant and looked over towards us.

"Is everything all right out here gentlemen?"

Parker gritted his teeth and forced a smile.

"This gentleman was just moving his car, Raif." To me, "weren't you?" Back to Raif, "No cause for concern."

Raif hesitated then nodded and stepped back inside the restaurant.

Hate radiated off Parker.

"This conversation is over!" he hissed. "Now get out of my way and move your damn car."

I smiled and winked. "Don't say I didn't warn you."

I made a show of looking for the keys while sitting in my car and starting the engine.

Seconds later, as I turned onto Marine Parade. I glanced in my rear-view mirror and he was still standing in the same spot watching me.

27

If you cast your net just a little further from the fast food places, surf shops and trashy souvenir shops of Surfers Paradise, you have about 60% of the city's real estate tax revenue in the form of multimillion-dollar homes with swimming pools and the occasional tennis court. Sovereign Island. Aptly named. The absolute prime real estate location on the Gold Coast, just close enough to the Strip and Marina Mirage but far enough away from the riff raff.

The assessment of personal real estate can be classified according to a few yardsticks. The size and location of the property is always given first priority. Then, the longer the driveways, the more points scored. Beyond that, more factors are reflecting pools, topiary and excessive outdoor lighting.

Real estate material refers to this area as a 'sparkling jewel in a parklike setting' and the views are always described as 'breathtaking', 'stunning', or 'spectacular'. Words like 'serenity' and 'tranquillity' abound. Every noun has an adjective attached to give it the proper tone and substance. The 'lush, well-manicured' lots are large and the 'elegant, spacious' homes are set well away from the roads and 'dotted' with palms amid tropical gardens. Lots of 'dotteds' and 'amids'.

It has always been my observation that the rich like to separate themselves into the haves and the have-mores. This part of town was classed as very exclusive, favoured by the well-to-do, overlooking water and populated by what is commonly called 'new money'. They have an insular approach to living where they believe the chaos of other parts of town could not touch them. Pre-dominantly, they were correct because as far as crime went, nothing much happened here. The worst offences were teenage kids having parties while their parents were away, producing a string of drink-driving charges.

As I looked at the smouldering ruins of the mansion, the main thought in my head was *someone will have to pay big for this.*

The house would have been something you'd read about in a *'Rich and Famous'* magazine. A Mediterranean mansion you'd see nestled on the side of a cliff on some Greek Island complete with rose gardens, manicured lawn and swaying palm trees.

After ducking under the crime scene tape, I stood in what had once been a courtyard beside a winding path that snaked around a Japanese garden to the right. To my left was a koi pond. Well, former koi pond. The pond was now sodden with ashes and the koi were dead, floating on top. The main section that didn't burn was a mess, drenched with water and the acrid stench of smoke.

The Fire Chief greeted me with his hardhat under one arm. He rubbed his hand down his white paper overalls before sticking it out to shake mine. He was maybe fifty with hair that had once been red and wavy but was now orange. His face and hands were smudged with soot and I knew he'd been working inside only minutes before my arrival.

"Good morning," he said. "I'm Terry Bryson. I assume you're Detective Curtis?"

"Good morning, Chief," I said as I held my own hand out to shake. "Just Mister Curtis. I'm private now, just consulting with the police on this case."

I looked around and said, "Bit of a mess."

He nodded. "You could say that."

There was no need to explain why I was here at the crime scene. Sam would have already informed him.

"What have you got for me?"

He took a small notebook and glasses from inside his overalls and placed the glasses on the end of his nose as he flicked through the pages. From that small gesture I knew he was someone who would be reliable in court when he had to relay the information.

"Well, as you know, we found a body in the debris. It was an adult male and from experience I'd say we have a man drinking and smoking in bed. He passes out, spills the booze, drops the cigarette and cooks himself."

He looked down at the water that had formed puddles around our feet and even to my untrained eye it showed traces of iridescence.

Bryson handed me a pair of white paper coveralls that slip over your feet like kid's pyjamas, a pair of yellow gloves and a hard hat. I knew once I was in the overalls, I'd end up looking like a bit of long-grain rice.

"You'll have to put these on before you come inside. It's not safe to examine too much the building until we check it out thoroughly but I can show you the ground floor, and some of the top floor," he said.

I pulled some Ziploc bags I'd thought to bring with me out of my back pants pocket, ready to put them into the overalls. If I needed to collect some samples, I'd be prepared. You never know.

I pulled the overalls on and shoved the bags into a side pocket.

We stepped over the debris carefully and stood at the entrance to what would probably have been the formal entry flanked by two large wings set at about a thirty-degree angle towards the back of the house just as a forensic photographer was coming out. His pallor told me everything I needed to know. He shakily lit a cigarette and drew in deeply with shaking hands and exhaled slowly as he watched us walk towards him.

"Don't go in if you've eaten lunch," he stated.

I knew he was referring to the lingering smell of burnt flesh. Murder scenes are bad but for overall vomit-inducing horror, it's hard to beat the burnt remains of a body. The smell stays in your nostrils, in your hair, and on your clothes for days. As horrific as seeing features twisted in fear and bodies mutilated by fellow human beings is, they fade into insignificance when the sickly smell of burnt flesh hits your senses. After twelve years on the job, there were few things that shocked me more.

Standing there I could see the central and western section of the house were still pretty much intact, smoke damaged and water damaged, but otherwise structurally sound. The eastern wing to the right was a different story altogether.

The spacious central structure had a huge winding staircase straight out of the movies that would have led to the bedrooms and a walkway on either side that I assumed led right out to a back deck.

You didn't have to be a rocket scientist to figure out the fire started in the eastern wing. Generally, the part of the house that has the most damage is the part of the house where the fire started, that is, where the fire burned the longest.

The easiest way to the outside of the house would have been to walk through the central section and I found myself glancing out towards the back boundary. Further on, I glimpsed the ocean glistening in the afternoon sun.

The big glass bifold doors had been blown out with the intensity of the blaze but they had once overlooked miles and miles of sky, horizon and blue ocean. Considering the size of the property, you're talking a million plus just for the view alone. Below the deck was a sloping rectangle of green lawn, and in the green there was another rectangle of blue, which was the swimming pool. Down to the left was a tennis court hidden by a bank of melaleucas. The view was magnificent.

He nodded towards the sooty glass doors. "You think you've got it all solved except what about that? That soot can only mean that the residue on the inside of the glass came from some kind of hydrocarbon fuel inside the house. Also, the glass was cracked into small, irregular patterns, which means it was fairly near the origin of the fire and that the fire built up fast and hot."

You can't argue with evidence but I didn't want to get too far ahead of myself.

"Could there be any other explanation for the oily soot?" I asked. I could see myself being cross-examined by the plaintiff's lawyer trying to make it seem like I was prejudiced from the beginning. I could hear the lawyer now: *"You were focused on the possibility of murder from the start, weren't you?"* Which is why it becomes valuable for an off-the-record opinion from someone like Terry Bryson with over twenty years' experience.

"I suppose," he said. "If the wood inside the room didn't burn completely, it might leave that kind of residue or there could be any number of petroleum-based products in the house quite innocently."

See? There you go.

I turned and walked back towards the east wing. There was a modern brick fireplace, which I couldn't imagine ever having been used in this climate, and the remains of a door that led to a kitchen, which would have run the length of the rear wall. The intensity of the blaze in this room was such that it was no longer possible to determine the state of the furnishings or decorations: everything was charred beyond recognition with plaster stripped from the walls. The ceiling had collapsed; bringing with it the contents of the room above, and daylight was visible through a hole in the roof.

"How did you see anything in this mess?" I muttered.

"You're looking at debris that has fallen from the ceiling and the upstairs room. The debris was moved sufficiently for me to carry out an initial examination, but the whole area was saturated with water and fouled by fire residues. What we *did* find was a body in the room you're looking at. Since the body was still on a bed, and I assumed this would have been the lounge room, I'd say it fell from the room above us."

He pointed at some shards of glass around the debris. "That's why I thought he'd been drinking in bed. There's no window over here but there was glass. Looked like a broken bottle to me."

We stood amongst the debris of the fatal room smelling the unmistakeable smell of burned flesh before I finally said, "Okay chief. Let it talk to us."

That's why they say, *'tongues of flame'*. The fire will tell you everything you need to know just by the colour of the flame, colour of smoke and the sound it makes with different substances.

"Not much to tell from down here." He pointed to the bed with the twisted, congealed bedsprings. "Like I told the police yesterday. It takes a 2,000-degree Fahrenheit fire to do that." He looked up at the ceiling. "Then there's the hole in the roof above where the bed was situated in the bedroom. That's known as the chimney effect. The fire ignites at the point of origin, that would be the bed, and the superheated gases rise and form a fireball. The fireball hits the ceiling and whoosh."

I looked up at the hole in the floor above. The bed had been the only thing to fall down through the floor.

"You are what you eat and the same goes for a fire. You can determine the severity of it, its origin, its direction and the rate that it spread by the amount of fuel in the building. For a fire to spread, it has to have material that is conductive. Paper for example is highly conductive because it's made up of about 20% oxygen. Some materials give off more heat than others. Wood gives off about 8,000 thermal units, coal is higher and flammable liquids, such as methylated spirits and kerosene are somewhere between 16,000 and 21,000 thermal units."

"Is it safe to go upstairs?" I asked.

He nodded. "Must be. The insurance assessor was up there this morning."

"Okay. Let's go."

We made our way back to the entrance and walked up the stairs gingerly. Surprisingly, they weren't too bad.

In the bedroom, I looked down and saw where the assessor had dug through the ashes around the floor where the bed would have been. I kept looking, trying to keep an open mind with no preconceptions.

The first thing I noticed was that the fire had burned a whole lot of stuff in this room judging by the amount of ash on the floor.

Terry Bryson must have read my mind.

"This much ash can only mean that it was a hot fire simply because the fire had enough time to consume a lot of stuff – *fast*. Don't forget we were here within ten minutes of the first call."

He looked down at his feet. "This fire had to be really *moving*. See this?" He toed a mound of ash. "This ash has a ripple effect. What happens is the hot fire burns quickly and moves fast, so it leaves sharp lines of demarcation between what it burns and what it doesn't. The hotter the fire, the faster it burns, the bigger the ripple. Are you keeping up with me?"

"So far."

"This is one big ripple." He looked up at the ceiling. "See that hole in the roof? That's what's known as a boiling liquid evaporation explosion. Also known as a chimney effect. The fire ignites at the point of origin, and the superheated gases rise and form a fireball. The fireball hits the ceiling and boom."

My eyes swept around the room. Pale marks, like reverse silhouettes, on the walls meant that furniture had shielded the wall from the initial flashover. Heavy char was on the rafters around the hole in the ceiling, which you'd expect because the fire burned the longest above the bed.

What I didn't expect to see was that there were several areas of the rafters that showed heavy char. One over by the opposite wall, one by the walk-in wardrobe and another by the door that led to the bathroom. Three places where the fire burned longest?

I pointed to the ceiling.

"Is that normal? Would you expect to see more than one point of origin?"

Terry Bryson thought for a few moments. "Not normally. There'd be a lot of char on the ceiling if there was something that burned well in those areas. But for an accidental fire, there should only be one point of origin."

"That's what I would have thought."

He was nodding his head. "What you should look for is V patterns."

"What do they mean?"

"Fire burns up. Right?"

I nodded.

"It ignites at the base of the V and the flames shoot upwards where the oxygen is. So in reality, the bottom of the V points to where the fire started. Because there is no surface left for the fire to mark, you look for a circular pattern on the ceiling above the point of origin."

Which there certainly was. Above the bed there wasn't a circular burn pattern, there's a bloody *hole* burned through the roof. What we had was ankle deep ash on the floor, deep char on *several* places on the rafters and a hole in the roof.

I walked over to the walk-in-wardrobe, which was slightly smaller than Tasmania. Again, ankle deep ash but then again, you'd expect to see a lot because there's a lot of stuff in wardrobes that fires just love to eat. And you'd expect to have lots of ash because you're going to have 'fall-down'.

From over my shoulder, Terry Bryson said, "That's pretty normal. A fire burns upwards and finds fuel like clothing, boxes and shelving. That's why sometimes you go into a fire and the floor hasn't burnt. A lot of times there's enough fall-down to smother the fire on the floor. See, fire goes up and then *across*. The fire isn't even burning across the floor; it's up on the ceiling. It burns hotter and hotter until the fire up top generates so much heat that the *heat*, not the flames, ignites the material on the floor and *then* the floor goes up."

"Yeah, but it all has to start somewhere."

"Which is the base of the V."

I've been called dogged and unrelenting among a few other choice names that I won't mention right now. Cynical is another name I've been called. That's why I was looking in the wardrobe because it seems that's a pretty good place to start a fire with all that fuel where the fall-down effect is not immediately visible because it's been obscured by the ash.

I squatted down on my haunches and began to dig away the ash from the back wall of the wardrobe. And there it was: a tall narrow V marking on the wall.

"What've you got there?" Terry asked, leaning over my shoulder.

"Another V pattern." I was feeling the first stirrings of instinct and excitement.

"Are you sure?" he asked, a frown creasing his forehead.

"Look for yourself."

I stood up and let Bryson get a closer look.

"Now that's really odd," he mumbled as the frown deepened. "A wide V tells you that the fire spread normally, just the usual grazing on the usual feed. A narrow V is the fire telling you something else." He looked up at me. "This fire was *hot*. And fast." He looked back down again. "Something else, too."

He pointed to the bottom of the V.

"See the apex doesn't come to a point? It looks like a V with the point cut off, doesn't it?"

I squatted down again. He was right.

"Why would it do that?" I asked.

"It means that maybe the fire had a little help to get it started." He blinked a few times. "I didn't see that the first time around."

My stomach did a little somersault. Bingo.

"Go on," I said.

"Well, in an accidental fire, the V will be pointed. But if the fire had a boost, say someone poured a little accelerant on the floor, then the apex of the V is going to be as wide as the pool of the accelerant. See here? You don't so much have a point of origin; you have a *pool* of origin, which ignites all at the same time."

So now, I had two points of origin. Which is one too many. If there's anything I know about an accidental fire, is that you have *one* not *two* points of origin.

I pushed aside some more of the ash and guess what? A hole in the floor as wide as the base of the V stared back at me.

"A fire burns up, you said?" I asked Bryson.

"You've got it. That's where the oxygen is." He was looking at the hole. "Unless it has a reason to burn down."

What I was seeing in my head was something being poured on the floor to get the fire going. An accelerant. It seeps down into the flooring and the fire follows it down because now it has a reason. An accelerant is better than oxygen. The fire eats up the accelerant and *then* burns up.

"You've got yourself a problem here," Bryson said. "Most people think it's easy to burn a house down but they'd be wrong these days. A fire needs a lot of oxygen and a lot of fuel to sustain it. Not just that, it needs time before the fire trucks roll in. In the old days it was different. You had homes a long way from the fire stations and nobody had fire alarms. But now, everybody has smoke alarms. It's the law. And don't forget, the fire station is only ten minutes away. If you want to burn the house down, or burn a wing of the house, it's a race against the clock. If you start a fire in just one place, you're going to lose the race. Physics is against you and it never lies. So you help it along. Firstly, you get some fossil fuel and secondly, you start more than one fire. You need several accelerated fires to get enough heat going so that the flames don't necessarily have to spread the fire. The heat will reach the ignition point of the materials and then WHOOSH. You have flashover and the fire is out of control."

No lawyer in the world can dispute the laws of nature. You throw a ball into the air, it comes down. Fire ignites and it burns *up* unless it has a physical reason to burn down.

I knelt there in my paper overalls with the smell of ash penetrating my sinuses going over it all in my mind. From the pocket of the overalls, I took out the Ziploc bags and scraped a little of the ash into one of them. I repeated the process a few times, taking a small chunk of wood from around the hole and putting it in to another bag. Then I went to a different part of the wardrobe and repeated the process. This was for comparison and hopefully it didn't contain accelerants. Otherwise, if all the samples contained accelerants, the argument would be that they're inherent in the wood itself. Pine flooring, for example, can have a lot of turpentine in it. I was hoping for a clean sample to show the difference.

While I was collecting the samples and writing on the white strip on each bag what sample it contained, Terry Bryson was moving ash around. By the time I looked up, he'd moved ash from the wardrobe in the direction of the bed.

He harrumphed. "Go figure."

He was looking down at a pour pattern that started in the wardrobe and lead towards where the bed had been.

I stood up. "Let me get this straight," I said looking down at the floor. "Someone poured accelerant in the wardrobe because the flooring is burned clear through and then they poured a trail of accelerant over to the bed?"

I was standing in the wardrobe with a hole in the floor, there was a hole where the bed had been and a hole in the roof.

"You've got it," Terry said, a look of confusion on his.

"Jesus Christ!" I whispered. "Whoever poured the accelerant poured it under the bed then doused him with it and lit a match."

Bryson nodded. "Looks like it. Does a professional arsonist do that?"

"Not if it's a strictly business fire, he doesn't. You douse a person in bed and it's personal. It comes from rage."

The best thing would be if I could walk a jury through the room because photographs aren't going to show it for what it really is. The place was too dark and they would end up being dark too. But the jury being here wasn't going to happen. For one, getting a court order to halt the reconstruction would be almost impossible and two, judges rarely allow a site visit especially when there's been a fatality. It would prove to be too emotional for a jury to see.

All I could hope to do was take samples from around the pour pattern and around the bed. For each potential 'dirty' sample I'd have a 'clean' sample for comparison. If there were accelerants present, it would shoot the 'smoking-in-bed' theory out the window. Because now it wasn't accidental: it was arson. And murder.

I had the icing but no cake to put it on.

Yet.

28

The afternoon was bright and sunny and after opening my window to clear the smell of ash out from my nose, the air smelled of salt and the sea. The sun was sitting low in the sky, pulling the shadows longer and longer, as the afternoon heat shimmered off the roads and gave everything an illusion of a silver lining. White gulls floated and circled overhead and girls in minuscule bikinis were still soaking up the remains of the sun with no regard for the ads on television about slip, slop and slapping. Surfers Paradise is Australia's answer to 77 Sunset Strip.

Right now, the samples were everything. If they tested positive for accelerants, it would blow the theory about 'drinking and smoking in bed' right out of the water. It would also mean that it wasn't an accidental fire of accidental death. It was arson. And murder.

What I didn't have was time.

I snaked up and down the streets around the station looking for a park. You need a degree in civil engineering to understand when and where it's legal to park in Surfers Paradise and the luck of a Lotto winner to find one. On my fifth go-around, a Mini pulled out half a block up. I shot forward and with much shifting and swearing, wedged my Mazda into the vacated space.

Hurrying along the sidewalk, I could see the grey hulk of the station looming in the distance. Somehow, the brooding structure looked wrong against the cheery blue sky. I was rounding the corner, head down, legs pumping, when a bicycle blasted into my side.

I went flying. I landed on my bum first, but quickly ten-pinned onto my chin, the wind knocked out of me somewhere into tomorrow. For a moment I could only focus on taking in oxygen.

Wobbling wildly, the bike rider continued for a few seconds, then stopped and turned to face me five metres away.

"Whoo hoo!" Laughing, the kid pointed a finger at me. "You looked just like my grandpa when you fell."

"You look like you should have left the training wheels on," I muttered.

The kid was tall, maybe up to my chin, and thin. Scarecrow-thin. I guessed his weight at about forty kilos soaking wet, his age at approximately twelve or thirteen. Maybe fourteen at a push.

I lurched to my feet and the kid moved closer. He had dark eyes and dark hair poking out from under a cap too large for him and if he had a bit more weight on him, he'd would have been considered good looking.

"Man, that was some fall," he grinned. "Probably Alzheimer's. Just like my grandpa used to have."

"Maybe your grandpa should have taught you some manners," I muttered as I dusted the seat of my pants with my hands.

I ran my hands through my hair before checking the samples were still secure in my pocket. Relieved they were still safe, I started to walk towards the station and the kid pedalled along beside me.

"I saw you the other night at the service station," he said.

I hesitated but kept walking. The only time in the last couple of days I'd been at a service station was when I'd cornered Jason with the baseball bat.

"Great. Now run along. I'm out of lollipops."

"You were watching someone."

Slowing down, I glanced at the kid. His expression was cocky but it held no malice.

"Maybe a bit more than watching."

I stopped and turned.

"What do you want?"

He grinned broadly. "You're close."

"Pardon?"

"Very close."

"To what?"

"Come on, old man," he chuckled.

"What's your name?" I asked.

"Benny."

"Benny what?"

"Benny never-you-mind."

I began walking again and I was sure Benny would peel off and ride away when I neared the station. He didn't. We were half a block away when a thought struck me.

I stopped. Benny hesitated, then dropped one sneaker to the sidewalk to brace himself.

"Hey shrimp."

"Yeah, grandpa?"

"Do you know a guy called Cruz?"

"Everyone knows Cruz."

"Why is that?"

"Cruz is into fucking everything. You need to watch your back with him."

"Does your grandpa approve of your foul language?"

A flicker of embarrassment crossed his face.

"Why aren't you in school?" I asked.

"I've got chicken pox," he lied.

His face was angled away from mine. "You've got a knack for making people mad," he mumbled.

Curious.

"What people?" I asked.

He shrugged a bony shoulder. "I'm just sayin'."

"Saying what? You need to make yourself clear here."

We were only metres away from the entrance to the station, near the parking area for police officers, when something suddenly jumped into my mind. When Frank was telling me the story, he told me Elizabeth had walked in on her john with a young boy. With everything that had happened, I'd forgotten about the boy. What had happened to him?

Suddenly I could barely breath.

Thoughts leapfrogged in my brain, coming from everywhere at once, but beginning with the Tamborine Mountain case over a year ago. Was it just the fact that Elizabeth walked in on the boy with Simon Parker that made him furious or was there more to it than that? Was this all connected to a paedophile ring?

I sucked in a ragged breath. "You know something, don't you, kid?"

He looked at me from under the ridiculously large bill of his cap.

"I know a lot more than you do," he smirked.

I hesitated. "Do you feel like some KFC?"

The bill tilted upwards. "You buying?"

"If you talk to me about Cruz, I am."

He grinned. "Fire up your hearing aids. But if you say you got anything from me, I'll say you're a liar and a paedophile."

Just then, the sound of an engine caused us to glance over towards the exit of the police parking area. Sam was at the wheel.

"Where the hell have you been?" she demanded, glancing momentarily at Benny. "I've tried calling and sending you messages and what, you're too busy to reply?"

Beside me, Benny's fingers tightened on the handlebar grips and one sneaker lifted to the pedal of his bike.

Knowing the kid was about to bolt, I tried a little humour.

"Well, you can cancel the choppers and the dogs." I grinned, spreading my arms wide. "Here I am."

"Very funny Jack. But this isn't amateur hour."

Amateur? That did it. My smile crumbled.

"Are you accusing me of being unprofessional, Sam?"

"Sloppy. Inconsiderate. Irresponsible. Shall I continue?" She glanced at Benny again. "And who's the kid?"

With that Benny turned and fired back up the block, skinny legs pumping like mad. At the corner, he cut a left and disappeared from view.

"Now *that* was unprofessional." I met her glare with one of my own. "I've been at the scene of the fire, remember? And that kid had some information he was about to impart."

In the icy silence, I noticed the reflection in her rear passenger window. It showed a ruffled man with a mouth hooked down at the corners, angry eyes the colour of day-old coffee and a grazed chin that had donated some skin to the pavement a block back. A few tentative greys were sending out feelers from behind the ears.

Sam had the grace to blush a little. Her shoulders slumped and she dropped her head.

"I'm sorry, Jack," she said shaking her head. "It's been a long day and Grayson is on the warpath. We're no closer to closing this case than we were a week ago and now we have Jason Brady's death on top of it." She looked up. "But that's no excuse. I'm sorry," she sighed. "I'm heading home for a break."

With that, she turned into the traffic and was gone.

I turned to see if Benny was hovering close by but he'd been spooked. I mouthed a silent curse and turned into the entrance of the station.

Once I was in the empty squad room, I pulled out a laminated A4 sheet from Sam's top drawer that had the extension numbers of different departments. At the same time, I pulled the phone over in front of me. I found the number I wanted and dialled. As the phone rang, I checked my watch. Five-thirty. He was probably gone. Everyone was gone.

"Come on. Come on," I whispered. "Answer the damn phone."

If you wanted to know why a train crashed or a bridge collapsed or a fire happened, Wayne Grant from Forensics could tell you, everyone said. They also said, he worked his butt off and was a great witness.

On the tenth ring, he picked up the phone and I almost yelped with joy.

"What?" he asked.

"Obviously, you haven't done the 'Phone Manners' module in your job manual yet."

There was a slight hesitation before he said, "Curtis? Is that you?" he asked with exasperation in his voice.

"Right first time. How are you?"

"How am I? How am I?" His voice got louder with the second question. "How the hell do I sound?"

"Charming."

I could hear him sigh. "This had better be good. I was just leaving and I'm already late. If I don't get home on time tonight I'll miss Jenny's band recital and my wife will never let me forget it. I promised I'd be home on time so this had better be good."

I could see him now. Whenever he got flustered, he ran his hand through his wild hair making it stand on end. The Einstein look. I pictured him squinting through grimy lenses, his prickly hair standing to attention.

"It's important, Wayne. I wouldn't ring you at this time of day if it wasn't. Heaven knows I'd like more regular hours myself."

There was silence over the line.

Eventually he said, "I thought you'd resigned."

"I'm consulting, Wayne. Just for this case."

I could hear a clock ticking in the background. "I need you to run some samples for me. Like yesterday," I added.

"Does Grayson know about this?"

"He does." I made a mental note to shoot an email to him immediately after I hung up. "You can check with Sam if you need to but it's getting late and she's already left for the day."

"What sort of samples?"

He sounded exasperated but at least he didn't say no.

I told him a quick version of the story trying to leave nothing out.

"Well, the good news is that I can do it. The bad news is it will have to wait until tomorrow. I'll need a crew of techs to help me but you'll get the result the same day."

I smiled. "Well, if that's the best you can do."

"One thing you should know." I could hear the doubt in his voice. "We use a gas chromatograph with a mass spectrometer here. I'm not sure it can be totally accurate when determining traces of accelerants."

I could feel the floor opening up under my feet.

"What's wrong with it?" I asked.

"Well, we live in a plastic society these days. A modern house is chock full of plastic products every one of which, when they burn, produce thousands of chemicals that can be confused with hydrocarbons and accelerants. We can do the test. I just won't be able to stand up in a court and swear under oath to the absolute accuracy of the result, that all."

"That's the best you can do?"

"That's it. Unless you go to something that is still experimental and then you'd have another kind of trouble in a court of law. It's just experimental."

"Okay. Do what you can. Do it until you're satisfied with the results. But do it quick."

"You get the samples to me, and I mean NOW, I'll start on them first thing in the morning."

"I'm on my way."

After shooting the email to Grayson, I delivered the samples and headed back to my car. The plan was to drive home and relieve Frank for a few hours before heading out to pay Jimmy Preston a visit in the quiet hours of the night.

                             ❧ 29 ❧

Frank opted not to leave the house for a break, preferring to sit and watch television with Hayley and eat the mountain of junk food bought on my credit card. Not that Hayley did much watching. Like any teenager, she sat monotonously scrolling through her phone while the television blared in the background. Frank looked contented with his feet up on the coffee table and I silently wondered if he intended to move in with me permanently.

It had taken me five minutes to get Jimmy's address from Bazza who was still holding a grudge against Jimmy. Anything he could do to tie Jimmy up in a big bow to hand to the police the happier he would be.

Oblivious of my presence, Jimmy's neighbourhood had shut down for the night. Houses rested in the darkness and all sound had subsided except for the occasional bark of a dog.

Jimmy's rental house was no different from the others in the street. It looked like an old meccano set. It was a structure of pipes, beams, joists, wood and bricks. Sort of like how you'd arrange things in your shopping trolley.

No car was parked in the driveway or under the carport and except for a faint light that glowed through the front room curtains that were falling off the railings, you could be forgiven for thinking Jimmy wasn't even at home.

Still I wanted to be sure. I had questions to ask but from my last encounter with him, he had a short fuse and a strong punch. I wasn't sure if he would be willing to part with information about Cruz, but I had some persuasion abilities of my own.

Because of that one light, I suspected Jimmy was at home so I decided to wait outside in my car until he turned it off. My plan was to creep around to the back door and surprise him, thus not giving him time to pick up a knife to skillet me or even a saucepan to dent my skull.

After an eon of waiting and watching bats jockeying for position on the overhead wires, my enthusiasm for surveillance had dropped and a million arguments for leaving the boredom of my car swirled around in my brain.

Occasionally, I give myself good advice. In rare instances, I take it. Whatever advice this turned out to be, confronting Jimmy was better than sitting in the darkness my car, waiting for ... anything.

Skin tingling with apprehension, I reached into the back seat and grabbed my baseball bat before opening the door and stepping out.

With the streetlights behind me, I pulled my cap down over my face and held the bat behind my back as I walked as quietly as I could, past dying shrubs and lumpy weeds, to the front door. I passed the empty carport and stepped on to the brick path on my way to the front door. I had a moment of hesitation, a heart flutter, thinking maybe sensor lights would suddenly illuminate me, bat in hand, enroute. But no lights. No flower pots. No birdbaths. No stone lions. No Venus de Milo statues.

Just in case Jimmy had heard me rustling through the weeds in the front yard, I inched my way along, back pressed firmly to the wall, until I reached the front door. Still no sound from inside the house although I could still see the faint light from deep inside the house. My guess was it was on in either the kitchen or a bedroom.

Peeking through a glass panel, Salvation Army chic furniture loomed in a room that hadn't seen a paintbrush since it was built in the 1960s. Tuffs of stuffing dotted the worn sofa and a full ashtray sat forlornly on a scarred coffee table in front of an ancient television on a wobbly-looking metal stand. Recently I'd read an article on the variety of fauna inhabiting couches. Head lice. Bedbugs. Fleas. Mites. The ratty sofa looked like it held all that and more, maybe even some vermin.

I scurried past the door and shuffled sideways through some more overgrown shrubs as I moved along a side wall toward the rear of the house. Halfway along, I reached into my back pocket with my spare hand and took out my torch.

A small frosted window at eye level appeared, grey with grime and a trillion bacteria. It would have been the bathroom and it was hiding nothing except contagious disease. Thankfully I was never going to fit through it. I turned my beam fast, lighting things up like a stroboscope. No sign of Jimmy.

A thought suddenly occurred to me. Did Jimmy own a dog? Just in case, I killed the light and inched around to the far back corner of the house on grass that was slick with night mist. Then I stood still and listened. Nothing. No Rottweiler barked. No pit bull lunged.

Around me, the house sat in darkness with the only light coming from a white streetlight a little way down the road. Everywhere, people were in bed. Every now and then, I saw a flicker of a blue television as some night owl watched a movie. That was it. I was hunting a giant in the dark.

I slid around to the rear of the house, pausing a beat to listen, then slid further around and moved along the back wall. The air felt suddenly still, like someone was watching me. It was my imagination, I know, but still I held my breath. No birds cooed and no leaves rustled.

The first window on my left looked to be the kitchen. It sat in darkness but I could see the dim light further inside the house. As I stared in, the reflection stared back at me showing a strained white face in a baseball cap. Sweat glistened on its top lip and I brushed it away with the back of my hand.

All seemed still and quiet on the inside. Hopefully Jimmy was asleep with a nightlight on, not listening and hiding behind the back door with something heavy in *his* hand.

Next to the window was a door made of solid wood with no window. Matching the age of the house, there was no locking system. Just a rounded doorknob that probably locked from the inside, maybe with a chain.

I shoved the torch back into my pocket and adjusted the grip on the bat before turning the knob slowly. Miraculously, it opened. I pushed it gently with spread fingers, praying silently it didn't creak. Old wooden doors had a nasty habit of doing that.

I was lucky. No creaking and no Jimmy.

Inside there were dark wood cabinets and an ancient stove that was cold to the touch. Everything smelt still and stale. Dirty dishes lay in the sink so I knew if Jimmy wasn't here now, he had been recently. The only occupants were startled roaches scampering away from my torchlight.

A fetid, cloying odour filled the air, sour like rotting vegetables. And faeces. I smelt faeces as well. Most of the stench came from an overflowing kitchen waste pail but my bet was most was coming from the bathroom I was yet to find.

I crept further, past an ancient Formica table and a single wooden chair, moving towards a hallway with threadbare carpeting. In front of me, I waved the bat like someone from an Anne Rice novel waving a crucifix.

The bathroom was on my left and I glanced in. The vanity top held a used bar of soap, a grimy plastic cup, a badly chipped ceramic toothbrush holder and a dead cockroach. Warm air moving through the open window fluttered the toilet paper hanging beside the commode where a slimy brown oval rimmed the bowl. Dead insects completed the assemblage.

I turned my attention to across the hallway, to a closed door that I imagined would be a small bedroom. Further on were two more rooms, presumably more bedrooms, one with the door half-open where light filtered out.

That's when I noticed another smell and the hair on the back of my neck prickled and rose, my instincts on full alert.

I inched further along with my back against the hallway wall, my bat held high in front of me pointing towards the ceiling, until I reached the door. My stomach turned a bit, leaving an unpleasant taste in my mouth. I looked at the door again and took a deep breath, in through my mouth and out through my nose, silently preparing myself. Then I stepped around and held the bat in front of me.

The sallow yellow light from the overhead opaque lightshade, that was multi-tasking as a crypt for dead insects, was enough to highlight the body tucked up in a foetal position on the single bed with fair hair fanning the pillow. He was fully dressed in jeans and a Guns and Roses t-shirt and even in the dim light, I could see his eyes were wide open and staring.

I reached out to support myself with one hand on the wall and dropped the bat to cover my nose. I'd found Jimmy.

There was no need to see if he was alive. His skin was a ghostly white with tinges of green and there was dried blood everywhere. A dark circle saturated the filthy bedding beneath his body as well as the ground below the bed. Decomposition wasn't visible yet but it wasn't too far off. The first wave of blowflies had found their way in somehow and had begun to settle on his body. Some maggots glistened in the eyes, nose and mouth suggesting death had been a minimum of twenty-four hours beforehand, but looking closer at them, I guessed longer.

I reached into my back pocket and pulled out my phone, ready to call the police.

While I waited for them to arrive, I did what I do best. I snooped. I didn't know what I was looking for but I'd know it when I found it.

As my mind worked, my eyes circled clockwise as thoughts, crashing against each other, emerged in the adrenaline and shock.

I stepped over a plastic bag of weed and a pack of papers and a small cloud of flies rose in whine of protest from Jimmy's body. Resting on the floor beside the weed was a fairly new black mobile phone. I put my torch in my back pocket ready to check the contact list and recent calls of the mobile. They were going to be invaluable. I was surprised at that snap decision because I knew how wrong it was. Tampering with evidence was a criminal offence and I'd just crossed the line. Again.

I needn't have bothered. It required a password. I pulled my shirt out of my pants and wiped off my fingerprints before placing it back on the floor where I found it.

More Salvation Army chic furniture in the shape of a gouged and broken dresser sat despondently against a wall, one broken leg supported by an inverted saucepan. On the top sat a hairbrush, an opened box of bullets and a single picture frame with a picture of Jimmy and Jason, arms around each other's shoulders, and smiling widely in front of a house.

I recognised that house. It was Jason's house because sitting in the driveway was the same Hyundai I'd seen when I spoke to Pauline Brady. It was a recent photo because both looked pretty much as they had the last time I'd seen them, buffed and happy with themselves.

At last a solid connection. Jason and Jimmy knew each other. I'd seen Jimmy's picture in the news article with Cruz when they were in Sydney and I knew Jason had worked for Cruz because I'd seen the confrontation in the Starbucks carpark. And here they were, arms around each other, wearing matching green sweatshirts like they were Siamese twins.

I did a quick scan for the gun but either the killer had taken it with him or Jimmy had a safe tucked away somewhere behind a Picasso. I went with the first option.

A thought suddenly jumped into my head. Was the gun Jason waved at me in fact Jimmy's gun? Was Jason the killer? Had he come here to talk to Jimmy and ended up killing him with Jimmy's own gun? Had Jason then taken the gun with him? Was that what Cruz had been berating Jason about in the car park? Killing Jimmy? The question then was who had killed Jason? And why?

Round and round it went. Images. Speculation. Questions. Mostly questions.

I had to be careful to leave something behind for the police to find and the bullets and picture frame were the most obvious items. If the bullets were the same calibre as the bullets found in both Jason and Jimmy's bodies, they would connect Jimmy to Jason, making Jason the obvious suspect for Jimmy's murder, prior to his own death. Even Cavanaugh would be able to join those dots.

I continued my quick scan of the room. A standalone wardrobe against the far wall held very little: a worn faux leather jacket, another pair of jeans and a pair of sneakers. Either he was waiting for the rest of his clothes to arrive from somewhere or he only owned two sets of clothes: the one he was currently wearing and the other in the wardrobe.

Outside a siren screamed its arrival at the top end of the street, leaving me no more time to search. I walked towards the front door and that's when I saw the dog. He was panting and cowering in a corner, almost hidden behind the sofa so as not to draw attention to himself. Not too far from him was a small turd and a puddle.

He looked like a concoction slapped together by a blind Frankenstein. He was the size of a Labrador with a mottled, wiry coat of a terrier and the large floppy ears of a spaniel. He had a hairless tail that looked like he'd chewed it off himself.

As the sirens grew louder, the two of us eyed each other, neither of us making a move. Seconds ticked by and in the silence, his panting became more frantic. And he was shaking as if he was about to have a seizure.

He's terrified, I thought.

"Easy boy," I said in a soft voice, just in case he was working himself up to pounce.

The dog flinched at my voice but then cocked his head cautiously, one ear up, one ear down.

"I'm going to open the door, okay?"

More panting. More shaking. I had no doubt that Jimmy had badly mistreated the animal.

I took a small step towards the door and opened it slowly as two ambulances screeched to a halt outside. He let out a soft whimper.

"Easy now boy." My hands were out in front of me, ready to defend myself if he launched at me.

Doors slammed. Voices called out. Others answered. Boots stamped up the path.

I had no need to worry. As two paramedics filled the doorway, the dog let out another nervous whimper and divided his attention between them and me, his eyes as big as saucers.

"Are you the guy who called this in?" one paramedic called out.

My hands were still out, one calming the dog the other pointing towards the bedroom where Jimmy's body lay.

I nodded. "First door on the left," I said, taking slow steps towards the dog.

I knelt down slowly, jerkily, ready to bounce backwards. The dog retreated further into the corner. As I moved to pet him, he bowed his head, not to make the back of his ears or neck more accessible to stroking but to indicate that he was subservient and harmless. He was shaking enough to loosen teeth, as if I was going to hit him. Somehow he needed to know I wasn't going to hurt him.

I kept my voice low and soft as I spoke.

"What's your opinion on this dog-show thing?"

His rear end moved a little but the tail didn't quite move.

"You're a dog, after all. You must have an opinion. These are your people being exploited."

Either he was a dog of extreme caution when it came to discussing current affairs or he was just a mutt with no position on the weightiest social issues of his species.

"I would hate to think," I continued, "that you are a dropout, resigned to the status of a lumpen animal, unconcerned about being exploited, all fur and no fury."

I began moving my hand slowly forward towards him as I spoke. His eyes dropped to my hand as I moved it closer. This time, there was not as much panting.

"Aren't you outraged that purebred females are forbidden to have sex with mongrels like you, forced to submit only to purebred males? Just to make puppies destined for the degradation of showrings?"

The mutt's tail began to thump softly against the floor.

"Good dog," I whispered and moved my hand close enough for him to crane his head forward and lick my outstretched hand.

"Do you need to go outside and do some business?" I asked gently.

The dog kept his head down, huddling warily but not trembling as much under my hand, remaining in a humble posture.

I slipped one hand tentatively under his chin, forcing his head up. After briefly trying to pull away, he ceased all resistance.

When we were eye to eye, I repeated, "You want to go outside?"

The dog looked away, down and left.

I lifted his muzzle gently again, trying to keep his attention. "We keep our head up boy. Always proud, okay? Look people in the eye. You got that?"

He slipped his tongue between his half-clenched teeth and licked the fingers gripping his muzzle.

"I'll take that as a yes."

I let him go and stood up.

"Let's go outside."

He jumped up as I walked towards the open door. Two more paramedics rushed through carrying a stretcher. I almost said, "No need to hurry," but I let them go.

The dog followed me to the front lawn and crouched down, urinating for a good minute. He must have been ready to burst.

Just as he was finishing up, another car screamed to a halt and Sam and Cavanaugh jumped out pacing quickly towards me.

"Well if it isn't Doctor Death," Cavanaugh goaded.

"Nice to see you too Cavanaugh."

Half an hour later, I was behind the wheel of my car, engine running, ready to follow them to the station. The dog was in the back seat of the squad car staring out, nose pressed to the window, one ear pricked, one ear drooping, watching me. Beside him sat a large bag of dry dog food I'd found in a kitchen cupboard while looking for a bowl to fill with water.

His breath was fogging the glass, but he wasn't barking. He just stared and waited. He was just thirty kilos of patience and longing.

❧ 30 ❧

"Interview conducted by Detective Cavanaugh and Detective Samantha Neil with Jack Curtis. Surfers Paradise Police Station. 11.20pm, 16th March."

Five minutes beforehand, I watched as Cavanaugh and Sam walked towards the interview room, him bent over talking earnestly to her while she listened stony-faced. It had given me a shred of hope that whatever he was saying, she wasn't going to let him hoodwink her in believing anything without listening to what I had to say first. That's what I was hoping anyway.

Watching them as they sat on the other side of the table, eyes intent and staring at me, my heart and stomach took it in turns to do cartwheels.

I waited while Cavanaugh paused, his eyes unreadable. Sam sat beside him, glowering at me. The light of the video camera flickered on and off every second or so.

"Let's start with why you're here." Cavanaugh's iceberg demeanour was in place.

As he talked, he pulled a file closer and flipped the cover. The file only held two thin pages.

"In your own words, Mr Curtis, can you fill me in on your whereabouts for the past forty-eight hours and why you came to be at the residence of James Preston this evening."

His eyes bored into mine as I cleared my throat, feeling uncomfortable. Sam's eyes dropped to her lap and I had an unnerving feeling I was being accused of killing Jimmy myself. What Cavanaugh wanted to know I couldn't tell him because a big part of the story included me beating Jason with a baseball bat outside a petrol station and heading to *Dolly's* with Sam to talk to a prostitute, sans Cavanaugh.

Not knowing when Jimmy had been murdered, I ran through the last couple of days in my mind. At around 10am two days ago, Frank was sitting in my office telling me about Cruz and Jimmy and the accident that had happened a year ago. I had to keep this piece of information to myself because well, this is Frank we're talking about and he wasn't exactly an upstanding member of society. He also plays a major part in the next part of my story.

Then I'd gone to Hayley's house and talked to Hayley, which was another thing I couldn't tell Cavanaugh. Then there was Jason and the baseball bat episode followed by hiding Hayley in my house with Frank babysitting her while I put my insomnia to good use, and interviewed Simone Tanner at *Dolly's* with Sam. Which was why she was staring at her lap right now, praying I'd keep my mouth shut. It was only after that, the next day, I'd decided to look for Jimmy.

All in all, there was nothing I could tell Cavanaugh. But I had to tell him something and that something could be how I had come to know Jimmy lived at that address. I could tell him how I'd recognised Jimmy's face beside Cruz's in the news article from a year ago and that Bazza had given the address to me. What I couldn't tell him was *why* I'd asked Bazza for the address in the first place without telling him about Frank. Dilemma.

Instead of telling him anything, I asked, "Do I need to call my lawyer? Karen is representing me and may want to sit in on this."

I had no idea if Karen still wanted to represent me. There'd been no contact with her since the Simon Parker incident and I very much doubted that things would return to the same camaraderie we once shared.

I watched Sam's head lift at the mention of Karen's name at the same time the shadow of frustration crossed Cavanaugh's face before he answered.

"Dead bodies have a tendency to stack up when you're around, don't they Mr Curtis," Cavanaugh said, visibly trying to stay calm while the recording rolled on.

Any other time, I'd have resented the remark. Now I thought he was on the right track.

I gave him my calm face to show him that I did not in any shape or form appear concerned by his remark.

"Is that a question you need me to answer, Detective Cavanaugh?"

As my stomach did another flip, I tried to stare him down. He stared right back.

People believe maintaining eye contact is a sure sign of honesty. But like most things, too much indicates an issue. Besides that, eye contact is the first thing cops learn at the academy. Module 101.

One thing I was certain of was that Cavanaugh knew I hadn't killed Jimmy. From what I'd seen, Jimmy had been dead for a couple of days before I found him a few hours ago. If I was the one who killed Jimmy, wouldn't I just leave him there hoping no one would find him until they came to turn off the electricity? Why would I be stupid enough to go back to the house and 'discover' Jimmy's dead body and put myself in this vulnerable situation?

What I was certain of was Cavanaugh wanted me to be nervous enough to open up and tell them everything I'd discovered. On the record. And he wanted me to panic.

None of that wasn't going to happen.

Instead, I said, "Don't be stupid, Cavanaugh." I smirked at him as he grit his teeth. "I didn't kill him and you know it. Rigor has set in and was dissipating which means he's been dead for about two days. But it's always nice for the seals at the zoo to have a new ball to play with."

For a moment, no one spoke. The implication was clear. Cavanaugh was trying to implicate me but he'd been outsmarted. My stomach began to settle down now that I felt like I was on top of the situation again.

"Have forensics finished fingerprinting the house?" I asked in the silence, hoping they would remember that Grayson had included me in on the investigation as a consultant. Every chance I got, I was going to remind them.

Cavanaugh hesitated before answering. It meant I'd asked a question he didn't want to answer and it bolstered my ego a little more.

"Yes."

I was going to have to work hard for this.

"And?"

Cavanaugh was slapping a pen held between his thumb and forefinger onto the palm of his other hand as he grit his teeth some more.

"They found some prints that matched with the second set of prints found on the gun that killed Jason Brady."

I scraped my chair back and stood so suddenly, the screeching sound filling the room, that Sam and Cavanaugh both jerked backwards in their chairs.

"I'm finished here. You've had your fun. You dragged me in here to grill me like this knowing full well I had nothing to do with this?"

Sam leant forward and spoke into the recorder. "Interview concluded with Jack Curtis by Detective Samantha Neil and Detective Cavanaugh at," she glanced at the clock on the wall, "11.33pm, 16th March." The light of the video camera flickered off.

Cavanaugh inhaled angrily, about to object no doubt, but Sam held her hand up to stop him, as if gesturing to a dog to stay.

"Enough of the theatrics," she growled at him.

She turned to me, finger in the air, and pointed to the chair I'd just vacated. I sat down obediently.

"Just tell us what you know, Jack. I know you haven't been sitting on your hands for two days."

I grinned. "You show me yours. I'll show you mine." It was part of our code in the good old days for swapping information.

Recognition of the phrase registered in her eyes and she took a few breaths before continuing.

"You've heard of the name Fleming." Her voice had softened and I like to think it was because of the reference to our past.

My eyes moved from Sam to Cavanaugh and back again as I settled myself back in my seat. I was thrown by the change of names from Jimmy to Fleming but for Sam to take over, I knew there had to be something else besides Elizabeth Delaney's disappearance linking the pair. I'd heard Fleming's name mentioned in the past few days from Frank but I didn't want to tell her that just yet.

"Rings a bell," I said.

She smirked but played along with me. "David Fleming is Manuel de la Cruz's accountant. He cooks the books for Cruz but so far there's nothing we can pin on him. The Feds have been watching him for years but they've been sitting on their hands because they want to get the whole team."

She glanced briefly at Cavanaugh, still grinding his teeth beside her.

"In light of Elizabeth Delaney's disappearance," she continued, "and our mention of Cruz's possible involvement, the Federal Government has decided to bring Fleming in for questioning. Unfortunately, it seems he's gone on an unscheduled overseas trip and can't be located."

I leant back and rested both arms on the armrests, my hands knitted together over my stomach.

"What about Cruz? Have you managed to find out where he's holed up?" I asked.

They both stared at me.

My eyes went from one to the other.

"You were going to put a tag on him after he left Starbucks. Where did he go?" I asked.

Sam hesitated before glancing at Cavanaugh. "We lost him," she said.

Cavanaugh began slapping the pen again as he grit his teeth some more. He was going to need a dentist by the end of this investigation.

"We'll find him," he muttered, his voice frosty.

"Faster than you lost him?" I asked.

Sam shot me a squinty-eyed look that was meant as a warning at the same time Cavanaugh's pen stopped moving. His jaw did the clampy thing while the look he shot me could have frozen peas.

I ignored both looks and asked, "Have you at least run a search on the registration plate to see who it's registered to and their address?"

"Gee," he said, his voice full of sarcasm as he palm-smacked his forehead, "Why didn't *I* think of that?" His Viking blue eyes simmered with anger.

"And?" I persisted.

His teeth ground again before he reluctantly answered. "It's registered to him but the address is old."

"So basically, he's gone." I stated. "Again."

Sam dropped her eyes to the table and sighed. "Can you both stop beating your chests here for a minute and focus on the case?"

On the tip of my tongue was *'he started it'*. Instead, I kept my silence. I had other questions that needed to be asked.

She lifted her eyes to me and said, "Now it's your turn, Jack."

She was opening the door for me to walk through. The question was how much did I tell them without getting myself into all sorts of trouble? I could think of two problems straight off: obstructing justice and withholding information.

According to Karen, I'd crossed a lot of barriers in the past few days, starting with Jason and the baseball bat incident. Then there was Hayley. And once they found out about Hayley, the shit would really hit the fan.

Then I had a light bulb moment. What I had to do was pretend to remove myself from the case without them getting suspicious.

I sighed theatrically. "Look Sam. This is all getting a little out of hand. I've been dragged in here as a suspect on two occasions while trying to help you both out." I glanced at Cavanaugh. "I've been badgered and bullied," I turned back to Sam, "and assaulted. I've been beaten and my life has been threatened with a deadly weapon. And at the end of it all, I'm not seeing a cent for all my hard work."

I let that sink in.

"That's not good business sense in anybody's book. I need to pay my bills like everyone else and as pleasant as it's been working with you both, I'm done here. I am politely extricating myself from this circus."

I stood up and straightened my jacket, ready to make a dramatic exit when I remembered the dog.

I turned to Sam. "Where's the dog, Sam?"

She hesitated and gave me strange look. "In a holding cell. We'll keep it overnight until the RSPCA can pick it up in the morning and take it to the pound."

Nobody was going to adopt him. The only resort would be to put him down. When a dog is as emotionally damaged as he was, they wouldn't bother to find a place for him. I had no idea what Jimmy subjected him to, and I didn't want to know. Ignorance is bliss and ignorance makes it possible for all of us to sleep at night.

I made an instant decision I hoped both me and Sherlock would not regret.

"I'm taking him with me."

She raised her eyebrows and blinked. "You want him?"

"His prospects are better with me than they are with them."

Sam nodded slowly. Perhaps she understood that the two of us were meant for each other. Both of us damaged and both of us needing a little unconditional love.

"I'll have him brought up when we're finished in here," she said softly.

"We're finished now," I said, straightening my jacket some more. "Send for him."

Cavanaugh exhaled sharply with the first hint of colour creeping up his neck.

"You're just going to walk out of here and forget all about Elizabeth Delaney? Is that what you're saying?"

"Why not? You've been trying to get rid of me from the very beginning." I shrugged. "You win."

A ghost of a smile crept across his face. He shook his head and snorted.

"You're actually going to abandon the case?"

"Apart from your sparkling repartee, what will I be losing?"

As his eyes held mine, he gave me a sceptical look I deserved. I had an unsettling feeling he could see the workings of my mind.

"I don't believe that for a second. That would be spitefulness without purpose. And nothing about you suggests you are a spiteful man."

For the first time there was a hint of warmth in his voice. It was enough to unbalance me into silence.

"So where were we?" he continued. It was his turn to point at the chair I'd vacated.

I was still off-guard by the change of tactics so I sat down meekly again.

Sam turned her attention to me. I'd had a glimpse of a Cavanaugh I'd never seen before, but the Sam of old was still lurking.

"Cruz. Fleming," she insisted sharply. "What do you know?"

It was time to give a little. Not everything, but a little.

"Maybe Fleming's disappeared but Hayley hasn't," I allowed.

Sam's face darkened and her eyebrows shot up. Cavanaugh's eyes bulged.

She held him back, the palm of her hand on his chest, and leant forward again. "And how would you know that, Jack?"

I spread my arms but said nothing.

"Certain laws apply even for you, Curtis," Cavanaugh warned. "You could be charged with withholding vital information from the police in an active investigation."

Gone was the Kumbaya moment. Maybe he was so used to playing the bad cop to Sam's good cop, he was set on automatic.

Seconds ticked by before I said, "Oh, Sorry. I was waiting for the dramatic music." It was needless needling but I have to admit, I loved being the bad guy.

"Do you know Hayley's current location?" Sam asked, stressing each word individually, visibly trying to stay calm.

My patience suddenly evaporated. "Okay, guys. Let's pretend I was a trained police officer for twelve years." My eyes flicked from Sam to Cavanaugh as I spoke. "Let's pretend I know that certain *other* laws come into play when a citizen talks to police," I said, ignoring Sam now and glaring at Cavanaugh. I was in full rant now. "Mostly the ones about saving your breath by skipping the bullshit."

Cavanaugh smirked. "Jack, Jack, Jack. Twelve years of going through the motions and now look at yourself. A private investigator with barely enough clients to make ends meet."

His nostrils flared. "You think you're so smart. But you're as simple as a school kid's lunchbox." He nodded slowly, a knowing look on his face. "I've checked your police file."

Sam's head swung to face him, her eyes wide with surprise.

"You were always a failure waiting to happen," he continued, ignoring Sam's look. "And now you're looking for a case to bring you back into the limelight." His Adam's apple bobbed in his neck as he chuckled. "After this you'll be lucky if Grayson lets you fetch our coffee."

The insult hit home. I didn't like the things he said but I couldn't fault the logic. I *had* been a loose cannon. I *was* headstrong. And I paid the price of those faults every single day of my life.

I eased air into my lungs through clenched teeth as a sudden rush of heat flushed through my body, the raw edge exposed.

"Ouch." I faked a cringe but the anger was building.

The mocking sneer on his face finally did it. I lost it.

"Let me tell you something, *Detective* Cavanaugh. I'm not an idiot. I know how things go," I snapped as anger knotted my gut. "You think I'm looking for some drama to bring me back into the fold? Well what *I* know is that you had a Plan A, which was to find Cruz, and we all know how *that* turned out. So, to redeem yourself, you've come up with a Plan B, which is to find Hayley so that Inspector Grayson will place a notch on your holster."

I gave a knowing nod as I was struggled to keep the emotion out of my voice.

"You've failed brilliantly to do either. But finding Hayley would have been a serious blunder on your part because that would have led the media to the reason behind Jason's death. The papers will print before and after shots of Jason and portray him as a sweet kid caught up in your failures. Then they'll show you bending down looking at a body with half a head. The backlash on your career would have been devastating."

I could hear his teeth grinding from across the table.

It was as if my outburst hadn't happened. "Do. You. Know. Where. She. Is?" he repeated calmly.

I smirked. "Yes. I know where she is. And she's safe."

"What??!!" Sam's eyes were nearly popping out of her head. "You have *got* to be *shitting* me!"

Cavanaugh's face turned red but he kept his voice calm.

"Are you refusing to answer my question?"

"I thought I just did," I smiled. "Yes, I know where she is. And I'll answer all your questions when I deliver her in two days time."

Sam gave me a WTF look but Cavanaugh just frowned.

"Why two days time?" Cavanaugh asked.

I had a vision of Simon Parker lying on the ground looking up at me with malevolence written all over his face. I figured with an ego like that, two days would be about right. He'd be wanting to even up the score and in his rush for vengeance, he'd make a mistake.

"Two days should be enough. I've already set the wheels in motion."

"You're negotiating with us? Seriously? Is that what you're doing?" Cavanaugh asked, almost spluttering.

"Then suggest an alternative approach." I pointed my index finger at the ceiling.

"Oh wait. There isn't one." I did a little wiggle of my head to show how smart I was.

Cavanaugh snorted a muted laugh. "Oh yeah. I really like how this *partnership* thing is going. You make all the decisions while we get to nod dumbly like idiots."

"Look. I'm not out to screw you. I'm doing you a favour. It's one of the lucky things that happen from time to time. It'll give you a promotion and make you a hero and the publicity will help my business."

Cavanaugh said nothing. Checkmate.

"Do you believe in hunches?" I turned to Sam, pretending Cavanaugh wasn't glaring at me from the other side of the table. "Because I certainly do."

"Every stupid mistake you've made comes from a hunch," she snorted.

I looked away to hide the hurt. But mostly to hide the guilt. Because deep down, I knew she was right.

"Well, think about this hunch for a while. The judge..."

"OH, COME ON! Not again," Cavanaugh exploded.

I glared at him. "Hear me out!"

Sam shook her head as Cavanagh gave her an *I told you so look*. But they kept quiet.

"I met with Terry Bryson the Fire Chief this afternoon and he walked me around the crime scene."

Sam was shaking her head. "It's not a crime scene, Jack. The report said accidental death. Did it not?"

I nodded. "It did. But I don't think it was."

Cavanaugh and Sam both sighed at the same time. Like they were twins. Both shaking their heads and sighing simultaneously.

Somewhere deep inside anger fizzed and I fought to keep it down. *You're just jealous* my good angel said. *Punch him* said my bad one. I much preferred the second option.

"And why do you think that, Jack?" Sam asked. Her cordial voice sounded forced, like a school teacher patiently talking to a disruptive, unruly student.

I made quote marks with my fingers, "A hunch."

I watched them both shake their heads in unison.

"And it looks like that hunch may just have paid off because Bryson and I found an anomaly."

That caught Cavanaugh's attention. "An anomaly?"

"The top floor where the bed once was is covered in accelerant. You could smell it but it wasn't just that. There's at least two, maybe three, pour patterns."

"Pour patterns?" Cavanaugh parroted.

"Pour patterns," I agreed. "Where accelerant was poured. One pattern started in the wardrobe and led straight to the bed where someone then poured the fuel *over* the bed."

In the silence, the clock ticked noisily as Sam and Cavanaugh both stared opened-mouthed at me in disbelief.

"They doused him in it and then lit a match and torched him," I concluded.

Sam blinked. "Bryson said that?"

"Yes, he did. And I've taken samples of the ash to Wayne Grant this afternoon for analysis. Results will be back tomorrow." I showed them my crossed fingers. "Hopefully in our favour."

I waited for a response. When none came, I said, "You're welcome."

Sam spoke first but more to herself. "You were right," she almost whispered. "This is all connected to Elizabeth Delaney's disappearance."

"Good thing I'm not the 'I told you so' type because I'd be saying it about now. You just haven't been listening to anything I've said. But we'll know for certain tomorrow when the results come back."

My eyes travelled from one to the other.

"Now that we all seem to be on the same side," I began, "I have a question for you. One thing no one seems to be concerned with is where's the kid that Elizabeth Delaney walked in on a year ago? Everyone's been concentrating on *her* disappearance but what about where this all started a year ago? What about the kid?"

Two sets of eyes bulged at me from across the table.

"Where the hell did you get *that* information?" Cavanaugh spluttered.

I waved the question off.

"Spare me the drama. I know, okay. What I want to know is if anyone looked into this a year ago?"

Sam and Cavanaugh both shook their heads.

"Sam," I admonished. "You, more than anyone else, knows about the murder of those kids eighteen months ago. There were five murders, remember? All boys of about fourteen years old and all killed over a few years' time span."

Realisation sparked in Sam's eyes. "You don't think...?"

"What?" Cavanaugh asked, his eyes swivelling from Sam to me. "What? Tell me!"

I turned to him.

"It was my last case here. A hiker stumbled over the body of a young boy who'd been murdered the day before. Sam and I were called to the scene at Tamborine Mountain. Over two days, we found four more bodies, a couple were just skeletons, but all were young boys and all were buried at varying times, going back three or four years."

I turned to Sam. "We never solved those crimes, Sam."

I didn't have to say anything else. The insinuation was enough. I just left the statement sit heavily in the silence.

Sam was shaking her head in disbelief.

"Who found Jason's body Sam?" I asked.

"A local resident and his dog." Sam sounded disgusted. "You saw the footage on television. By the time we got there a dozen other people had trampled all over the crime scene. There wasn't much to find after that."

"I want to see the crime scene at Tamborine Mountain for myself."

Cavanaugh leaned forward and snarled. "To do what exactly?"

I raised both hands in a *who knows* gesture. "I don't know. But fresh eyes can't hurt."

That's when the phone rang. A few strands of hair had fallen in Sam's eyes and she pushed them away absently as she checked the screen. She frowned and cocked her head to the side as she lifted the phone to her ear.

"Neil," she said.

In the silence as she listened, her eyes widened with each passing moment. A series of single word questions followed. "When?" Tinny words sounded through the speaker. "How?" More tin. "Where?" She glanced at Cavanaugh, then at me, before saying, "Shit! We're on our way."

"What?" Cavanaugh asked as Sam reached for the bag at her feet.

"I know why we can't find Cruz."

Cavanaugh and I both waited.

"Cruz is dead," Sam stated.

"What?" we both yelled in unison.

"How?" Cavanaugh asked first.

"He was found knifed in an alley off Tedder Avenue. He was killed sometime during the night. They found his wallet on him so they ran his name through the system and found the report I made, linking him to Elizabeth Delaney."

All three of us stood up at the same time, chairs scraping on the tiles. Sam's head spun around to me.

"Not you, Jack. Not this time."

Cavanaugh shrugged on his coat jacket and exited quickly, leaving me gaping at Sam.

"But Grayson said I could," I stuttered.

"He said you could help but he didn't say you could come to crime scenes," she said as she turned to watch Cavanaugh open a drawer and pull out some car keys. "Don't argue with me Jack. The answer will still be no."

I stared at the table top, thinking. She was right. There was no use going to the crime scene. I'd see the report tomorrow anyway. I had more important things on my mind. I wanted to go to the site where Jason was murdered and I had a plan to work on that included finding Elizabeth by using Hayley as a decoy.

"Are you coming?" Cavanaugh called out to Sam as he waited beside his desk.

I raised my face and sighed. "It must be exhausting to be so narcissistic." I turned to Sam. "I'm nowhere near as narcissistic, am I?"

Sam smiled but didn't argue the point.

"You know he's a real shithead," I added.

She sighed. "He has many fine qualities as a policeman, Jack. He's intelligent, passionate and he's tireless."

"But as a partner?"

She nodded. "He's a pain in the arse."

I laughed.

"Go." I jerked my head in Cavanaugh's direction. "He's waiting." And then, "But first the dog. Get him sent up here." I grinned. "He'll be my guard dog."

She turned to leave then stopped and turned back to me. "Oh God. Now what are you planning?"

She knew me too well.

My voice was gentle, nothing like I was feeling. What I was planning was to put myself at risk and go against every creed I have followed religiously for twelve years. And for what? A girl I picked up one rainy night who means nothing to me?

Except that's not true anymore. In my lonely existence, she had risen to the surface and given me purpose.

"You know what?" I began. "You keep telling me I'm not a cop anymore. And I get it. But the way I see it, that means I can do a lot of things you can't. I don't need a warrant to ask a few questions and I don't need shithead's permission." I smiled. "It's liberating in a way."

"I don't know what you're planning Jack," she put her hand up to stop me from interrupting, "and please don't tell me."

Cavanaugh stopped and turned at her raised voice.

"Are you coming or what?" he called out again.

She spun towards him, said, "I'm coming for Chrissakes!" Then she spun back to me.

"You can't go off half-cocked!" she hissed. "Haven't you learnt anything? I'm the one with resources now. You have to learn to rely on me."

"And shithead too?"

"And shithead too."

A truce. Of sorts.

"I promise I'll be good," I lied and grinned. I was hoping my survival would be a happy bi-product.

"Come on, Jack. Are you serious?"

"Nah. Just tired. I'm raving. I'm actually going home."

I pushed myself off the chair using both hands. To be honest, I *was* tired.

"Go. Shithead's waiting."

She glanced at Cavanaugh then back to me. "Were you serious about going to Mount Tamborine?"

The look on her face told me she knew how hard it would be for me to return to where five tiny bodies were found a year ago. She was right. The pounding in my chest was supersonic.

"I'll be fine. Can I please have the address, mum?"

She nodded her head once. "I'll text you the location."

Then she turned to join Cavanaugh. Over her shoulder she called out, "The dog's in Holding cell 1. You know where that is."

❧ 31 ❧

Frank and I spoke very little the next morning.

On the way home the night before, the dog sat on the front passenger seat of the car drooling, looking straight ahead at the quiet streets. The sky was as grey as crematorium ashes but in a few hours, it would begin to lighten with the promise of dawn. When I got into bed, he lay down at my side, his nose inches from my hand, as if he wasn't about to let me out of his sight.

Frank and I both rose late, Hayley later still, and it was almost 9.30 by the time the two of us were taking our first sips of coffee on the back veranda. As I filled him in on the night before, the dog rested his muzzle on my shoes just as Sherlock loped onto the veranda. Sherlock screeched to a halt, hissing and arching his back, but the dog simply raised his head and watched silently before dropping his muzzle back on to my shoes.

"Sherlock. Meet the dog," I said. "Get used to him. He's here to stay." Five minutes later, the two were touching noses in an early truce.

Frank sipped his coffee. "What are you gonna call the mutt?"

"Right now, *dog* will have to do."

Frank snorted. "Jeez mate. You can't call it *dog*. Where's your imagination?"

"Right now, my brain is stretched as far as it can possibly go with this case and I don't want to push it any further by trying to think of a suitable name for an animal."

I checked my phone. As promised, Sam's text with the address of the person who found Jason's body was sitting in my message box. She'd contacted him and he was willing to show me where he'd found the body. The time scheduled to meet with him was 1.30pm today. There was no answering reply to my message questioning her about Cruz's death and after last night's discussions, I didn't expect one. They were locking me out of that investigation for the moment but I wasn't too concerned. I'd get the report later today. Until then, I had a trip to Tamborine Mountain to keep me busy. It also meant I had the morning free to write up my notes and settle the dog into his new environment.

Since Hayley was still asleep, I offered Frank a few hours away from the house but once again, he waved the offer away. He was showing no signs of boredom with his babysitting job but from the couple of times I'd seen Hayley, she was showing an edginess that was disquieting. When I spoke to him about it, he waved his hand at me again.

"Kids," he scoffed. "They need to be entertained the whole blimmin' time." He glanced down at the dog. "Maybe the dog will give her something to do."

The trill of my mobile interrupted my thoughts and Wayne Grant's voice boomed at me over the phone.

"Got your results, Jack."

"You're a man of your word, Wayne. What have you got for me?"

"I tested the composition of your clean sample first before I tested the dirty sample. All the accelerants I test are like cake mixtures. They're made up of many different substances, each present in different amounts. All of the substances present in any given mixture will produce a unique signature of a given mixture."

"Umm okay."

"Let me explain it this way. Suppose you throw a pot plant onto the ground. It'll shatter in a lot of different pieces. Every time. And no two pieces will ever be alike. But a molecule is different. Every time you break it, it will break into exactly the same size and number of fragments. Each substance has its own unique signature."

I heard a shuffle at the other end of the phone, like he was changing the earpiece from one side to the other.

"Now the computer automatically compares the signatures against the mass spectral library profile of certain substances and comes up with a match."

"Come on, Wayne. Spare me the chemistry lesson. Have you got a result or not?

"Yes, Jack. I have."

There was silence down the line. It was like pulling teeth.

"The samples are different, Jack. The dirty sample is soaked in kerosene. No way are they even remotely the same. You've got a murder on your hands."

His words bounced around in my head.

"I was right," I almost whispered.

$\ast$ 32 $\ast$

The drive up to Tamborine Mountain starts off pleasantly enough but ends up steep and windy as you thread your way through the bushland and rainforest towards the top. As I climbed, I kept my speedometer on a steady 40kms an hour and took in the scenery as I followed the squiggle of road up to the top.

If you've read the brochures of Tamborine Mountain, you'll know that it *oozes* charm. Situated 70kms south of Brisbane and 25kms inland from Surfers Paradise, its plateau rises 580 metres above the surrounding countryside and is the home for about 6000 residents who share it with tourists visiting the wineries, B & B's, bush walks and markets.

All seemed pretty quiet but to me, the air buzzed with a nervousness it gets when the wind begins to blow, dry as a bone, cooking the hillsides into kindling that can snap into flames hot enough to melt a car chassis. Even with the windows closed, the air smelt of smoke and a column of smoke rose off towards a distant ridgeline where the Gold Coast City Council had been conducting 'controlled burning' to halt the devastation that happens around this time every year. When it does happen, it's big news.

Unlike the open grasslands, the Tamborine valley looked lush and green. The low foliage glowed a deep lush green while thick coarse vines wound themselves around trees in their attempt to reach the sun. Along with the smoke, I could smell the sweet, cloying odour of eucalyptus mixed in with a musky animal smell.

The road continued over an old wooden bridge crossing a stream before Siri told me to take a dead-end tributary off the main road into a heavily wooded area. Suddenly she chirped, *'You have reached your destination'*.

I turned into a driveway and peered through the windscreen. The house was overgrown with ivy and an eight-foot-high stonewall separated it from the road that wound on further into the distance, following the road uphill and disappearing over the rise. On both sides of the fence, there were eucalyptus trees and melaleucas, gnarled grey and well established, which probably meant they had been here well before I was born. Through a gate, the path disappeared around the corner of the house, curling through callistemon that were in the final throws of blooming. In a month's time, the delicate red brushes would be turning a soft brown and the seeds would be filtering through the air ready to settle in the soft earth to germinate again.

I opened the car door and eased myself out, groaning as I unfolded.

There is one disadvantage to glorious summers in the hinterland of the Gold Coast. Man-eating insects. Mosquitoes struck the instant I stepped out of the Mazda, whining around me and telegraphing the happy news to others of a new food source. I flicked my hands around my head and took in the surrounding area.

From where I was standing, I couldn't see much of the house. I couldn't see much of *anything* because the trees were so thick, making everything look gloomy. Here I was in the middle of a hot summer's day at one-thirty in the afternoon and it was so dark and quiet, it felt ominous. It made me feel like I was a kid sneaking out to do something bad and not wanting anyone to hear or see me. This place did that to you. It was so quiet the ticking of the car's cooling engine sounded like finger snaps and I made a mental note to carry a crucifix and a sharpened wooden stake if I had to come here again.

The clear sky was streaked with wispy strips of residual smoke but otherwise it was like a sheet of stainless steel spray-painted blue and I blinked against the brassy sun in my eyes. Judging by the heat and humidity, if I didn't make a move soon, I'd be a puddle.

A man stepped out through the front door of the house and placed his hand over his eyes, shading them from the glare. Pale, watery blue eyes watched me as I crunched up the driveway towards him. Beside him sat an odd-looking dog, tongue lolling out, watching my progress with greater interest. Halfway up the driveway, the dog dropped to the ground, all four limbs spread out from his body, as if it was too much effort to stay standing.

The man was over six feet and could not be called a soft man but at the same time there was no muscle or definition of his body, as if he bypassed conventional sports. His hair was wet, freshly combed with the part a razor sharp straight pink line in his white scalp and his eyebrows were an unruly tangle. His teeth were set slightly askew as if they needed to be adjusted. Despite the warmth, he was wearing a lightweight long-sleeved white shirt with white slacks. Just looking at him was making me sweat.

I held out my hand. "Good afternoon, sir. Detective Neil may have called? My name is Jack Curtis."

He shook my hand and nodded. "Yes, she called, Mr Curtis. My name is Philip Marshall."

"That's an amazing looking dog," I commented conversationally, looking at the prostrate dog at his feet.

"This is Napoleon," he said, bending down and ruffling the dog's head. "He's of no particular breed," Marshall said unnecessarily. "He has Labrador in him somewhere and a bit of German Shepherd too, looking at the displacement of his hips. For a while when he was a puppy, he used to give me a lot of trouble eating everything in sight. He's getting on in age now, like me, so he sleeps most of the day away."

Napoleon raised its head for a second as if he knew we were talking about him. If the French general were alive today, he'd chop Marshall's head off for the insult.

Almost as if his head was too heavy to hold up for long, Napoleon yawned widely and a great bacon strip of a tongue lolled from his mouth. I could imagine my hand disappearing in one bite but he dropped his head back onto his paws again, although he still watched me closely.

"Nice dog," I lied, hoping the gods wouldn't smite me down. "May I come inside?"

Even in the shade, I could feel my shirt sticking to my back.

"Yes, of course. This way."

He led the way through the front door where a delicious coolness greeted us. Napoleon groaned loudly as he stood up and pushed his way past me to collapse again near a sofa.

"Can I get you something to drink?" Marshall asked.

"Water would be nice, thanks," I replied, thinking to myself, *a beer would be perfect.*

Minutes later, we were both sitting in the lounge room on opposite sides of a coffee table, a glass of water in our hands.

"Would you mind going over what happened two days ago, Mr Marshall?"

He took a breath and glanced out the window, gathering his thoughts.

"I wish I'd never taken him off his leash," he said wearily. "It was just like any other day. Napoleon likes a walk in the morning and when I can, I take the leash off and let him run. He likes to do that. When I whistle, he comes back, only this time he didn't."

Marshall was talking slowly and haltingly as if the memory was difficult for him. As he spoke, Napoleon sat between us, staring at me with nearly human intelligence. Sometimes he panted with what looked almost like a grin, tongue dangling. I had met other Napoleons before. He was a drooler. His eyes shifted as the old man spoke, gauging our tones. I had no doubt he would intervene if he didn't like what he heard.

"I whistled again thinking he must have gone a little further than usual and he came running back with what looked like a baseball cap in his mouth. At first, I thought it was something left behind by a hiker but as he got closer, I saw it was covered in blood. I took it off him," he looked down at the dog, "and had a bit of a fight with him. Then I called the police."

"Do you mind putting the dog back on a leash and taking me to where he bought the cap back to you?"

"No. No. Not at all. I'll get the leash."

He turned and made his way to a door to his right, leaving me alone with the dog. As he left the room Napoleon slowly stood up, as quiet as a sentinel, and lumbered towards me, head down. He eyed me silently through hooded eyes and took a step closer just as Marshall entered the room.

"Here we go."

Marshall jiggled the leash at the dog and Napoleon sprang to attention as if he'd been shot out of a rubber band. He issued a high-pitched yelp and squirmed as the doctor connected the leash his collar.

"After you," I said to Marshall, keeping my eye on Napoleon as he bounded down the front steps.

The overhead canopy of the trees blocked out most of the light and provided a slight relief from the hot sun. Circling in the sky was a hawk, its wingspan stretched out as gracefully as a soaring kite. I knew I was close to the creek because the bush was alive with the sound of chirping crickets, buzzing mosquitoes and churning rapids.

I wiped the sweat away from the side of my face and the insects went nuts when they smelled my flesh. For a while, I tried the Zen trick of ignoring them but after a few hundred bites or so, I gave up. Confucius never had to live in ninety percent humidity on a thirty-plus-degree centigrade day. If he had, he'd have felt like I did and would have decided to hack off a few heads instead.

The ground was covered in pine needles that were spongy beneath my shoes and I struggled for purchase as I trudged behind Marshal and the dog like I was part of a straggly entourage. My hands were beginning to get sappy from grabbing hold of trees to keep myself upright.

But if there was any place to escape the heat, we had found it. We were in the shade and a light breeze swirled around us. If I wasn't preternaturally opposed to biting insects, snakes, heat, stinging nettles and dirt, I might have enjoyed the rumoured serenity of the eucalyptus forest.

Twenty minutes later, the ground levelled off slightly and the trees thinned.

"This is about where I let him go," Marshall called to me over his shoulder.

I heard him slap a mosquito as the dog sprang off in a weaving pattern towards a bank of trees, moving in long steady paces instead of running full bore. Sniffing the breeze, Napoleon stopped every now and then, sometimes doubling back a short distance but always moving forward. Marshall encouraged him with an occasional "Good boy" and Napoleon sprang off well ahead of us. In the distance, I could hear him thrashing around in the undergrowth.

As I lost another pint of blood to the mosquitoes, Napoleon began zigzagging more erratically through the trees, obviously pleased to be out again but not giving any indication that he was close to finding the spot where he'd found the cap.

Hearing stories from dog handlers, I had an idea that a dog's nose should be on the ground not up in the air most of the time like Napoleon's nose seemed to be. Trained to respond to the smell of rotting human flesh, cadaver dogs find hidden bodies like infrared systems pinpoint heat. A truly skilled sniffer can nail the former resting place of a corpse even after its removal. Some are good, some are lousy and watching Napoleon now, I had an idea he was the latter. That and the fact that he wasn't baying as I'd have expected made me wonder if we were wasting our time.

As if reading my thoughts, Napoleon began barking and in the distance the trees parted. As we neared, I could see twigs scattered around and to my right the landscape was marred by the yellow crime scene tape marking where the body had been found.

"Just a minute." Marshall walked over to Napoleon and held him by the collar. He told him to sit and said, "Good boy," as the dog shifted around on his front paws like a kid that needs to go to the toilet. Reacting to the firmness of his owner's voice, Napoleon obeyed and sat panting, watching my approach with large caramel eyes.

"Thank you Mr Marshall. If you like, you can take Napoleon back to the house now. I can find my way back from here."

At the look of uncertainty in his eyes, I added with an encouraging nod, "Thank you for your help."

As I listened to Marshall crunching through the pine leaves, I stared at the spot for a few moments then looked around, not knowing exactly what I was looking for. I had precious little to work on and the medical examiner had already catalogued everything two days ago.

Still, I hoped to find something.

The dirt track we came in on was the obvious point of entry to the scene. I needn't bother looking for tyre tracks. After talking to Walt, I knew the killer had made him walk from the car to here, probably hands behind his back, picking their way through the scrub. He would have known that when he got to where the killer had planned to stop, he was going to die. Jesus, how frightened would you be?

Fifteen minutes later, I knew I was looking at a dead end. Whoever had killed Jason had covered their tracks well. There was nothing left behind. No shell casings. No footprints. No note saying, *'You got me.'*

I was used to detecting in a crowded office surrounded by colleagues and friends who would roll their eyes at me and eavesdrop on my calls. Now I was on my own and as the leads dropped away, there was nothing left for me but the sound of mosquitoes laughing at me from the trees. It had been a waste of time.

I fell twice in the first five minutes on the way back and I didn't see a small leafless branch until it raked across my cheek, cutting it open. I cursed under my breath and pulled the front of my shirt out of my pants to wipe the blood away from my cheek. The wound stung from the sweat that was dripping down my face and the mosquitoes went nuts again.

And that's when I saw it. Almost hidden in the green foliage of a nearby bush was a small piece of green material. I reached over and plucked the snagged fragment from the bush and stared at it. The material was lined with pale green fleece but the outside was a deep green that blended with the trees. As I examined it, I realised it was from a tracksuit. Or a sweat shirt. Maybe even a hoodie.

Forensics had missed it, firstly because it wasn't anywhere near the crime scene, and secondly because it blended in so well with the environment. If the branch hadn't raked my cheek and if I hadn't stopped to wipe the blood away, I would have missed it as well.

Something was working its way through my brain as I stared at the scrap of material in my hand. I was missing something that was important but I didn't know what it was.

I tucked it into the pocket of my pants and trudged on, telling myself it may mean nothing at all. Up in this terrain, hundreds of hikers pass this way every month. Odds were it had come from one of them and I could almost hear Cavanaugh's snide remarks now. Still, it was something and it was worth looking into.

Twenty minutes later, I was back at the car. I pulled my phone out of the glove compartment as well as another Ziploc bag and placed the scrap of material inside the bag before switching my phone on.

Seven messages. All from Sam and all pretty much the same.

'Call me for Chrissakes! Call me!'

'Jack. Pick up!'

'Where the hell are you? Call me back now!'

'What is going on with you? Call me!'

The last one was a little calmer. *'Jack, you have to call me. For all I know these guys know who you are and you're dead. Please call me.'*

I pushed the reply button and listened to the buzz for a couple of seconds before Sam picked up. "Thank God, Jack. Where are you?"

"You know where I am. Mount Tamborine searching Jason's crime scene."

I'd decided to wait until I was back at the station before mentioning my prize. Before anything, I had to check Walt's report to see what Jason was wearing when he died. I'd already read the report but I was too involved with the gun to take much notice of what he was wearing. If it was a green sweat shirt then it showed the path he had followed to his death. If it wasn't a green sweat shirt, I just may have struck pay dirt. It wasn't much and I had no idea how I was going to tie it in with the crimes.

The thought of a green sweat shirt made me hesitate again and something shifted in my brain. Why did that ring a bell?

I mentally shook myself. "What about you?" I asked Sam. "Have you finished processing Cruz's crime scene?"

"Only just. We're back at the station now and the body is with Walt at the morgue. He'll try to autopsy it today." I heard her sigh. "He was stabbed, Jack. Five times around the heart. The murderer must have been covered in blood. But not one damn person saw or heard anything and no murder weapon. Why do you stab someone five times?"

Because you hate them the voice inside my head said. Instead I said, "Vengeance."

"If that's the case then half of Surfers Paradise are on the suspect list."

I could hear the weariness in her voice and I only just realised she had worked through the night with minimum rest between shifts.

"Grayson is having a fit." She was sounding agitated. "Three dead bodies and not one damn shitty clue. The crime scene was clean. Absolute bullshit!"

I laughed. It felt weird to hear prim-and-proper Sam drop curse words like it was the most natural thing in the world. What it meant was the stress and the strain was beginning to show. I wanted to ask if there was something else wrong, to say I was here if she wanted to talk but I didn't. I'd wait for the right time and it wasn't now.

"Well, it is," she stated. "How can you kill three people and not leave a damn clue behind?"

"Well I have something that might cheer you up."

"Well, I could certainly use that."

"Wayne Grant got back to me this morning. The killer *did* slip up."

I heard an intake of breath. I had her attention.

"He's finished processing the samples. And my hunch paid off. The samples contained kerosene." I let that sink in before continuing. "The judge was definitely murdered."

I heard a groan through the phone and I knew Sam's mood had gone from morose to despair in the matter of seconds.

"Shit, Jack! How is *that* supposed to make me feel better? All it means is we have another related death! Now I've got something else to tell Grayson and he'll be apoplectic."

I hesitated. Should I tell her about the scrap of material as well? Almost immediately, I decided against it. I wanted to produce it like a magician's rabbit from a hat and I wanted to see Cavanaugh's face when I did.

"When are you coming into the station?" she asked. "We need to tell Grayson about this."

"I'm finished here now. I can be there in half an hour."

❦ 33 ❦

It took me an hour instead to get to the office. I stopped off first at McDonalds drive-through for a Big Mac, large fries, apple pie and coffee and I ate the meal while sitting in the car during heavy traffic travelling slower than a glacier.

I was doing what I always did when I was on the job. I slept badly. I drank too much. And I ate irregular meals, if I ate at all. And I survived on caffeine. My body was beginning to show signs of stress but there was no way I was going to give in to the pressure right now. We were so close. I could feel it.

"Where's shithead?" I asked Sam when I walked into the office nursing the remains of my coffee. I'd already shoved the waxy wrapper of the burger into the grease-stained bag and mashed my contribution into the overfilled rubbish bin outside the station. I was regretting my menu selection and the speed with which I'd consumed the damn thing.

Without hesitating, Sam said, "He's been called into Grayson office."

"Really?" I smiled.

"Don't be a moron." Her eyes drifted back top Grayson's office where loud voices floated across the empty room. "I filled Grayson in on the results of the accelerant and he wanted a full update on the case. He also wanted to know why it was you who found evidence that the death of the judge was murder and not Cavanaugh. As lead, Cavanaugh has to face the music."

"How's he taking it?"

"He's livid. He started off with how you're not being open with us and Grayson cut him short."

I was beginning to enjoy the feeling of euphoria just as my phone buzzed. I pulled it out of my pocket and glanced at the screen. Frank's name appeared with a message. *'Call me.'*

I closed the message app on my phone and immediately the phone rang. The caller ID said, *Frank*. For Frank to call straight after leaving a message meant something was up. I wanted to tell Sam about the fabric that was burning a hole in my pocket but I also wanted Cavanaugh to be present when I produced it. But first, I had to see what Frank wanted.

I held my phone out to Sam. "I need to talk to you about what I found at Tamborine Mountain but first I have to take this. It could be important."

She nodded absently but barely registered my exit to the corridor.

I pressed the answer button but before I could say anything, Frank jumped in.

"Where are you, mate?"

Somewhere in the back of my mind, the urgent tone of his voice registered. I had an uneasy feeling in the pit of my stomach and something with a hundred sticky feet crawled along my spine.

"What's up, Frank? Is the dog okay?"

The pause was so long I thought the connection had dropped out.

"It's not the bloody dog. It's Hayley. She's done a runner."

My heart jumped into my throat. "What? Oh shit! Tell me she didn't give you the slip. Don't tell me that Frank."

"What was I supposed to do? Piss my pants?"

"Shit, Frank. SHIT!"

In the background, I could hear engine noise. I knew he was already in the car searching for her.

"She's on foot so she can't be far. I'm in the car so I'll find her mate."

"Jesus, Frank."

I ran my hand through my hair. Jason and Jimmy were both dead. Both murdered. As was the judge. And now Cruz. And Elizabeth Delaney was still missing. What I didn't need was for Hayley to join the group of dead and missing.

"Jesus Christ, Frank!" I repeated.

"She can't be far, mate. I was gone for what, a minute? Two tops. There's nowhere she could go from your place. She's around here, and I'll find her. Settle yerself down. You'll blow a gasket."

"You keep my informed!" I yelled.

I glanced over to see if Sam was watching but she was on her way to Grayson's office, unaware of my raised voice. I turned my back to her and whispered angrily into the phone.

"Do you hear me? I want to know when you find her. Not *if*, Frank. Definitely not *if.* *When*, you find her."

"I will, I will." I heard a mumbled curse before he hung up.

Where the hell had she gone? And why? We couldn't afford to lose her. She was the hinge that kept it all together. Just this morning, everything seemed fine. Frank and Hayley were getting on just fine. What had caused her to disappear now?

I saw Sam walk out of Grayson's office followed by Cavanaugh looking like he was ready to explode. He took one look at me and his face reddened even more. The look didn't escape Sam's attention and she mumbled something that barely settled him down. He glared hard at me as he stomped towards me standing in the doorway.

For a second I thought he was about to start an open brawl in the office. His gaze was murderous and his jaw flexed as he ground his teeth together. He was barely keeping it together. But then he was past me, bumping my shoulder hard on his way through to the corridor without saying a word.

Any other time, I would have reacted to the jolt. But something made me hesitate. I recognised the look on his face. It was frustration and it made me hesitate because I knew that look and I knew that feeling. That was me twelve months ago and within a short amount of time, I had a meltdown that ended my career. It made me pause and give him a little latitude.

I glanced at Sam and saw her shoulders drop with relief. Her reaction sent a jolt through my body because she had expected me to react. Badly.

For the second time in a minute, I hesitated. Was Cavanaugh right? Had I been a failure waiting to happen? Was I just looking for a case to bring me back into the limelight? It was a sobering thought.

I walked over to Sam as she sat down heavily at her desk.

"Okay, Jack. Tell me what you found," she said wearily.

Her body was guzzling up all the reserves of her energy leaving her exhausted. I could see it in the way she slouched in her seat, in the weary tone of her voice and the slight tremor of her fingers as they rubbed her chin. She was slowly burning out and I had a feeling it wasn't just the case that was causing the exhaustion.

I softened my voice. "You once regarded me as a friend, Sam. I'm still that same person. I know something else besides the case is eating you up. Talk to me."

Her eyes lifted and met mine, and as always, when someone speaks gently to you at fragile times, emotion takes over. Her chin trembled making her lips turn inwards and her eyes reddened. Still she said nothing. She was barely keeping it together.

"Is it the divorce, Sam? Is your ex-husband bothering you?"

She snorted, wiping the back of her hand under her nose.

"He couldn't care less about the divorce. Neither can I. It was doomed from the start. We're both professional people with jobs that take up all of our time, even our spare time at home. We spent four years trying to make it work but in the end, we drew further apart when we were barely communicating in the first place."

"Then what's the matter?" I asked softly again.

I watched her swallow and take a deep breath.

"My mother died," she said simply.

I blinked a few times.

"Then why are you still here?" I asked.

She sighed. "It's a long story but we weren't on good terms. My mother was pure Irish and our family had issues," she did speakie fingers with both hands, "with another Irish family that lived in our small town near Strachan in Tassie. I crossed a boundary and she never forgot or forgave me for it. It got so bad and so hard to see those eyes condemning me every day of my life that I left home fifteen years ago. I haven't seen my family since Christmas five years ago. Even after all that time, it was pretty dreadful."

"What family, Sam?"

"An elder sister who endlessly berates me for leaving her alone to care for our aging mother." She sniffled. "She has a point but there's more to it than that and I don't have the time to explain." She shook her head. "Forget it, Jack. It's none of your concern. I'll work it out."

"But you're going home for the funeral, right? Tell me you're doing that."

She sighed. "Yes. In a week's time. If we ever solve this case."

I grinned. "In that case, I'll unwrap my present now." I jerked my head towards the door Cavanaugh had walked through minutes before. "But won't shithead want to see this?"

"For God's sake, will you two just kiss and make up and get it over and done with? Just no obvious love bites, okay. It would be hard to explain to Grayson."

She took a few breaths to calm herself down as she rubbed her forehead, like she was trying to wipe away a headache. "Just tell me what you've got, okay?" she whispered.

Before showing Sam the scrap of material, I glanced down at my phone to see if there was a message from Frank. Nothing. I wanted to get back to the house but I had a few questions to ask first.

I pulled the bag containing the scrap of material out of my pocket and held it out to her.

"I found this up at Tamborine Mountain."

She frowned at the bag. "What's that?"

I explained what I'd done, from following the dog to the crime scene and finding nothing there. I told her how I'd walked back alone and raked my cheek on a branch. Her eyes glanced at the cut but she said nothing. Dark circles were etched under her eyes and I realised the strain she was under to produce a result for Grayson. He may like her but he had to answer to people higher up on the food chain. The pressure always filtered down and the investigating detectives were always at the bottom and responsible for results.

I held the bag out to her.

"Forensics missed it. Maybe it has nothing to do with Jason." I shrugged. "Hikers are everywhere up there."

She stared down at the bag in her hand, a frown pulling her eyebrows together.

"What was Jason wearing when he died?" I asked.

"Jeans and a black t-shirt. And a green hoodie." She looked up at me. "But I know for a fact that the hoodie was intact. I've been over the report a million times and I know it backwards," she said handing the scrap back to me.

I stared down at it. That meant it was from a hiker and not related to the crime. But for some reason, I just couldn't believe that. It was too coincidental to be on the exact same path that Jason had taken and the exact same colour.

That niggling feeling telling me I was missing something vital surfaced again. What was I missing?

I tried to focus. If it wasn't from Jason's hoodie, and it wasn't from an unrelated hiker, then it had to have been the killer. That was the only other alternative.

But who?

My breath suddenly caught in my throat. The world went deathly quiet and all sounds were obscured by the emotions roiling inside me.

There's a moment in film and television shows when a particular shot or word signifies that moment when the penny drops. Sometimes, it's something little that goes 'click' and everything seems to fall into place. For real people it triggers something in the memory and we remember where we left our car keys or the name of that someone or that song we've been wracking our brains to think of. For Harry Callahan, it's usually a darker revelation. It's the instant that signifies the break in a case. Then when comprehension dawns, the camera zooms towards the face of the hero and the music reaches a crescendo as the light of realisation grows in their eyes.

The certainty hit me like a cricket bat. I felt a bead of sweat on my top lip, tingling hot then cold. I felt so sick, my stomach felt like there were 100 snakes in there and all of them were fighting. Even as I felt my stomach contract, even as I felt my heart turn to ice, I somehow managed to detach. I felt something in me harden.

I didn't feel the remaining coffee from my cup spilling as I stood silently in the room. What I felt was that old familiar surge of adrenaline rushing through me when pieces start to join up. My blood starts to spark as the pieces of the puzzle come together.

Sam saw the expression on my face and said, "What?"

My heart was racing and my skin crawled with apprehension. Bells were ringing like crazy inside my head and dozens of pieces of ignored information were clamouring to the front of my brain.

Focus, Curtis. Focus on the facts.

Memory is an amazing thing. Sometimes it's something as obvious as a photo that triggers the memory. Other times it's merely a scent or gesture that sends your mind in action.

What I was seeing was the photo of Jason and Jimmy on the dresser in Jimmy's house. One single picture frame with a picture of them both, arms around each other's shoulders, buffed and happy with themselves, and smiling widely at the camera in front of Jason's house. Both had been wearing matching green hoodies.

But there had been no green hoodie at Jimmy's house when I searched. Just a worn faux leather jacket, another pair of jeans and a pair of sneakers. I even remember thinking he was either waiting for the rest of his clothes to arrive from somewhere or he only owned two sets of clothes: the one he was currently wearing and the other in the wardrobe. But there was no green hoodie.

Jason had worn his to his death but where was Jimmy's?

And then another memory surfaced and I almost gasped. The banging in my ears told me my pulse was going apeshit.

Memory may be amazing but it's also unreliable. It's not even good. Cops don't catch a killer by sitting around remembering stuff. They collect facts not recollections. Facts, not memories. That's how we investigate. Memory can change the shape of a room. Change the colour of a car. Memories can be distorted. They're just interpretations, not a record and they're irrelevant if you have the facts. They're like clouds you can't see through. Like smoke in the air obscuring everything.

But this was different. I was absolutely positive. Why hadn't I seen it before? It was all there. I couldn't dispute it. Disparate facts jostled. Pieces. Photos. Evidence.

I almost collapsed into a chair as Sam continued to stare at me.

"Is this an episode of Skippy the Bush Kangaroo, Jack? Say something."

Sam was at my shoulder now, her voice sounded concerned as she stared at me.

"I think I know the truth." I whispered. I raised my eyes to meet hers.

Time seemed suspended as I stared disbelievingly at the wall. I blinked a few times. I know I did.

Just then, my phone buzzed with a message and I hurriedly pulled it out to read. The screen said *Frank*. I clicked the message icon and the message opened.

Back at the house. All good. New development. Get here asap.

I stood up, in a hurry to get home. Sam jumped up and followed me, grabbing my arm and spinning me around, her hands like talons.

"Don't you DARE walk out on me like this! You tell me what you're thinking."

I blinked again. Thoughts were crashing around in my head.

"When we were in Starbucks," I began. "The day Cruz pulled up in his Porsche?"

She nodded, her eyes bright.

"How many customers did you notice?"

She frowned as she tried to remember. "The old couple in the corner." She hesitated. "A couple of mothers with kids in strollers." She folded her lips together in thought. "And a kid nursing a coffee a few tables away."

I waited for her to put the pieces together.

Her eyes opened and her mouth made a small O. "In a green hoodie." she mumbled in awe. Seconds passed as thoughts ran through her mind. "A girl."

I nodded. "Yep."

"She was watching us?" she asked. Her head tipped backwards. "Elizabeth's alive? And she's been watching?"

"That would be my guess."

I was as stunned as Sam. For almost a week, I'd been searching for Elizabeth and she had been hovering in the background all the time, watching and waiting.

"Is she the one who's been killing everyone?" Sam asked in a stunned voice.

"I don't know, Sam. She may not be the murderer but she's connected some way. That's a fact."

"Then where the hell is she? And if she's innocent, why is she hiding?"

"That's what I'm going to try and find out."

And why was she wearing a green hoodie that could only have been Jimmy's I thought that but didn't say.

❧ 34 ❧

The kid was leaning against a graffiti littered concrete wall in the darkness of the quiet back street. His shoulders were hunched and his eyes had settled on the cracked pavement in front of him. His bike rested on the ground at his side.

I was only a block past the police station so I knew the kid must have been watching me walk in and waited for me to come out. Once again, annoyance surfaced at my inability to notice that I was being watched. It was becoming a bad habit. First Elizabeth and now a kid. I was slipping.

I pulled over into a parking space on the opposite side of the road, and his head jerked up. Part of me wanted to sprint across the road and grab him before he sped off again. Another part of me hinted that in my present state of unfitness, he'd easily outrun me and I'd look like a desperate paedophile shuffling down the road, chasing him. But then, he had waited for me.

Before I even stepped out of the car, two figures rounded the corner of the building out of the darkness and jerked to a stop before elbowing each other and laughing as they approached him. Both were the steroid type wearing tourniquet-tight black t-shirts over camouflage pants that hung low on their hips.

The kid, visibly frightened, pressed his back against the wall and put his hands in front of him in a typical defensive pose. The two figures moved in close and towered over him threateningly, and that's when I made my move.

"Gentlemen," I called out as I crossed the street.

Both camouflages spun at the sound of my voice. At first, their expressions were those of Neanderthal men hearing a strange noise for the first time. Then they looked me up and down and the smiles returned to their lips because I'm not a physically imposing figure.

They watched me walk the last few steps across the road and I could feel their confidence growing. I liked that. In my present frame of mind, I was itching to show them what an angry middle-aged man can do.

The beauty of their attire was that it was highly unlikely they were carrying a weapon. Not just are guns hard to procure, they are hard to hide. Knives, however, are another matter.

My eyes did a quick body scan for locations where they might be concealing a weapon and came up negative. Their clothing was more for show not weapon concealment. Even if a knife was hidden in the deep pockets of their pants legs, they'd lose precious time reaching in and digging around trying to get it out. By then, I'd have made my move.

"You should leave now," I said, spreading my arms wide as I stood in front of them. I had nothing in my hands and I wanted them to see that.

Camouflage on the right looked at Camouflage on the left and I in turn switched my gaze from one to the other. I'm not usually confrontational but like I said, in my present frame of mind, I would be a worthy adversary. I wasn't about to lose the kid again.

Camouflage One looked at me hard and I winked at him. His eyebrows jumped high in shock.

"Hit him," Camouflage Two said. "And break him."

As he spoke, Camouflage One actually started cracking his knuckles.

"Isn't that a bit over the top?" I smirked.

"What?" Definitely Neanderthal.

"Cracking your knuckles." I glanced at his hands. "I get it. You're a tough guy. But come on." I snickered.

"Oh man," Camouflage One sneered. "I'm really going to enjoy this."

He started walking towards me like an ocean predator approaching a guppy, lurching from side to side. There was no reason to wait. I locked my index and middle fingers together into a spear, cupped my hand slightly, and struck him straight in the throat. Hard.

The blow landed like a dart. Both hands went to his neck and he gagged, leaving him totally exposed. I quickly swept his legs from under him, knocking him backwards to the ground.

I turned to Camouflage Two and grinned, waving him on with both hands. "Your turn."

He was having none of it. He'd just watched his friend get taken down easily. He turned and ran. Camouflage One rolled over and was scuttling along on all fours behind him.

I turned to the kid. "Are you okay?"

The kid was breathing heavily as he nodded silently. He was visibly shaken and I wasn't sure if it was because of my combat skills or the thought of what could have happened if I hadn't happened along at that particular time.

I watched him collect himself as I made a few assumptions in my head.

"How come you're working the streets?" I asked. "You look like a smart kid. Where are your parents?"

The kid tried looking tough but as with most kids, his reply came out as sullen rather than threatening.

"None of your business," he muttered.

"So why'd you wait for me?"

"Someone I know wants to talk to you."

"And I should just follow you like an idiot?"

"This someone wants to help you."

"You'll have to do better than that, kid."

"Okay, old man." The cocky grin had returned. "How's this? You're looking for a girl, right? A girl who knows a lot about a certain lawyer who likes kids like me."

He watched my eyes widen and he smirked. "That got your attention."

"Why does he want to help me?"

He snorted. "*She* said you'd be suspicious. *She* said to tell you not to look a gift horse in the mouth."

He turned and started walking away from me. "Follow me. She's waiting."

Two streets away, the pavement outside Adventureland was crowded and noisy. Inside the store, the cacophony of sounds was deafening.

There was the digital ding-ding and siren sounds coming from machines as kids scored, together with the artificial noises of virtual planes being struck down and monsters dying under heavy armed assault. There were flashing neon lights, racing car simulators and claw cranes trying to snag generic stuffed animals from within a glass cage. Towards the back there was a ping-pong table and a pool table. Together, the noises were chaotic. And there were a lot of hooting teenaged boys taking the noise up another level.

My eyes swept the room as the kid weaved through the room towards an area called Laser Maze, which looked like one of the scenes from *Mission: Impossible* where someone tries to move without crossing a beam and setting of an alarm. Behind it was a door marked EMERGENCY EXIT where two security guards stood with their hands folded in front of them, like they were protecting their family jewels from an imminent attack.

The kid didn't pay much attention to them and they, in turn, looked so bored I wondered if they'd both had a lobotomy.

The kid stood between the guards and looked up at a surveillance camera. Then he motioned for me to do the same. Seconds later, there was a clanging noise and the door, made of reinforced steel, swung open. The kid walked through first and I followed.

Another guard stood on the other side and waved a mental wand over my body. Satisfied I didn't have a weapon on me, he waved us through another door. By now, I was wondering why a dump like Adventureland, with arcade games that had seen better days, would warrant such security.

The room we stepped into was nothing like the arcade outside. This room was sleek and modern with a dozen high-end monitors and screens on walls, on desks, everywhere. I counted four men sitting in front of monitors.

Standing in the middle of the room was a heavy-set woman with greying hair pulled back into a ponytail watching the screens, seemingly relaxed and almost casual.

She turned and eyes the colour of freshly brewed coffee appraised me.

"Give me a second, will you?" she said to me before she turned back to the monitors.

All eyes were on the centre screen on the wall and all four men were busy watching, reading and typing. I could see their reflections, intense and concentrating, from the screens in front of them.

There was obviously a conversation going on and all four were participating. There was however, five names involved in the conversation.

That's when I noticed the names. BANDITO, GAME BOY, BLAZER and JUPITER. Communicating with them was HUNGSTALLION12.

"Keep the conversation going, Thomas," the woman said. "Find out as much as you can. Don't let him go until you make a date with him."

She patted the man on the shoulder I assumed was Thomas and then turned to me.

"Welcome to my humble office, Jack Curtis," she said simply. "My name is Sandra Burton."

I glanced at the kid and he was looking at her like she was the Virgin Mary descended amongst them.

"Not so humble," I stated.

"Aren't you going to ask how I know your name?"

"With all this high-tech equipment, finding out who I am would be pretty simple."

She smiled and spread her arms wide, sweeping them to encompass the monitors over every wall.

"This is my nerve centre."

Nerve centre. This woman should have been petting a hairless cat like some Bond villain.

"Do you know why I'm not worried that you have seen all this?" she asked.

"I'm sure you're going to tell me."

She nodded and smiled. "I like you Jack."

She glanced back to the monitors and was seemingly satisfied enough with the conversation that was still in progress to turn back to me.

"I'm not worried because there is nothing you could really do," she grinned, "even if you wanted to. You've noticed the security and you may have noticed that there's no hard drives. Everything we dig up on these fine upstanding citizens out there," she waved to the monitors, "is kept in a cloud. So, if anyone breaks in, we push a button and voila," she snapped her fingers, "there's nothing to be found."

"Clever."

"I'm not boasting. I'm just letting you know who you're dealing with like I made it my responsibility to know who *I* would be dealing with."

She snapped her fingers again.

"Once Benny here found out your name, it didn't take long to learn everything about you."

She pointed to a screen behind her. Someone had paused the screen on an article from The Gold Coast Bulletin.

DETECTIVE JACK CURTIS TAKES LEAVE OF ABSENCE FROM THE POLICE FORCE

Under the headlines was the article covering everything about the case that had almost taken my mind. The bodies of five teenaged boys discovered on Tamborine Mountain and my eventual mental breakdown when I was unable to uncover the murderer. Under that was the headlines from six months later.

HAS DETECTIVE JACK CURTIS RETURNED TO HELP THE POLICE INVESTIGATE THE MURDER OF A YOUNG WOMAN FOUND IN AN ASHMORE HOME?

Shannon.

I closed my eyes and I could see her face again. The wounded eyes that showed a depth of hurt that no one could ever imagine. The red of her lipstick the same colour as the blood that oozed from her body where the bullet had entered her chest. The dragonfly pendant she always wore because she believed it promised her a better future than her destructive past. The softness of her lips that last time I kissed her as she promised me we'd be together soon, just one day before she was brutally murdered.

Everything about Shannon was burned into my brain and I didn't want to dredge it all up again.

When I opened my eyes, the screen had gone blank.

"I don't mean to be cruel," the woman said. "I just want you to know that I have people working for me who are resourceful. And we would like you to help us."

"Do what?" I asked, dumbfounded.

She turned and smiled down at Benny like a benevolent aunt. "Find the people who abuse and kill young boys and bring these people to justice."

She turned back to me, her eyes penetrating. "I know the story of the night Christine Buchanan disappeared and I know why she was forced to run. She was a plucky young lady."

I knew she was about to tell me something important and I realised I was holding my breath, waiting for her to continue. In the background, fingers tapped away at keyboards as her words echoed in the room.

"I know about the boy, and the other ones too," she continued in a soft voice, disguising the emotion evident in her eyes. "The ones degenerate men like to abuse."

She looked down at Benny again and smiled. "I've heard the story from the one person who knows better than anyone else."

Benny was watching his feet as he shuffled them on the concrete floor.

"That was you?" I asked him.

Benny's head shot up, a defiant look on his face.

"I've grown up since then, grandpa, so don't you go feeling sorry for me." His dark eyes burned with resentment. "That isn't who I am anymore. I don't need your pity!"

Sandra Burton tsked a couple of times.

"Benny. Don't embarrass me. Jack is our guest and I've asked him here to ask him for help and to tell him everything we know. We're all on the same side."

In the silence, Benny shuffled his feet contritely.

She waved me to a table with two chairs at the back of the room and before following her, I glanced at my watch. Frank would be waiting for me but there was no way I could leave here until I knew what she had in mind.

My chair made a small screech as I dragged it along the concrete floor and sat down opposite her. Benny continued to stand beside her.

"What do you know?" I finally asked.

She leaned back and folded her hands in her lap, her eyes settling on mine. "I know you are looking for Elizabeth Delaney, who disappeared almost two weeks ago. As you know, Elizabeth is actually Christine Buchanan who disappeared almost twelve months ago."

I nodded but kept quiet, letting her continue.

"I also know the name of one of the men who set all of this in motion." She gave me a sad smile. "As do you. You've already met him."

A silent moment passed while I wondered if she was playing me. Did she know or was she fishing?

She nodded. "Simon Parker."

My gaze drifted to Benny who lifted his eyes to me. For Sandra Burton to know that I had met with Simon Parker meant that Benny had been watching me for days. Some detective I was.

Sandra took a deep breath, her shoulders rising and falling with the breath. "Simon Parker was the one who blackened Christine's eyes and split her lips. And he was the one who scarred that beautiful face."

My eyes shifted to Benny again as my mind began turning things over. Did Benny lead Elizabeth to Sandra Burton? How did she know about the scar otherwise? And where was Elizabeth now?

"Yes," Sandra said, reading my mind. "I've met Elizabeth and she is safe now. With me." She looked at Benny. "Benny has been very useful to my operation. He has repaid my kindness to him in full."

She blinked for a few seconds then folded her lips together.

"But Simon Parker is not the one who supplies these degenerates with young boys." She clenched her teeth. "There are others who do that."

Her eyes flicked to me. "Parker is just one of many high-profile customers who use their services."

As I watched her face, a transformation took place. One minute ago, tears were shining brightly in her eyes as she told me Christine's story. But in the blink of an eye, a sneer distorted her face into something dark and ugly. The change stunned me.

"This operation we are talking about is a small one with only two members," she continued. "But it's just one of many operating on the Gold Coast that connects to a bigger operation controlled by the same men. These men have operations all over the country and they survive by keeping each operation small. But trust me, there are hundreds. This one however is different because they only supply to selective clientele like Parker who trusts them to keep their dirty habits a secret. These men have a lot to lose."

She glanced over to the monitors and waved an arm to include the four men sitting at the monitors. "These upstanding gentlemen here have certain ways of contacting these people and it's only been of late that we have been able to intercept those messages."

She glanced back at me with a small smile on her face. "Recently those people had a stroke of bad luck. One of the members of the team met with an untimely death leaving the other member to handle the operation alone. Which is when Benny made his timely escape."

Asking me to come to her and have this conversation meant that I must know the name of the person who had run the paedophile ring and had met with an 'untimely' death.

Names chased each other in my mind. Elmer Fudd. Jason Brady. Jimmy Preston. Cruz. All had recently met with an untimely death but which one had the accomplice?

Suddenly, it clicked. Jason Brady.

My mind spun back to the first confrontation with Jason Brady outside the tavern. *Tricky,* he called me. Then I saw myself, dishevelled and dirty with a bruise on my face, standing in front of Pauline Brady as she looked me up and down. In my anger and frustration, I'd missed the clue to it all. The noise from inside the house that had sounded like something being knocked over. She'd said it was a cat but if I'd been thinking straight, I'd have realised it was something else entirely. Giving myself a little leeway, I had no idea of the bigger picture at the time. I was simply looking for Elizabeth Delaney, not a paedophile ring.

Sandra Burton smiled. "I can see you know who it was. Jason Brady and his mother." She smirked. "And Parker, ever the business man, stepped into the void after Jason's death and take over the business."

She glanced down at Benny again. "Benny has been invaluable to us."

In the silence Benny blushed and Sandra smiled.

"Benny has told me everything we need to know. From how they ensnared the boys to how they kept them under lock and key until they had need of their," she hesitated, "*services.*"

She gave a little cough, throaty and moist and I knew it was emotion that was causing the irritation.

"Benny managed to escape and it was my good fortune that he ran into our arcade that day trying to evade recapture. He has been with me ever since and it only because of him that we know the full story."

She looked over at the monitors and the four men still typing.

"We are also working on uncovering as many of the degenerates who think they are so smart that they can lure young boys by saying sweet things to them online."

She turned back to me. "I can understand why you had a break down a year ago, Jack, and I believe you're a good man."

She hesitated as her eyes bored into mine. "I know for a fact that this operation was connected to the Tamborine Mountain case you were investigating." She nodded and let that sink in and I felt the colour drain from my face. "You were unable to solve that case, Jack. But it wasn't your fault."

She leant over and patted my hand like my mother used to do. "There were outside forces at work. People high up on the food chain had a lot to lose if the truth came out."

She sat back and took a deep breath preparing herself for...I wasn't sure. As I watched her gather herself, Benny shuffled his feet nervously. My eyes moved from one to the other and I knew they were about to tell me something that would change everything for me forever. My principles. My morals. My rules. My life.

The air crackled around us and I found myself holding my own breath again.

"We have had to take matters into our own hands."

There it was. Like a bomb being dropped. It was a confession of sorts from her, not quite admitting she had instigated crimes, but leaving my imagination to join the dots together. The judge's death. Jimmy's death. Jason's death. Even Cruz's death. All seemingly separate murders but I knew they had to be connected. What I hadn't known was how.

Not even an hour ago, Elizabeth became my prime suspect. She had the best motive in the world: vengeance. *This girl has killed,* a voice had whispered in my head. Now Sandra Burton sat silently on the other side of the table, with her hands resting softly in her lap, watching every emotion travel across my face after telling me it was her, not Elizabeth, who had taken matters into her own hands.

A thrumming sound echoed in my ears as my heart raced. Someone had drugged Jason and walked him up to the top of a mountain and brutally killed him. Someone had doused the judge with petrol and set fire to him while he slept in his bed. Someone shot Jimmy and someone stabbed Cruz five times in the heart. A voice in my head said, *And you thought that slip of a girl was capable of doing that? Are you kidding me?*

Without consciously thinking about it, my hands formed fists at my side.

I knew *why* Sandra had arranged to kill all four men. I just couldn't condone the murders.

Could I?

"You?" I whispered.

She smiled sadly. "Not me personally, Jack. I had help from like-minded people who know that if we just sit back and wait for the authorities to do something, nothing will ever happen." She hesitated as her eyes bored into mine. "Because the authorities are the ones who are part of this problem."

She looked down at the table before looking back up at me. "It's all about money, Jack. The rich want to be richer and they don't care how they do it. Money means power, which creates more money. It's greed, pure and simple."

"I didn't set out to kill them, Jack," she continued. "That just happened when Elizabeth was threatened by Simon Parker at the restaurant. *He* contacted the judge and Cruz, and *he* started this whole thing in motion. They would have killed her, Jack. Have no doubt about that. And they would have felt justified in doing so."

Sadness washed over her face.

"When I found her, she was a wreck. She tried so hard to escape them. A year, Jack. A whole year of thinking she was finally free only to find that the nightmare was returning. I brought her here and I am happy that she trusted me so much."

She smiled down at Benny. "And you too, Benny."

Benny blushed but didn't say anything.

"Suddenly I knew that there was a first time for everything," she continued. "The first idea. The first step. The first kill. Sometimes you just know when the time is right."

She sat up straighter, her back stiff. "And I have no regrets, Jack. If I have saved just a couple of boys, and that lovely young lady by stepping in, I will have done a good thing."

There wasn't a day in my life when I didn't remember the events of Tamborine Mountain that ended my career. I watched those tiny bones coming out of the ground, one by one. Small lives cut short when they should have been laughing and kicking balls around a park. They should have been allowed to grow up and feel the first pangs of love. They should have had children of their own to love and nurture. Instead, immoral men had cut their lives short because of their own perversions. How could I not agree with her?

That, of course, was my dilemma.

Her voice cut in. "But we still have serious problems. There will still be paedophile rings out there that we will never find. But we can do something about this one."

I'm not one for theatrics or even feeling much of what might be labelled astonishment. I have seen a lot in my forty-plus years. I have killed and I've nearly been killed. I have seen depravity that most would find difficult to comprehend and I have learnt over the years to try and control my emotions and reactions during stressful and volatile situations. These qualities have saved me from time to time.

"Are you asking me to help you commit more murders?" I asked, my voice husky with emotion.

She shook her head. "No Jack. You are too good a man for that." She patted my hand again. "But there are other ways to skin a cat."

"Did Elizabeth have anything to do with these killings?"

She shook her head again. "No. She almost lost her life once. I couldn't ask her to risk it again. But she gave us names."

She looked over at Benny who was riveted on every word she spoke. "As did Benny. And she has helped me in other ways."

She waited a few seconds, watching me closely, probably assessing whether she should tell me the ways Elizabeth had helped.

She nodded slowly, coming to a decision, and smiled.

"It was Elizabeth who helped me by luring Jason to Tamborine Mountain. She met with him after you saw him at the petrol station." She laughed softly. "You're not always a '*by the books*' man are you?"

I felt my face burn and once again, I felt like a hypocrite.

She waved the emotion away.

"Apparently Jason always had a soft spot for Elizabeth. She had dinner with him and during that meal she drugged him. Not too much but just enough to make him groggy and in need of assistance. Then she and my friend drove him to Tamborine Mountain where ..." she stopped. "You know the rest, Jack. Because of her help, we have managed a sort of justice."

The word *vigilante* crossed my mind. Killing for the sake of justice without legal authority. Was I actually condoning this?

"But we still have Simon Parker to deal with. And Jason's mother, who is evil personified." A deep frown creased her forehead. "For a woman to do this to young boys..."

She left the sentence unfinished as she gritted her teeth. When she turned back to me, determination burned in her eyes.

"I have already put a plan in motion." She grinned and looked at Benny. "Well, Benny has actually. He was waiting on the footpath for Simon Parker to exit the office carpark this afternoon while you were inside the police station. When he did, Benny made sure he saw him. Benny waved and took off on his bike, leaving Parker staring open-mouthed through the windscreen."

She grinned at Benny. "I wish I'd been there to see his face."

The two chuckled for a few seconds before Sandra turned back to me.

"Now I want *you* to help me bring them all to justice."

The smile she gave me sent a chill through my body. I remember once hearing someone say that the scariest thing in the world was watching Glenn Close smile at you. That was the look Sandra Burton gave me now.

"What can I do to help?" I finally asked.

✼ 35 ✼

The drive back home was excruciating. There were so many thoughts running around in my head and I needed to sort through what Sandra Burton had told me. Without a doubt, I needed to contact Sam and fill her in on our plan to snare Simon Parker. But I couldn't tell Sam everything I'd heard tonight. I had to be careful and not let anything slip that could incriminate Sandra Burton or Elizabeth.

Along with those thoughts were the many questions I needed to ask Hayley. I needed to know why she had left the house. I needed to know where she'd gone and I wanted to know if she knew where Elizabeth was now. A lot depended on her cooperation and running off in the middle of the night was not helping things.

Frank's car was parked on the kerb outside my house but most of the lights were off inside the house as I pulled into the driveway. Just a dim light from the kitchen was lighting up the grevilleas hugging the back fence.

The garage door finally finished opening. I drove in and pressed the button for the door to slowly rumble shut as I headed towards the door leading through the study to the lounge room.

Frank and Hayley looked up from the dining table, both heads turning towards me like they were synchronised swimmers. On the table was another opened pizza box with several pieces missing. Sitting on the floor beside Hayley was the dog, his tongue licking his lips after finishing a pizza slice.

Hayley smiled warily at me. What I wanted to do was shake her and make her realise this wasn't a game we were all playing. As I took a step towards her, ready to give her a lecture, a movement from the kitchen caught my attention, and I turned.

Standing near the back door was a girl, her hair stripped of dark dye and back to its natural blonde shade. Eyes the colour of a clear summer sky stared back at me warily and the scar almost shimmered in the dimness. Slung over her shoulder, like a baby being burped, was Sherlock.

Beside her stood Jasmine, my thirteen-year-old daughter.

Jasmine looked like she was heading off to a Renaissance Festival. Her choice of clothing was a claret-coloured, crushed velvet, ankle-length dress with a ruffled collar, long sleeves, black tights, and high-top black gym boots. Her hair was loose and wild and the colour of mulberries, thanks to Clairol. A variety of thick silver bracelets adorned one wrist while a leather cuff studded with brass and silver nails adorned the other. Nails the colour of blood peeked out from the sleeves. The result was almost comical.

As I stared at my daughter in shock, a loud purring filled the silence as Elizabeth ran her hands along Sherlock's back. Jasmine simply stared defiantly at me.

She had my colouring and her mother's bone structure but that had changed enough in recent years to bear no resemblance to either of us. Her cheekbones were high, her full lips were glossed red and her eyes were heavily lined. The freckles on her nose were obliterated with lots of make-up that made her look beige.

I turned to Frank and his ugly face was creased in a smile.

"Your tiara's back in place, mate. And your daughter's come to visit."

It's not often I'm lost for words, but right at that moment, there was nothing I could think to say.

Elizabeth was silent, teeth biting her bottom lip as she eyed me across the room. Jasmine stood silently, waiting for my reaction.

Elizabeth seemed to come to a decision. She placed Sherlock gently on the ground and he grizzled a little but settled with collapsing beside the dog.

Tension showed on her face but she spoke confidently.

"Sandra called to say she'd spoken to you and you both have a plan."

No nonsense. Straight to the heart of it.

I nodded agreement then turned to Jasmine.

"And what's your story, Jasmine?"

"Christ! My name's Jazz. I've told you that before."

She folded her arms across her chest in the same defensive pose I remembered so well from Sally. "I ran away from home," she added.

I sighed and thought, *Right now? Today?*

The pose used to infuriate me when I was married to Sally, but I can't say I blamed her. Looking back on my marriage, there were times I wished I'd listened to her more. What I remember most was the pain and the anger. Like Jazz standing before me, Sally's face was a mirror to every emotion she felt. No matter how hard I tried, I always ended up alienating Sally. It's easy to see the faults in others but not so easy to see your own.

"Does your mother know you're here?" I asked patiently.

"She doesn't understand me."

And I do? I felt like asking. She was at that rotten age when everything is everyone else's fault.

"But does she know you're here?"

Her eyes shone with anger and small spots of red glowed through the make-up on her cheeks. I remembered when she was little and about to throw a tantrum, those small red spots would always appear just before the onslaught. This time, instead of the expected tantrum, she jerked her head in what I can only assume meant *no*.

I nodded because I didn't know what to say. It had been a long day and this conversation was not the one I would have wished for after a month of not seeing her.

"What doesn't she understand?" I eventually asked, somewhat wearily.

Jazz sighed dramatically. "I got suspended from school."

I hesitated before asking. "Did you go dressed like that?"

The glare she gave me was pure Sally. "What's wrong with what I'm wearing?"

I suppressed a sigh. "Did you go dressed like that?" I repeated.

After a brief hesitation, she replied quietly, and a little sheepishly, "What if I did?"

"I assume that's why you were suspended?"

Her eyes flashed at me as she harrumphed. "The younger grades have to wear uniforms but for the upper grades," she hesitated, making a face that said *like me*, "it's left up to our individual discretion."

The attitude was back and I could only feel sorry for Sally.

In my peripheral vision, I saw Frank and Hayley's heads swivelling from side to side following the conversation silently. Beside Jazz, Elizabeth had found something very interesting at her feet to stare at.

"And you don't think this outfit," I waved my hand at the ensemble, "is outside the guidelines?"

She snorted derisively like she couldn't believe how stupid I was. "The rules state no skirts or dresses with hemlines above the knees, no tank tops, no T-shirts with slogans, no underwear showing and no flip-flops." She tossed her hair. "As far as I can see, I'm playing by the rules. As it turned out it was a big no-no."

She harrumphed again and did a side-to-side jiggle with her head, mimicking the teacher's tone. "Non-communicative. Non-compliance with the teachers. Needs a change of attitude," she singsonged.

Her right hand rotated in a circle indicating an endless dialogue.

Gone was the little girl running through the kitchen at an age when kids were always in a hurry. Gone was the little girl with eyes full of innocence. Little unconnected memories surfaced. The maple tree in our backyard in Hobart dropping its fiery red leaves as four-year-old Jazz scooped them up and threw them above her head, laughing. Rain falling softly onto the leaves of the Leopard tree with a soft pitter-patter as Sally rocked a tiny five-year-old Jazz to sleep.

I looked at the defiant child before me who was almost a woman. In a few years' time, a different sort of problem would raise its head and I was beginning to wonder which one was the worst.

Hayley popped up. "I like your style, girl."

I spun my head towards her, Exorcist style, "Do I need to ask you to leave?"

Both hands came up, surrender style. "Just saying," she muttered.

We grew silent. Eventually, Jazz asked, "So, what now?"

I was wondering that myself.

I took a deep breath. "We all need to sit down and talk," was the best I could manage. "First I call your mother. She'll be worried."

Jazz interjected and muttered petulantly, "She *likes* to worry."

I ignored the statement and continued, "Then I'll take you home when she's calmed down."

She rolled her eyes at Hayley who turned to Frank and said, "*Now* he wants to talk."

Frank chuckled and pushed the pizza box towards me. "Pizza?"

I was getting one of those headaches you get when you know nothing you say is going to be right. Maybe my blood sugar was just low. All I'd eaten all day was a coffee at breakfast and the Big Mac at lunch. Suddenly, I was starving.

"With anchovies?" I asked.

"You're finicky now?" His eyebrows floated up.

Sally looked drawn with dark rings circling her eyes and Jazz had the grace to look ashamed. What I could see more than anything else was the pain. Pain and anger.

Her arms were folded over her chest, the same way Jazz's had an hour before, and my mind flashed back to a memory of Sally reading on the lounge with her legs tucked under her, wearing a big baggy sweater she always wore. The past came back at me so hard, I nearly stepped backwards.

"You've got some explaining to do, young lady," Sally began as Jazz pushed past both of us and made for the stairs.

"Jazz," I called out. We'd spoken in the car and she'd agreed that an apology was needed.

Jazz hesitated and turned around, sighing dramatically. "Sorry, mum." Then she was gone.

"Bye," I called out, and a soft voice from an upstairs room warbled, "Bye."

Sally opened her mouth to say something just as a male voice called out from inside the house. She glanced over her shoulder and the moment was gone.

She turned back to me with a tight smile and said, "Thanks Jack," before she closed the door softly.

It was well into the night by the time the plan was in place and we were sure of how it would work and the stories we were going to tell afterwards would fit. In the future, when it was all over and Parker and Pauline Brady were behind bars, a lot depended on everyone telling the same story, secure in the fact that no one would deviate from that story.

Elizabeth stayed the night, huddled with Hayley in the back bedroom. Every now and then giggles erupted which meant the healing was well on its way.

While the dog snored softly at my feet, Frank settled himself at the dining table in front of the computer trying to explain the working of the dark web. It was going to take a long time, maybe weeks, maybe more, before it became clear to me. But I realised I had to drag myself into this new world if I was going to make my new career a worthwhile one.

The plan was a simple one. Elizabeth would call Parker early the next evening around six o'clock to set the plan in motion. The last person he would expect to receive a call from would be Elizabeth and she would take full advantage of the shock. It was her job to make him believe that she and Benny were on their way to release the other boys at Pauline Brady's house before going to the police. They knew his name and they would tell the police the whole story.

I filled Sam in on most of the story the next day, phoning her rather than going to the station. I didn't want to see Cavanaugh and I didn't want Sam to interrogate me or talk me out of the plan. She'd given me two days, I said, and it had only taken one. I told her about Pauline Brady and the boys she had locked away in back rooms. I told her about the paedophile ring and I inferred that it was Simon Parker who had organised to have the others in the ring eliminated. With them out of the way, the profits did not have to be divided between so many. There would only be Pauline Brady because after all, someone had to look after the boys and keep them securely locked away. Finally, I told her that Elizabeth had come forward and together she and Hayley had hatched this plan.

I didn't tell her about Sandra Burton and I didn't tell her about Benny. There was actually quite a lot I couldn't tell her and what I did tell her was mostly lies. Maybe after the case was solved and she could listen without exploding, I'd tell her the truth. Maybe. Until then, she was doing it my way.

She huffed and puffed and told me I was leaving a whole lot out, which I was, but finally she realised that she would be solving cases that looked like never being solved at all so she calmed down.

Sam won the argument the next afternoon about who would drive to Pauline Brady's house while Elizabeth made the call. *Her* car, she said, so she would drive. While I rode shotgun, Cavanaugh sat broodily in the back seat.

A light drizzle had begun to fall as we wound through the streets and a kaleidoscope of blurred colour and shadows slipped past my window. Fragmented neon glistened on the pavements and splashed across signs and cars as our wipers beat a slow metronome on the windscreen. Here and there smokers lingered in doorways, enduring the wind and damp for a nicotine fix.

Ten minutes out, we turned into the street and were in full view of the Brady house. Lights were coming on inside but apart from that, the street and the house was quiet. As Sam cut the headlights and killed the engine half a dozen houses away from the house, the drizzle slowed to a stop.

It was almost half past six and the ticking noise from the cooling engine had ceased when headlights appeared up ahead. They were dimmed, at a moderate height and not too far apart, which meant the vehicle was of normal size and not an SUV.

As it came closer, I recognised it.

"A black BMW. That's Parker. It's showtime." My heart was doing somersaults inside my chest. "Now we wait until he's inside."

The car turned into the Brady driveway, parked neatly and Simon Parker got out wearing dark pants and a black long-sleeved shirt. Good for blending into the dark shadows.

He stood and looked around cautiously before walking up to the garage door and did something with his fob. The door clattered up slowly, getting faster as it rose.

Even in the darkness, I saw the glint of a gun as he pushed it into the space between his belted pants and the small of his back. Something you see gangsters do in shows like *The Sopranos*.

In my peripheral vision, I saw Cavanaugh in the back seat reaching under his coat to pull out his own gun.

"Tell Dirty Harry back there to ease up on the firepower," I whispered to Sam loud enough for Cavanaugh to hear.

"Shut up, Curtis," he growled fiercely back. "Believe it or not, I know what I'm doing."

"Well I hope so. Just remember the plan. We don't want to alarm him. We wait until he's inside and then we call for backup. We want the boys, Parker and Pauline Brady together in one search if these charges are going to stick."

"I know the grill. Just you stay behind Sam and me when we go in. *We're* the ones with the badges here. Not you. No matter what you think, you're not in charge."

Sam muttered, *Jesus Christ,* as I shook my head melodramatically.

While we bickered, Parker walked into the garage and a minute later there was a muted repeat of the same noise as the garage door began to lower slowly.

I took my own gun out from my shoulder holster and put my hand up indicating for both Sam and Cavanaugh to wait a little longer.

I should have known Cavanaugh wasn't about to follow my lead. He was out of the car, his gun held out in front of him with both hands, walking towards Parker in a crouch with his gun pointed at him.

"HANDS IN THE AIR AND STAY WHERE YOU ARE!" Cavanaugh yelled.

"What the ..." I muttered to the empty back seat.

Beside me, Sam muttered, "SHIT!"

As Sam and I jumped out of the car, Parker glanced our way and stepped back a pace as the door continued to descend slowly. His hand was above his eyes trying to block the glare of the florescent light, searching for the owner of the voice. Then he did what I expected he'd do. He reached behind him and pulled out his gun.

"STOP! DROP YOUR WEAPON!" Cavanaugh shouted, dropping to a crouch.

The door closed with a clunk and Parker was gone.

I turned to Cavanaugh as he stood up and I lost it.

"ARE YOU FUCKING MAD?" I yelled, shoving him against the car.

"What happened to the plan? We were going to wait until he was inside and then call for backup." I waved my hands at the closed garage door. "Now he's inside and you can bet he's busy hiding anything incriminating and planning an escape. If he gets out with those kids and hides them, we won't be able to prove a thing."

Cavanaugh shoved me away from him and yelled back. "Like I said before, Curtis. You are not in charge. You need to calm down."

"Calm down? *Calm down?*" I lunged forward again and thrust my face into his. "You think I'm just some has-been looking for drama?"

Cavanaugh leaned back and I felt Sam's hand on my shoulder but I was in full rant.

"Let me tell you something, Cavanaugh." I jammed my finger at his chest. "The combined fucking genius of the Southport Police couldn't find Hayley Johnson, Elizabeth Delaney or proof that Parker was the head of a paedophile ring. But I did!"

My voice echoed in the silence. Lights had come on in a couple of houses. Curtains moved and irritated faces were peeking out. Pretty soon, they'd be calling ooo.

I spun around to Sam. "I'm going around the back to make sure he doesn't get those kids out of there before we can finish this. You can either come with me or you can stay here and cover the front with this idiot. One thing is for sure, he's not coming with me. Your choice." I glanced towards the house. "But make it quick."

Without hesitating, Sam said, "I'm coming with you."

I turned to Cavanaugh. "You fucking stay here and cover the front while Sam and I go around and cover the back," I ordered. "While we're gone, call this in and ask for backup to seal the street off. See if you can at least do that much."

I glanced over at the neighbouring houses where lights glowed inside dark exteriors then turned back to him.

"After your little charade, the neighbours may already have done your job so pretty soon, all hell will break lose around here."

Even under the streetlights, I could see colour flood Cavanaugh's face. He opened his mouth but before he could speak, I said, "Shut the fuck up! Just do it."

As I turned and ran towards the house, I knew there was no need to keep quiet. Parker knew we were here, and so did Pauline Brady. Speed was the essence now.

Behind me, I heard a curse from Cavanaugh as Sam and I squelched our way towards the house, our soles leaving shallow depressions in the soft grass and bark. Whether it was the adrenaline or the fact that I'm not as fit as I used to be, my breath was coming out in sharp gasps even before we reached the house.

When the grinding noise of the garage door abruptly broke the silence, I stopped and Sam ran into me from behind. In unison, our eyes swivelled towards the sound, watching the door slowly rise. Even as it rose, the nose of the black BMW edged its way out, eager to make an exit before the door had risen completely.

It took me too many precious seconds to register what Parker was doing. He was taking away the only evidence of his complicity in the crime. The boys. I had no idea where he was taking them but I knew their lives were in danger. He couldn't afford to leave any loose ends. His whole existence depended on getting rid of those boys.

I turned, avoiding Sam, and raced back to the car, my feet slipping on the moist grass.

"You bloody idiot," I spat at Cavanaugh. "Look what you've done. He's been warned and now he's running."

I glanced over my shoulder and saw the BMW almost free of the garage. Another couple of seconds, and there would be enough room for the car to speed away, leaving us flat-footed and scrambling to follow him.

"I'm going after him," I said as I ran towards the driver's side of the car. Without looking, I could hear Sam running behind me heading towards the passenger side.

"Call this in and fill them in on what's happening," I shouted to Cavanaugh over my shoulder. "If we do this right, we can still catch him before he gets away."

Defiance flared in Cavanaugh's eyes for a second before he stopped and closed both eyes. He was about to step onto a tightrope without a net and the realisation stopped him short. He opened his eyes and gave me the smallest of nods.

The BMW was out of the garage and Parker was flooring it down the driveway towards the street. He glanced over towards us, his eyes burning with fury as the car hurtled over the gutter, the back end crashing loudly as it met with concrete.

Bouncing around in the back seat, three terrified young faces stared open-mouthed, all wearing studded dog collars, proclaiming their current profession in the worst possible way.

Benny had told me there were two others. What we had here was three. They'd recruited in the past week.

I turned the key in the ignition, slammed the gear into drive and floored the accelerator. As I sped past Cavanaugh, I glanced in my rear mirror and saw him shouting into his phone.

"Watch the road!" Sam yelled.

My attention snatched back at Sam's outburst as I jerked the car through the chicane-like cluster of cars parked on the otherwise empty street. I followed through a swirling cloud of trash flying through the air from rubbish bin Parker had upended on his exit.

With both Same and me following close behind, Parker's car sped along the street before making a screaming right at a T-junction. Angry horns sounded as the BMW leapt onto the main road. Moments later, I did the same.

I darted looks left and right while I tried to avoid the rushing traffic. In the chaos, cars scattered in all directions.

"There," Sam yelled, pointing.

I shot a look, hit the brakes and hung a tyre-smoking right just as the BMW turned into a narrow street, swiping garbage dumpsters and sending sparks flying down the side of his car.

This time, there were no horns from angry motorists. The street was only crowded with parked cars and over the screaming of the engine, I heard the crash of metal on metal as the BMW ripped fenders and hubcaps from them. The impacts were fleeting but it was enough to slow him down.

Another right turn and this time, I saw signs announcing the exit to the M1. If he made it to the motorway, I knew I'd lose him.

Out of the corner of my eye, I saw Sam's gun resting in her lap, her hand gripped tightly around the butt.

"Don't risk it," I said. "There's three kids in the car with him." *And causing the car to crash at this speed would be a disaster*, I thought.

Up ahead, I saw something emerge from the driver's window of the BMW.

I couldn't be a gun, I thought. *He'd have to be stupid to drive and shoot at the same time.*

Even as I thought the words, a flash appeared and smoke blossomed.

"Hang on," I yelled, swinging the wheel and fishtailing through chain link fencing into a vacant lot, raising a cloud of dust. Seconds later, I spun out and turned the car back on the BMW's trail, grateful it wasn't my car I was trashing.

Parker turned in the direction of the M1, scattering pedestrians who were ambling over a pedestrian crossing. As I struggled to control the car, a woman walking her German Shepherd cannoned into a delivery man carrying a couple of pizza boxes sending them and the pizzas tumbling into my path. I jerked the wheel, narrowly missing the people, but not the boxes, one of which bounced up and over the hood, smearing the contents over the windscreen. Along with the food was a mobile phone and as it hit the windscreen, a spiderweb of cracks appeared.

"I can't see a thing," I shouted in the deafening noise.

Sam, using the butt of her gun, pounded the windscreen and on the third blow, it burst out and flipped upwards, flying over the car and spinning to a rest on the roof of a parked car.

Screwing up my eyes to the buffeting wind, I saw Parker turn onto the exit road of the motorway. A NO ENTRY sign flashed past. If a car was exiting the motorway, he was a goner. And so were the kids.

Spotting an opening on this right-hand side, metres from the no-entry sign, I pushed my foot harder on the accelerator, hoping to push him into the bushes before he made the turn.

"I'm going to ram him," I yelled to Sam. "Hang on tight."

Her head jerked to look at me and I noticed her face was white.

The move worked. I jerked the steering wheel to the left and Sam's side of the car crashed into the side of Parker's car, sending him careening towards the bushes. I saw a flash of brake lights seconds before he turned towards a narrow street on his left, just as I jerked the car back from the off ramp.

I was gaining on him as he fishtailed wildly, three heads in the back seat of the car swinging wildly from side to side.

I floored the accelerator again, gaining more on him, and as I saw smoke coming from his rear right wheel, I silently cheered. When I'd hit him, it must have jammed the bodywork onto the tyre. It was going to slow him down even more.

Sam noticed how dangerously close we were to Parker.

"What are you doing, Jack?" Her voice came out as a squeak.

I didn't have time to answer or warn her. I rammed my car into the rear of the BMW, the jolt cannoning through my neck and shoulders.

Boom. Once. *Boom.* Twice.

I dropped back, floored it, and rammed him a third time.

This time, the BMW went into a helpless spin before lurching over a gutter and a sidewalk then catapulted into a low brick fence. In the darkness, I saw a body fly through the windscreen.

I brought the car to a screeching halt and Sam and I both scrambled out, running to the wreck of the BMW. Sam held her gun out at the ready but I knew it wouldn't be needed.

Parker had been thrown from the car through the windscreen and was lying face down amidst broken glass, twisted metal and bricks.

As Sam stood over me, gun pointed at the body, I bent down and felt for a pulse. I knew there wouldn't be one. His head was bent at an impossible angle and the visible side of his face was pulp.

I stood up and put my hand over Sam's gun, pointing it to the ground as I shook my head. That's when the back door of the BMW groaned open, metal screeching, and a boy fell out. Following him were two others, bleeding from minor cuts, as they collapsed at our feet.

Sam pulled out her phone calling for an ambulance as I bent down to one of them.

"Are you okay?" I asked. "Don't move. Stay still. An ambulance is on the way."

The boy looked up at me and grinned. His hair was dishevelled and blood oozed down the side of his face from a cut on his temple.

"Man," he mumbled. "That was better than any Dreamworld ride I've ever been on."

＊ 37 ＊

The term 'media circus' has been bantered around for decades and for good reason. The only things missing were the tents and the dancing elephants although as Sol Mendelssohn lumbered around the group, I noticed he'd put on a lot of weight since the last time I'd seen him a year ago.

I had become the overseer to the small army that arrived, ready to begin work on the crime scene. Sam left me to talk to Mary O'Brien, the medical examiner, just as her phone rang. Sam muttered, "Sorry," and turned to answer it just as Mary turned to me. She merely nodded and glanced at my left arm, crossed over my mid-section, where the seat belt had held me in place. I wasn't complaining. If the belt hadn't been on, I'd been lying on the damp grass beside Simon Parker.

"Hello again, Jack," she smiled. "Do you need a doctor?" she asked. "The way you're holding yourself, you may have damaged a few ribs."

I shook my head. "I'm fine, Mary. Really."

She looked as if she was about to say something. Instead, she hesitated before patting my arm and said, "Take care, Jack."

She squatted down next to the body and as expected, her expression was wretched. I heard a mumbled, "Oh my Lord," but when I glanced at Sam, the only word I could use to describe her expression was joyous.

From eavesdropping on her conversation, I gathered Cavanaugh had done as I'd ordered and called for backup back at the house. He had Pauline Brady in custody at the station and was interviewing her as we finished up at the accident site.

"I'm free to leave?" I asked Sam as I watched her shove her phone in the back pocket of her jeans, obviously finished with Cavanaugh.

She nodded. "Sure Jack. There's nothing more for you to do here. I'll wait for Mary to finish then head on home myself. A social worker has already picked up the boys but I'll probably see them again first thing in the morning at the station when they all give their statements. You'll need to be there too." As an afterthought she said, "and bring Elizabeth and Hayley too."

I nodded.

"Looks like you'll make the funeral after all," I commented.

"Must be my lucky day," she sighed.

I reached out and touched her arm gently. "Call me if you need a friend," I said softly before turning towards the remaining gaggle of reporters blocking my way.

Sol took a few steps towards me, microphone in hand, and they rest noticed his movement and turned, expectantly holding their own microphones at the ready. Instantly, flashbulbs burst in my eyes and microphones were pressed up to my face.

"Can you tell us if it's true the body belonged to a partner in a major law firm, Jack?" Sol asked.

"No," I said as I pushed forward.

"Can you give us a statement then?"

"No."

"Come on, Jack," I heard Sol mumble, "give us a break."

"No."

He smiled sardonically as he stepped in front of me, barring my way, holding a microphone close to my mouth. "One tip, Jack. Just one."

"Yeah. Here's one for you, Sol," I said. "Get out of my way and I won't shoot you."

I tried to look reasonable but at this time of night, I had no time for Bob Hope repartee and I've always said the only two things you can believe in a newspaper is the date and the price.

Behind me, I heard Sol call out, "Keep taking those blue pills, Jack," followed by a few snickers. I kept my eyes focused ahead and pushed my way through the crowd between camera flashes.

A card was suddenly thrust into my hand and my eyes glanced down, then up at the person standing to my side, being jostled by the gaggle of reporters. The eyes of the stranger were sharp, at odds with the shabbiness of both his clothes and general appearance.

"Call me, Jack," he yelled over the chaos as he nodded at the card in my hand. I glanced down again and saw *Peter Murray* printed above letters flying haphazardly from an opened book. Put together, the letters spelled *Author*. Under that was a mobile number and an email address.

He was elbowed aside again just as I raised my eyes to him again. My last sight of him was as he disappeared back into the crowd but I knew the fire in those eyes would stay in my memory for a long time.

I had no idea what he wanted but I shoved the card into my coat pocket anyway and kept walking until I reached the main road. I was lucky enough to hail a cab and fifteen minutes later, I was at the police station car park, getting into my own car, grateful I'd listened to Sam and let her drive hers.

I stopped at a McDonalds on the way home and bought two Big Mac combos and a vanilla shake to take home.

As I drove through the dark streets, I remembered first coming to Surfers Paradise when I was accustomed to seeing the skies of Hobart bright with a light that only comes from brilliant stars. Surfers Paradise is bright all right, but it comes from streetlights, bars, shops and skyscrapers. I used to joke that it was the absence of stars that made people lose their bearings and morals in life.

Now I know better.

❦ 38 ❦

The house was dark and quiet when I walked in. The only sound in the silence was the ticking of the clock and the thumping of a tail on the floorboards.

"Hello dog. Here boy," I called into the darkness before switching on the lights.

The dog walked slowly towards me, head down with his tail not quite between his legs, which told me he was on his way to trusting me. He raised his head and his nostrils twitched at the two bags in my hands.

I let him out the back door into the yard and he made for a cluster of bushes in a corner seeking privacy for his toilet. Sherlock lay curled up in one of the two chairs on the veranda and only managed to raise his head and open one eye, *oh it's you*, before snuggling down and returning to sleep.

"Wait, wait, wait," I called to the dog, and he stopped to look at me.

"You'll come back with your coat full of burrs, and it'll take me an hour to comb them all out."

The dog seemed to understand because he stopped short of the bushes and raised his leg while I went inside for a beer.

I opened the can and took the bags out to the back veranda and the dog used his best sad-eyed look, his most pathetic whine, his wagging tail, to tell me he was hungry.

I opened one of the burgers and put it on its wrapper on the floor. By the time I'd extracted my own Big Mac and taken a single bite, the dog had wolfed down the meat patty and most of the bun. He gazed yearningly at mine and whined.

"Mine," I said.

He whined again. Not a whine of pain but a whine that said *oh-look-at-poor-cute-hungry-me-and-see-how-much-I'd-like-that-hamburger-with-special-sauce-and-maybe-even-the-pickle-on-a-sesame-seed-bun*.

"Do you understand the word *mine?*"

The dog fixated on the bag of French fries in my lap instead.

I dug into the bag of fries and dropped a handful onto the wrapper. They vanished as I took another bite of my burger and then he looked longingly at the others. I tipped the rest from his bag onto the wrapper and he wolfed them down too.

I took the lid off the shake and his head cocked in interest.

"See what I bought for you? Now aren't you ashamed of thinking all those bad thoughts you had when I wouldn't give you my burger?"

I tossed the water from his bowl over the balcony and tipped the shake into it and he attacked it, consuming it in a frenzy of lapping. When he was finished, he looked up at me, his snout smeared with milkshake.

"You have disgusting manners."

With an amazing rotation of his tongue, he licked most of the mess off his snout.

I walked inside to the kitchen and filled the bowl with water and placed it down in front of him. He dug into that as well then looked up, his muzzle dripping, and burped.

"Come here, slob."

Eye-to-eye with the dog, I leant over and wiped his snout with my serviette.

"We're all going to get along just fine, aren't we?" I said, scratching behind his ears. "We're going to be the best of friends."

While I wiped and scratched, the dog's tail wagged furiously.

"I think I may have made a big mistake tonight, dog."

More wagging.

"Tomorrow you will see this handsome face plastered all over the news.

Papers too, no doubt. And I know you're asking yourself, why does he look so worried? It's good for business, right?"

More panting.

"Maybe so, but this operation I helped to close down tonight, well, it was only part of a much bigger one operated by some very powerful men. And they are not going to be pleased when they find that yours truly has put their operation in jeopardy. What they will want is payback because with their type of business, secrecy and privacy is of the utmost priority. What I did tonight was the opposite. I put it in the limelight."

The dog was listening intently, one ear up, one ear down.

"The way I see it, I've put us all in danger. And I'm sorry for that."

The tone of my voice was tender and apologetic as I stroked his head.

"I know I did this to further my career and my business. But after tonight," I hesitated and shook my head, "I think I will have to shut it down."

The dog blinked.

"We'll be fine," I assured him. "Maybe not so many burgers and fries in the future, but we'll be okay. With Frank's help. And Sandra Burton's."

More blinking.

"Frank helped me download a VPN today and showed me how to gain access to a lot of computers. The phone company. Main Roads. The Police Department. Even the Government. The list of places I can now access is endless. Which means I can still do detecting work but it will be under the radar from now on. By the way, this work will pay more because there are people who are willing to pay big money for certain types of information, especially if what they do isn't quite...," I hesitated. "I was going to say legal. But that's not the word. Authorised is probably a better word."

Hypocrite, my good angel whispered. *Whoo hoo*, yelled the bad one.

I nodded.

"And both Sandra Burton and Frank know a lot of people who are under the radar too. People who want things to stay that way. Word of mouth will get around and we'll be eating burgers, fries and shakes again in no time," I assured him with a smile.

He whined.

"But that's just the beginning. Now that I have this know-how, I can see things these bad people don't want me to see. I'll know ahead of time what they're planning. And I can change things." I grinned. "Smart, eh?"

He sneezed.

"How about we go to the beach tomorrow? Have you ever been to the beach?"

More wagging.

"You'll love it. It's calming and it's consistent. Nothing you do will ever make it go away. And that's us too, dog. Together against the world. Right?"

Wag. Wag.